Prais

"Kramer's uniqu____ is a delight: funn___ than the show. With Kramer's enchanting sense of humor, the blonde, lovely Brady girls and their irascible brothers, loving parents, and housekeeper Alice are off on a romp that rivals Shakespeare for a comedy of errors. Readers will be up all night before drifting off to dream of a love story like this." —*RT Book Reviews*

"Kramer scores with the inaugural House of Brady imbroglio. . . . Though [she] includes her characteristic lighthearted touches, she's smart and confident enough to take her characters and their situations seriously, turning what could have been a one-line joke into a deep and appealing story." —*Publishers Weekly*

"The Impossible Bachelors feature[s] delightfully witty and vibrant prose to match the books' unforgettable titles. . . . Kramer's clever and engaging style is now employed in the service of finding the perfect mate for each of the six Brady siblings. Libraries should buy a bunch." —*Library Journal*

"An emotional story that will leave readers loving Lady Marcia." —*Romance Reviews Today*

"[An] entertaining homage to [the] television series." —*Night Owl Reviews*

"Fans of the TV sitcom *The Brady Bunch* will be amazed at how cleverly and unexpectedly Kramer improvises on the show in her latest incandescently witty, completely captivating Regency historical." —*Booklist*

MORE . . .

Praise for Kieran Kramer's Impossible Bachelors series

When Harry Met Molly

"A delectable debut . . . I simply adored it!"
—Julia Quinn, #1 *New York Times* bestselling
author of the Bridgerton series

"Clever banter, stellar pacing, and appealing, exceptionally well-drawn characters make this fresh, sexy, and gloriously funny debut a knockout and a perfect start to Kramer's Regency-set quartet."   —*Library Journal* (starred review)

"In her exceptionally entertaining literary debut, Kramer deftly sifts deliciously humorous writing, a cast of exceptionally entertaining characters, an outrageously inventive yet convincing plot, and a splendidly sexy love story into a delectable literary confection that will have Regency historical readers begging for seconds."   —*Booklist* (starred review)

"You'll smile and even laugh out loud reading Kramer's delectable debut—even the title's nod to the famous film elicits a grin. With her perfect sense of pacing, comic timing, poignancy, and marvelous characterization, this utterly enchanting new voice will have you eager for more."
—*RT Book Reviews*, 4½ Stars, Hot Top Pick

"At once frothy and heartfelt, *When Harry Met Molly* satisfies. This book is better than dessert!"
—Celeste Bradley, *New York Times* bestselling
author of *When She Said I Do*

"Kieran Kramer pens a delightful Regency confection . . . a wonderfully bright debut."
—Julia London, *New York Times* bestselling author

"I couldn't put it down . . . a charming delight!"
—Lynsay Sands, *New York Times* bestselling author

"A wickedly witty treat . . . an exquisite debut!"
    —Kathryn Caskie, *New York Times* bestselling author

Dukes to the Left of Me, Princes to the Right

"Utterly charming and delightful with a twisted spy plot mixed in with Russian royalty, unruly dogs, and gossipy cooks."   —*Publishers Weekly*

"Kramer's captivating Impossible Bachelors series returns with another memorable, well-crafted, deftly plotted story as enchanting and romantic as the first. There is great joy in her storytelling (and titles) that compels readers to smile and laugh with her characters. You'll be up all night until the satisfying conclusion to this delicious romance."
                    —*RT Book Reviews*, 4½ Stars, Top Pick

Cloudy with a Chance of Marriage

"Quirky, fresh, and filled with brilliant dialogue and whimsy, this sexy confection from the talented Kramer is pure sunshine."   —*Library Journal* (starred review)

"Wonderfully quirky characters, a devilishly clever plot, and writing that is both laugh-out-loud funny and sweetly romantic all add up to a completely captivating Regency historical from one of the romance genre's most dazzling new authors."   —*Booklist* (starred review)

If You Give a Girl a Viscount

"A smart, resourceful heroine, a clever, worthy hero, two stepsisters you want to shake, and a rotten-to-the-core stepmother combine in a delectable, most rewarding story that sees the last of the quartet of 'Impossible Bachelors' happily wed and a delightful series put to bed."   —*Library Journal*

Also by KIERAN KRAMER

THE HOUSE OF BRADY
Loving Lady Marcia
The Earl Is Mine

THE IMPOSSIBLE BACHELORS
When Harry Met Molly
Dukes to the Left of Me, Princes to the Right
Cloudy with a Chance of Marriage
If You Give a Girl a Viscount

Say Yes to the Duke

KIERAN KRAMER

St. Martin's Paperbacks

This is a work of fiction. All of the characters, organizations, and events portrayed in this novel are either products of the author's imagination or are used fictitiously.

SAY YES TO THE DUKE

Copyright © 2013 by Kieran Kramer.

For information address St. Martin's Press, 175 Fifth Avenue, New York, NY 10010.

ISBN: 978-1-250-00990-6

Printed in the United States of America

St. Martin's Paperbacks edition / September 2013

St. Martin's Paperbacks are published by St. Martin's Press, 175 Fifth Avenue, New York, NY 10010.

10 9 8 7 6 5 4 3 2 1

To my darling sister-in-law Sharon Brennan Wray.
This is your time.

Acknowledgments

As always, I would like to thank the terrific team at St. Martin's Press for making my writing life such a joy—especially Jen Enderlin, my wonderful editor. And I'm always grateful to my fabulous agent Jenny Bent for her unceasing support and encouragement.

I'd also like to thank all my readers for tagging along with me on this journey . . . your good cheer and unflagging loyalty mean the world to me. I hope we share many more story adventures together.

Of course, having my family to share in my happiness is a blessing I can't begin to measure. Thank you, Chuck, Steven, Margaret, and Jack! Thanks, Mom, Dad, my in-laws, Ted and Dottie, my siblings, and outlaws on both sides of the family! And thanks to Benny and Joon for crouching next to my laptop and to Striker for curling up at my feet from Chapter One until I write <u>The End</u>.

Chapter One

Lady Janice Sherwood—the one with the gorgeous older sister—had literally waltzed, however inelegantly, through several London Seasons and still hadn't found a husband. Everyone knew what a proper young lady did when she wasn't in demand. She rusticated in the English countryside in the hopes she'd be missed. And it went without saying that if she were wise, she'd develop her own magical charm while she was there— perhaps even catch the attention of an eligible gentleman in residence.

The chances that the dowager's grandson, the fabulously handsome Duke of Halsey, would fall madly in love with Janice when she was to stay at his house as a guest of his grandmother were next to nil. But Janice's parents, knowing the duke was to be there hovering about his prize horses, hoped the impossible would happen.

"But it won't," Janice said that very frosty morning she left London. "Me? Marry a duke?"

It was a ridiculous notion. She was going to the country to *hide,* for goodness' sake!

"If you have to fall in love, it might as well be with a duke," Mama said in utter seriousness, Daddy nodding solemnly behind her.

They actually believed that Janice, in her diminished

state, was capable of attracting such a lofty personage. Which was touching, of course, if a bit deluded, the way all parents' hopes were.

She might not be able to fulfill her parents' dreams of glory for her—after all, her three best suitors had deserted her last Season—but she could be sporting about it. So when Lord Brady's glossy black carriage broke a wheel at the beginning of the long drive leading to the ducal manor, Janice put down her book and was willing to walk the rest of the way. But Oscar said no, she should wait for him to return with a fully equipped carriage from His Grace's stables.

"Because the daughter of a marquess doesn't arrive on foot at the front door of a duke's house," he said. "Nor does she ride in a cart."

Of all the Brady drivers, only Oscar had the privilege of speaking so freely.

"I thought you told me nothing happens in the country, my lady," her maid, Isobel, fretted.

Oh, dear. Perhaps Isobel had that privilege, too.

"Nothing ever *does* happen," Janice asserted, hoping her confident delivery would lend her words extra power. A month dawdling in the country would allow her to forget for a while that she was the invisible sister, wedged between a glorious beauty—Marcia—and an adorable charmer, Cynthia, who'd soon make her own debut. "We'll play cards until Oscar comes back, shall we?"

"Very well," said the maid, "but you're not very good at cards, my lady. Do you think you'll have better luck with the duke?"

"Izzy!"

"Don't you want to marry him? Every eligible young lady should if she's got a head on her shoulders."

"But I want to marry for love." Janice did, too. Not that she had much hope for it, at the rate she was going.

Isobel dealt out the cards. "I should think loving a duke would be easier than loving someone else." Her tongue stuck out of the corner of her mouth as she eyed her hand.

"The question is how easy it is for a duke to fall in love with someone like *me*," Janice murmured. "And we both know the answer."

"You're being much too hard on yourself," protested Isobel. "You're very agreeable, my lady. And you had plenty of beaus in London."

"*Had* is the operative term." Janice sighed.

Isobel gave a luxurious laugh. "Perhaps you were too sparing with your kisses. . . ."

Janice likely had been. She drew a card. Another heart! "I refuse to think any more of love," she said. "It's much too overwhelming a subject." And kissing was dull. It had been a grave disappointment to her to discover that fact. "Now let's play cards until Oscar returns. I vow to beat you this time."

But when the carriage door opened fifteen minutes later, Janice had lost yet again and the person standing there wasn't Oscar. From what she could see of the stranger through the new-falling snow, he was tall, broad shouldered, in his late twenties, she guessed—likely one of the duke's grooms, in his well-cut but serviceable coat and simply tied cravat. Beneath his beaver hat, his hair was like coal, curling around his ears and framing a square, shaven jaw.

His horse stood waiting patiently behind him.

Janice's spine straightened. The man's eyes, thickly fringed in black lashes, were deep blue, the color of Daddy's sapphire ring. And his mouth—ah, his mouth.

It was a work of art. Hard, male, yet as expressive as his eyes, which radiated intelligence, good humor, and a bold, restless intensity that proclaimed him his own man, despite his servant's garb.

The slight imperfection of his aquiline nose suggested he'd been in a fight or two. But the mystery and threat its crooked line hinted at only made his sheer masculine beauty more compelling. Indeed, his appearance was a shock, especially when she was expecting potato-eared—but perfectly lovable—Oscar.

Isobel, too, found the stranger riveting, judging from the way her chin dropped onto the thick violet muffler with extra pom-poms Janice had knitted for her.

The man's eyes glittered with interest when he perused Janice's face, setting her heart racing. *What on earth?* He was a servant, of all things. He shouldn't be looking at her that way.

"You're obviously unhurt," he said, "so I'll dispense with the niceties." His voice was rich yet faintly bitter, like one of the coffeehouse brews she craved on a regular basis and sneaked out to get when Mama wasn't looking. "State your business, my lovelies. No one with good intentions comes down this road."

"Of course we've good intentions," said Janice, mortified. "We've been traveling for hours with good intentions, and we intend to get out of this carriage and have a cup of tea with His Grace and the dowager duchess." Her heart pounded like a herd of stallions crossing a plain. She was dressed modestly, in a navy cape and simple matching bonnet. And as for her hair, she'd taken no time to pin it back up after a few ringlets had fallen out at their last stop.

Yet the man eyed her as if she was a fascinating creature. He was the only man who'd ever looked at her that way, and she immediately thought of her underthings, all of them practical but with scraps of the finest Avignon lace sewn here and there. Mama had made them and stitched Janice's initials on every garment.

"You're after more than tea with the duke and the dowager." He grinned, exposing strong, white teeth. "We received no notice of your arrival, yet you've enough trunks to stay for weeks."

"Your impertinence is remarkable," said Janice. "We *are* staying longer than tea. We plan to stay for a month." She sat up higher on her seat and, despite her pique with this man, felt an insane desire to lean forward, lay the flat of her palm against his jaw, and cup it, just so she could trap that grin and stare at it all day long. She didn't need the rest of him. Oh, no. The rest of him could jump in a lake. "The dowager summoned me herself."

"How can that be when she's incapable of summoning anyone? She thinks she's the Queen."

A great shock course through Janice. "Well, queens do summon people."

His skeptical glance didn't faze her.

"I'll have you know she was quite lucid in her letter." Janice's tone was cool, but inside her heart was clamoring. How could the dowager think she was the Queen? "I have that letter in my trunk and am ready to produce it for the appropriate person, who wouldn't be *you*. Who are you, pray tell? A tenant farmer? One of the duke's grooms?"

The man lofted an elegant brow and opened his mouth to speak.

"I knew it!" gasped Isobel before he could say anything. "He's the duke himself!"

"*Izzy!*" Janice cried, embarrassed.

His mouth twitched in amusement. "I *am* a groom,

actually." He sounded quite proud of the fact. "My skills venture beyond the stables, however. I'm tasked with preserving the integrity of the place, so don't bother making up a wild story about why you simply have to stay. I've heard them all, I assure you."

The twinkle in his eye unnerved Janice like nothing else. What was so amusing? And even if something was, how dare he look that way at her? She was a marquess's daughter, and while she didn't often flaunt that fact, she was owed at least a bit of dignity, wasn't she?

She looked down her nose at him. "But we haven't done anything wrong. The dowager *did* summon me, I have the letter and seal to prove it, and you're the most disrespectful"—*handsome*—"groom I've ever met—"

"I assume your driver has gone ahead with the horses," he interrupted her smoothly. "This road is impeccably kept, not a pothole in it. Which of you engineered that? Or was that your driver's trick? The letter is easy enough to discount—forgers abound—but a broken wheel permits a second chance at staying while the letter is examined. An ingenious complication to the ploy, ladies."

"There *is* no ploy," Janice returned hotly.

But she could hardly hold on to her shock and anger. His eyes had filled with jealous admiration. Or perhaps it was reluctant respect, not the kind she usually got— the *I'm looking through you* token respect that men, servants, and everyone gave her as the stepdaughter of a marquess.

It was very much like the respect she'd earned from her old friend Dickon. When she was eight and he was nine, she could balance on one leg much longer than he could. This man was looking at her the same way, as if she had a talent. A skill of some kind. A special trick.

And you do, the thought came to her. *You've got all sorts of special tricks and talents.*

It was a big, wonderful notion, and it hadn't occurred to her in a very long while. Confidence surged through her. "I'd like to know what trick *you're* up to, sirrah. I'm Lady Janice Sherwood. And this is my abigail, Miss Isobel Jenkins."

"Of the traveling circus Jenkinses," Isobel interjected proudly.

He raised a brow, and Janice let him wonder. Izzy never passed up an opportunity to speak of her family and their interesting way of life, and Janice, for one, adored her all the more for it.

"You're being most irregular suggesting we're here under false pretenses and planned our little accident," Janice accused him. He leaned lazily against the carriage door frame, presumably unaffected by her ire. "Had I not been rattled by the shock of hearing that the dowager isn't well, coupled with the tumble we nearly took within this carriage, I'd take even more offense. What's your name?"

"Luke Callahan," he said in serious tones. "Thank you for asking. You're the first ever to ask, of all the strumpets who've come to see the duke in the six weeks I've been here."

Oh, goodness. His eyes. The pupils were like little black diamonds inside those sapphire irises.

"You're welcome, Mr. Callahan." Janice swallowed. "Wait a minute, what did you say?" She stared at Izzy. "Did he call me a strumpet?"

Izzy nodded, her eyes wide.

"I'll take it back"—his tone was completely unapologetic, but his gaze felt like a caress—"if you'll cooperate. It's too late to return you to the village. The snow has lent you the best excuse yet to stay—even better than that broken wheel. But you'd best behave while you're here."

"Behave?" Janice practically squeaked the word, she felt so prim at the moment—and she only felt prim whenever she was in over her head. "I don't know what you're about, but it makes no sense. No sense at all. Why, look at my bonnet and cloak! They're perfectly respectable—"

"Come now." He shot her a sympathetic grin. "You and I both know they don't disguise your true hot nature."

"My *what*?" She inhaled a breath. "If you don't stop spouting nonsense—"

"Let me explain a little closer," he said, and, without ceremony, half-entered the carriage, grabbed her by the hand, and pulled.

Janice's heart went wild. "What in heaven's *name*? Just what do you think you're doing?" Shock turned to anger, and anger made her fierce. She clung to the door of the carriage with every ounce of strength in her.

Yet with one quick motion the groom tugged her free, and she fell into his arms, like a fly into a spider's web.

Isobel screamed just as he kicked the door shut and set Janice on the ground. "You're good," he said in an approving tone while holding her pinned tightly against his chest. "Not many know the dowager is in residence. And that wheel . . . you must be hell-bent on deliverance. From what, though? Why would a spitfire like you need saving?"

"Unhand me," Janice said, low. From behind her, she heard Isobel opening the carriage window. "I'm the daughter of a marquess."

"That's what they all say," he said with relish, and captured her arm behind her back. "I must warn you. If you expect anything worthwhile from that excuse for a duke you're after, you'll be disappointed. If you're wise, you'll leave as soon as the roads clear." He paused long enough to rake her from head to toe with an appreciative glance—she put every ounce of scorn in her possession into the haughty expression she shot back at him—and then he kissed her, a bawdy, lush kiss that demanded immediate compliance.

It was a miracle how quickly he redefined kissing for her, a marvel how well her lips fit with his in the brief second before she gathered her wits and attempted to knee the blackguard in the groin. She caught him on his thigh instead.

"What the devil?" He drew back and stared at her, not releasing her arm, which he still held vice-like behind her back.

"See?" Janice was breathing hard. "I really am here to see the dowager, you reckless rogue of a man!"

Snow fell between them, and she had the uncanny feeling she was in a dream. *It's he,* her heart said—her foolish, foolish heart —even as her lips stung, her throat tightened with white-hot anger, and her brain immediately pegged him as no good.

The man like no other.

The one Mama had told her she'd find someday, who Marcia had also assured her would come her way despite the fact that her experience with Finn Lattimore had shaken her to the core and made her distrust men entirely.

But Luke Callahan—this groom—couldn't be he. He wasn't a gentleman, not by half.

He grinned. "So I've erred."

"You most certainly have." She gave a yank on her arm.

He let it go, but now he put his hands on the small of

her back and pressed her close. "Devil take it," he said in that easy way he had of speaking, "you're a luscious mistake I don't regret." He perused her face. "Do you? Do you wish I'd never supposed you were anything other than a proper lady?"

She blinked several times. "I can't answer that," she whispered. "And you're a blackguard to ask."

He roared with laughter. "I like you, Lady Janice. You and your circus maid. She's watching right now. Let's ignore her, shall we?" And with a wicked gleam in his eye he bent down and kissed Janice again.

What was she *doing*?

But he was good . . . oh, so good. If a man could be called *good* the way she called a warm fire good, or a cup of steaming chocolate, or a . . . a mouth that spoke to her without speaking, the way his was.

You're made for love.

You tantalize me.

I want you.

Messages that made her entire body wake up in a way it never had before. She was quivery, like a newborn lamb. Her eyes were closed, but the world unfolded like a bright spring meadow.

His lips brushed soft yet insistent against her own, but hardness was what she was thinking of, the solid weight of him—of his chest, and his belly, and the security of his thighs against hers.

Mr. Callahan's thighs.

Three words she never knew she'd say. She'd never even heard of the middle one, *Callahan*. But in that moment, they were the three most important words she'd ever put together.

Life was full of surprises.

Chapter Two

Janice's mouth was still scorched twenty minutes later when she arrived at the Duke of Halsey's Elizabethan manor. Every snowflake that touched her lips practically sizzled off them. Never, *ever* had she envisioned that a fire could spring up so quickly between a man and a woman—and on a slush-filled rut in a road, no less, with clouds of their breath mingling in the frigid air and the musky smell of wet wool and leather in their nostrils.

It was the sort of surprise that she could dwell on for days, weeks, months.

Which was why she was relieved to see that the house was as indifferent to her presence as any upper-crust English pile of stone could be. She didn't need any more surprises today. The ducal manor would make a fine place at which to pass time, to look up suddenly and realize that she'd wiled away a month stitching pillows, playing the pianoforte, and providing solace to an ill older woman while the busy outside world passed her by.

"What is it, my lady?" Isobel asked her, a pucker on her forehead. "You look ready to jump out of your skin."

Janice kept her eyes on the house. "I don't want a duke," she muttered grimly.

"Of course you don't," Isobel said. "All you want to

do is forget the rest of the world for a while. Am I right, my lady?"

"Yes." Janice sighed. "I'm tired of trying to meet everyone's expectations."

"And you think the best way to forget them is to kiss that groom again."

"Please don't remind me." Janice's insides jangled with a confusing mix of anger and longing. "I can't stop thinking about it. About *him*. Blast Mr. Callahan's hide. And blast yours, too, Izzy, for being so perceptive. You mustn't tell anyone. I'll recover eventually."

"I won't. I promise, although"—the maid looked over her shoulder—"I have to tell you, when you slapped his face, it was the most exciting thing I've ever witnessed in my life. It had been going *so well* up to that point."

Janice sighed. "I wish you'd looked the other way."

"How could I possibly have done that? I felt as if I was at a play and I was watching two perfect lovers meet onstage. Except one was a very handsome, naughty groom and the other was a lady. It wasn't proper at all. It was the opposite of proper, which made it even more exciting. And then *you*—"

"I know. I had to slap him. He was . . . oh, never mind." He'd been caressing her bottom, and she'd actually moaned aloud. Even now, as she thought about it, her cheeks grew hot. She looked around, feeling completely skittish.

"I understand, my lady," Isobel reassured her. "With my own ears I heard him laugh and then tell you to slap the duke, too, if he ever dared touch you."

Janice got huffy just remembering. "How many women did he say had slapped him before? A hundred?"

"No, my lady. He said over a hundred *should* have,

but none actually had. You were the only one. Ever. And he liked it." Isobel giggled.

"He said that to make me angry. Surely if he's kissed at least a hundred women another one would have put him in his place by now."

"Oh?" Isobel's answer was arch. "Perhaps he's such a good kisser, everyone else forgot to. In fact, I'd have done far worse than moan, as you did, my lady—I'd have fainted dead away with pleasure."

"*Izzy.* I didn't moan, for goodness' sake. I-I was struggling to get away. Sort of. As soon as I heard Oscar and the duke's carriage approaching . . ."

But the maid threw her a sideways glance and sidled over to the unfamiliar vehicle—borrowed from the duke's own stables—to watch Oscar overseeing the removal of their bags. It was Isobel's way of disagreeing with her mistress without outright contradicting her.

All right, heaven help her, Janice *had* moaned and clung tightly to the man's muscular neck long enough that her knees gave out and a delicious tingle between her thighs stole her breath away. And she wasn't proud of it. She'd behaved like the desperate spinster she was fast becoming.

How had she reached such a point?

Her first Season had gone splendidly. She'd turned down several proposals, being in no rush. But her second Season was different. Her callers dropped off. At balls, men looked right through her, as if she didn't exist.

Perhaps she'd done it to herself. After her humiliating romance with the no-good Finn Lattimore, she'd read more books. Been less willing to speak up. Was more wary. She thought she'd gotten over him—no, she *knew* she had.

But still. She persisted in being a failure. Somehow this visit to the country was supposed to help restore her luster. She'd wondered how, but now she knew: *more kisses from Luke Callahan*. She'd been like a tarnished silver teapot that had just been rubbed to a gleaming finish.

She didn't want to tarnish again.

Meanwhile, Mr. Callahan's warning about the duke echoed in her brain, but she shrugged it off. *I'll make up my own mind about His Grace,* she thought, and prayed the duke knew she was arriving. One more person in this large place wouldn't be too much a burden, would it? She didn't believe that he'd be vastly pleased to hear she was coming—he was a duke, after all, and had more important matters to attend to than the comings-and-goings of his grandmother's friends—but in Janice's daydreams she wished that he'd be pleased.

Lady Janice is at my door? she imagined him saying. *The Lady Janice? The one with tremendous powers of observation and a quick wit? She spilled lemonade on me once, and I've never forgotten.*

He'd run to his bedchamber and change his cravat before he was to meet her because he'd be slightly nervous. And in this musing of hers he'd show her round his library and tell her it was hers to peruse at any time of day or night. He'd watch to see which books she'd take down. . . .

Oh, she needed to stop weaving these girlish fantasies, as if she were an ingénue who could afford to indulge in them.

No duke was going to notice *her*.

The windows at the ground level were heavily curtained in a deep maroon velvet. Within she caught a glimpse of bookcase, a chair, a portrait. The face of a maid, and then her swift withdrawal.

Janice wondered what rooms the dowager had and another sweep of dread rushed through her: Mama didn't know a thing about the dowager believing she was the Queen and never would have let Janice be chaperoned by her had she been aware of the state of things.

But Janice didn't want to return to London. She'd do anything to stay.

And hide.

And . . . and maybe kiss that groom again. If she could ever find him. He'd led the way back to the house but disappeared as soon as the vehicle stopped near the front steps. No doubt he'd returned his own mount to the massive stable block, which housed some of England's finest horses.

The snow was back to downy flakes, sweetly falling, while perfectly formed curlicues of smoke drifted lazily away from the chimneys. She was counting them when the Duke of Halsey himself appeared in the distance, coming from the stables, surrounded by a pack of dark gray hounds and two other men. A cheroot hung from his lips, and he was outfitted in a heavy coat beneath which she caught a glimpse of impeccably cut country tweeds. His friends dressed in similar impressive fashion.

Janice's heart picked up its pace as he neared.

Although the duke wasn't the tallest of the group, he bulged with muscle, exuding a solid masculinity the men trailing him lacked. With his almond-shaped eyes, swarthy complexion, and rolling gait, he reminded Janice of Pan . . . a hot, seething Pan. She half-expected the snow behind him to melt in his trail. A blush heated her cheeks as she recalled the images she'd seen of the half human, half beast, all of which portrayed him with a wildly large portion of the male anatomy she really shouldn't be thinking of right now.

But she couldn't help it. Only a few minutes ago, she'd been wrapped in the arms of a man who'd made it abundantly clear that *he'd* been aroused by her.

Her toes curled and her belly tightened just thinking about Luke Callahan.

Now the duke snapped his fingers at the hounds, and they all took off in a pack and huddled, restless, near the front steps, not wanting to lower their haunches onto the snow. Then he tossed away his cheroot, a nonchalant gesture that spoke volumes. There was no one he needed to impress here, yet he would greet a lady as a lady should be greeted.

Be agreeable, she thought when he bent over her hand murmuring polite words of welcome while his friends hovered nearby, pale moons in his orbit. She was often dismissed easily. And she might be nearly on the shelf. But she could win awards for friendliness.

The august personage before her straightened again yet still held to her gloved hand. They were of the same height, she realized, a fact she hadn't noticed the one time she'd met him in London and managed to spill that lemonade on his arm at a ball.

Up close, she could see that his lips were dry and chapped, his cheeks ruddy with cold, and his hair a tangled mess of brown, coarse and abundant, like a horse's mane. He was clearly a man meant to live outdoors, and she wondered if he gave his valet fits.

In London, he'd been packaged to a fault as a duke—he'd had a restrained, immaculate appearance. But here . . .

He was Pan.

"So, Lady Janice." His eyes bored into hers with cool disinterest. "You're of the prolific House of Brady."

"Yes, Your Grace," she said. "I'm the second of three daughters, the fourth oldest of six siblings."

And probably the last to get married—if ever. She imagined herself doddering about with a cane and sneaking sweets to all her nephews and nieces while their parents weren't looking.

"How interesting," the duke murmured in the smooth, unhurried tone that suggested buckets of money, ancient bloodlines, and an Oxford education.

She could tell he was lying. He was bored by her already. She was ready to leave him, go to her room, and become invisible.

"Are you enjoying the snow?" he asked her.

"Yes," she said. "It's lovely." But she wouldn't wax on about how gorgeous it was coating the eaves of the house like sugar, making it appear like something from a fairy tale. It was true, but she was cold and ready to go indoors.

He looked over his shoulder at the two gentlemen huddled behind him. "This sort of weather clears the lungs, isn't that right, men?"

The more Janice heard the duke speak, the more his rich man's accent became too nasal and contrived for her liking.

"Of course, Your Grace," said the short older man, wincing as a gust of wind caused him to hold on to his hat.

"Right," returned the other, who was much younger and strove to sound spirited.

One didn't contradict a duke, did one?

Janice would have chuckled at the misery evident in their expressions if it hadn't also been a pity that there didn't seem to be true affection between the men and their host—the kind that she'd seen her brothers and father share with one another and their friends.

When the duke introduced them—the older one was Lord Rowntree and the younger Lord Yarrow—he was all that was courteous, as were they.

But there was still something different about Halsey. Beneath that layer of polite ducal behavior was something exotic in his demeanor. Janice wondered if he'd traveled far and well, perhaps experienced extraordinary things.

Dark things.

Her scalp prickled with a sinister awareness, but she quickly discounted it. Mr. Callahan's influence, of course. And maybe there was still some caution of her own—well-earned caution after Finn.

By now her ears were frozen. Her entire face was, and as for her toes . . . well, they were like ice. She should really discuss with His Grace the matter of her not having a proper chaperone, now that she knew his grandmother wasn't well enough to serve as one. But she'd bring the matter up inside, before a fire.

If they'd ever get there.

"I understand you're here to see my grandmother." He spread his legs and crossed his arms as if he were prepared to stand there indefinitely.

"Yes." She gave a little involuntary shiver, but he made no move toward the house. "The dowager duchess wrote my parents and asked me to stay a month. But I understand she's not herself."

"She *is* ill. Who told you?"

A stab of alarm shot through her. "A groom, Your Grace." Surely he wouldn't be upset with Mr. Callahan and construe his telling her about the dowager as gossip. "He was only looking out for your best interests. When he found us on the property and asked us our business, I told him the dowager had invited me. He said that was unlikely as she was ill."

"She believes she's the Queen." His Grace spoke with a simple frankness that lent his words a measure of poignancy.

"I'm so sorry." She wrapped her arms around herself in hopes he'd take the hint. "Did you have any idea I was coming to see her? I would hate for my visit to have taken you by surprise."

His eyes gave nothing away. "Dukes don't always know the particulars of the daily goings-on at their homes," he said, "but I assure you, nothing is done at Halsey House unless it's my express wish."

How that could possibly be Janice couldn't fathom. It seemed quite the paradox. But polite answers often were ambiguous, and who was she to question a duke?

"We're glad to have you here, Lady Janice." He must have seen the doubt on her face. "You'll enjoy your stay—although I'm sure you'll want to return to London as soon as the roads clear."

Return to London?

"Oh," was all she managed to say. Her kissing groom had told her the same thing.

"You didn't come here to be a nurse," the duke went on, "but that's exactly the sort of companion my grandmother needs." He allowed his mouth to curve in a small smile. "You should be at parties in Town, my lady, enjoying yourself."

Oh, right. Enjoying herself in Town. Janice took her mind off the memory of Luke Callahan long enough to remember everything she was missing in London—

Which wasn't much. This was most awkward. His Grace had no idea how unpopular she was, obviously.

And he was basically telling her to leave. But in such a charming way.

She felt momentarily overwhelmed. "I-I'm so sorry about this, Your Grace. Yes, of course, as soon as the snow clears I should head back to Grosvenor Square." She bit her lip. What a disappointment this trip was turning out to be. Mama and Daddy would be devastated. "I'm afraid, meanwhile, that I have a further complication. I can tell you about it inside."

"Oh?" He took another deep, cleansing breath. "Why put it off? We'll discuss it now."

He would want to, wouldn't he?

"Very well." An eddy of cold air swept up her skirt. "I didn't bring a companion. My mother believed Her Grace was to chaperone."

"An understandable mistake. Your maid will serve as a chaperone just as well."

What he was proposing wasn't exactly proper. Surely he must know. But he was striving to accommodate her, wasn't he? She didn't want to be churlish and overly demanding. She was an uninvited guest, really. Her invitation hadn't counted, not if the dowager wasn't in her right mind when she wrote it.

Which was why Janice said, "Yes, my maid will do," although Isobel most certainly wouldn't. She and Janice were the same age—down to the same birthday—and Izzy was the opposite of strict and mature, not to mention she had the colorful manners of a girl who'd grown up in a traveling circus and regularly ridden on elephants as a child.

But Janice would agree to anything at the moment. She looked longingly at the front door.

"Your maid will do until I procure you a genuine chaperone, of course," the duke clarified. "We can't have your mother concerned."

There was that enigmatic half smile again, the one that made her heart beat faster with the slightest twinge of worry. "That's good of you, Your Grace," she said. "Thank you."

"I have just the person," he said with alacrity. "A widow who recently moved to the estate. A former schoolteacher. Her name is Mrs. Friday. I'll send someone for her immediately."

"Thank you, Your Grace." A shaft of icy air angled down from the roof and flung snowflakes beneath Janice's bonnet. "Are you sure she won't mind having her routine disrupted?"

"She'll welcome a change; I'm sure of it." He raised a hand and snapped his fingers. A footman came running over, and Halsey gave him directions. "Send someone to fetch Mrs. Friday straightaway. Tell her I'll compromise her well"—there was a cough from one of his friends, and Janice felt her eyes go wide—"*compensate* her well," he went on smoothly, "especially as we're giving her such short notice."

He turned back to Janice, completely unfazed by his outrageous faux pas. Dukes didn't need to feel embarrassed about such things.

"Thank you, Your Grace." Janice tried to smile. "I look forward to meeting your grandmother. I may not be a nurse, but I can . . ."—She paused, her entire body heating up when she saw Luke Callahan walk with quiet resolve behind Halsey toward the carriage, where he put his hand on the horse's harness and made direct eye contact with her—"keep her company," she finished lamely.

Even through the snowfall, the groom's gaze was bold. Unyielding. The message was clear: *Don't forget what I said about him.*

The duke, of course.

But who was he to talk, this Mr. Callahan? Hadn't he agreed with her that he was no saint himself?

Janice looked away from him as fast as she could. Warring with her annoyance with the man was the ridiculous exhilaration that rushed through her at the sight of him.

He'd kissed her.

Really kissed her.

And she'd never forget.

Never, ever.

Although she wished she could. He was a blackguard, a ne'er-do-well. And he'd laughed at her when she'd slapped him.

The hounds began to whine and wag their massive tails at him, which caused the duke and his friends to look in his direction.

"You! Groom!" His Grace shouted. "Get over here and pick this up." He pointed to the still-smoking cheroot in the snow.

Inwardly, Janice winced. Despite her disapproval of Mr. Callahan on general principles, she couldn't help feeling very strongly that he didn't deserve to be addressed with so little dignity. He was intelligent. Shrewd. All virile man. This she knew from experience. Very *close* experience.

She sensed a split second's hesitation before he left the horse, but then he walked toward Janice and the duke with a fearless gait and she found herself bracing. *For heaven's sakes,* she reminded herself. *He's a* groom.

But it was no good. Her pulse quickened even further as he approached. He'd unlocked a door to a deeply pleasurable place within her with his kisses, which was reason enough to lose her breath. In his groom's garb, he somehow managed to exude an aura of power, something that went beyond his impressive physique. It shone from his eyes and seasoned his stride with confidence. She had to struggle to maintain an even expression and thought back to what she'd told Isobel in the carriage: nothing happened in the country.

And then he strode past her.

She felt a searing disappointment. The next moment, he was only a few feet away from her, bending over the cheroot, smashing it out in the snow, and picking it up. He straightened and faced Halsey and her both. The feel of his mouth on hers was still fresh in her memory.

"Move swiftly when I beckon you." The duke spoke without heat but with an implied sense of supremacy.

Mr. Callahan stood directly between His Grace and the house. "An old leg injury, Your Grace."

It was no apology. And he hadn't appeared to have a leg injury earlier. Oh, no. He'd been a firm rock of a man who'd held steady all the while that she'd kissed him, kneed him, and then slapped him.

The duke's face, implacable as it was, took on a curious cast. "Was it you who told Lady Janice my grandmother might be ill?" There was no chiding in his tone. But there was something else. . . .

Control. That's what it was. The duke was very controlled, Janice thought, and held her breath.

"Yes, Your Grace."

She was fascinated to see that Luke Callahan appeared equally in control. It was like watching a chess game between two well-matched opponents.

"It's not your place to speak to the young lady at all." Halsey was still cool and composed. But the tension around his mouth belied his words, making Janice's heart beat faster.

"Their carriage wheel broke," Mr. Callahan replied

calmly, "and her driver needed assistance. Naturally, I asked why they were on the estate. It was a matter of security, Your Grace."

Yes, that's right, Janice thought. He'd told her he was under orders to preserve the integrity of the estate.

"I make those decisions, not you," said the duke. "Whatever carriage comes through those gates will be free to arrive at this house. All inquiries will be left to me. Have you questioned visitors before?"

"Never, Your Grace," the groom replied.

Janice blinked. He was lying right there. He'd told her he had, that it was his job.

The duke observed him through narrowed eyes. Mr. Callahan looked steadily back.

"I'll fire you for your insolence if you do it again," His Grace said. "The only reason I won't this time is because it might distress the lady. Now get the snow off those steps. And do it quickly." He finally showed some irritation in his tone.

"Very well, Your Grace." Mr. Callahan turned to do as he was bid.

Janice was flummoxed.

Mr. Callahan had won that match.

It made no sense, but he'd somehow bested the duke in a game that should never have been played. She wasn't even sure His Grace knew he'd been defeated.

The gritty sound of Mr. Callahan's boot on the stone and the sheer conviction of his movements—shouldn't he have at least pretended to have a weak leg?—only added to her sense that he was the vanquisher and not the vanquished.

Yet he was a servant doing a servant's job. How could he be as enthralling a figure as a duke?

He's not. *He's a* groom.

But when she was very young, she'd been a shopgirl. *And you always will be, you fool, if you can't keep your eyes off the help.*

The crowning moment came when Mr. Callahan finished his chore and walked purposefully down the steps. "All finished, Your Grace." He stood at relaxed attention, his gloved hands dangling at his sides, while the dogs stared avidly at him, their tongues lolling.

He was a Very Bad Man, Janice thought. And, God help her, she couldn't look away.

Except she must when, seconds later, she walked past him. Even with snow pelting her cheeks, she felt his heat. And his gaze. Yet she wouldn't look at him. That wouldn't be proper. Kissing him wasn't proper, either. But what was done was done. She could be proper starting *now*. She would behave as a real lady should.

But as she cautiously ascended the freshly cleared steps to the front door with the duke—finally!—his unremarkable friends following behind in much the same way the hounds were, she had an odd craving, considering how fortunate she was to be with His Grace: she wished a wayward groom were escorting her up these stairs instead.

Was it exhaustion or desperation that made her think this way? Every woman in London would like to trade places with her right now. The duke's grip was firm and his body next to hers intimidating. Beneath his coat, his calves strained with muscle, and his belly was flat as a washing board. He was clearly in the prime of life.

And he was without a wife.

She looked one more time over her right shoulder to see Mr. Callahan, and her heart skipped a beat. There he was, watching her steadily, his mouth grim. Forbidding. As if he was ready to do someone bodily damage.

Yet there was also that element of amusement behind his eyes, barely concealed, when they locked gazes.

Janice bristled. This was the man who'd devoured her lips as if he were partaking of a rich gateau, who'd raked the length of her body with his hot, shameless gaze.

He was a savage. And he had no right to be amused by her.

But her body didn't lie.

She wanted him, nonetheless.

Chapter Three

A butler magically appeared to throw the door wide in welcome. Janice was never so ready to cross a threshold. The duke and his friends came behind her, and then the hounds. When the door finally shut, sealing the scoundrel groom out, she breathed a sigh of relief. She could focus on why she was here—and then she remembered she wouldn't be here long.

Her heart sank fast to her feet. And she knew it was because once the roads cleared she would be sent back to London.

But at least now she was warm. And somehow the hodgepodge of a décor, faded but still dignified—from the suit of armor in the corner to the tall case clock ticking laboriously at the base of the staircase to the ancient hat stand—spoke to her. The home seemed ducal in the noblest sense of the word, achieving an air that overlooked mere pomp in favor of depth and substance.

Perhaps Halsey was the same way. She hoped so. She'd forgive him his self-importance outside in the snow, as well as his apparent indifference to her. What duke didn't feel important? And as for his lack of interest in her, perhaps he was wise to maintain his distance. For all he knew, she—like the other women who'd come before her to Halsey House—was after him, and if she followed her parents' wishes he'd be correct.

Embarrassed at the very idea of scheming to win a man she didn't know, especially a duke, she stared upward at the house's beams and rich, well-worn tapestries hung on its high walls. *Welcome,* it seemed to say. *I have stories to tell, great and small.* A slant of light from the transom above the front door fell on a crystal vase on the massive sideboard, throwing little diamonds over the black-and-white tile floor.

She might not be Irish, like Daddy, but she was fey in her own way. She got a sure impression that much laughter had echoed through this home's spaces at one time or another, that abundant love had flowed as copiously as wine at a wedding.

She had a sudden wish that one of the house's stories would be hers.

But it won't be, she reminded herself. *You're leaving.*

As soon as the roads cleared and her wheel was fixed. It would be a week at most. And it was a good thing. His Grace, his friends . . . they didn't want her here. She could tell.

She tried not to think of the way Mr. Callahan had kissed her, as if he wanted her very much.

From somewhere far away on the next floor, several women could be heard chatting and laughing. The duke looked sharply up at the top of the wide staircase and then directed his butler to send the housekeeper to the drawing room straightaway. "Tell her that until Lady Janice's maid has had an opportunity to put away her things or Mrs. Friday arrives, she'll serve as Lady Janice's chaperone." The duke looked to her. "I'm going to tell my grandmother myself you're here. I'll see you in a few minutes. Meanwhile, don't wait. The tea tray should be ready."

"Very well, Your Grace."

Daddy would be so glad that His Grace was a stick-
ler for the proprieties.

Luke Callahan, Janice was sure, had completely mis-
judged the duke, but she'd forgive the groom for malign-
ing his employer so. She knew too well how difficult it
was to be looked down upon. Servants met with glaring
lapses in kindness toward them every day, and resent-
ments, naturally, could grow very heated.

"My other houseguests should appear any moment,"
His Grace added. "I'm sure they're anxious to meet you."

Before she could reply, he bowed and left her with his
cohorts. She really preferred to go straight to her room
to unpack first and clean off her travel dirt, but how
could she say no to her host? He had a way of speaking
that was different from everyone else of her acquain-
tance—as if he never second-guessed himself but always assumed everyone would do his bidding. And he
was deucedly unapologetic about that fact.

It was entirely mortifying, really, to be left alone
with Halsey's two friends, neither of whom looked at
her with any real warmth in their eyes. She understood
why the highly eligible duke was on the defensive. But
these two?

They had no excuse.

But Janice refused to surrender to the awkward situation. A footman led them to a vast space filled with oil
paintings of horses. There were bold red accents everywhere: in the fabrics, on the vases, and even on the
china on the tea tray. The dogs had collapsed before the
fire.

It was a man's drawing room.

It needs a woman's touch, she couldn't help thinking
as she took a seat by a low table, where the teapot sat at
the ready. She hoped Isobel and Oscar would get their

own tea very soon, but they probably hadn't yet. Isobel would soon be upstairs with Janice's trunks. And Oscar would no doubt go to the stables to the horses.

She must admit, she even hoped Mr. Callahan would get his tea, although she shouldn't care whether he did or not. She wouldn't think of his shapely legs or broad shoulders, nor would she think of the way he'd kissed her, as if he couldn't get enough of her. She must remind herself that she had many misgivings about him, however glorious a masculine specimen he was.

The housekeeper, an older woman with a large bosom and a kindly face, glided in. "Don't mind me, my lords and my lady," she said quietly.

"Thank you." Janice felt as if she'd put out the entire household with her arrival.

Isobel liked to take her time putting away Janice's things, so unless Mrs. Friday arrived soon, the poor housekeeper would have to ignore her regular duties. She took a seat near the window and opened a small book that she pulled from her apron.

Lord Yarrow, whose face was long and his nose markedly hooked beneath his jet-black hair, sat opposite Janice. "So you're Brady's stepdaughter by his second marriage?" His voice carried that tonnish ennui that she so despised.

"Yes." She poured him a cup of tea. "Although my parents make no distinction between siblings. We're all one happy family."

"Happy? Is that so?" Predictably, the older, rounder Lord Rowntree didn't sound terribly interested as he flung out his tails and took his own seat on a red silk settee. He had silver sideburns and a strong cleft in his chin.

"It *is* so." Janice handed him a brimming cup, too.

"Your older sister is very beautiful." Lord Yarrow

gazed at her with open curiosity, as if he hoped she'd react strongly.

But he'd be disappointed. Janice was used to hearing such compliments about her sister, and contrary to what everyone assumed, she was quite proud to be related to Marcia.

"Yes," Janice said, "she's the most beautiful woman in Town, apart from Mama. Of course"—she smiled—"I'm most prejudiced in their favor."

Janice felt a strong longing to retreat to her room and crawl into bed with a good book, not make small talk with these world-weary fellows who were the last men on earth she'd ever want to marry. They certainly didn't stand out the way the duke did—

Or Luke Callahan.

Oh, dear. Him again. She added two lumps of sugar to distract herself. His Grace, she told herself sternly, was the man she should be thinking of. Yes, he was intimidating and indifferent to most of the rest of the world, but he acted as a duke should.

Yet . . . that wasn't nearly as memorable as a *groom* acting as a duke should.

It was shocking and inappropriate, how Mr. Callahan behaved.

But fascinating nonetheless.

Janice restrained a sigh and looked over her own dish of tea to see Lord Rowntree cross one leg over the other, and the words *Mr. Callahan's thighs* popped into her head. An instant rush of warmth to the apex of her own thighs ensued, followed by a strong dose of guilt that made her temples pound. She drank a sip of tea and wondered if she was a wanton or merely prone to outlandish daydreams.

Mama would be appalled either way.

Janice was grateful to hear more feminine laughter

and the muted sounds of many feet on the stairs. The men paused in their conversation just as three women came into the room, all of them elegantly attired but looking rather hastily put together. Sleepy, even. It was quite a shock this late in the day.

"Sorry we're late," said the first young woman in a strong American accent. "We stayed up past midnight . . . reading novels." Dressed in a plum muslin gown and with a mess of black curls framing her dainty face, she gave a giant yawn and plopped down next to Lord Rowntree. "I'm Lilith Branson of Boston," she said, and extended a hand to Janice.

For the briefest moment, Janice stared at it, not quite sure what to do. So she put down her cup and held her hand out, too. Miss Branson gripped her palm and shook it hard. "Nice to meet you."

"And you." Janice was excited to meet someone new. It was a rare thing to see an American socialite, especially one as bold and friendly as Miss Branson. "I'm Lady Janice Sherwood. My father is the Marquess of Brady."

"I've heard much of your sister Lady Chadwick," said another young lady in a rather dated yellow silk gown. She had brown hair and bright green eyes. "I'm Lady Opal, and this is my sister, Lady Rose."

"Pleased to meet you both." Janice smiled, happy they had each other. She knew the value of sisters and suddenly missed her own.

Rose was freckle faced, with strawberry blonde hair, and wore a soft blue gown that Janice could swear had nearly threadbare sleeves, although she wouldn't gaze upon them long enough to find out.

Despite the sad state of their gowns, the sisters, with their wide-set eyes, were equally pretty. Neither outshone the other. And Miss Branson was attractive, too.

She had dimples on either side of her heart-shaped mouth and a pert nose.

Janice poured them each a cup of tea. "Were you invited here by the dowager, as well?" she asked with sympathy. Perhaps they'd been caught in an awkward situation, too. It would explain their lack of chaperone. They were certainly of an age to require one.

The two men watched them all as if attending a play.

"Oh, no." Lilith gave a hearty laugh. "I came on my own. I'd read about the Duke of Halsey's stables. I've got my own back home. I figured he wouldn't mind a visit from an American heiress with a know-how for horses." She winked. "Don't tell my father. He thinks I'm over here visiting a boarding-school friend in London."

Janice was shocked but tried not to show it.

"And we're on our way further north," explained Lady Rose with a sweet smile, "to our aunt's house in Manchester."

"Our late mother knew the duke's mother," said Lady Opal. "We stopped to pay our regards."

"I see," said Janice, trying her best to be understanding. But they mentioned nothing of an invitation, either.

"Our usual companion was ill when we left our home in Kent," Lady Rose said. "She should be arriving any day now. As soon as she does, we'll make our way north again."

"This companion of theirs must be very ill," Lilith said to Janice. "They've been here a month."

Lady Rose's brow puckered. "And you've been here three weeks, have you not?"

"That I have." Lilith stared back at her and drank her tea down in one gulp as the men exchanged amused glances. "But if anyone told me I needed a chaperone, I'd tell them to jump in a lake. I'm rich, I'm American, and I do what I want."

Good God, Janice thought. *How marvelous that must be!*

But she couldn't get away from the fact that these women were highly questionable guests. Mama would be appalled that they were here. As for the men, from their poor manners alone Janice didn't think much of them at all.

She'd seen Daddy struggle with problematic visitors, too. When one had a great deal of power and wealth, one attracted all sorts. Of course, if the Duke of Halsey had a wife these awkward social situations wouldn't happen. His wife would see to it that the house was run properly, that guests were only of the invited sort, of excellent character, and assiduously looked after.

Poor, beleaguered duke. He needed to marry.

But Janice wasn't to be a candidate for the position of duchess. A week wasn't enough time to win a duke, surely, especially a duke who appeared to want one gone.

And she didn't want him anyway.

Just as she finished that thought, the object of her musings swept into the room, fully in command, and very regally so.

"My grandmother was demanding the crown jewels," the duke said, "which I, of course, couldn't give her. She had to be satisfied with the cup of tea I poured her instead."

It was a sad situation. And Janice couldn't help thinking that he was a thoughtful grandson.

"You do your best with her, Halsey," Lord Rowntree said on a sigh.

"Yes, you do, Your Grace." Lady Rose batted her eyes at him. "Any woman would love to drink a cup of tea you poured."

His Grace brushed off the compliments and made sure Janice had been properly introduced to everyone before he sat next to her and observed her with a quiet, confident gaze. "You play the pianoforte, I suppose."

It was a bald statement, but she was becoming used to his style of speaking—as if her answers didn't matter and he was merely being polite.

"Yes, I do play. Passably." She was quite good, actually, but she got very nervous playing in front of anyone who wasn't a family member.

His Grace accepted the cup of tea she poured him. "I assume you sing as well."

"Yes, I suppose I do." She loved to sing. Mama had told her she had one of the most beautiful voices she'd ever heard. Yet Janice was terrified to sing in front of company, too, and never had beyond her immediate family.

Her host stirred his tea. "You'll play and sing for us tonight after dinner."

It wasn't an invitation. It was a command. A very ducal one, at that.

Janice felt immediately queasy. "Yes, of course, Your Grace."

It was the last thing she wanted to do. But he was the Duke of Halsey. What choice did she have? Especially as she was an uninvited guest, in her own way?

There was general conversation for a few minutes, desultory and quite proper, although Janice noticed an underlying tension in the room. But it could be coming from her. After all, she was the newest arrival at this unusual house party—because that was what this gathering apparently was.

Without warning, the duke stood. "I'll show you round the house now, Lady Janice. The portrait gallery and the conservatory are particularly worth seeing. Your parents can't have you return home without a few interesting details about the house to share."

Return home.

She noticed how carelessly he'd injected those two words into his speech.

He probably assumed she'd be flattered that he was showing her so much attention, but it was entirely wrong of her to stroll about the house with him unchaperoned.

Just as it's wrong of you to kiss a groom, a little voice in her head chided her.

"Shall—shall all your friends accompany us?" she asked him.

"I've already given them the tour," His Grace returned easily.

"And an exciting one it was." Lord Rowntree nodded, his wattle quivering.

"Indeed," Miss Branson echoed him. "I look forward to hearing which portrait is your favorite, Lady Janice."

Janice swallowed and smiled. "I suppose that will be all right."

But it wasn't. She knew it wasn't. Mama might want Janice to capture the duke's attention, but she wouldn't want her to do anything inappropriate.

"Wait," she found herself blurting out. "I can't believe I forgot. I should see the dowager immediately, now that I've had my tea and an opportunity to warm up." She also wanted to retreat to her room to refresh her toilette after her long day in the carriage, but no one seemed to notice she'd not been granted that basic courtesy.

A wife in residence would have noticed, of course.

"Granny's not going anywhere," the duke said mildly. "She's sleeping at the moment, as it is."

"Very well," Janice conceded, with some regret. "However"—she looked down at her gown's rumpled skirt—"I really should remove this travel dirt."

"You can do that after the tour," he replied. "You'll have plenty of time before dinner."

She was entirely flummoxed. *Say no,* she thought. *Say you need a chaperone and that you need to change your gown!*

And then she saw that the housekeeper had disappeared from her corner. Janice hated to make a scene and demand the woman be found and dragged along. Nor did she want to insist on calling Isobel down from her bedchamber. And if Janice demanded to change her gown, it might seem churlish in light of the duke's efforts to be a good host.

"Well, my lady?" he asked her.

She looked into his alert amber eyes and decided that she was being silly. One little tour of the house . . . it was such an innocent thing. And he was obviously proud of it, the way a boy is proud when he lines up his tin soldiers.

Besides, he was a *duke*—a duke who was used to getting his way, as no doubt all dukes were.

"Y-yes," she said slowly. "Yes, you're right. Everything can wait until after the tour."

She could do this. She could survive without a chaperone for a few minutes. His grandmother could wait, too, as could Janice's travel dirt.

She took a step toward him to take his proffered arm, but the butler came to the door. "A note for Lady Janice," he said, "from the stables."

"Oh?" she said lightly. Oscar must need something. Perhaps it was her emergency flask of Daddy's whiskey. Oscar had been in their employ so long, he was like family and would think nothing of making such a request if his own flask had run dry.

Relief flooded through her. She'd had a temporary

reprieve from an awkward situation. Yet it was still a painful sensation to endure feeling all eyes upon her as she walked lightly past the duke and his friends and took the note from the butler's outstretched hand.

Unfolding it, she read in a careless male scrawl: *I found a dog outside the stables—she's about to become a mother. You'll want to see her.*

It was signed only *LC*.

Luke Callahan, of course. The name should inspire indignation in Janice. And there he was presuming that he knew how she'd respond—just as the Duke of Halsey did.

But something warm wrapped around her heart. All her annoyance at the groom was temporarily forgotten. How did Mr. Callahan know—how could he have known that she loved strays so much?

There was only one answer to his question: *Yes,* she thought as she folded the note back up and made a brief excuse to the company.

And she meant it for so many different reasons.

Chapter Four

Four of the stable hands were sitting around a coal stove with Oscar when Janice burst through the door, bringing with her the blinding white light that came with snow, along with a flurry of downy flakes. Behind her was a friendly junior groom named Aaron, who'd delivered Mr. Callahan's note to the house.

"Hello!" she said with a broad smile to the circle of men.

She was tremendously excited that she'd found a way to leave the house—without her gloves, but she didn't care. All the grooms stood from their chairs, but she didn't see Mr. Callahan among them.

"Lady Janice, what in devil's name are you doing here?" asked Oscar.

"To check on the stray dog, of course," she said. "And to see if she's produced any puppies."

Mr. Callahan stepped forward from the shadows.

Janice swiveled to look at him and saw that nothing in his eyes suggested they'd ever shared a long, heated kiss. Of course, that was a relief. She replaced her smile with a contained, formal expression.

"The dog's this way." His tone was polite but not at all deferential. "And no, she hasn't produced puppies. Not yet."

"Let's see her then," Janice said crisply. It was an

order. Not a request. The kind a well-brought-up young lady would give a groom.

Oscar stayed by her side—clearly hovering—and the three of them walked back to the remote stall that held a glowing lantern, even though the day hadn't quite waned.

"Does the duke know why you're here, my lady?" Oscar asked her.

She chuckled. "I told him a little white lie. I said you were ailing but not enough to need a doctor. Just a reminder of home." She pulled a flask from her coat pocket.

The driver glowered. "'Tisn't right for you to be coming to the stables. And I've got my own flask of Lord Brady's whiskey as it is."

"I know you do," she said, "but I couldn't simply walk out and say I was visiting a stray dog."

"All the more reason you shouldn't be here," Oscar admonished her.

"It harms no one that I want to see her," she chided him gently back, and then saw the animal sprawled in the hay. "Oh, my," she whispered, and with fumbling fingers tried to pull open the stall door.

"Let me." With one quick motion of his brawny arm and a deft twist of his fingers, Mr. Callahan opened the door.

"Thank you," she returned politely, but she remembered those fingers in her hair and that arm wrapping her close. She'd try her very best to steer clear of him, but when she passed in front of him she felt ridiculous enjoyment at his nearness.

Once in the stall, she walked carefully across sweet-smelling hay to crouch near the soon-to-be mother. The dog was a mid-sized, long-haired black-and-white thing of no particular breed, but Janice guessed she might be a shepherding sort of animal who'd lost her family.

"I wonder what your name is?" After petting the dog's sleek head, Janice looked up at Mr. Callahan. "This is a lovely bed. Thank you for preparing it."

"I did next to nothing." Again, it was as if they were meeting for the first time.

Janice was grateful for his discretion, yet a small, hidden part of her was also disappointed. What a shame that people were trapped in their own special roles and not able to do exactly what they wanted. According to her parents, her role was to be a respectable member of the Beau Monde. The thought had never bothered her before—indeed, she'd been grateful that Daddy had saved them from penury—but it certainly did now.

If Mr. Callahan had been dressed by Weston and wore boots by Hoby—if he had a title and properties— he'd be an eligible suitor. But instead, she was supposed not to notice that he existed, beyond the services he provided as a groom, such as lifting her foot into the saddle if she required assistance.

She looked away from him to the dog. "She has to have a name. I think I'll call her Esmeralda."

Oscar chuckled.

"Why such an elegant name?" Mr. Callahan asked.

"It's the least we can do for her," Janice answered serenely.

"Of course."

She heard the groom's light sarcasm but chose to ignore it.

Esmeralda got to her feet. Shook her head. Looked miserably at her visitors. Sat on her haunches, whined, and stood again. Then collapsed and focused on her hindquarters.

"I think she's ready," Mr. Callahan said.

"Aye." Oscar kneaded his hat in his large hands.

"All right," Janice whispered. "Good luck, dear girl."

She stood and went slowly to Oscar's side, almost all of her attention focused on Esmeralda. But part of her was constantly aware of the groom—of Mr. Callahan.

"You'll come back in the morning," Oscar reassured her, "to a litter of puppies for you to admire."

"No." Janice pressed her lips firmly together. "I want to see them being born."

"It could take hours," Mr. Callahan said. "The duke will be expecting you back soon."

"And it's not fitting for you to stay and watch anyway," Oscar added.

"Of course it is," she replied softly. "It's natural. And I can't leave her."

And then it happened, what they'd all been waiting for. At that very moment, Esmeralda gave birth to a black-and-white puppy. She made quick work of freeing the tiny thing of its cord and licking it clean.

Janice pressed both hands to her face, her eyes filling with tears at the sight. "She knows exactly what to do, doesn't she?"

The squirming puppy sought its mother, and Esmeralda tended to it with calm purpose. "She's a good little mother. Oscar, isn't it marvelous?" Janice turned around.

But Oscar wasn't there. He lay sprawled in a heap on the straw-covered floor.

Chapter Five

"Oh, no," Janice whispered, and crouched in the straw next to Oscar's inert form. At least he was breathing. And his color was good. "I can't believe he fainted."

Mr. Callahan chuckled and knelt next to her—mere inches from her. "It's always the toughest who go down at birthings."

She could feel his heat. Smell his clean, soapy scent, mingled with a whiff of leather and linen. But she must focus on Oscar, not on the groom, who laid two fingers on the older man's neck.

"His pulse is strong and steady," Mr. Callahan said. "He'll come round."

At that, Oscar's eyes opened and he looked quizzically about him. "What the devil?"

"You fainted," Janice told him gently.

"No," he whispered. "I don't faint." He sat up on his elbows. "Last thing I remember, we were watching the dog—" He swallowed hard.

Janice looked over her shoulder at Esmeralda and gasped. "Another puppy!"

Esmeralda once more did what her instincts told her to do, cleaning the wriggling newborn and nudging him to snuggle with his sibling.

Oscar groaned and laid his head back down.

"It's not uncommon to get a bit dizzy at things like this," Mr. Callahan told him lightly, which Janice appreciated very much. Oscar had his dignity, after all. "Let me help you up and get you upstairs."

Oscar winced. "I suppose that's best."

Janice laid her hand on the older man's grizzled jaw. "I want to give you a sip of Daddy's whiskey right now, and once you get to your bed, take some more from your own flask. Will you promise me that?"

"Aye." Oscar didn't even wince as she dribbled some of the potent liquid into his mouth. He swallowed it as if it were the elixir of the gods. "I want to stand up," he rasped after a moment.

Mr. Callahan helped him to his feet.

"Are you sure you're fine?" Janice couldn't help but worry.

"I'm right as rain." There was gravel—and perhaps a bit of annoyance—in Oscar's tone.

Mr. Callahan exchanged a brief look with her. The slight upward curve of one side of his mouth mirrored her own amusement—and relief.

Aaron appeared at the stall door and peered around them to Esmeralda and her family. "Look at that, will you?" Then he seemed to notice Oscar's distressed expression. "What's wrong? Do you need a doctor, Mr Camp?"

"No, I don't need a doctor." Oscar lowered his bushy eyebrows at the boy, who drew back an inch or two.

"Sorry," Aaron said.

"No need to be." Mr. Callahan explained in very few words to the junior groom that Oscar needed to be taken upstairs to his bed—but that he was just fine.

"Right as rain," Oscar said again.

Aaron grinned at him. "Let me help you. I can do it."

"All right," the old servant grumbled. "Let's go, son."

"His name is Aaron," Mr. Callahan clarified, then lifted his chin at the boy. "Help Mr. Camp find his flask when he gets there."

Aaron nodded. "Yes, sir."

Janice couldn't help but approve of Mr. Callahan at the moment. He was good at looking after strays, wasn't he? Aaron was the lowliest of the grooms. She knew from her walk with him to the stables that he had only a sister and she'd emigrated several years ago. And while Oscar wasn't a stray, exactly, he needed careful handling.

"All right." Oscar grimaced. "Let's go—Aaron."

Janice looked after both of them as they departed, and when they were a decent length away she actually chuckled. "I know I shouldn't laugh at Oscar's fainting."

"You're right." Mr. Callahan had a twinkle in his eye when he looked at her.

"I never imagined Oscar as sensitive," she said. "He doesn't come across that way, usually. As you see, he can be quite the curmudgeon."

The groom extended his palm, indicating that she could exit the stall first. "No man likes to be seen as weak. And no man likes to be fussed over by a woman."

On the other side of Esmeralda's wall, Janice said, "But women add a sense of civility and ease to any situation."

"Ease?" Mr. Callahan pulled the door shut behind him.

"Yes." Janice knew she sounded lofty, but he brought that out in her.

"I don't feel ease around *you,* Lady Janice." He seemed especially interested in the tendril of hair tumbling down one side of her face.

She wondered if her cheeks were as red as they felt. "You should," she said, and heard that prim tone in her voice that came when she was in over her head. "I'm perfectly agreeable."

"Agreeable?" He gave a short laugh. "That's an interesting choice of words." He leaned his elbow on the edge of the stall, put his chin in his hand, and looked at her as if he could stare at her for hours.

She'd never experienced such absorbed interest from a man and was entirely flummoxed. "Being agreeable is what I'm best at. Marcia is the great beauty and Cynthia is adorable. I get to be the sister who gets along well with everyone, and I don't mind in the least."

"I can't believe that you do." He chuckled. "You're not a pushover, as I well know. You've got yourself a temper, my lady."

She raised her chin. "I only behave that way when I'm required to, Mr. Callahan. When I'm put into a corner and need to fight back. And so far, you're the first man who's ever brought that out in me."

"Oh." He gave her a lazy grin. "You should behave that way more often." There was smoke in his voice.

Her heart beat faster. "You're being silly."

"I don't think so."

"Please change the subject." Her voice came out as a mere squeak. She could have simply turned and left him, but—

She couldn't.

She craved every second she could get in his company.

It was foolish.

But she couldn't help herself. He was like a drug.

"All right." He stood up straight and folded those massive arms over his chest. "What do you think of the duke so far?"

She blinked several times, overwhelmed by the leashed power she sensed in those muscles of his. She didn't think Gregory could take him down, nor Daddy. And certainly not Peter or Robert.

"His Grace," she said in a thin voice, "is perfectly courteous and pleasant—if a bit demanding and unconventional."

She didn't care about His Grace. Especially when she looked into this man's sapphire blue eyes. She wanted to know how he could have possibly kissed a hundred women. Of course, she couldn't *ask*. And she prayed he couldn't tell what she was thinking.

"I know what you're thinking," he said with a gleam in his eye.

"You couldn't possibly," she said immediately, her pulse pounding in her throat.

"Oh, yes, I do." He grinned. "You want to know . . . how is it that this man has kissed so many women? He's a groom, for goodness' sake. He lives in the stables. Where in heaven's name are all the women?"

Mortification made her hot. "You're—you're wrong."

"Am I?" he said easily, as if he didn't mind in the least her curiosity. "But we were discussing the duke. . . . What did he do to merit your observation that he's demanding and unconventional?"

She couldn't understand how Mr. Callahan was nothing more than a groom—not that the position wasn't respectable, but he radiated such intelligence and confidence, surely he could have become a scholarship student and become a country doctor, or, at the least, a tenant farmer who managed his own lands.

She dragged her wandering thoughts, like rebellious runaway children, back to the question at hand. "His Grace wanted to show me his conservatory and the family portraits without anyone to chaperone us."

"I'm not surprised." Mr. Callahan lifted and dropped his sculpted shoulders. "I told you—beware of him."

"It was enthusiasm for his treasures that caused him to forget the proprieties," she said. "Nothing nefarious. Besides, he himself is arranging a chaperone for me."

"Which he hasn't provided the other ladies, who should have them, too."

Her cheeks flushed. "Yes, well, I haven't deduced exactly why they're here yet."

"Remain naïve," the groom warned her, "but it will be at your peril." He looked over her head. "Look. In all the commotion, we've missed something." He turned her delicate shoulders—which stiffened immediately at his touch—so that she faced Esmeralda. "More puppies."

"Two more!" Janice cried softly. "But . . . one of them is . . . brown?" She turned to the groom and lofted a quizzical brow.

"It must look like its father."

She gave a bright laugh. "How wonderful!"

They watched in silence as another one was born, this one white with a large black spot on his side. Esmeralda went to work on him, nipping, cleaning, pushing him with her nose. But he didn't respond the way the others did. There was no wriggling. No blind clawing about, seeking warmth and solace.

He lay there in the straw, mute and motionless. But Esmeralda, dedicated mother that she was, wouldn't stop trying. The other puppies stayed busy climbing over one another while she worked.

"Mr. Callahan—," Janice said, a catch in her voice.

But he was already there, through the stall door and kneeling in the straw. He rubbed the newcomer's belly, his tiny chest, and stroked his muzzle. "Come on," he urged the puppy.

But nothing happened. Esmeralda nosed around him, clearly worried.

The groom picked up the scrawny parcel, cupped the puppy in his palm, and gave him another massage.

"Oh, wake up," Janice murmured. "Please, little one."

Nothing.

It pained her to see the puppy so lifeless, but she couldn't afford to succumb to the feeling. She couldn't distract Mr. Callahan from saving him.

"You're going to wake up," the groom told the prone pup. Opening the newborn's mouth and clearing it, Mr. Callahan blew into it. The pup's ribs expanded and sank back.

One more try.

No, two.

And three. Why not? Janice was glad Mr. Callahan couldn't bear to give up just yet.

Four.

The puppy gave a little start. A wriggle. A tiny yelp.

"Yes!" said Janice. "Oh, please, be well."

Esmeralda nosed the tiny body cradled in Mr. Callahan's hand with the impatience that any new mother would have when she wanted to connect with her baby.

"Is it all right?" Janice couldn't help hoping.

"I believe so." Mr. Callahan sounded well satisfied when he laid the now-wriggling newest member of the family in the straw next to his siblings.

"Oh, thank God." Janice shot through the door and wiped away a tear on her way to Mr. Callahan's side again.

Together they watched Esmeralda line up her troops. The one that had been ailing seemed as frantic to get to her teats as the rest now.

"Thank you for saving it," Janice quietly told the man beside her.

"I was glad to do it." They sat in silence a moment,

watching the happy scene; then he added, "For Esmeralda."

Not for Janice, of course. He was making that clear.
But she was so grateful to him for saving the puppy, she
ignored the slight.

"I've already named almost all of them," she said.
"Pinky, Walnut, Sweetie, and Beanie. Whether they're
boys or girls, the names will fit."

"How did you do that so fast?"

"The names just came to me." She grinned at him. "I
left the last one for you." She dared to touch the groom's
arm, and it instantly brought her back to that kiss in the
road. "You saved him. He's your puppy. Or she. So *you'll*
name that one."

And she stood before Mr. Callahan could react or
respond.

"Wait a minute." He stood, too. "I don't name puppies."

"You'll name this one." Despite her fascination with
the canine family, Janice was even more fascinated with
Mr. Callahan. She put the stall door between them. "I
plan to tell your friends that you saved it and must
name it—"

"For the love of God, don't do that." He didn't look a
bit repentant when he opened the stall door and came
around himself. "I'll name the damned thing; just don't
go out there telling them I saved a puppy."

"Mr. Callahan." His nearness set off alarms in her.
"It is not a damned thing."

Funny squeaks started soft and grew insistent, near
frantic—puppies seeking their mother's warmth. The
sounds made Janice's whole being soften.

Who couldn't be moved by them?

When she turned back to look at the groom, she saw
that he was taking it all in, too.

"Puppy noises," he murmured, observing the little family with obvious pleasure. "Puppy noises and a strong, beautiful woman next to me. It does get better—when you get that particular woman alone, *really* alone. But this will do . . . in the meantime."

The meantime? Was there going to be a time when he got her alone? "You can't—" Janice felt her face heat up and her heart pound. "We can't be alone. You shouldn't say things like that. It's wrong. I-I should report you, Mr. Callahan."

"But you won't, will you?" He turned to look at her then, and it happened again, that odd, compelling connection, like a beam of invisible light suffusing her and him alone.

"No." The urge to reach up and lay her palms on his chest, lift her face, and part her lips for a kiss was so strong, she had to fight to contain it.

Did he want to kiss her, too?

Surely he must—this feeling couldn't be one-sided. It wasn't something she even wanted. It was silly of her to kiss a groom—not only would Mother be appalled; it would lead nowhere.

But Janice wanted to. Oh, how she did!

"You're wondering how I've kissed so many women." His voice was laced with cynical amusement. "It's because I excel at attracting the type who needs comforting—and that's an awful lot of women, Lady Janice. Every town is brimming with them, women who've been hurt. Who need reassurance. Who want to believe that there's more to life than scrubbing and child rearing, hiking up their skirts and painting their faces to please men they don't even like and who never thank them for anything they do." He paused and tipped up her chin. "But you're not one of those women. You don't need me."

"Of course not." *But I want* you.

She couldn't tell him so, of course.

His gaze seared into her. Her pulse quickened at his nearness. She remembered the feel of his hard chest, the demanding pliancy of his lips.

One side of his mouth lifted. "I still know what you're thinking." His voice was extra low now, and her belly did a little flip-flop of pleasure. "But the duke's looking for you."

He took a step back, and she felt the vastness of the space separating them.

Remember, he's a groom. You're a lady. And ne'er the twain shall meet.

She pressed down her coat. "I'll leave, sir, but if you have any concerns at all about Esmeralda and the puppies—or if there are any surprising developments—I expect to be alerted. If it's too late to send a note, put a lantern in that large arched window facing the house."

She wouldn't even say *please*. It was meant to be an order. It was all she had, really, to defend herself against him.

He knew full well, too. "Very well, my lady," he murmured, his eyes lingering too long on her to be considered proper.

She whirled around and strode down the row, her back ramrod straight, her curls jouncing. The tips of her ears felt hot, and her fingers curled stiffly.

Why couldn't she be cool around him?

He knew he'd gotten to her.

Again.

"Lady Janice!" he called after her.

She stopped walking but didn't look over her shoulder. "Yes?"

She heard his boots move across the stone floor, coming closer. With every step he took, her belly clenched tighter. When he was at her back, she felt him lift that loose tendril of hair off her shoulder.

Was he weighing it in his hand? She wouldn't turn to see.

"I told you that the puppies would serve to temporarily distract me from the ultimate pleasure of getting you alone," he said. "But you mustn't listen when I say such things, no matter how convincing I am."

"Of course I don't." Her palms were wet when she clenched her fists. "Aren't you satisfied that you've won over all those other women? Why do you taunt *me* with such nonsense?"

"Good." He dropped the curl. "Keep fighting back," he said in her ear. "Don't give me an inch, because I'll take it." He ran a finger down the side of her face. "I'll take more than an inch, my lady. I'll take it all."

All? What did he mean by that?

Her heart pounded in her ears. She gulped and took a step forward, away from him. "I really must be going." Her voice sounded pinched, she knew.

"You do that," he said.

And without another word, she stalked away from him, feeling decidedly unnerved.

Chapter Six

With a footman in tow, Janice returned to the house furious at herself. It appeared that kissing a groom and wanting to do it again because he'd saved a darling puppy was a more complicated scenario than she'd ever imagined. There was nothing easy about the charming Luke Callahan. He posed a threat that she wasn't sure she understood.

Think about the pups!

She tried; she really did. But instead of focusing on images of tiny wet noses and scrabbling paws, her mind slid to recollections of Luke Callahan's chiseled mouth, his strong back, and the way he lowered himself in the straw on muscular haunches to cradle a limp puppy in his hands.

Janice actually smiled to herself thinking of how he'd appeared when the near-dead puppy stirred. Mr. Callahan had been shocked and pleased—and there was a brief moment when tenderness appeared around his eyes, in the curve of his lips.

It had done something to Janice's heart, that look. She'd felt an ache like nothing she'd ever known, a desire to touch that tenderness—

To touch him.

He'd charmed her thoroughly. But in the end, he'd

made it clear that he wasn't to be trusted. And yet . . . she couldn't help being drawn to him, even so.

Perhaps it was his honesty—she'd take an honest scoundrel over a sly one any day, she supposed.

But what did that say about *her*, that she was attracted to a rogue of the worst sort, a self-confessed one who teased her one minute and pushed her away the next?

When she entered Halsey House, she was still seething as the butler took her coat and bonnet. The hounds sniffed her up and down. They smelled dog. And hay.

The butler shooed them away. "Everyone's gone off to the billiard room," he informed her quietly.

"I think I'll seek out the duchess, then." Janice had yet to freshen up, but it was time to visit Her Grace—the sooner the better. She'd most certainly take Janice's mind off what had happened in the stables.

"Your chaperone, Mrs. Friday, is putting away her things," the butler said. "She'll be down for dinner."

"Oh. Very good." The news was a boost to Janice's spirits. Mrs. Friday's presence would make everything easier.

A maid led Janice up the enormous staircase, down two long corridors upstairs and around several corners, and finally across a balcony running the length of the ballroom. "Almost there, my lady."

"Goodness, the duchess appears far removed from the rest of the household," Janice said, and surreptitiously smoothed down her skirt. She didn't know why she should feel so nervous. She knew eccentric people. London abounded with them. This woman couldn't be any more eccentric than they.

"In her own wing, she is," said the maid.

"Why is that?"

"The duke said it's for her own protection. He thinks the quiet is good for her."

Was quiet beneficial for a person who didn't live in her own mind? Shouldn't there be distractions? Familiar sights and sounds? "I suppose the doctor agreed," Janice said.

"I have no idea if one's been consulted." The maid eyed her balefully. "This is a *family* matter, the duke told us, and we're to remain silent about it."

Janice refused to cringe. So she'd been caught fishing, but who could blame her? She'd been invited by the dowager, and she had a right to know something of what was going on.

Surely a doctor had been consulted if Her Grace's condition was so dire. Janice felt a sudden sense of urgency to see her. *This is why you're here,* she thought, *to check on this woman. Not to win a duke. And definitely not to daydream about kissing a groom.*

Her heart lifted. Perhaps the complications she'd faced here would quickly fade away if she could be of real use. She hadn't felt truly useful to anyone since Mama had left her sewing shop behind and married Daddy. Everyone around Janice these days was entirely too competent. Even her younger siblings, Robert and Cynthia—despite their occasional foray into high jinx that made no sense to her—were generally sensible and able to handle their own business.

The maid brought Janice to a large door and opened it quietly. "Lady Janice Sherwood to see you, Your Majesty."

"Send her in," a tiny voice proclaimed with a great deal of haughtiness.

Janice walked shyly into the room, which was small and dark, entirely inappropriate for an elderly convalescent *or* a queen.

A nurse stood in the corner, folding cloths. Deep in the pillows was a petite elderly lady with a proud chin and nose. She had silver hair and wore a beautiful mauve muslin dressing gown. "I've been anticipating your arrival." Her eyes were narrowed, her gaze unrelenting. "Don't you know that one must never, ever keep a queen waiting?"

Janice felt a moment's shock but tried not to show it. Without hesitating, she went to the woman's bedside and sat down in a chair already placed there. "I'm so glad to be here, Your . . . *Majesty*."

The old lady extended her tiny, wrinkled hand. There was a giant ruby ring upon it.

The duchess might be frail, but she managed to keep her hand aloft. Obviously, she wanted Janice to kiss that ring. Gingerly, Janice lifted the bony fingers to her mouth and pressed her lips to the cold red stone. She felt silly. But immediately the dowager withdrew her hand, so Janice supposed she'd done the right thing.

"I didn't send for you so that I can reminisce of my childhood and bore you to tears," her hostess said testily, "so don't you dare imagine we'll be sitting here all day wasting time. I'm not an invalid. I have things to do. Places to be. If only Halsey would let me out."

"Won't he?" Janice didn't know what to think.

"No, he won't." The dowager's eyes filled with the most interesting mix of scorn and bravado. "How does he expect me to find my crown jewels?"

"Oh. . . ."

"Do *you* know where they are?" Her tone was accusing.

"I-I don't at the moment." It must be awful to be so worried about something that is entirely in one's head, Janice thought. "But I'm sure they can be found."

The old woman gave a gusty sigh. "Perhaps a princess

is borrowing them. If that's the case, she'd best bring them back. Do you know if there's a ball tonight?"

"Yes," Janice said. "I believe there *is* a ball."

The old lady stretched out her other hand, which was completely bare. *Ah.* She simply wanted someone to hold it. Janice took it and felt a great tenderness toward her. Her nerves disappeared. The duchess was only someone who wanted love and attention. Janice could manage that easily.

"Where are the festivities to take place?" the dowager asked impatiently, even as she clung to Janice's hand as if she never wanted to let go.

"Down the street." Janice was surprised how easily she was able to lie. But the dowager was like a little girl in this state, even if she was rather haughty, too. Janice wanted to please her. "There'll be loads of women in bright gowns. And the men will look quite elegant, I should imagine. Flowers will spill from every window, and the chandeliers will blaze with candles."

"What address?"

"Somewhere on Half Moon." Janice smiled just thinking of the lovely residential street.

The dowager frowned. "Must be Lord and Lady Foster, then. He's entirely too cocky, and she—well, she's a watering pot, cries at the least little thing. No wonder he has no patience with her." She released a gusty sigh. "I knew I could trust you to tell me all the goings-on."

"Of course," murmured Janice.

The dowager lifted an enormous handkerchief to her nose with her free hand and sneezed.

"Bless you." Janice saw the nurse pause in her housekeeping for a moment, then return to folding a cloth with a sure, steady motion.

The dowager fisted her handkerchief and leaned toward Janice as if seeing her for the first time. "You're

Lady Janice, are you not?" Her eyes were softer now, even friendly.

"Yes, Your Majesty."

"Your Majesty?" The duchess gave an indulgent little laugh and waved her free hand. "You must be travel weary, my dear. I'm merely the Dowager Duchess of Halsey. Not the Queen."

Oh, dear. This wasn't going to be easy. Janice caught the nurse's eye—the woman shrugged and continued about her business.

"I'm sorry, Your Grace." Janice wondered how long the dowager's moment of clarity would last. "Of course. My mistake."

"It's all right." She eyed Janice kindly. "I had my secretary write you. Would you like to know why?"

"I did wonder. But I was very glad, Your—Your Grace."

A fond smile passed over the old woman's face. "Your mother used to sew for me. She made me a gown, and you were there when it was being fitted. You held up a scrap of velvet cut from the same cloth and said that someday you'd be a duchess, too. You said no one ever made fun of duchesses nor pounded on their door for the rent. I never forgot that. Your mother was terribly embarrassed. You were a pale little thing sitting in a corner with a book. I almost didn't see you."

Janice blushed. "I wish I could remember. I must have been very young."

"It doesn't matter," said the dowager. "*I* remembered. I kept track of your mother. She made me a good many more gowns, and I referred all my friends to her until she became quite the thing among seamstresses. She deserved the business—her talent is remarkable— but in my mind's eye, I always saw you, the little girl who wanted to be a duchess."

"Your Grace." Janice blinked back tears. "How very kind of you to help my mother so."

"And I was so happy to see her meet her marquess. I knew that would make you a lady. Lady Janice. No longer the little shopgirl."

"No, I no longer am." Janice swallowed the lump in her throat. In a very odd way, the duchess had contributed to Janice's mother's success . . . and even to her meeting Daddy. Life was certainly funny.

The dowager sneezed again into her giant handkerchief.

Janice blinked. "I'm sorry you've a cold."

But when the old lady looked up, her eyes were different. They were narrowed once more. "Enough of colds," she said in the same superior tone she'd employed when Janice had first entered the room. "There's something you must do for England, young lady."

She was being the Queen again!

"Really?" Janice wasn't so taken aback this time. In fact, it was rather exciting talking to the dowager—illness aside, of course. She was a challenge, to be certain, but terribly interesting. "What's that, Your Majesty? Aside from finding the crown jewels?"

The duchess threw a suspicious glance at the nurse, then crooked a finger at Janice.

Janice came closer.

"I have a mission for you," the dowager whispered in her ear. "You're a girl after my own heart."

Janice laid a hand on her heart, which was thumping wildly. *Me?*

"Yes, you."

"But why do you say so? You don't even know my name."

"You've got a look in your eye," the dowager whispered again. "You're clever; I can tell. And I see the same sense of frustration in you that was in me at your age. You're a competitive spirit denied a chance to shine, all because you're too frightened to speak up."

"How can you see all that? We've only just met."

"I'm the Queen," said the duchess in a patronizing voice. "Do you think I don't know my own subjects? Halsey, for example, needs a wife in the worst way."

"I-I suppose he does," Janice said low, "as he's a duke."

"Indeed," said the dowager, "but not just any wife." She poked Janice in the shoulder. *"You."*

Chapter Seven

"Oh, no, Your Majesty," Janice told the Dowager Duchess of Halsey. "I'm not suited to be a duchess."

"Of course you are." The woman who thought she was the Queen curled her fists in her lap. "He needs a wife who'll make the most of her power. That's why you'll suit him well."

"I don't want power," Janice said. "I want to read and take long walks and be with my family. I don't *need* power."

"Certainly you do," said Her Majesty. "And there's only one way to win the Duke of Halsey."

"Perhaps you should tell Lady Opal and Lady Rose. Or Miss Branson." Janice almost giggled at the thought of one of them becoming the next Duchess of Halsey, but she decided that would be churlish of her.

"Absolutely not," said the dowager. "This is a state secret, and only I know it. Whoever I divulge it to will win Halsey, no matter what she looks like. No matter how big a dowry she has, or whether she's even from a good family. None of those things will matter."

"I see," Janice replied uncertainly. The conversation was getting to be more interesting—and nerve-wracking—by the second. "But you needn't bother telling me the secret. I can't marry him. I need to love the man I marry. And I don't even know Halsey. Not to mention that he's a duke and I'm—I'm simply a girl who's had two Seasons and didn't take."

"Pah," said the dowager with a wicked gleam in her eye. "He'll want you, all right, once I tell you what to do."

"No, thank you." Janice stood up. "Really. You're too kind. But I'm here in Surrey to see *you,* Your Majesty."

"Of course you are." The old woman grabbed her wrist and held it tight. "And to hide from all those London gossips who'll relish seeing you on the shelf. But are you going to let this opportunity slip through your fingers? It's time for you to shine." She leaned forward. "I know it must frustrate you no end that you're not more influential."

Janice's hand flew to her heart. "Why would you say that, Your Majesty?"

The dowager slapped her coverlet. "An astute monarch always recognizes hidden ambition."

Janice sighed. "I'm not ambitious."

"Ridiculous." The dowager curled her lip in scorn. "What's wrong with you? You're young! You should be reaching for the stars, child, not simpering in fear that you'll offend someone." She thrust out her shriveled chin. "I don't believe you. You're lying to me and to yourself."

"But there are rules, Your Majesty, and a girl in my position must adhere to them."

"Proper is as proper does. It only takes you so far. Life is short. You must live it while you can."

"I appreciate the sentiment—"

"Oh, leave my sight." The dowager flung her hand out. "I've no patience for flatterers. If you insist on becoming a spinster, suit yourself. But in your dotage, you'll remember this day. You'll remember that you could have become a duchess, and you threw the opportunity away."

Janice opened her mouth to speak, but she was so

astonished by the vehemence of the dowager's words and the shock of her actual proposal that she didn't know what to say.

The old woman grabbed her handkerchief and sneezed again. "This blasted sneezing. I can't seem to rid myself of it." She paused and looked indignantly over the lacy edge. "I blame Parliament."

"Your Majesty," Janice said softly, "please don't upset yourself."

The old woman continued muttering as she leaned back against her pillows and closed her eyes, but within thirty seconds she began to snore.

Janice bit her lower lip. She was confused, yet at the same time it was really quite simple. The dowager duchess had two distinct facets to her identity, one real and one imagined. And the Queen in her wanted Janice to marry the Duke of Halsey!

"How long has she been like this?" Janice asked the nurse.

"For *years-s-s-s,* they say." The nurse had a gap between her teeth and whistled on her *s*'s. 'I've been with her only since she moved here from the dower house last year."

"That explains why she hasn't been in Town. Does it happen often, her switching back and forth like that . . . between the Queen and the dowager?"

"Many *times-s-s-s* a day."

Goodness, that whistle was quite pronounced.

"As you can *s-s-s-see,*" the nurse went on, and Janice tried not to wince, "it happens every time she *s-s-s-sneezes.*"

"That's the oddest thing. Has a doctor been in to see her?"

"Of course. He recommends rest and *s-s-s-seclusion.*"

Janice was glad a physician had attended upon the

old lady, after all, but something felt terribly wrong about his advice. "How can seclusion help anyone?" She watched the sleeping duchess. "It's all very sad."

"It might be, but it ain't my business." The nurse shrugged.

"You don't seem to care about her." Anger made Janice bold.

"I'm not supposed to care," the woman replied in a huff.

"Of course you are. She's your charge. She's obviously in need of affection and understanding."

"*That's-s-s-s* not what I'm paid for," the nurse said. "I'm paid to keep her room clean, to feed her, and make sure she's bathed and properly *dress-s-s-sed*."

The whistles were going a mile a minute at the moment.

"Those are all very important things," Janice said. "But there's more an invalid needs than that."

"You heard her—she doesn't think she's an invalid. She wants out of here. But where can she go, *s-s-s-speaking* the way she does?"

Irony of ironies that a whistling nurse said that. "Don't you ever allow her to walk in the gardens?"

The woman shook her head. "She never leaves this room. Doctor's orders."

"That's reprehensible. I'm going to talk to the duke about that."

"Good luck. His Grace believes the doctor is right. He doesn't want her hurting herself."

"I still intend to speak with him," Janice said. "And what about Her Grace's secretary? Does he have a role here? Who mailed the note to my mother in London?"

"Her secretary"—the woman gave a short laugh—"is the fishmonger who comes once a week. She pays him to mail things out for her."

"He comes up here?"

"Her Grace insists that he does. She tells the duke she wants to discuss fishing with him, and His Grace allows it but only because Her Grace creates a fuss. She likes to remind him that fishing is a favorite family pastime, that his own father—her son Russell—used to love it, he and his big brother, Everett, both. Supposedly, they'd spend hours a day in a rowboat on the estate pond. She waxes on about it to the fishmonger, and he just nods, then mails her correspondence out. But it's none of my business. No, it's not."

"I never thought I'd say this"—Janice advanced to within a foot of the nurse—"but in this instance I'm glad that you believe so. Because that's how she got a letter to *me*. What's your name?"

"Martha. Mrs. Martha Poole."

"Well, Mrs. Poole, if you can't tell me at this very moment that you'll show more heart to this woman, then I'll go to the duke immediately and call for your replacement. Furthermore, if you can't drum up even one iota of affection for Her Grace, I expect you to pretend that you can. And you'd better be a very good actress. Is that understood?"

The woman's eyes widened. "Who are you to talk to me this way?"

"I'm Lady Janice Sherwood, as you know very well."

Mrs. Poole glowered. "All right."

Janice put every bit of cool threat she could into the look she sent the nurse at that moment. She'd seen Mama use the same expression when they were poor and up against the tough nuts who comprised London's rough population. She'd also seen Mama use it as the marchioness—with unruly servants, rude guests, and her own brood of six children.

"My lady," Mrs. Poole tacked on to the end of her sentence as if it physically pained her to do so.

"Thank you, Mrs. Poole," Janice said in a pleasant tone. "Carry on."

It took her another minute to return to her room, where Isobel was waiting with a freshly pressed gown for dinner.

"But you must clean up first, my lady," the maid said.

"Of course." Janice sat on the edge of her bed, her knees weak. She couldn't believe how naturally it had come to her to defend the duchess, but it had. Mama would be proud, she knew. "I haven't had a moment's rest, Izzy, since I arrived."

"Have you not? Tell me all about going to the stables, my lady. I've been enjoying my tea and some delicious biscuits while I put away your things."

"I'm glad for you." Janice told her all about the puppies, Oscar's fainting, and Mr. Callahan's reviving the ailing pup.

"*That man* saved a puppy?" Izzy asked.

That man being the same one who'd kissed Janice mercilessly in the falling snow that afternoon. "Yes, he did." She blushed thinking about how for a few heady moments she'd responded to his passionate ministrations with equal ardor.

"Oh, my lady"—Isobel crushed one of Janice's gowns to her chest—"are you all right? Just talking about *him* makes me shiver." She paused. "But somehow in a good way." She gave a little giggle and hung the gown in an armoire.

"Really, Izzy." Janice pretended to be shocked, but she wasn't. She understood, unfortunately, her maid's reaction to the man.

Isobel strode to the small dressing table and began to arrange Janice's combs in a neat line. "What are you going to do about him? Especially now that he's saved a puppy? I'd be lost, I would. Don't you crave—?"

"That's enough." Janice stood and approached the dressing table. She bent low over it to see her reflection in the looking glass. Did she have hidden ambition? Was she so frustrated at being invisible that an ill old woman could tell? "I'll grant you that it was good of him to save a puppy. But—"

The maid's expression turned bright. "Wouldn't it be wonderful if the duke kissed you the way *he* kissed you?"

Janice held on to her patience. "It would be enlightening," she admitted. "But I must ask you not to tell anyone that I kissed a groom. Promise me?" She handed her a brush.

Isobel patted the dressing-table seat, and Janice sat down. For a few seconds, the maid worked to restore Janice's hair to a semblance of order. "I'd never reveal your secret, my lady. Never. Not even to my mum. Or my three sisters. Or my grandmother, although up until now I've told her everything. Polly, too, the upstairs maid in London. As well as Jude, my childhood friend whose father tamed tigers. I don't see him often, but when I do, we tell each other *everything*."

"Did you leave anyone out?" Janice said warily to Isobel's reflection.

"No, my lady."

Janice chuckled. "I'm glad I can count on you."

Isobel lifted a casual shoulder and added a pin to the back of Janice's coiffure. "He was the most handsome groom I've ever seen in my life. I think I'll have to go out to the stables to look at him again—while I visit the puppies, of course."

"We should be done speaking of him—"

"Yes, but I think he might even be the most handsome *man* I've ever seen in my life, too," Isobel gushed. "The duke is one to admire, as well, but you can't imagine him moving boulders. Mr. Callahan could, I'm sure. I'd like to see him chop wood, too. Wouldn't you?"

"No, Izzy," Janice said evenly. "I would *not* like to see him chop wood."

Which was a lie. She most certainly would. And if she looked out her bedchamber window long enough, she just might see him at work. The stable block's south side faced the house, and already she couldn't help wanting to peek out whenever she could to catch a glimpse of him walking to and fro.

Isobel bit her lip and stepped back from the dressing table. "Sorry, my lady. I don't mean to dwell on him."

Guilt made Janice sigh as she pinched her cheeks to add some color. "It's all right. I know how easy it is to lose one's head over a man. I've done so once before, and it wasn't at all comfortable when it ended. So I try not to find myself in that position again."

Stupid Finn. Thank God he was long gone.

"But that was ages ago, wasn't it, my lady?"

"Long enough that I should put it behind me, and I have." Janice stood once more. "But it took some time. The heart is a fragile thing."

"You're right," Isobel said. "I know my heart is extremely fragile. All of me is, my lady." She looked down modestly.

"Right." Janice smiled, remembering how Isobel once hoisted two full trunks over her head.

"What is it?" Isobel raised her head and gazed suspiciously at her.

"Nothing." Janice's tone was light and brisk. "As usual, you lift my spirits without even trying. We really must stop talking of this morning's events, memorable as they were. It's time to get ready for dinner. Unless you think I have a few moments in which to read."

There was a knock on the door, and she exchanged a wry glance with her supposedly fragile servant. "I suppose you'll have to answer it."

"I'll get rid of whoever it is." Isobel's eyes narrowed with purpose, and she opened the door wide, as if to confront a lion.

The nurse stood there, looking as taciturn as she had upstairs.

In a way she was a lion, but one Janice intended to tame. "Come in, Mrs. Poole." There wasn't a question about wanting to see her. Anything to do with the duchess was important.

"My lady," Mrs. Poole said, "I've *mess-s-s-age*."

Isobel blinked fast, probably at the strong whistle on the *s* in *message*.

"And your message is?" Janice prodded the nurse.

Mrs. Poole folded her hands. "The dowager awoke and said she never got to tell you good-bye."

"Oh." Janice was puzzled that the nurse had come all this way to tell her so. "She sneezed and fell asleep quickly. Neither of us was able to make our farewells."

"She tends to fall asleep fast, but she woke up shortly after you left." The woman hesitated.

"As . . . the Queen?" Janice asked.

Isobel drew in her chin, and no wonder. Janice hadn't told her yet that Mr. Callahan was right—the dowager *did* think she was the Queen, at least some of the time.

"No," said Mrs. Poole, "she woke up as Her Grace."

Isobel's eyes widened.

"She was asking after her grandson," Mrs. Poole went on, "and I told her that he was soon to visit. But she wasn't satisfied with that. She got a little teary."

"Oh, dear," Janice said, her heart pained. "That's a terrible shame."

"I-I offered her a new handkerchief." Mrs. Poole looked over Janice's head.

"You did? That was good of you, Mrs. Poole."

"Yes, well, I opened the curtains, too, which seemed to cheer her."

"Very nicely done." There was hope for this nurse, after all.

Mrs. Poole returned her reluctant gaze to Janice's. "But then she sneezed and . . . well, you know what happened."

"Right. She became the Queen."

Isobel dropped the hatbox she was carrying in the far corner of the room.

The nurse paused to frown at her.

"Don't mind me." Isobel said airily. But her eyes gave her away. She was intensely curious and desperate to hear more.

Mrs. Poole looked back at Janice. "Her Majesty told me to pass this message on immediately to the young lady who recently visited her—'the clever, frustrated one,' she said."

Janice scratched the side of her nose. "I suppose she might mean me."

"Of course she means you, my lady!" Isobel interjected. There was a moment's pause, and her face went red. "I don't know about the 'frustrated' part. But you *are* clever."

"Thank you, Isobel," Janice said. "Do go on, Mrs. Poole."

The nurse drew a deep breath. "I also assume you're the young lady to whom the dowager refers because you're the only one who's visited her since she became ill."

Janice's heart sank. "You mean, Ladies Opal and Rose haven't? Nor Miss Branson?"

"No, they haven't. Nor have the other ladies who've been in residence."

"Have there been many?" Isobel asked, agog.

"Yes," the nurse said coolly, "not that it's your business."

Isobel's mouth opened, but Janice held up a hand to silence her. "That's unfortunate, that the dowager has had little feminine company other than yourself, Mrs. Poole. But the duke visits regularly, doesn't he?"

"Once a day," said the nurse. "He insists on sitting with Her Grace alone every afternoon at three o'clock. That's when I take my tea."

"How good of him." Janice had arrived at that time and found his absence at tea rather touching, now that she knew exactly why he'd left her.

Mrs. Poole nodded. "He's very devoted to her."

He certainly appeared to be. "So what *is* this message?" Janice tried to curb her impatience. "I think I should be getting downstairs."

"I don't understand it myself." The nurse's manner was more stiff than ever. "But Her Majesty says . . ."

She hesitated.

"What?" Janice wasn't certain she wanted to know.

Mrs. Poole's lips thinned. "She says that you must say no. And that if you ignore her advice, you're a fool."

Janice felt her own mouth fall open—she'd been too long around Isobel—and quickly shut it. "That's all?"

The nurse nodded. "She was quite emphatic about it, too. 'No, no, no,' she said as she fell asleep again."

Hm-m-m. . . . Janice was almost dizzy thinking of the implications. "Thank you for passing that on." She managed to smile calmly in farewell to Mrs. Poole.

The nurse, of course, refused to smile back.

Oh, well. There was only so much one could accomplish in a day.

"Goodness." Isobel stared at Janice. "She whistles like a bird all day long. You'd think that would make her cheerful, but no. She's as sour as a lemon. Do you know what she meant by that message, my lady?"

"I think I do." Janice leaned her back against the door, her whole body fraught with tension. "The dowager told me there's only one way to win over the duke, but she fell asleep before she could tell me. That was her one way."

"'Tell him no,'" Isobel said in a dramatic whisper. "How very clever of her. Everyone knows you must say yes to a duke. Whatever he wants he gets."

"Exactly." Janice swallowed to quell the butterflies in her stomach. "Not that it matters. I'm not interested in winning the duke. I'm here for the dowager's sake."

"But, my lady! Why won't you at least *try* to win him? Imagine . . . you could be a duchess."

Janice pushed off the door and began to pace in a small circle on the rich burgundy Aubusson carpet in front of the hearth. "I've already told you, Izzy. I'll marry for love if I marry at all."

"But think of how it would feel," Isobel said, "to make those jealous women who say you're the invisible sister upset? They'd have to pretend to be happy for you. And you could give them the cut direct if you chose."

Janice sighed. "I have to admit, something to that effect would be satisfying for a few fleeting seconds. But seeking that sort of petty revenge isn't a good reason to spend the rest of your life with a man you don't love."

"Even if he's rich?"

"Yes, Isobel, even so." Janice patted Izzy's arm. "I know you mean well. But trust me that money doesn't solve all one's woes."

"It doesn't?"

"No. It doesn't," she said softly. "It seems to me that only love makes things truly better."

"I hope so," Isobel said with a short chuckle, "as I'm never going to be rich."

"Neither one of us knows what our futures hold. Besides"—Janice sighed—"I can't say no to people. I think it comes from living in a large family. One has to compromise."

"You *are* agreeable, my lady," said Isobel. "Perhaps too nice. . . ."

"Isobel. One can never be *too* nice."

"I don't know, miss. I remember the circus trainers cracking their whips at the tigers. If they didn't frighten them a little bit, they'd get eaten up."

"I don't propose to crack any whips," said Janice, "nor shall I be devoured. I promise."

They shared bemused smiles.

"Well, I'm off." She looked one more time at her reflection and didn't see an ounce of the lurking ambition that the dowager—as the Queen—seemed to think she had. "Wish me luck downstairs."

"You don't need it." Isobel winked. "You know the *secret*."

"Right," said Janice dryly. "I suppose I do."

Say no.

Say no, and if the dowager was right the world would be Janice's, whether she magically blossomed out here in the country—per her mother's wishes—or not.

Chapter Eight

On her way to the drawing room, Janice got lost. She thought she was going down the corridor that led to the staircase, but instead she found herself in a vast hall—the portrait gallery. One stunning portrait in particular caught her eye. It was of a beautiful lady with a spark of something—a glow—in her eye.

She's in love, Janice thought. *That's what love looks like.* She'd seen the same look on Marcia's face and on Mama's.

And then Janice wondered if the woman in the portrait was the dowager when she was young. The clothes would have been from about that time.

Janice had turned back, determined to find her way to the stairs—it was a simple enough correction she had to make—when she found the most wonderful sitting room with an enormous window, in front of which were three wingback chairs. She skirted around them and stood before the panes, where a blanket of cold air made her shiver as she looked out to a snow-covered garden.

She was so glad Esmeralda was no longer trembling out there in the cold but was instead snug in her straw bed with her puppies.

Thanks to Mr. Callahan, Janice couldn't help thinking, and wondered what he was doing at the moment. Talking to Oscar? Looking in on Esmeralda?

Or . . . thinking of her?

No. She really had to rein in her too-vivid imagination. She didn't even like him. How could she like a man who'd warned her away from him himself? And he didn't like her. He'd made that obvious. He'd not helped Esmeralda for Janice but for the dog's sake alone. Had it really been necessary to tell her that?

No. Which proved that he didn't give a fig for her. He simply liked to *kiss* her. As she did him.

She decided the dramatic yet pristine view deserved her attention more than Mr. Callahan did, so she'd linger over it another minute. She sank into the middle chair, curled up her feet, put her chin in her palm, and gazed upon the portion of sky where the setting sun lent an orange glow to the tops of the tree line. For a few seconds she closed her eyes and let herself drift . . .

Right back into Luke Callahan's arms.

"I left them in here, I'm sure."

Her eyes flew open at the sound, and she felt a moment's embarrassment, as if she'd been caught out doing something entirely wrong. But of course, no one could see inside her head. Nor could anyone see *her*, not unless they came round to the window.

It was one of the sisters. Lady Opal, she was sure. She had the softer voice of the two.

There was a further swish of skirts.

"You're so absent-minded," said Lady Rose. "There they are. On the table."

"Oh." More rustling. "They're not even smudged."

Spectacles, probably. Janice should really let the two women know she was there. But she'd been so cozy. They'd leave any second and she could grab another minute's wicked daydreaming about Mr. Callahan and that kiss this afternoon before she had to head downstairs. She didn't look forward to trying to be charming during dinner, after which she'd be required to sing and play the pianoforte, something she dreaded.

"After tonight, we'll know if she's after him," said Lady Rose.

Janice's heart lurched. She had the sickening feeling that she was the subject of their tête-à-tête.

"I wonder what she'll wear to dinner," said Lady Opal.

"It was too difficult to tell her intentions today at tea," Lady Rose answered her. "Perhaps she really is here to see the dowager."

Heavens. They *were* speaking about her!

"It's just so hard to believe." Lady Opal's tone had an edge of scorn to it. "You know her parents must have sent her here to capture the duke's interest."

Janice squeezed her eyes shut. They had—they had sent her here for that very reason!

"I've heard she can't hold a candle to her older sister," said Lady Rose.

"Then her older sister must be extraordinarily beautiful," said Lady Opal, "because Lady Janice is quite pretty."

Janice supposed she should be complimented. But instead she felt a bit seasick listening to them speak about her with no feeling.

Please leave, she willed them silently.

"What are we going to do if he makes us go?" asked Lady Rose.

Janice heard a sigh.

"We'll try Scotland," said Lady Opal. "There are plenty of lairds seeking feminine company."

A frisson of shock went through Janice, and she opened her eyes again. What exactly did Lady Opal mean by that? Her statement could be taken any number of ways.

"In this weather?" Lady Rose sounded entirely bleak. "Surely we won't have to worry about traveling for a while."

"I hope not."

There was a heavy silence.

"No pitying ourselves," said Lady Opal. "For one shining Season, we had our chance. Now we make do."

"If only you'd said yes to Lord Archibald—," began Lady Rose.

"If only *you'd* encouraged Sir Kevin instead of Lord Boxwood. He was never going to be interested. I told you so." Lady Opal sounded bitter.

"Oh, do be quiet," whispered Lady Rose.

"Lady Janice will never be like us," said Lady Opal. "She has a family to take her in."

"That's its own sort of misery," said Lady Rose, "traveling from relation to relation. And you're wrong—she is quite like us. I see it in her face."

"What do you mean?" asked Lady Opal.

"She has the air of someone who's afraid to chase her own happiness."

Janice's middle clenched.

"Like us," said Lady Rose. "Why did we never think we were good enough to be happy?"

"I don't know," replied her sister. "Perhaps because our parents didn't like us terribly much."

Lady Rose sighed. "She doesn't have that excuse. They're supposedly a very loving family."

"But she may have another excuse equally as good," said Lady Opal.

Shame made Janice's cheeks hot. She didn't have any defense at all.

"Well, whatever her reasons, she's too timid to chase

a duke," Lady Rose said. "And come to think of it, surely her parents must know that. Perhaps they really did send her here to see the dowager. Get her out of the way, so to speak. She's had every opportunity to make a good match. No doubt they're ashamed she hasn't."

A stab of horror went through Janice. Could Mama and Daddy be ashamed of her? She knew they pitied her, but shame was something else entirely!

"You're suggesting she's a millstone?" Lady Opal's voice went up an octave.

"No one likes to be around a failure." Lady Rose sounded a bit smug, as if she weren't a failure herself. "It's bad luck, especially if one has a reputation of excellence to uphold."

Janice swallowed. Her parents weren't like that. They loved her.

But then she remembered all the important events she was missing, how Mama had brushed them off and so had Daddy. And then they'd practically pushed her into the coach.

Did they really not *want* her at Mama's grand ball? Or at the dinner parties that they'd surely hold in Gregory and Pippa's honor?

Was her presence becoming a burden?

"I do recall that she made a bit of a fool of herself over some man," said Lady Opal.

Janice's eyes widened.

"Finnian Lattimore." Lady Rose was quiet. "He was gorgeous. Don't tell me you don't remember the details."

Breathe, Janice told herself, and laid a palm on her breast in hopes of slowing her heartbeat down.

"Remember what?" asked Opal.

"There's an old rumor that won't die," Lady Rose said with some amusement. "A very dark rumor, and no one who's heard it would dare repeat it to the family."

"Why don't I know of it?"

"It must have been when you were bedridden those six months. Yes, that was it. You were deathly ill, and I wouldn't share certain *on-dits* with you. And then it never came up again."

"What is it?" Lady Opal asked. "You're driving me mad."

"It is said that she might have given herself to him. Long ago. In Ireland. At some wedding. And then later at Vauxhall, of all places."

No.

Janice was glad she was seated and not standing. They had it all wrong! That was Marcia Finn had taken advantage of in Ireland and left high and dry—

Marcia!

Not *her.*

The injustice of it all made her dizzy.

She wasn't angry at Marcia . . . poor Marcia. She'd had an awful experience.

But it was frustrating for Janice.

Entirely *too* frustrating.

Because how could she ever defend herself? She'd never be able to. Never in a million years would she correct that statement—

Not without putting a blight on her own beloved sister's reputation. Janice would have to bear it with a smile. She'd have to pretend she'd never heard it. Mama always told them to ignore gossip anyway. Never to dignify it with a response.

And Janice must admit, too, that the skewed tale hadn't come from nothing. She *had* attended a few events with Finn in London. Of course, she'd had no idea of Marcia and Finn's painful past at that point.

He and Janice had never—

They'd never done what Lady Rose said they'd done.

They'd kissed at Vauxhall. Nothing more. They'd shared several kisses, yes, down a dark path, away from the glow of the lanterns. But nothing else. She hadn't dared! At the time, she'd felt guilty, and she knew she'd been careless to disappear with him like that, but she thought nothing would ever come of it.

But wouldn't you know . . . Mama had always told her that gossip was wicked, that words got twisted and innocent people hurt. And Mama had also told her to behave appropriately at all times—that bad decisions always came back to haunt one.

Janice was nearly ill now with horror, humiliation, and fury.

Damn that Finnian Lattimore for still wreaking havoc in their lives!

But she was more furious with herself for ever falling for his false charm.

"Who told you such a thing?" Lady Opal asked her sister.

"Mrs. Barrett, the doctor's wife who brought you your special possets. She'd just been to London and heard it from one of her dear friends."

"It can't be true," said Lady Opal. "Lady Janice would be married to him if it were."

"Exactly. Or he'd have been challenged to a duel by her brothers or father," said Lady Rose. "No decent family would allow such scandal to go unchallenged."

"But he *is* gone." Lady Opal sounded speculative. "Banished, perhaps?"

"*Opal*. His brother married her sister. It can't be true."

Opal chuckled. "You're right. But it's the sort of delicious gossip that doesn't die, does it? Not for years."

"Not until she marries, most likely."

"Well, if it's as widespread as all that, perhaps she never will."

"That's the thing. It's not widespread, and I'm sure it's because the family is extremely popular. They're known for their integrity and kindness. Not only that, Lady Janice's older sister has an impeccable reputation. Anyone passing this gossip on would seriously think twice—and would likely do so only if they consider it imperative."

"Why would Mrs. Barrett have told you, then? And her friend in London tell her?"

"Mrs. Barrett has a son, an artist with a studio in Mayfair"—that would be Eugene! One of Janice's favorite beaus!—"who was very interested in Lady Janice. That's why her friend felt compelled to tell her. And she only found out because her son, too, was considering Lady Janice as a marriage prospect."

"Oh, dear. Who was this friend?"

"Lady Corcoran."

Janice put her fingers over her eyes. Lady Corcoran's son Marcus had been Janice's most serious beau. She'd never understood why he'd suddenly . . . disappeared.

Now she knew.

"And Mrs. Barrett told *you* all this because . . . ?"

"Because she found me crying," Lady Rose said, "lamenting the fact that I had no suitors. She felt sorry for me, so she told me there was one girl who had it worse and I should think of her whenever I pitied myself— Lady Janice. She told me to keep it close to my chest."

Dear God. Janice could barely tolerate listening. The pain nearly made her ill.

"I see," Lady Opal said. "Then there really have been no ill effects. The parents are invited everywhere. Lady Chadwick's school has a waiting list. And here Lady Janice has been invited to a duke's house."

"By his addled grandmother," her sister reminded her in a wry tone. "It's going to be dreadfully dull until she departs. Whether the rumor's true or not, no doubt she'll be on her best behavior."

"What a trial for us all, I'm sure," said Lady Opal. "Yet now I'm quite curious about her."

"We'll endure, I suppose," Lady Rose conceded. "Did you see the men? They're not looking forward to her stay, either. I don't think they know that rumor. Or they'd at least have given her the time of day."

Both women giggled. Not long, but enough that Janice's breath grew even more shallow.

"She really is like us," said Lady Rose. *"Before."*

"Yes, when we thought we had choices."

"But we didn't. We wasted time imagining that we had."

"And now we have nothing," said Lady Opal, her voice hollow.

There was another silence.

"Perhaps we should tell her that her luck has nearly run out," said Lady Rose. "Maybe she could find a man whose mother doesn't know—"

"We don't have time to look after her." Lady Opal was brisk. "We have our own problems. And she has that family. She can always fall back on their support."

"That's true," said Lady Rose quietly.

And they both departed.

Janice took a deep, slow breath.

No wonder.

No wonder her three serious beaus had disappeared one by one. Her good reputation was clinging by a thread. All it would take was one indiscretion . . .

Say, with a groom?

She swallowed hard, stunned by the sudden knowledge that she'd been in such a precarious social position for a long time and had never known it. The situation would be laughable if it weren't also so damnably serious.

All she had that was her own was her good character. Everything else came to her from either Mama or Daddy or both: her wealth, education, appearance, and even talents.

Yes, she was bookish and tended to be shy and unable to command a room the way Marcia and Mama always had. But Janice had managed to have a perfectly acceptable social life, until—

Now that she thought about it, everything had gone distinctly downhill after Finn had left. She'd gone to Ballybrook for the summer, but when she'd returned to London in the autumn things had changed. Something had to have been said by someone . . . likely by Finn himself before he was banished.

And in the process, as gossip tends to do, Marcia's torrid history with him and Janice's flirtatious one had become as entangled as Daddy's rose vines and grown into one sad story with Janice as the unfortunate subject.

She'd never tell her sister that her painful, long-ago indiscretion had now become, in a way, Janice's. Marcia would be devastated. So would Duncan, her husband. And God forbid that Mama and Daddy ever found out, either.

Janice would never tell them. Everyone was so happy now. Things had worked out for Marcia in the best possible way. Janice prayed the rumor would wither away and die. Surely it would eventually.

About Ladies Opal and Rose . . . Janice didn't even care that they'd spoken so carelessly about her. She was glad not to be in their unenviable position. No wonder they were a bit cruel. To be all alone in the world . . . the very idea made Janice shudder.

Yet they'd said she was similar to them, too.

That observation gave her pause. What if Mama and Daddy really were embarrassed by her persistent failure to secure a husband? Panic began to creep up on her when she thought back to that morning's breakfast, which seemed an eternity ago now.

"But Mama, I'll miss your birthday ball," she'd said. "Hundreds of people come."

Mama had flung out her hand. "Oh, that old thing." As if the fete in her honor were nothing special.

"And Gregory and Pippa's visit," Janice had added. "I don't want to miss that. They'll have Bertie."

"You'll see them *next* time," Mama had replied in that serene way she had.

"But you'll have so many dinner parties in their honor." Janice loved Mama's dinner parties. "Think of all the august personages I'll miss. Why, the King might come to wish Gregory and Pippa well."

"Even if he did," Daddy said, "you've seen His Majesty before."

"You need to go to the country," Mama told her.

Daddy nodded vigorously.

And an hour later, they'd practically pushed her into the coach.

When it sprang forward, she'd looked back and waved. Mama's face had lost that steely resolve. Her entire slender body exuded relief as she waved madly at Janice. Daddy stood with one arm around Mama's shoulders, a satisfied smile on his face.

Now Janice had to wonder as she stared at the stark tree line outside the window if Mama and Daddy might never have believed she could win the duke's notice. However, they might have enjoyed having her absent for a while. . . .

Her face was extremely hot when she stood. She was angry at herself for not seeing all the possible reasons she was here at Halsey House. But even more, she was humiliated—by that rumor, yes, but just as much by the idea that she might be an encumbrance to her family.

Dear God, if they were ashamed of her—

And now here she was . . . not wanted at Halsey House, either.

She belonged nowhere.

She and the two spinster sisters Opal and Rose *were* alike.

Well, she would have to change that. She wouldn't continue allowing people to look right through her, to push her, to pull her hither and yon, to treat her as if she didn't matter.

She'd carve out her own place in the world.

Deep inside her, something began to glow hot and bright: a need to prove herself, that was what it was. Maybe it was the ambition the dowager had noticed.

Unleashed.

Janice was ready to crack the metaphorical whip Isobel had mentioned.

To become a questionable guest.

To dangle after a duke!

If she could become the next Duchess of Halsey, Mama and Daddy would be so proud. Her brothers Peter and Robert and her sister Cynthia would look at her over the breakfast table in a new, respectful light. Marcia, Gregory, and their spouses would also be impressed. And Janice's friends and acquaintances would cock their heads and say, *I never knew she had it in her. She's the bookworm, after all. The middle sister whom no one noticed. The one who carried the shadow of a nasty rumor around with her like a ball and chain.*

But she did. She *did* have it in her!

The dowager had been right. If Janice let this opportunity to gain the Duke of Halsey's notice pass her by, she was a fool. As Mama had said, if Janice had to fall in love, it might as well be with a duke.

And if he'd heard of the rumor?

Well, she'd simply have to rise above it. She'd act as a duchess-to-be would. Whoever applied the secret would win him—

". . . no matter what she looks like," according to the dowager. "No matter how big a dowry she has, or whether she's even from a good family. None of those things will matter."

Not even a nasty rumor.

She'd do it, Janice decided as she marched over to a looking glass and crossed her arms. "No," she practiced aloud. "Absolutely not."

Hm-m-m. She'd better try again. It wasn't quite believable enough.

And she knew why. It was because Luke Callahan's admonishing face swam before her eyes. The duke was dangerous. That was what the groom had said repeatedly. She must beware.

But she thought upon what would become of her if she lost her good name, her family's support, and her ability to choose her destiny.

Now *those* were dangers she never wanted to encounter.

One duke who came with a warning from a source she wasn't sure she could trust yet? Or one life that went nowhere, that drifted aimlessly and desperately until she faded away?

Janice knew which risk she'd take her chances on.

"No, I tell you." Her eyes glittered with resolve. *"No."*

That was better.

She headed downstairs to the red drawing room, prepared for battle.

Chapter Nine

Everything was different now. Janice was different. Other than Ladies Opal and Rose, which of the occupants of the drawing room—none of whom apparently wanted Janice there—knew the rumor about her and Finn? Who believed it? Who didn't?

It was such an overwhelming question, she actually couldn't care. What could she do about it anyway? The ugly tittle-tattle, it seemed, had unlocked a place in her that had always feared the worst—that she wouldn't be liked, that she wasn't good enough.

She still couldn't believe that unbeknownst to her, she'd been the victim of gossip. Of a spurious story.

Yet she'd survived, thanks to her family's good name.

And she'd continue surviving—but now it would be because she took an active role in her own future.

In the corner by the fire, a lovely woman, no more than twenty-five, sat quietly stitching. She wore a modest pale lavender muslin gown and matching lavender paisley shawl, the colors of light mourning. But the garments couldn't disguise the luxuriousness of her hair—a rich walnut hue—or her beautiful cream-and-rose complexion.

The other members of the house party were gathered in their usual spots around the low table.

The men stood when Janice arrived.

"I trust you've settled in?" There was nothing beyond politeness in the duke's question.

"Yes, very well, thanks," she told him.

The lady by the fire directed an endearing smile Janice's way. She had bright, intelligent eyes, and Janice immediately got the feeling that at least *she* wanted her there.

Halsey introduced them. "This is Mrs. Friday, a widow, former schoolteacher, and your new chaperone. She recently moved in with her sister, whose husband is one of our farmers."

"Thank you for coming to stay," Janice told her, "and I'm so sorry for your loss." She couldn't imagine how Mrs. Friday was feeling.

"It's been a little over a year now." Mrs. Friday smiled a sweet half smile. "And I'm glad to be here, if only to get some peace. My sister has three young boys. It's a happy household but a loud one."

"I hope your sister can do without you." Janice smiled back. "I have three brothers, so I know what havoc they can wreak."

Mrs. Friday laughed. "She'll do well, I promise you. The boys assure me they'll take fine care of her."

They both grinned at that.

With some hope in her heart that she might have acquired a friend as well as a chaperone, Janice took a seat next to Miss Branson. When the duke's male friends sat down again, Janice didn't even attempt to guess what they were thinking, although Lady Rose's earlier insistence that they wanted her gone, too, gave her reason to tilt her chin up a fraction of an inch more than usual.

"Good evening," she told the company.

They had no idea what they were in for. But as resolute

as she was to proceed as she'd planned, fear over what she was about to do made her severely mute.

The Duke of Halsey was an excellent conversationalist. Lord Yarrow and Lord Rowntree made the occasional bland remark, reinforcing her impression that they weren't very distinguished themselves, and the questionable women—Lady Opal, Lady Rose, and Miss Branson—interjected fairly amusing comments as well.

But the duke steered the topics and set the tone. Janice stayed quiet, murmuring only a few words of agreement.

But she would have to change that. *Now.* She took a deep, quiet breath and in the back of her mind hoped that Mrs. Friday, at least, would be happy with what she was about to say.

"Your Grace"—she noticed that Mrs. Friday looked up from her stitching with a warm smile of encouragement—"I enjoyed meeting your grandmother very much. In fact, rather than leave when the roads clear and my carriage wheel is fixed, I've decided to stay the full month as she requested I do in the letter, as long as Mrs. Friday can spare the additional time away from her sister."

"Of course I can." Mrs. Friday's enthusiasm was touching.

The duke hesitated only a fraction of a second. "Oh, but that won't be necessary, Lady Janice. You're very kind, but we have plenty of people in the household to provide my grandmother company."

"Oh? According to Her Grace's nurse, no one but you has been to visit her, Your Grace." Janice looked round at the other guests. "Since some of you have been here at least several weeks, I made the assumption that you'd have done so by now had you intended to."

There was a brief pause.

"I'll be happy to go see her," said Miss Branson. "I *like* old ladies. I simply forgot about her. I never *see* her, for God's sake."

Janice was tempted to smile. She did enjoy Miss Branson's over-the-top speech.

"We're only following doctor's orders," the duke said on the heels of Miss Branson's colorful remark. "My grandmother needs peace and solace. But perhaps the occasional visit won't be untoward."

"I'll go," said Lady Opal. "I'm sure we'll find something to talk about."

"We'll all go together, shall we?" Lady Rose spoke as if she, her sister, and Miss Brandon would be entering a tiger's lair rather than an elderly woman's bedchamber.

"Damn tootin'," said Miss Branson.

Lady Opal nodded vigorously in assent.

Janice wished she could be happier about their enthusiasm, but she saw, of course, that this was their way of helping her leave the house party and return to London while they maintained guilt-free consciences.

"I'm sure your grandmother would enjoy seeing Lords Rowntree and Yarrow as well." Janice looked at them expectantly.

Lord Rowntree cleared his throat. "I-I'll be happy to visit Her Grace."

"As will I," said Lord Yarrow.

"Wonderful." She couldn't help smiling at the two men, who looked stonily back at her. "All these visitors will do her good."

"True, my lady," said the duke. "Which means that when the roads clear, you may return to your family with no worries about Granny."

Janice didn't know if she should laugh or cry at how blatant His Grace was being about wanting to be rid of her, but she decided she'd find greater satisfaction in focusing on her new plan instead: making him want her to *stay*.

"*No*, Your Grace," she said lightly but firmly. "But thank you for your thoughtful offer. I intend to follow through on my promise to the dowager and stay the entire month."

Janice gazed at him without blinking and smiled graciously, as she'd been taught by Mama to do. For a few seconds, the only thing she heard was the snap of a log in the fireplace and the ticking of the clock on the mantel.

"Lady Janice," he said in serious tones, "you do yourself credit by volunteering to stay. But I must insist you go. My grandmother never should have written you. It's all an unfortunate mistake, and you shouldn't have to pay the price for our lapse in not better overseeing her activities. Go back to London. Enjoy the Little Season. Be frivolous. A girl your age shouldn't be burdened with the needs of an ill old woman."

Janice inhaled a light breath through her nose. "No, thank you, Your Grace. Nothing shall change my mind. I'm a guest of the dowager." *Not your guest* was her distinct implication. "I'll remain the month, per her wishes."

She felt the weight of every eye in the room on her, all of them disapproving, save for Mrs. Friday, who still watched her as if she found her interesting and even likeable.

"Well, then." The duke cocked his head at her and shot her another half smile that didn't quite reach his eyes. "You shall stay. *Granny*, I'm sure, will be delighted."

His implication? That he wouldn't be.
Touché.

She would give him that paltry success.

Little did he know that soon he'd be begging her to stay himself.

Their gazes locked, and although there was no shift of power, she saw a glimmer of interest—*real* interest—in his eyes. However cool it was, it was better than his previous indifference.

The women exchanged uneasy glances while Lord Yarrow stroked his chin and watched her. Lord Rowntree's mouth curled in what could only be termed a light sneer.

Move on while you're ahead, Janice told herself. This was a game. A giant game. And she intended to win.

"From what I saw of them this afternoon," she told the duke, "your stables appear quite filled with prime goers."

It wasn't much, but it was something.

"They are, indeed." He had a lazy yet demanding way of speaking that made one feel in the presence of a powerful man, which he was, of course. "Speaking of the stables, is your coachman well?"

"He had a fainting spell." Ironically, it had happened *after* Janice told the fib that Oscar was ill. "But he's doing better, thank you." She wanted to go again to the stables to see him and the puppies—*and Mr. Callahan,* a wicked portion of her brain taunted her. "I think I'll check on him later tonight to ensure that he's back to his old self."

"Very good." The duke crossed his legs nonchalantly and took a sip of something golden in his glass. "And tomorrow you'll take a tour of the stables and choose a horse to ride when the weather improves."

There he went, ordering her about again.

"Just ask the head groom to show you around," the duke added. Because *he* certainly wasn't interested in escorting her there, she knew. "I assume you're a good rider."

Again, it wasn't a question.

Janice gave a soft shrug. "According to my brothers, I am, Your Grace, and they're tough critics."

"Ah." He took a sip of his drink. "The young men of the Brady household. I've seen them at Tattersalls. All excellent horsemen themselves." His indifferent gaze wandered to a piece of lint on his boot, which he flicked off with his index finger. "When the weather improves, we'll ride out together to the dower house. I stop by once a month. You'll want to see the stove house where the exotic flowers are grown."

That sounded lovely! And then she remembered the dowager's advice. . . .

"No, thank you." Janice was kind but firm. Her heart was going so fast, she was sure everyone could see it.

"Really?" The duke's brow furrowed. "Why not?"

Her mind raced as she looked around at the other guests, all of whom were watching her most curiously, including Mrs. Friday. "I-I don't mind riding out with women." She hoped she sounded calm and collected. "But not men."

Oh, heavens. That sounded so peculiar.

"Why?" asked Lord Rowntree, his brow furrowed deeply.

She didn't know why. But she'd had to think of *something* to resist the duke's wishes. "I-I find I want to challenge men to races and quite lose my temper if I lose." Actually, she'd done this on several occasions with her brothers, so it wasn't really a lie. "You see, I become too hoydenish, at least according to my brothers Peter and Robert." She chuckled, feeling more confident as she called upon amusing memories to fill out her elaborate explanation. "So I simply avoid those circumstances. Not for my sake. But for others'. I can be quite frightening, the boys tell me."

She smiled and shrugged. Let them think what they would. She was done with being agreeable all the time.

"You? Frightening?" asked Lord Yarrow in astonishment.

"I think so," she said brightly. "Perhaps you need to be a brother of mine to believe it possible."

"And you enjoy losing your temper?" asked Lady Opal.

Janice thought about it a moment. "I never realized I did until now, but yes. I believe I do. But it doesn't happen very often. Perhaps I should lose it more."

She said the last part playfully, but there was another silence. The duke watched her intently, his mouth curved slightly at one corner.

"Ladies," Janice forged on, "when the weather improves, I'll be happy to ride with you to the stove house, and the men can follow later. Would you consider it?"

Mrs. Friday moved the needle through the frame with such regularity that Janice found her presence comforting. Now she looked up. "Of course," she said, smiling.

But winces of various degrees appeared on the faces of the other women.

"Without the men?" said Lady Opal. "I think not."

"No, thank you." Lady Rose stared at Janice as if she were mad.

"Over my dead body," said Miss Branson with a huff, then looked at His Grace. "And I thought we Americans were the brash ones."

"What a shame." Janice took a slow sip of ratafia, astonished that she didn't feel foolish for turning a ridiculous lie about not wanting to ride with men into the semblance of the truth. She *was* a bit competitive in the saddle. "Perhaps you ladies can ride out with the men then. I'll stay behind with Mrs. Friday and the dowager."

What did the duke think of her outrageous speech? She wished she could tell.

He uncrossed his legs and leaned forward. "I've a solution, Lady Janice. We'll go while there's snow on the ground. We'll ride in two sleighs. That way you'll have no chance of being hoydenish around men on horseback and we can all arrive together. We'll bring a picnic of strawberries and sparkling wine."

She was somewhat taken aback, but she kept a calm smile glued to her lips.

Strawberries? Sparkling wine? Those were rather whimsical picnic items. . . .

Could the dowager be right, that telling the duke no was the way to win him?

"That sounds a lovely compromise to me," she said. "But"—oh, dear God, how could she say this politely?— "I don't like strawberries, nor do I like sparkling wine, Your Grace. I prefer bread and cheese, please. And lemonade." She kept her expression politely neutral.

Thank God her brothers had taught her how to keep a straight face while playing cards.

The other women's mouths hung open, all but Mrs. Friday's. She merely paused in her stitching and watched Janice with a mildly amused expression in her eyes. Lord Yarrow stared avidly at Janice, as if she were an odd scientific experiment. Lord Rowntree watched her steadily, his expression unreadable. But she sensed that even he was unsettled by her remark. His knuckles were tight around the stem of his wineglass.

It was a new experience for her to draw so much attention.

"There will be no strawberries or sparkling wine,

then," the duke said in a low tone, sounding neither pleased nor unpleased.

"Thank you, Your Grace." Janice took another sip of ratafia and looked at something random—a very beautiful set of candlesticks, the tapers of which were lit and glowing. She forced herself to think of mundane things, such as the fact that her new kid gloves had already lost a button. She was terrible at buttons and lost them constantly. Isobel, thank goodness, was excellent at finding them. Janice had never met anyone quite as good, in fact.

After a moment, she took a peek at the duke and found him looking at her again, a furrow in his brow. As a little experiment, she forced herself to think, *No, no,* no.

And his eyes flamed with something dark and hot.

Her heart hammered in her chest. Good God, she'd had no idea how easy it was to be the object of fascination! If only she'd known how in London. Because clearly, everyone in the room was riveted by her behavior at the moment.

Especially the duke.

Chapter Ten

And Janice's success continued. When Halsey tried to escort her in to dinner, she said no, thank you. She preferred to walk in at the rear. It had something to do with . . .

"With an Irish superstition my father told me once," she lied. "It would be bad luck for me to go first when I'm not married. Lord Rowntree, I'm quite content going into dinner with *you*." And without even waiting for the duke's reply—or Lord Rowntree's permission—she took the earl's arm. Lady Opal was on his other side.

Lady Rose wound up going in with the duke.

Mrs. Friday was on Lord Yarrow's arm, along with Miss Branson, who made a terrible face at Janice—her eyes bulging out and her nose flaring. But Mrs. Friday winked. *She* knew something was going on and wasn't fazed, obviously.

Janice liked her even more.

The duke registered no expression when everyone arrived in the dining room, but there was a new intensity about him that could be seriously intimidating if one was a middle daughter with two failed Seasons. But when he pulled out Janice's chair near the head of the table—clearly a place of honor—she still refused it.

"Another Irish superstition?" His Grace drawled.

Janice detected an edge of pique in his tone and wondered if she might be thrown out of the house for her impertinence. But she refused to dwell on the possibility. "No, Your Grace," she said in an easy manner. "No superstition."

He looked at her, obviously waiting for a reason. But in a moment of inspiration she decided that making excuses only incensed him further. It sounded so weak, in a way, to make excuses, didn't it? Best to leave her reasons to the duke's imagination.

So she said nothing and simply took a seat farther down the table. Lord Rowntree rushed to be seated on her left and Lord Yarrow across from her. Mrs. Friday sat at the end of the table.

"No, Yarrow," His Grace said tersely. "You're up here, on my right. Lady Opal, you're to the right of him." He went on to tell everyone else where they were to be seated

Except for Janice.

She took that as a triumph. Either that or she'd already fallen into his bad books tonight and lost all her chances of capturing his notice. It was a risk, of course. But life *had* been dull in London for a good while.

Today, however, had been outrageous but exciting ever since that kiss she'd shared with Luke Callahan.

Ah, that kiss. And what about the way he'd looked at her as if she were up to tricks? And clever? And desirable?

She held the memory close to her—like armor—while she continued on her campaign to win the duke by saying no. In a matter of minutes, she said no to trying out His Grace's telescope after dinner. That was difficult, as she loved looking at the stars and here in the country no doubt they'd be extra bright. She also refused his request to tell the story of her parents' romance, which everyone at the table seemed anxious to hear.

"No, I'm afraid I can't," she said. "It's private. Of course you understand."

She looked at the duke.

"Of course," he said. But he didn't sound convinced.

She also denied His Grace's assertion that Edinburgh ranked below Paris as a cultural mecca. "No, I believe it's leaps and bounds ahead of Paris," she told him when he asked if she agreed.

That assertion wasn't too outrageous. Many people thought Edinburgh ranked high that way. She wasn't sure that it was leaps and bounds ahead of Paris, but she did love the Scottish city the one time she'd been.

But the next question was more difficult. When His Grace asked her if she cared for his favorite opera, *Il Barbiere di Siviglia* (which was secretly her favorite, too), she was forced to reply, "No, not in the least."

"Why?" asked Lady Opal. "Raise your hand if it's your favorite." Everyone around the table raised their hands, except the duke. He rested his chin on his palm, his index finger straight and nearly poking him in the eye, his elbow on the table in a most disgraceful fashion, and stared at Janice as if she were from another world.

"See?" Miss Brandon said, looking around at the raised hands. "How could you not like it?"

"Easily," said Janice, and sawed off a piece of beef on her plate. She looked straight at the duke and popped the meat in her mouth. Her stomach was in knots, and she had no appetite at all. She forced herself to swallow the bite of food with wine. She was already on her second glass of a standard selection and seriously wished she hadn't had to turn down the special vintage the duke had recommended earlier.

He leaned forward now. "Do you care for Shakespeare's comedies?"

Oh, heavens. This was going to be the most difficult one of all to deny. Janice laid down her fork. "No, I don't." She put her hands in her lap so no one would see her fingers tremble.

The duke's eyes blazed with intensity. "His tragedies, then?"

"No," Janice said. Her fingers were laced so tightly, they almost hurt.

There was utter silence in the room.

"Do you like anything about Shakespeare?" asked His Grace.

"No, Your Grace." Janice felt her cheeks heat. This saying no—besides making her look extremely foolish—was quite fatiguing. But it seemed to be having some sort of an effect. The duke drained his entire glass of wine while not taking his eyes off her.

Lord Yarrow groaned into his hands. "Lady Janice," he said, "I can't believe I've never heard of your quirky conversational style in London. How could anyone meet you and walk away unaffected?"

She wasn't sure if that was a compliment or not, so she simply smiled like the *Mona Lisa* and wished for an end to the dinner.

"You promised us earlier," the duke reminded her when his two footmen brought out cheese and fruit, "that you would sing for us tonight. And play the pianoforte."

"I'm afraid I've changed my mind," she said right away.

The duke was about to eat a piece of cheese, but he put it down.

Miss Branson tossed a grape onto her plate. "That's enough of your obstinacy, Lady Janice. Why are you here if you're not going to be pleasing to the company?"

Janice tapped her linen serviette to her mouth. "I assure you, my declining to sing and play will please you more than your being forced to listen to my performance."

"Is that so?" said Miss Branson.

"Yes." Janice truly believed it to be so. She was a lovely performer in private, yet she might falter among strangers. She might cry. She might faint. She had no idea, and she wouldn't attempt to find out.

"Doesn't your sister Marcia sing like a bird?" asked Lord Yarrow.

"Yes, she does," Janice replied quietly.

It was good to be able to say yes occasionally—to anyone but the duke, of course.

"Most young ladies would never admit to being ill suited to playing the pianoforte and singing," said Lady Rose. "I commend you for your honesty, Lady Janice."

She felt terribly grateful for Lady Rose's understanding, although Janice was being the opposite of honest.

Another huff of disgust came from Miss Branson.

"I know that you'll understand that to change one's mind isn't a sign of weakness." Janice kept her gaze on the duke. "It signals one's desire to follow one's own heart rather than abide by others' whims, however highly ranked those persons may be."

"Brava," said Lord Rowntree.

The duke stared at her with that penetrating yet inscrutable expression and said nothing.

Janice felt so prickly and hot returning his gaze that for a ghastly ten seconds she sincerely regretted listening to the dowager's advice. The woman thought she was the Queen, after all. What did she really know about what it would take to captivate her grandson?

But what did Janice have to lose by experimenting? Nothing. Nothing at all.

Ladies Opal and Rose were correct. It wasn't as if Janice would go back to a successful life when she left Halsey House to return to London.

A few moments later, the men rose to adjourn to the library for brandy.

"Oh, Lady Janice," His Grace said.

"Yes?" His hair, she noticed, had been arranged in a more civilized manner.

"You mentioned returning to the stables tonight. We'll send a footman out to get a report on your driver and bring it back to you instead. "

"No, thank you," she said. "I'd prefer to go myself."

"But there's no need for you to endure the elements again this evening." His eyes gleamed in the candlelight, but even now she had no idea what he was thinking.

"I like a bit of fresh air at night, truly." She smiled politely. "I'll walk with the footman. Thank you, Your Grace."

"*No*, Lady Janice. You're staying." His words weren't clipped. Nor did he speak coldly.

Nevertheless, a chill permeated the room in an instant, so fast that Janice felt goose bumps rise on her arms. She opened her mouth to protest, but nothing came out.

Luke Callahan's warning came back to her.

Beware.

She knew that she wouldn't defy His Grace this time. Seeing the puppies, Oscar, and the groom she couldn't forget—all of it would have to wait until the morning. She wished she could be angry at being thwarted, but she was still a tad . . . afraid. And everyone else in the room appeared as stunned into submission as she.

"Cat got your tongue, my lady?" A flicker of something dark in the duke's eyes flamed and then disappeared.

"No, Your Grace." At least she could still say no.

He gave a short laugh, which broke the spell.

Perhaps he's not wicked, she thought as he told the other women good night. *Perhaps he's simply being a duke.* She'd crossed him the entire evening, after all. It was expected that he'd be impatient with her. And dukes were bossy. It was their right to be.

But when he left the room with his friends, she was glad to see him go, all the same.

Chapter Eleven

Lanterns in windows had never been a pleasant sight for Luke. They reminded him of all the houses he'd passed by over the years. Walking as he did, always alone, he'd often catch a glimpse of people eating and drinking around a table, a woman sewing, a dog before a fire, children playing. Each glowing window was a reminder that he didn't belong.

So now here he was, with a lamp in the window of a large stable—the closest he'd ever come to a home since the orphanage he'd been forced to leave at age eleven—and he was waiting to welcome a guest.

Lady Janice.

It was an odd sensation to be a host. Perhaps it was more accurate to say that he was the spider to her fly—which didn't give him a good feeling, but it must be done.

It was better this way.

He allowed himself to linger over the memory of their meeting on the road—how the obstinate young lady's lips had collided with his while his gloved hand pressed hard against the wool of her coat. The craving to caress the warm flesh of her hip had driven him nearly mad. She'd been like a potion. For a moment there—just a moment—he'd looked into her eyes and was astonished that he recognized her.

Knew her.

But, of course, he didn't.

She shouldn't have come to Halsey House, he remembered thinking.

But she was here now.

And she might be the best mistake of his life.

He sat near the coal stove and worked on his latest whittling project, a figure of a galloping horse, half the size of his hand. He had a whole collection of carved animals under his bed in a box. He couldn't stop whittling them, although he no longer needed to. They'd helped him survive when he was younger. On the streets, he'd always kept several in his bag, and when money was short he'd sell one for a meal.

The door opened when he was beginning to carve away at the shape of the horse's head. And there Lady Janice stood, red cheeked and openmouthed, as if preparing herself to be shocked. "Are the puppies all right?" she asked without preamble. "I'm not supposed to be here. But I came."

He rose from his seat and dropped the wooden form into a canvas bag. Something in him—the foolish part—was temporarily overcome with a nonsensical delight in seeing her face. "The puppies are fine," he said easily.

"*All* of them?"

"Yes."

"And Esmeralda?" Janice pulled the door shut behind her.

"Exhausted but well."

Janice's brow furrowed. "This isn't about Oscar, is it? He's not—"

"He's recovered nicely."

"Good." Luke saw a visible relaxing of her shoulders. "Then what is it? You put the lantern in the window. Is there an astonishing development—in a good way? If so, what could it be?" she asked before he could answer. "Have their eyes opened?"

"Not a one."

"Then why did you put the lantern in the window?"

Ribbons of heat from the coal stove warmed his back, but she'd let in cold air and his face, belly, and thighs were freezing. *She can make them warm again,* he couldn't help thinking as she pulled off her bonnet, revealing a long, blond braid.

He had a sudden sense of indecision. Perhaps he shouldn't tell her what he was going to tell her. She was sweet. Innocent. Kind. He was wrong to involve her. He should wait. There would be other women coming up the drive, and one of them might work.

Or not.

Should he choose a random hope—or a sure prospect?

"Because I named the last puppy," he said calmly, although he wasn't calm at all. She agitated him in a way he never had been before. And he'd not named the puppy.

But he must lure her in.

Her face lit up. "What did you name it?"

"I'll tell you when we see it." He picked up the lantern and indicated with his hand that he wanted her to go ahead of him. "Esmeralda is anxious to show all of them off."

After dinner, he'd picked each pup up and told their mother what a fine specimen of dog it was. But he made sure to do so when no one was near.

Lady Janice's face registered even more pleasure. "Is she proud?" She advanced eagerly, and they walked side by side past the quiet stalls. "How can you tell?"

"She makes it very clear by her expression. Her upper

lip catches in her teeth, and her eyes follow me everywhere. It's as if she's waiting for me to notice them."

"Oh," Janice breathed. "How sweet."

She cast a brief, curious glance up at him, as if she
wasn't sure what to think of him. And he felt his own
reaction: half lust, half something else so compelling
that it made his natural tendency to lightheartedness
feel inadequate—for the first time since he could remember.

As soon as they turned a corner and she saw a glowing stall at the other end of the row, she left him behind.

He stifled his amusement. She was enthusiastic, to say
the least. And beautiful, walking swiftly with her braid
bouncing on her coat.

Too beautiful.

He forced himself to ignore the perfection of her
profile as she fumbled with the door. She was already
inside and crouched by Esmeralda when he hung the
lantern on a nail on the outer stall wall and walked
through the half door to join her.

Over her shoulder, she grinned. "They're having a late
supper."

He crossed his arms and decided he must wait patiently for her to get past her initial elation at the sight.
He owed her at least this small pleasure.

"When *will* their eyes open?" she asked, almost pet-
ulant.

"Perhaps in a week," he said.

A small pucker furrowed her brow at his answer, but
she moved on, holding up the white puppy who'd been
in such distress when he was born. "What's his name?"

"Theseus." Luke had only just now decided.

She laughed. "This little thing?" She put her nose up
to his own tiny one and laughed again, then looked up
at Luke. "So you know the Greek myths?"

"Of course."

She looked down, and he could see that she was embarrassed for having asked.

"I read," he explained with no heat. To show her that he wasn't offended, he sprawled next to her in the hay, his palms on the floor behind him, his legs spread wide.

She met his eyes again. "I'm so glad," she said shyly. "I think everyone should learn to read. My mother and younger sister and I have been teaching several lads in our stable in London."

When he didn't reply, she went back to looking at the wriggling white puppy. Luke simply watched her hold the furry creature—and could admit to himself that he enjoyed the sight very much.

Too much.

"Why Theseus, though?" She chuckled, her eye still on the pup. "Is he destined to save many other dogs from being eaten by a Minotaur?"

"One never knows where a Minotaur will pop up," Luke said. "They take many forms."

She cast him a sideways glance. "You tend to assume the worst, don't you? A monster around every corner . . ."

"There often is. I'd rather be prepared for them than not. And a good dog stays alert, too."

"Well, I'm glad he has such a weighty name." She laid the puppy back down. "It suits him, considering the drama he's already brought to the day of his birth."

Once again, Luke said nothing. He was trying to ascertain the best time to tell her she was working for him, whether she wanted to or not. He hated to ruin her agreeable mood—but he told himself that his reticence had nothing to do with the fact that when she was like this something dark and heavy in him dissolved. Disappeared. And left him—

Happy.

If happiness was wanting to stay in this moment.

No, he was delaying the inevitable. He knew he wouldn't enjoy having a furious female on his hands. He'd already seen this one in action when she was angry. A new onslaught was bound to come at him. And although the wall he'd built around himself was impenetrable, her flailing at it, useless as that thrashing was, made him—dare he say it?

Sad.

Gad, that was a feeble word. But if sadness was wishing that everything could change instantly, then it was the right word.

She sat facing him now, her hands wrapped around her knees. "I'm glad you signaled to me," she said quietly. "I had a rather difficult evening and wasn't sure how I should sleep."

Deuce take it, now she was confiding in him. He should stop this nonsense. He didn't *care* what her petty concerns were. Or he shouldn't. He actually did want to know why her evening was difficult.

Damn her for drawing him in. "Would this have anything to do with His Grace?" he asked dryly.

"You're very disrespectful," she said.

"I mean to be."

Her gaze slid away to the puppies. "Halsey's intimidating. But he's not shown any signs of being *wicked*." She was scornful on the last word.

"Oh?" Luke waited.

Esmeralda yawned loudly. One puppy whimpered and wriggled, but the rest had given up on their midnight snack and were sleeping soundly, their tiny rib cages rising and falling in unison.

Finally, Lady Janice turned away from the heartwarming sight to look at him. "I sense he has a temper when he doesn't get his way, all right?" Her cheeks reddened. "But he's a duke. They're supposed to get what they want. And he showed remarkable restraint with me tonight. Believe me, I pushed him to the brink of impatience."

"You?"

She nodded and sighed. "Don't ask me to tell you why. You won't approve. Not that I *need* your approval." She sent him a threatening look, which he refused to acknowledge.

"You want to tell me," he said. "Otherwise, you wouldn't have mentioned it."

They were speaking low. Neither wanted to disturb Esmeralda and the puppies or awaken one of Luke's fellow stable hands.

Lady Janice pressed her fingers to her eyelids and sighed. "All right. I'm pursuing the duke, after all. Me. The girl who didn't receive even one offer this past Season."

Everything in Luke hated her plan. He couldn't help leaning forward. "Why?"

She dropped her hands. "Because I'm tired of having no power. He's a duke. He has plenty. And he can share it." She let a beat of silence pass. "I know you thought I was after him when I arrived this afternoon. But I wasn't."

"Then why are you now? Don't you have a great deal of influence already, as the daughter of a marquess? Why do you suddenly want more?"

Her face took on a closed expression. "I have very little control over my own fate. And as for why I need more power, I won't discuss it, other than to say that I heard something today which changed everything for me. It made me realize that I have to take my future into my own hands. Which is why I'll throw my hat into the ring."

"Like the other women who appeared on the driveway." The irony wasn't lost upon Luke.

Or her, either. She looked none too happy. "I suppose so."

And it came to him then how wrong he was to make that sort of dig. "You're not like the others," he told her.

It took everything in him to say those words. It was an apology. But deep down, it was also an admission. He found her different from every woman he'd ever known. She was special somehow. To him. He didn't know why.

"What if I *am* like the others?" She looked at him with accusing eyes. "Who are you to judge? If a woman is scheming, it's because she's trying to survive."

He knew that. He *knew* that. He'd felt sorry for those women who'd come down the driveway before her. His own mother had become a desperate woman. But he wasn't going to tell Lady Janice she was right. He'd said his piece. She could take it or leave it.

He wasn't in the business of making people like him.

She sighed. "I know that was your way of trying to apologize, Mr. Callahan. As such, I accept it."

More irony. This time extremely bitter. She wouldn't accept any of his apologies if she knew that he planned to bring down the very man she hoped would solve her problems.

Luke wished he could tell her right now that she might as well give up on trying to win over the current master of Halsey House. That man was Grayson Hildebrand, Luke's first cousin. Their fathers had been brothers.

The circus maid had been right. Luke's real name was Lucius Seymour Peter George Hildebrand, and he was the rightful seventh Duke of Halsey. And if it was the last thing he did, he'd reclaim the title on behalf of every woman hurt by Grayson or Grayson's father, Russell—from Luke's own mother almost thirty years ago to the desperate women who entered Halsey House now, to the nuns running St. Mungo's Orphanage, the only home Luke had ever known, where his mother lay buried in an unmarked grave.

But he couldn't tell Lady Janice any part of his history. It would put both their lives—and his objective—in serious jeopardy. He despised being trapped this way. He'd never been pinned in a wrestling match. But he felt pinned now. He knew that marrying Halsey would only be a disaster for her, but Luke couldn't tell her that—yet. All he could do for now was keep reminding her that his cousin wasn't a good man.

"Pushing Halsey to the brink of impatience will help you win him?" he asked her now. "It seems an unlikely strategy."

"His grandmother told me that the only way to capture his interest is to tell him no," she said. "He's so used to everyone kowtowing to him, you see."

"So you're listening to his grandmother."

She nodded. "It's the oddest thing, her switching back and forth between being the dowager and being the Queen, but she's very convincing."

"Telling him no should be easy for you." Luke lofted a brow.

"What does that mean?"

"You're good at being defiant. Kicking. Slapping. Throwing. I've seen you do them all." He knew he was being unfair, but there was something illogical in him now, something that enjoyed goading her, and he had a feeling it had everything to do with the fact that he was frustrated. *Very* frustrated. And not only about the fact that he couldn't be honest with her about his own plans for Grayson.

Luke wanted her. She was so close, he could smell her hair and her skin.

And he couldn't have her.

She deserved a man who'd stay, not someone like him, who'd never be able to give her what she needed.

She sat up on her knees, her eyes glittering with indignation. "You earned all that. You shouldn't have yanked me out of my father's carriage and kissed me."

He grabbed her wrist. "I'd do it all over again."

She pulled back, but he held tight. Their gazes locked. She was so beautiful, he could barely breathe.

"I have something to tell you," he said, "and you're not going to like it. It's the real reason I brought you here tonight."

Her eyes widened. "It wasn't because you named the puppy?"

He released her. "Do you really think that counts as an astonishing development?"

"Yes." She rubbed her wrist and glared at him. "I was sure you wouldn't do it. I *was* surprised."

"Well, that was a ploy to get you over here."

"Oh?" She scrambled to her feet. "This had better be good, Mr. Callahan. I don't have patience with men who mislead me."

"Has one misled you before?"

"None of your business." She narrowed her eyes at him and crossed her arms over her chest.

He wasn't a laughing man. But part of him wanted to grin at how ineffectual her threatening expression was. And the other part of him wanted to strip her of her coat and clothes and kiss away that frown and any bad memories she'd accrued from whoever had hurt her.

All the more reason to be careful around her. He

didn't want to be the next man to cause her pain. "Sit, Lady Janice," he said gently.

She kept glaring at him.

"Sit," he insisted, "or I'll pull you down next to me. If you try to run away, I'll capture you. And if I have to do that, I promise I won't let you escape until I'm good and ready to let you go."

She let out a gusty sigh and lowered herself to the straw. "All right. This once, I'll sit. But don't threaten me again. You're still a groom, and I'm a woman of influence, as you've noted. I can get you removed from this property without a reference. I could make your life a living hell."

"Yes, you've mentioned that before." He gave a small yawn, just to rile her. "And you won't do it. You're too kind. And you don't really want me gone."

"That's ridiculous." She refused to look at him. "Why did you bring me here?"

"Because"—he slid over so that she could see his eyes—"there's something I have to find at the house. And you're going to find it for me."

"How dare you order me about?" she hissed. "If you need assistance, you should ask politely. I refuse to listen to anything you have to say until you show that basic courtesy."

He couldn't resist turning that rounded chin so that she faced him directly again. Her eyes were stormier than ever.

"I'm not asking," he told her. "I'm ordering. There's something I need that belongs to me—and you're going to look for it."

"You"—she gulped—"are extremely rude. And you're also out of your mind. You can't order me to do anything."

"Certainly I can," he said. "I'm doing it now. You have until the end of the week to find it—that's six more days—and if you don't, I'll tell Oscar you're in danger from the duke, and Oscar will feel compelled to take you home immediately."

She gasped. "Why are you doing this? Why can't you simply ask me to help you?"

"*Ask?* Why would I do that?"

"I can't believe you said that. You are *so* arrogant."

"I don't like to be beholden to anyone, my lady. Besides, if I had asked, you'd have said no."

"How do you know?"

"Would you have said yes?"

"No."

"See?"

She folded her arms again and glared at him. "So you think coercing me is an acceptable alternative?"

One of the puppies stirred. Esmeralda nudged it and looked at Luke and Lady Janice with worried eyes.

"Why not?" Luke pitched his voice lower so as not to disturb the dog. "If it works?"

"Well, it won't," Lady Janice whispered. But she was so adamant and agitated, her braid swung from one shoulder to the other.

"All right, then," Luke said. "Tomorrow morning, I'll tell Oscar that the duke is a dangerous man. You might be snowed in, but you can bet Oscar will find a way to get you to the village, even if it means he has to carry you over his shoulder."

"Don't you dare speak to Oscar!"

"You want to stay, don't you?"

"Yes. As you well know." She frowned at him. "So tell me what it is I'm looking for."

"A journal. It belonged to my mother, Emily March."

"Your mother?"

He nodded. "Why so shocked?"

"What's your mother's journal doing at Halsey House?"

Two puppies woke up and made little grunting noises. *You're too loud,* Esmeralda's expression seemed to say.

Luke gladly moved a few inches closer to the warm woman next to him. "She worked for the dowager duchess."

Lady Janice leaned away. "Really?"

"Yes. Long ago, before I was born." He couldn't stop looking into the blue depths of her eyes for the secret to her attractiveness. It was something he couldn't define. It went beyond standard good looks. She was very pretty, but he'd seen women who'd turn more heads. Yet none of them had ever captivated him the way she did.

He wondered if someone had put something in his tea. Some sort of potion.

"Stop staring at me that way," she murmured.

"What way?"

"Like that." She pushed on his chest. "And move back."

He didn't budge. "*S-s-sh.* You'll wake more puppies." He wanted very badly to kiss her, but it wouldn't be a good idea. "Look at Esmeralda," he said in a moment of inspiration. "She's bothered."

It took Lady Janice a good few seconds to drag her gaze away from his and look over her shoulder—a delay that tortured Luke. Her mouth was calling to him.

"Sorry," she whispered to the dog.

Esmeralda thumped her tail.

But when Lady Janice turned back to him, Luke's momentary reprieve from wanting to crush her to him and kiss her was over.

"Why can't you just knock on the door and ask Halsey for this journal?" she asked.

"Because he might not want to give it to me."

"Why?"

"You don't need to know."

"Then I refuse to help."

"You keep forgetting that I'm *making* you help."

She was wrong for the job, Luke knew. All wrong. But deuce take it, she could be right. He could make her so. He'd been seeking a *man* to help him, had been waiting six weeks for just the right one, someone sympathetic and intelligent—a footman, perhaps—who'd have the guts to search Halsey House for the diary and who could be trusted not to stab him in the back.

He'd no idea that the best candidate would turn out to be a woman.

Lady Janice grabbed his coat collar. "Tell me why the duke wouldn't want to give you the journal, Mr. Callahan. Or—or I'll turn the tables on *you*."

"Will you? How?" He pried her fingers loose from his coat.

"I need to think about it. But it will be devastating, I assure you."

He was amused by her robust attacks upon his person. But he also admired her nerve, so he would reward her with a small piece of the whole truth. "My mother may have been mistreated here. And if so, she likely would have written about it in her diary. That's why the occupants of the house might not want to hand it over."

"Oh," she said, seemingly pacified. "Did she tell you herself she might have been mistreated?"

"No, the nuns at St. Mungo's Orphanage told me."

"The *nuns*? And what's this about an orphanage?"

"It was Sister Brigid in particular, and my mother and I lived at the orphanage. It's a long story, and I'm not the sharing sort."

Lady Janice shook her head. "You'll have to get beyond that. If you want my help, I *must* know more. Why were you in the orphanage? And what happened to your mother?"

"Just go find the journal. There's a chance, of course, that it's no longer there. Perhaps someone found it long ago and threw it away. But on her deathbed, my mother confided in Sister Brigid that she hid it and wanted it found."

"She didn't say where it was?"

"No. She was practically incoherent. For all we know, this story was part of her delirium. But I want to find out for myself."

And for the residents of St. Mungo's. And for every person who'd had their happiness stolen away by Grayson or his father.

But Lady Janice didn't have to know that part.

"You have to tell me more." Lady Janice's voice was trembling with intensity. "I can't go looking for Emily March's journal and not know why she was delirious, why you were with the nuns, and why she hid her journal."

"Yes, you can. I'm coercing you."

Lady Janice closed her eyes. "You've no tact."

"No." He picked up her braid and caressed its golden silkiness with his thumb. "Why should I? I'm a groom."

She opened her eyes again and took her braid back. "You've given me six days to find this journal?"

"Yes." Was that pretty confusion in her voice? Was he distracting her somehow? Because he was certainly losing focus himself. The journal seemed less and less important. Touching Lady Janice—kissing her—seemed much more imperative a goal at the moment.

Could he give himself that moment? He knew the bigger picture. He did. But right now—near her—he wanted to stop thinking about it.

For a little while.

"If you expect me to have any luck at all"—she brushed a tendril of hair off her face—"I need to know everything *you* know about Emily March. I need to feel her as I'm searching. It's got to do with feminine instinct."

"I admire feminine instinct."

"Do you?" Her voice was a little breathy.

"Yes." He wanted—

Oh, dear God, he simply wanted.

Her.

It was stupid of him. Careless. It went against everything in him. But there she was, her concern for a woman she didn't know—a woman who wasn't even alive anymore—making a mockery of the rules of survival he lived by.

"There's a male instinct, too, you know." He picked up her hand and traced a circle over the back of it with his finger.

"Mr. Callahan—" The words were practically strangled in her throat.

He stopped tracing and looked up. "Yes?"

"I need my hand back."

"Are you sure? I'd like to borrow it another few seconds."

She shook her head. "That's not a good idea."

He lifted it to his mouth, palm up, and kissed its center. Her skin was sweet and warm. He couldn't help closing his eyes, inhaling her scent, and pressing that hand against his jaw.

"No," she whispered.

He opened his eyes. "Did you know that *no* means 'yes'? Just for today?"

She giggled. "You're outrageous, Luke Callahan."

He was, too. Still holding her fingers, but now cradling them in his lap, he leaned through the foot of air separating them, pulled her close, and kissed her lush mouth.

Chapter Twelve

The air in the stable stall smelled of straw, warm puppy, and virile man.

When Luke Callahan put his arm around Janice's shoulder, pulled her close, and slanted his mouth across her own, she knew that she'd asked him to put a lantern in the window for that very reason—so she could kiss him again, feel his body pressed close to hers.

Yes, she cared about Esmeralda and the puppies, but the truth was, Janice was just as eager to see the man whose mouth covered hers so possessively that she whimpered aloud.

She was worse than one of those puppies craving Esmeralda's maternal attention.

Janice craved this man. What was it about him that made her forget everything proper? She shouldn't kiss a groom. Plain and simple.

But ladylike reservations went out the window when he pressed her back into the straw. She let it happen, just as she allowed him to keep kissing her, his tongue delving deep into her own mouth, seeking out her response, which she gave wholeheartedly.

"You're beautiful," he murmured near her ear.

He kissed her jaw, caressed her temple, and ran his other hand over her coat near her hip.

As she had that afternoon on the long, snowy drive-way, Janice felt adored. It was such a heady feeling that she let her head fall back even farther into the tickly straw so that the impossible-to-resist groom could continue exploring her neck.

He nipped her ear and brought his head up.

She had to focus her eyes. "Yes?"

"This isn't working," he said in such a rough, manly voice, she ached to pull him down and kiss him again.

And then she heard what he said, and a dark rush of embarrassment flooded her being. "You're right," she breathed. "What was I thinking? I'm sorry."

She immediately pulled herself up onto her elbows and was struggling to get to a sitting position when he stood and held out a hand.

He didn't grin, exactly. But his eyes twinkled with something like amusement while the corner of his mouth tilted upward. "That's not what I meant. Here."

She took his hand, and he pulled her to a standing position.

"Your coat's in the way," he said. "And the straw is, too." He pulled four large pieces out of her hair.

"Oh, dear," she said. "But now that I'm standing again, I can see that we really shouldn't have—"

He wrapped his arms around her and kissed her long and deep.

By the time the kiss was over, Janice's knees were literally missing. At least it *felt* like they were. She was so wobbly that when he began to unbutton her coat she simply stood there and watched. And then she allowed him to turn her around while he removed it.

"There," he said when he was done.

He looked her up and down. "You came out in a night rail?" His pupils were dilated with what could only be shock at how silly she appeared.

"I had no idea I'd be taking off my coat," she said as primly as possible. "I should put it back on."

He didn't say a word. He merely took off his own coat, threw it in the straw, and advanced a step. A thrilling sort of fear shot through her, setting off shimmering sparks of desire at the juncture between her legs, which was moist and wanting.

Ready.

He'd made it so.

His eyes were half-lidded when he put a hand on either side of her face. Did his entire body feel as heavy as her own felt? When he kissed her again, his hands slowly descended to her shoulders, then her waist, and then her lower back and hips.

It was heaven. Absolute heaven.

And then he butted his masculine hardness against her belly.

Ah. So there was more to heaven, after all.

She pressed right back and moaned her wonder and pleasure into his mouth.

"*Damn* you," he murmured as he pressed kisses against her neck.

And then he kissed her mouth again, but this time there was something different. Something fierce. He ran his hand liberally over her body. And when he cupped her breast in his hand she reveled in the sensation even as she was still shocked at his words.

He was a man who enjoyed teasing.

The sensible part of her mind stirred. What did she mean to him beyond a temporary pleasure and a way to get to his precious journal?

Anything?

For that matter, how could he mean anything to her?

"Stop thinking." He caressed her buttocks. "Just feel."

She gasped in pleasure when he played with her nipple through the muslin of her night rail with his thumb and then ravished her neck with more kisses.

This was all about pleasure. About taking. Wanting. And *having*.

"But why is it so imperative that you have the diary now?" she managed to whisper.

He swung her up into his arms and kissed her hard before she could protest. "Because I don't know when I'm going to have another chance to get it. Open that door. I'm taking you someplace more private."

Something in her thrilled at the fact that he hadn't asked her permission before whisking her away. She pulled open the stall door and craned her neck for one last glimpse of Esmeralda and the puppies. They were all sleeping peacefully.

"Our coats," Janice reminded him.

"No one will come by. We'll get them in a little while."

A little while. What were they going to do in that little while? She had a suspicion that whatever it was, she'd like it very much.

"Why do you need *me* to help you?" she murmured in his ear, and enjoyed the steady rocking motion as he carried her in his arms. "And not someone else?"

"Because you're the first person I've met here whom I can bend to my wishes," he said.

She bristled. "I resent that."

He stopped a moment. "Are you sure? I plan to do just that in the tack room."

Bend me to his wishes?

Heat flooded Janice's belly at the thought. And then he kissed her again. Against her better judgment, she wrapped her hands around his neck and kissed him back. He was a glorious treat of a man when he kissed her—and she forgot about everything else.

But the sensible part of her continued to wage war with the wanton in her.

Coming up for air, she said, "Is trusting a servant in the house out of the question? You couldn't ask Cook? Or one of the footmen?"

"I'd have asked Cook or one of the footmen long ago if I'd had something I could use against them."

She sighed. "My point is, don't you have any *friends* to help you?"

"No."

"That's not good."

"It's not bad, either."

"Yes, it is."

"I work well alone." He grinned, and his teeth were bright white, even in shadow. "It goes against my nature to get involved with anyone else."

But here they were—*involved*. "Why didn't you force one of the other girls who came down the drive to help you?"

"I never learned anything about them other than the fact that they were after the duke."

"Wouldn't that have been enough fodder with which to threaten them? That's how you got me to do your bidding, after all."

He made a lazy perusal of her open neckline. "Are you sure about that?"

"I am not so easily swayed, sir," she protested. "*This* has nothing to do with *that*. They're two entirely separate matters, and quite frankly, I don't know why—"

She tried to wriggle out of his arms, but he held her fast. "Stop thinking," he said again, and this time when he kissed her he slid his hand beneath her gown and up her calf.

She shivered with delight, then felt great disappointment when he stopped.

"I was ready to bend you to my wishes even before you confessed tonight that you were after the duke," he said. "Remember? I put the lantern in the window. A ploy you didn't care for."

"True. So you were really calling me over for *this*. Not *that*."

"I won't deny that the thought crossed my mind." He kissed her again, and this time when he ran his hand up her leg he went all the way to her lacy drawers and fingered the edge.

More, she thought. *I want more.*

And was appalled at how hungry she was for his touch.

"However"—he pulled back—"I deduced very quickly that you were using this place to hide out. You wanted to go back to London as much as you wanted a tooth pulled. You'd have done anything to stay."

"You're right, but how did you know? You're rude. You're bossy. You've all the sensitivity of a porcupine."

"Open that door," he said.

"See?" She reached out and turned a knob, and they walked into a small, dark room. "You don't even care that I insulted you."

"Your insults are like feathers tickling my cheek." He laughed when he put her down and walked away. She heard the scratch of a tinderbox. A moment later, the glow from a small candle made a halo of light around him.

But when he turned she saw no angel but a handsome, strapping man, his face shrouded in shadow.

She had a sudden thought. "Are you even a groom? Or did you simply take that job to get here?"

"I'm many things," he answered cryptically.

He came toward her again, and this time she froze. "Please." She felt suddenly afraid. "Don't."

"Don't what?" He took her elbows firmly. "Kiss you again? Bring you pleasure?"

"N-no," she said. "I mean, yes. It's too much. *You're* too much."

"Not for you." He took her braid and unraveled it. And then he shook out her hair.

She closed her eyes. "I can't," she whispered. "I'm a good girl. I shouldn't be here with you. I don't know what's come over me."

"Shush." He walked her to a bench. "We won't do anything you don't want to do." He straddled it and patted its surface.

She sat with her hands pressed between her knees and her feet together and felt herself trembling from relief. But the fear hadn't left her, either—she was still afraid of the world she'd begun to explore with Mr. Callahan. It was nothing like the brief interlude she'd shared with Finn. This world was darker, primal. With the groom, she was not herself—at least as she knew herself to be. There were depths to her that she'd never broached.

"Why *did* you wait for me to look for the diary?" she asked. "Why didn't you ask one of the other girls?"

"Because I couldn't trust them to do what I wanted. They could have turned right around and said something to the duke and got me fired."

"You knew I wouldn't."

"Yes."

"How?"

"By the way you kissed me."

"Blast it all. You could have kissed *them*. Did you?"

"No. I wasn't interested. I don't do anything I don't want to do."

"Another way to say that is, 'I do what I want.' An entirely selfish notion."

"You ought to try it sometime."

"Huh." She crossed her arms and looked away from him.

"There's another reason I didn't consider any of those women candidates for finding my mother's journal."

"Why?"

"Even if they'd agreed to look, I couldn't be sure that they wouldn't accidentally— or on purpose—reveal themselves. I learned very quickly that you, on the other hand, are obviously resourceful, clever, and adept at keeping secrets."

"I know I'm resourceful and clever, but how would you know I'm adept at keeping secrets?"

"Because you hide yourself very well. On the surface, you're a bit bookish, stubborn, and wary. But the real you is adventurous, playful. Bold."

"You can't learn all that in one day."

"Oh?" He lifted her hair and planted a kiss on the back of her neck.

Her entire body tingled, and she felt compelled to turn to him. "Just as I can't know that you're an unusual groom. You're probably like all the others. I'm not thinking straight. It's the snow, and the dowager being the Queen. It's Esmeralda and the puppies, and Oscar fainting. Oh, and the duke's been very difficult to read, and Ladies Rose and Opal gossiping about me, and—and it's simply been an extremely long day." She released a sigh.

"I'll get your coat," he said.

She laid a hand on his arm. "Wait."

He said nothing.

"The two sisters"—she swallowed—"they said a terrible thing."

"What was it?"

She gave a hiccupping laugh. "That I was ruined by an old beau." Her eyes watered, but luckily, he couldn't see. "It's awful for a number of reasons."

"I can see why that would be." His voice was rumbly, like a comforting roll of thunder far away, the kind you hear when you're inside a house, safe and protected.

"So you understand why I'm even more foolish being here with you. Were I found out," she said low, "the rumor would be proved true."

He said nothing, but in the midst of the silence he laid his hand on her cheek. She leaned into his palm and closed her eyes. Shock at his sweet gesture quickly turned to longing. It was firm, that hand. Strong and warm.

She reached out and laid her own hand on his muscular thigh and marveled at its perfection—sturdy, rounded.

And then she turned to kiss his palm.

She felt him suddenly still. She kissed his palm again, and this time she opened her mouth and swirled her tongue around it, enjoying the salty roughness. His man's hand opened something inside her, something enigmatic and untried.

It called to her, whatever it was—a dark, slow beat that began in her veins and worked itself through her arms and legs, her belly, the tips of her breasts, her mouth, her cheekbones, her bottom pressed against the bench, and found its home in the nubbin between her legs.

And still he cradled her face, and she sighed against his hand.

She never wanted to leave this moment.

But she slid into another bit of bliss when his fingers began to work at her temple. The darkness behind her lids filled with reds and blues while her scalp was invigorated by the bold raking of his fingers through her hair.

"Mm-m," she said, her hand still claiming the curve of his thigh.

His fingers were no longer raking. His hand cupped

her hair now—petting in that slow, sure way she'd seen him calm Esmeralda. Her head bobbed ever so slightly with the on-off pressure. *Don't stop,* she thought, and mindlessly ran her hand over his thigh, quid pro quo.

It was such a lovely reciprocal activity.

He pulled her head closer and kissed her again. She turned at the waist to face him, the stretch of muscle and skin a welcome release of the tautness in her abdomen. But it came swiftly back, that tension, and left through her hands as she clung with one hand to his shirt and the other kneaded his thigh over and over.

"I don't want to go," she whispered against his mouth. "Don't get my coat. Yet."

"Straddle the bench with me." He hooked her left leg—her night rail ballooned softly—and then she was facing him.

Before she knew what was happening, he grabbed the hem of her night rail and pulled it up. *Bump* went her bottom. Her breasts were exposed, her arms cold. A flash of white and the gown was over her head.

She sat with her mouth open.

He stared into her eyes—her equal—and unlaced his shirt.

Inside her lacy drawers, the wanting grew, the beat of that primitive pulse lifting her nearly off the bench. She couldn't keep her eyes off his chest. With each loosening tug, more skin and curling hair were exposed, along with her own raw admiration.

And then there were his shoulders as the shirt came off, and his belly, ridged and hard.

She could barely breathe.

He tossed the shirt onto the floor with her gown and, without another word, pulled her close. The touch of his bare hands on the naked arch of her back made her cry out.

"I've got you," he said into her eyes. "No matter what happens, I've got you."

She believed him.

What came next?

The exquisite pleasure of her breasts crushed against his chest. Their thighs splayed and touching—her bare skin against his trousers as their tongues clashed. His hand lazily pushing through the barrier of her drawers and skimming her most tender flesh. Her moaning. His holding her. Her falling back on the bench while with one hand he teased that pearl at the center of her being and the other kneaded and played with her breasts.

The grinding of her bottom into the bench, the arching of her legs in the air, her heels leaving the ground.

The absolute ache for his fingers to enter her.

The out-of-body experience that brought her to wave after wave of pleasure while his body curved over hers—

His kissing her while she spoke the new wonder with guttural cries.

Luke pulling her up.

Her seeing the bulge in his trousers as he kissed away one stray tear of utter depletion from her cheek.

Her night rail that he put over her head and arms and smoothed down her body. The way he lifted her in his arms again, blew out the candle, and walked her silently back to Esmeralda's stall, where the little mother twitched in her sleep in haphazard time with nearly all her puppies, save one. The forlorn little thing lay a foot away and backward, facing the two of them—fellow night owls—his eyes sealed tight shut.

Theseus.

"I knew he'd be the first to wander," Mr. Callahan said proudly.

Janice giggled. "Esmeralda is going to have her hands full tomorrow."

A moment later, the groom walked the lady to the house under the moonlight.

"I won't be found out," she assured him.

"If you are, send me a note. You came out to see the puppies. I'll tell Oscar to verify that story. What door will you use?"

"The front." She felt suddenly shy.

"Of course. Thinking like a future duchess."

There was no recrimination in his tone. And she had nothing to apologize for. She was the daughter of a wealthy, influential marquess and would make a suitable wife for a duke. But her cheeks burned hot all the same.

He turned to go.

"Mr. Callahan—"

"Yes?"

"You never had to coerce me to help with the journal." She thought about how he'd bent her on the bench and the lingering pleasure she still felt between her thighs. "I would have looked for it anyway."

He looked at her a moment. "I know," he said eventually. "But old habits die hard."

She watched him make a new path through the snow back to the stables and mourned the boy who'd become the groom with the unyielding back, the shadowed eyes, and the heart so wounded he knew no other way.

Chapter Thirteen

"Wha'?" Grayson sat up in his huge bed—which he'd once dubbed the small country of Carnalia—and looked around him. There was usually one, two, or even three women sprawled upon the ducal sheets with him (not *under* the sheets; he never shared that way), but this morning he was alone.

He looked down at his erect member and didn't like that it was doomed to wilt. He never had to pleasure himself these days. That was someone else's job.

And something else was wrong. He winced, but his head didn't pound from too much drink.

Why not?

Then he remembered . . . that female, the blasted Sherwood girl, Lady Janice. She'd changed everything with her arrival at Halsey House. He'd finally gotten the Yankee chit to strike his rear end with a horsewhip with just the right amount of wrist action so that the sting was pleasurable. And as for the two sisters, he was ready for them to depart. The younger one cried every time he wanted all three women at once. And the older sister wasn't attractive enough to bed in daylight, which was his favorite time to rut.

He'd been on the verge of sending the two siblings packing, but he couldn't now. There was the snow, of course. But the primary reason they must remain was that he feared one of them might seek petty revenge by blurting out the truth to Lady Janice: not that he was wicked— which he could deny if he had to—but that he couldn't finish off any coital activity without wearing a certain diamond necklace he'd picked up in Venice. Supposedly, it had belonged to one of the former czar's concubines.

That would be a much more difficult story to fob off. It was too interesting, too detailed, to be entirely false.

Of course, it was entirely *true*. He looked longingly at the necklace on the dresser—unworn last night. Word certainly couldn't get out in London. He'd become a laughingstock.

He chuckled. Even *he* thought his fetish amusing. He might be wicked and indulge his sexual appetite in an unusual way, but at least he had a sense of humor. Not that he let other people know. It was much more exciting to let them be afraid of him.

Entirely naked, he slid out of bed. "Prescott!" he called.

A mere second later, his valet opened the bedchamber door, a silk banyan already over his arm.

"Where's Lady Janice?" Grayson asked him as he held out his arms.

"In the breakfast room," said the valet as he wrapped Grayson in the royal blue fabric.

"Is she being as obstinate this morning as she was last night?"

Prescott never made eye contact as he tied the banyan's belt in a smart knot. "According to the footmen, she's very agreeable."

"Agreeable? Hah." It was only Grayson that she said no to, and he didn't quite understand.

He stalked over to the looking glass and smoothed

back his hair. He wasn't a fool—some females recognized that men lusted after the unattainable and so threw up obstacles at every turn, but this young woman was carrying the age-old strategy to the extreme. He'd had a difficult time not laughing the night before when she'd said she hated all of Shakespeare, but no one else seemed to recognize her game.

Yarrow and Rowntree—the idiots—had fallen for it. For *her*.

They wanted her.

Grayson did, too. But only because he believed that she really *was* here to see his grandmother and that, despite her toying with him, she didn't give a fig for him.

Good God, why didn't she?

He was handsome, and he was a duke.

He didn't like when people didn't crave his company.

At first he'd been annoyed with Lady Janice for ruining his preferred country routine—ride, wench, drink, play cards, and wench—but she intrigued him enough that he was willing to forgo his regular schedule and instead focus on her. She seemed very clever indeed, apart from her foolish nay-saying. How amusing it would be to bed her.

But she was off-limits, of course. Her stepfather wouldn't stand for Grayson's ruining her—not unless there was a wedding involved, which was the last thing on his mind.

So as of that morning, he was undecided what to do, other than to observe her a bit more, see what he could see, lust after what he couldn't have, and wonder why he didn't appeal to her.

"Sir Milo Falstaff is here," said Prescott as he shaved him.

Grayson opened his eyes. "Is he? It's about time."

"Yes, he got snowed in at the village. He managed to

make his way over here this morning on his Arabian. He's in the stables now."

"He'd stay there all day if he could. Are Yarrow and Rowntree awake?"

"Yes. In fact, they just walked out to see him."

Grayson hated being left out of anything. It went back to the days of his childhood, when no one appeared to notice him at all—at least after his mother died. "Hurry up, then," he told the valet.

Ten minutes and an empty stomach later—Grayson really *did* hate being left out and so skipped his usual toast and coddled eggs—he and his hounds were in the stable block with his so-called friends, sycophants all. It really began to wear on one, to have to endure the false joviality of desperate men and women both.

Nevertheless, Grayson indulged them, knowing that at any moment he could toy with their lives and ruin them completely. He was a good man for choosing not to. His mother would have been proud, or at least relieved—so he liked to tell himself.

As a groom brushed Milo's black stallion, Grayson noted with jealousy the man's muscular back and bulging thighs. He was a prime specimen of manhood, the same servant Grayson had taken to task the day before in front of Lady Janice. Funny how he'd not noticed him before. He must have stayed out of Grayson's way in the stables.

Grayson would fire him as soon as the snow melted. No one on the estate was allowed to outshine the duke. That only made sense, of course, so he didn't feel guilty in the least. The title must be propped up, revered, respected. He was doing his share.

"There was a lovely barmaid I had to part with this morning in Bramblewood," said Milo.

"Good thing you got in a last romp." Grayson pulled

out a cheroot, held it up, and waved it back and forth. "What are you waiting for, groom?"

The servant paused in his brushing.

"Yes, you," Grayson said.

It felt so good to have power.

Just don't lose it.

God, he hated his father's voice. Grayson was practically haunted by him. He'd been the most vile, cold father a boy could ever imagine, and Grayson had been so relieved when he was near death—until Father had told him he wasn't the real duke and that some rotten bastard was roaming the earth at that very moment who was the actual Duke of Halsey, and that Grayson would have to take up his father's pursuit of him, whoever and wherever he was, and be rid of him.

It was such a miserable burden to endure, day in, day out.

How would he be rid of this supposed duke if he was ever to find him? Grayson wasn't a murderer, for God's sake. He wondered if his father was crazy enough to ever kill someone over a title and properties, and sometimes Grayson thought he might have been.

It wasn't a pleasant thought.

So Grayson preferred to ignore the entire problem, pay lip service to it by occasionally rattling the nerves of those nuns at St. Mungo's Orphanage, where the trail of the real heir had run cold years ago.

No wonder he drank and wenched incessantly when he was in the country. He frightened *nuns.* And at any moment he might lose everything, if this missing duke ever appeared.

The home estate was the only place Grayson could let go. In London, he had to pretend to be a sober, high-minded peer of the realm. Indeed, his glittering life there would have been quite amusing if he hadn't had this diabolical secret.

While Grayson's hounds milled about, the groom laid the brush on a wall, strode to the coal stove, and lit a small but tight twist of straw. He then approached Grayson with a purposeful stride and applied the flame to the end of his smoking stick.

Grayson inhaled, glad that he wasn't a stable hand. "We have to be on our best behavior for the time being," he muttered round the cheroot clamped in his teeth.

After a moment, the end of the cheroot began to glow, but before the groom could retreat Grayson blew a plume of smoke in his face.

Yarrow and Rowntree chuckled.

The servant refused to blink, and nothing registered in his eyes beyond a calm neutrality. *Bastard,* Grayson thought when the man sidestepped him and put the straw out in a pail of water. He took all Grayson's fun away.

"Why must we behave?" Milo squinted at him.

God, the baronet was ugly. The only reason Grayson put up with Milo was because he was unsurpassed at selecting prime goers for purchase.

"There's a decent chit in residence." Grayson hid it well, but he was always restless, like Milo's Arabian. "She's here to see Granny. And she intends to stay a full month."

Milo laughed. "For the love of God, Halsey, do you really expect us to be like choirboys? We're snowed in. There's nothing else to do but eat, drink, and be merry. Can't you put her on a sleigh to the dower house and let her molder away there, arranging the library for you or some such thing?"

"No." Grayson scowled at him. "She intrigues me."

"This is a first." Milo exchanged smug glances with Yarrow and Rowntree.

"Not that way." Grayson's tone was cold. "I'm not the marrying sort. But I'm not going to bed her, either. She's of good family. You'll behave. I won't have you damaging my standing among the ton by acting like degenerates in front of her. I won't tolerate her carrying tales back home. Is that clear?"

"But why do you care what anyone thinks, Halsey?" Milo said. "You're a duke. You can do anything you want. The King does. He's a reprobate, and everyone knows it."

For a man who wasn't even a peer, Milo never knew when to shut up.

Grayson took a few steps, grabbed him by the lapels, and yanked him close. "Vice is never as gratifying as when it's performed in secret," he hissed. "And the pleasures of depravity sharpen oh, so sweetly when one also has the adoration of innocents and the approval of men of good character, as I do. You won't endanger that." He threw him off, and the baronet stumbled backward. "You'll endure. And you'll do it with aplomb. Think of it this way: a little self-denial will make your next descent into base indulgence that much more satisfying."

There were several beats of tense silence—Grayson was good at causing those. Only the groom seemed oblivious. He lifted the rear left hoof of the Arabian and peered at it.

"Aren't you done yet, groom?" The man irked Grayson, like a splinter in his finger.

"In a moment, Your Grace," the servant said without looking up at him. But it wasn't out of deference. It was because he was so intent on examining that hoof.

Another reason to fire the man. He was too insolent by half.

"Who is this high-and-mighty female altering our plans?" Milo polished his fingernails on his jacket.

"The Marquess of Brady's daughter—Lady Janice," said Yarrow.

"Lady Janice?" The baronet's dour face registered astonishment, which was odd.

Grayson's pulse quickened. "Why are you shocked? You've heard of her? None of us have."

"All we know is that she's the middle daughter of the Marquess of Brady," offered Yarrow.

"I know who she is." Milo murmured. "Most know only of her older sister, Lady Chadwick. But there's a rumor. . . ." He trailed off with a chuckle.

"Spit it out," Grayson ordered.

Milo scratched his temple. "The Mayfair magpies— and my mother is one of them—are well aware that Lord Chadwick's brother, Finnian Lattimore, broke Lady Janice's heart before he left England."

"I'd not heard that," said Rowntree.

"Nor I," said Grayson. "I remember Lattimore well. A handsome ne'er-do-well."

"Most gentlemen wouldn't know the story," said Milo. "We don't keep up with women's affairs of the heart, do we? Especially women who don't command a great deal of attention on the social scene. As his brother married her sister, who'd ever suspect anything tawdry? But"—he looked round the company with a lascivious leer—"there are others who say the story between Lattimore and Lady Janice is even uglier than most people are aware."

"No," said Yarrow, his eyes alight with glee. "Uglier could only mean—"

"Oh, yes," answered Milo. "Some say he plucked her cherry before he sailed."

The men—save Grayson—burst into whoops of laughter.

He felt a cold satisfaction. He hadn't realized he'd put her on something of a pedestal for defying him, but he had, obviously. His relief that she wasn't any better than he was strong.

"The wily little vixen." His smile was patently false. "Here she defies me at every turn—as if she were a duchess and I were nothing."

"That's the brazenness of a strumpet for you." Yarrow shook his head.

"Hold on." Milo raised his hand. "The general feeling is that it didn't happen. The marquess never would have let Lattimore get away with it. Nor would he have given permission to Chadwick to marry her sister."

"Lady Chadwick *is* a paragon of virtue," said Milo.

"And a remarkable beauty," added Rowntree.

"But this little-known rumor about Lady Janice lingers"—Milo gave a sly chuckle—"as all scintillating rumors do."

"So there's more to her than meets the eye." Grayson blew a smoke ring and watched it hang lazily in the air. Beyond it, the groom led the Arabian to a nearby stall. "I like the overlooked girls. The wronged or rejected ones. They're odd ducks, but on the whole they're grateful for a little slap and tickle"—he broke up the ring with his finger, a crude representation of his lascivious intentions that made the other men grin—"especially if they think it might lead to marriage."

"Humph," said Yarrow. "Lady Janice has an unusual way of showing she's looking for a wedding ring. She was an outright bitch last night, turning down your offer of strawberries and sparkling wine. And then saying no to looking at your telescope."

Milo chuckled. "Perhaps she had another sort of ducal telescope in mind?"

Grayson curled his lip at the guffaws that ensued. He

never liked being upstaged, especially at the expense of his own dignity. His telescope would put theirs to shame, he was sure. "You seemed mesmerized by her last night, Yarrow."

"Weren't we all, to some extent?" Rowntree said. "I'd like to know why no one has told the marquess or his sons of this vile rumor. Surely, they'd have sent her to a convent by now."

"Lattimore's long gone," Milo said. "Why bring it up and risk a bullet to the heart? Her brothers and father are all magnificent shots."

"She's here to see my grandmother." Grayson took a long draw on his cheroot. "Or so she says."

"She must be," said Yarrow. "She doesn't like *you*, Halsey. That's all there is to it."

Grayson stared at him without speaking for a few seconds. "You're like a clucking hen. Let's put you in a gown and a turban and send you to a ball to natter on with all the matrons."

Yarrow clamped his mouth shut.

"I must agree with Yarrow that Lady Janice isn't fond of you," said Rowntree with a shrug. "Sorry, old boy."

Grayson scoffed. "Do you think I care whether this castoff likes me?"

"When was the last time you had a female who didn't have designs on you, Halsey?" asked Milo.

"Never." Grayson shrugged.

"Good God, *I* would marry you if I were a woman," Yarrow said. He always recovered easily from Grayson's insults.

Their laughter rattled the nearby horses enough that several of them whinnied. The groom reappeared and busied himself with some tack while Grayson's hounds sniffed his breeches for horse dung, their favorite scent.

"Whether the rumor is true or not"—Grayson looked round at them all—"I'll have her. I must have an answer. It will make good sport."

"It shouldn't take long," said Rowntree. "Even good girls have ambition."

"A hundred pounds that the story's valid," said Milo.

The mood became quite spirited.

"I'll take that bet," answered Yarrow.

In the end, it was two against two: Grayson and Milo would bet that Lady Janice was already a fallen woman, and Yarrow and Rowntree wagered she'd still be virgin when Halsey bedded her.

There was another round of smug laughter.

"Heaven help you if you get caught," Yarrow told Grayson. "Brady won't care that you outrank him. He'll kill you."

"I haven't been caught yet, have I?" With the tip of his shiny black Hessian boot, Grayson pushed away a cat stupid enough to come to greet him amid the hounds.

"You haven't," said Rowntree, "and even if she did squeal, who's going to believe a young girl over a duke, especially as she's already followed by a whisper of serious scandal?"

"No one," said Milo. "A girl nearly on the shelf is a pitiful creature. She'll go to any length, even telling stories, to gain attention." He gave a dramatic sigh.

More chuckles.

"If you get her with child, you can blame"—Yarrow looked around—"one of these Lotharios, eh?"

He pointed to the junior grooms now filling up a stall with hay. Both of them looked severely embarrassed as the four gentlemen laughed.

"When *are* you going to marry, Halsey?" Yarrow asked.

"That little niece of yours is how old?" Grayson replied testily.

"Fifteen." Yarrow sounded eager. "Only a few more years until her debut."

The fool. He couldn't even sense the scorn in Grayson's voice. "I'd as soon have your blood mingle with mine through marriage as I'd ask for the smallpox, Yarrow." He allowed his usually elegant tone to contain a savage edge. "Don't ever speak to me about the cursed connubial state again. None of you. I'll marry if and when it suits me."

"Is that so?" said Milo. "I just saw that fribble Henry Gordon at Court, and he asked after your health, as he always does."

"He's a swine," said Grayson. "And I told you—"

"I didn't mention marriage, Your Grace," said Milo lightly. "But if you stick your spoon in the wall, believe it or not, there are those who believe your third cousin will make a fine Duke of Halsey with his lace cuffs and preponderance of rings."

"Over my dead body." Grayson shuddered.

"Exactly." Milo bowed. "Good-bye, gentlemen. I'm not staying. No point."

"You can't be leaving." Grayson disliked the baronet, but it secretly pained him when anyone believed his company wasn't sufficient.

"Indeed, I am," said Milo. "There's that barmaid in Bramblewood."

"But it's starting to snow again," Rowntree said.

"I'm aware of that." Milo sniffed. "I'd rather be stuck with her for a few days than in this dreary place, even with His Grace's good whiskey. Groom!" he called the man over. "Saddle up Ormond again."

"He's into a bag of oats, sir," the groom replied.

Grayson eyed the man's strong jaw and noble brow and thought it a waste of good looks.

Milo sighed. "I'll wait a few minutes." He turned to Grayson. "Can you spare me a valet?"

"Absolutely not. If you want one, you'll stay here." Grayson could be sulky when he wanted to be, which was often.

"Fine," Milo told him. "I'll take this groom." He indicated Luke. "You won't be needing him."

"I can't be spared, sir," the servant said right away.

"Oh, yes, you can." Grayson waved him on. "It's not as if we'll be taking any horses out."

"But, Your Grace, I've been administering the daily poultice to Plutarch's lame leg." The groom's tone was cool.

Who the devil did he think he was, defying him? "Someone else can do that." Grayson didn't bother looking at him.

"And I've been overseeing the new mare's feeding schedule," the groom insisted. "She's only just beginning to cooperate."

Grayson reluctantly swiveled his gaze to his. "I can replace you in a bloody minute," he bit out. "Now get going."

"You're a good man, Halsey." Milo slapped him on the back.

And Grayson believed he truly was.

"When will we come back?" the damned groom had the temerity to ask Milo.

"*You're* asking *me*?" Milo gave a short laugh. "What do you care? You do as you're told."

"I only want to take care of the horses properly." The groom put his fists on his hips. "I know them best."

Good God, he was bold—Grayson wanted to explain his defiance by calling him a dolt, too, but he obviously wasn't. "You're not coming back," Grayson told him. "You're *done*."

The groom's eyes registered a flicker of surprise. "You're firing me, Your Grace?"

"Yes." Grayson was shocked to see that the man was *still* calm and unflappable. "What do you not understand about the word *done*?"

The groom was quiet a moment. "I don't recommend you do that," he said quietly.

Grayson waited for him to add *Your Grace*.

But with a dawning sense of incredulity, he saw he'd have to wait for a very long time.

"You're vastly entertaining," he lied. Truth be told, he found this encounter highly stressful. "I've never heard of a groom refusing to be fired. Tell me why I shouldn't. I want to share it with my friends at White's next time I'm in Town."

He waited for his friends to laugh, which they did. But it was forced. No doubt it was because this groom was behaving in a way no groom they'd met ever had. "Do you think you're that good with horses?"

The man's mouth became a thin line. "I *am* that good with horses. But I'm also that good with maintaining security here, Your Grace."

"You and security." Grayson gave a short laugh. "You mentioned that yesterday. I don't need a lowly stable hand looking after my estate. I've got an overseer. I have my tenant farmers. I have my stable master."

"He obviously has delusions of grandeur," said Lord Rowntree dryly.

"Not delusions," said the groom, looking round at them all. "The estate needs protection, and no one can shield it better than I."

"From what?" Grayson asked him.

"From threats, of course," the servant said plainly.

"Threats?" Grayson laughed out loud, and his friends joined in. "You really are deluded, aren't you? Like Granny. Perhaps it's something in the water. Next thing I know, you might think you're His Majesty and declare war on my nearest neighbor."

But there was something in the groom's face . . . something that caused the hair on the back of Grayson's neck to rise.

The man with the hero's face tossed the rope in his hand to the ground. "It's your choice, Your Grace. I'm a former boxer. I had to learn to anticipate strikes before they came. And I'm telling you now . . . you can choose to ignore possible danger, or you can guard yourself against it. I'm willing to stay here and watch over things for you. Or I can go."

They locked gazes, and somehow . . . somehow Grayson sensed a connection between them—an equality that made no sense, that offended his sensibilities yet also felt genuine.

It was so rare that he felt *any* authentic link with another person.

"His zeal to defend Halsey House is almost endearing, Your Grace," said Milo. "You should keep him on. I'll return him when I feel like it, and no sooner. Do you hear that, young man?"

"I do," said the groom, his eyes still on Grayson.

"You can stay," Grayson told him. "But you're hanging on by the skin of your teeth. And don't forget it."

"Yes, Your Grace."

And when the man moved away, Grayson felt it like a stab in the heart: *he* was the one actually hanging on by the skin of his teeth.

Pity he'd no one he trusted enough to tell.

Chapter Fourteen

Life wasn't fair.

Mama and Daddy had always told Janice so.

Long ago, she'd truly grasped the concept and accepted it. She'd been poor. Yet she was now rich. Marcia was beautiful, like a work of art, while Janice was merely pretty, like a child's drawing. Cynthia was an excellent poet, but Janice was the better singer. And people didn't always get what they deserved—good or bad. Sometimes, fate seemed fickle.

So what was the point in attempting anything?

But Janice had learned a valuable lesson from watching Mama and Daddy: A member of the House of Brady always tried one's best and had hope. One never gave up.

Which was why when she awoke that morning she wasn't happy. She lay in bed for ages looking at the silk canopy draped over her bed.

What was she to do?

For a few years now, she'd tried hard to win a husband because that was what wealthy young ladies of the ton did if they weren't anxious to enter the convent, serve as governesses or companions, or be maiden aunts. And she was still trying. The duke was eligible. She saw firsthand that he needed a wife. He must produce an heir, and Halsey House required a mistress to smooth out its rough edges. Even his grandmother wanted her to marry him.

Not only that, if Janice *did* marry him that wretched rumor about her and Finn would die a quick death. No one in the Beau Monde would dare repeat gossip about a powerful duchess for fear of being found out and left off invitations as a result. If anyone risked discussing the rumor, they'd say, *Of course it's silly. No duke would marry a ruined woman.*

So Janice knew she was doing the right thing. She wasn't giving up on marrying, and she was hopeful that she had a chance with the Duke of Halsey.

But . . .

She pulled the covers over her head.

She didn't *want* the Duke of Halsey. Blinking into the darkness, she knew there was only one man she wanted—

Luke Callahan.

She was obsessed with him.

But he was a *groom*.

She blinked back angry tears. She'd been a poor girl once. And she'd been glad to leave that life behind.

"But I didn't know what I'd be giving up," she said out loud. "I didn't know!"

She'd be giving up *him*. She wasn't sure how he felt about her, but she liked him. Very much. Even though he was silent sometimes, rude other times, and generally bossy. Last night, when he'd cradled her face in her palm, she'd seen that he was more.

More.

And she wanted him desperately.

Dear God, she prayed with her palms together. *Please make the lantern be in the window tonight and every night that I'm here.*

"My lady?" It was Isobel. "Are you all right? How

can you breathe in there? Look out the window. It's starting to snow again."

Slowly, Janice lowered the covers. The bright snow light reminded her that nighttime was a long way off. A well of disappointment formed in her stomach. But then she remembered she could go see the puppies—Mr. Callahan would surely be there.

"I'm fine." She threw her legs over the side of the bed and pretended to yawn. But the truth was, she was wide awake—her heart was already beginning to beat faster at the thought of seeing the groom. "I was talking to myself, is all."

"I know," said Isobel with a smirk. She enjoyed bustling about the room in the mornings. At the moment, she was brushing down Janice's coat again. "You're looking extra bright eyed and rosy cheeked this morning. Could you be coming down with something?"

"No. I'm fine. Really."

"At least tell me if there was an astonishing development last night."

"There was." Janice smiled. "Mr. Callahan named the last puppy."

"Is that all?" Isobel laughed softly and raised her eyebrow. "It sounds like a poor excuse he invented to get you over there."

"No. That wasn't it at all." Janice blushed.

"See?"

"No," she repeated firmly. "There was another reason—a very important one."

And she told Isobel about the journal.

The maid set aside the brush. "If that don't beat all. The groom's mother was a lady's maid for Her Grace and she was mistreated?"

"Apparently." Janice put her finger to her mouth.

"Sorry," Isobel whispered.

"We need to keep it a secret for the time being. You can help me look for the journal."

"It would be my pleasure." Isobel grinned. "But if it's thirty years old, where would it be?"

"All I can think is that it might be on a shelf somewhere with other books."

"I'll search every one in the housekeeping office near the kitchens as soon as I get you ready."

"Good," said Janice. "And I'll look in the duke's library. If he walks in, or anyone else does, it will be easy enough to tell them I'm an avid bibliophile."

"Of course. Whatever that means, it sounds grand." Isobel went back to bustling. "What if there are books in the attics? How could we find out?"

"Good point. I'll ask the housekeeper. I'll tell her my hobby is seeking out vintage ones."

"Perfect. We can't also forget to look in every escritoire in the house."

"That would involve going into rooms we're not supposed to be in." Janice was a little worried about that.

"Leave it to me." Isobel was insistent. "I can be furtive when I care to."

With her bright ginger hair, Janice somehow doubted that. "We'll split them up," she said. "If I'm caught, I'll say I was looking for a spare quill."

"And I'll say I was looking for a spare quill for you." The maid giggled.

Janice bit her lip, then said, "But if Emily hid her journal, she probably wouldn't have put it on a shelf. Or an escritoire."

"True"—Isobel's brow furrowed—"but if it were ever found by a maid or footman, no doubt they'd have slipped it onto a shelf or in a drawer somewhere."

"Right." Janice had a busy day ahead of her. Looking for the journal would mean she'd have little time to think about Luke Callahan, and that was likely a good thing. What could come of her involvement with him? "We'll hope for the best. And if we don't find it in any of those places, we'll think about other spots."

"It would help to know what room she slept in," said Isobel.

"But how to ask those sorts of questions without stirring people's curiosity?" Janice sighed.

"You do something else at the same time that interests them more," said Isobel. "They'll answer you, but they'll be focused on the other thing. I learned that from the animal trainers, too."

"Do you have an example?"

"Yes. While you ask the tiger to sit, you wave a bit of beef about on a stick, and he sits without a problem because he really wants that meat."

"Good God, how am I supposed to apply that to this situation?"

"I don't know, my lady," Isobel said serenely.

She enjoyed stirring Janice up, without a doubt.

A half hour later, Janice indulged in a large breakfast. She had such an appetite!

Mrs. Friday was there before her. "You're looking well this morning."

"Thank you." Janice swathed more butter on her toast. "As are you."

Mrs. Friday was so beautiful she would look good in a flour sack.

"Thank you," Janice's new friend said, "but I must say that color becomes you particularly well." Janice was wearing a periwinkle blue muslin. "Either that, or it's the country air that's brought a bloom to your cheeks. And your lips are a lovely cherry red."

Goodness. She was the second person to have

mentioned that. Janice couldn't help thinking that perhaps what she'd done last night with Luke Callahan had altered her appearance for the better.

It would be her secret.

And it was the most delicious one she'd ever kept.

Miss Branson, Lady Opal, and Lady Rose joined them.

"The butler tells me that the duke's in the stables greeting a new guest," Miss Branson said. "A baronet called Sir Milo. He's a runt of a man, but he knows horses. Other than that, I don't know what the duke sees in him."

Janice didn't know what His Grace saw in his friends Lord Rowntree or Lord Yarrow, either. She wiped her mouth with her serviette and stood. "I'm going to visit the dowager now." After that, she'd look for the journal, and of course she had to go see those puppies.

And Luke Callahan.

Mrs. Friday stood as well. "I'm off to prepare the noon meal with Cook. I'm to stir the sauces."

"I'd like to go with you," said Lady Opal. "I'm curious about the culinary arts."

"What are you talking about, Opal?" said Rose over her shirred eggs. "We both cooked for our parents when they were alive. You're an excellent cook."

Lady Opal turned red. "Yes, but—but that wasn't culinary. I want to learn something new and exciting from a duke's chef."

"Don't ever call Cook a chef," said Mrs. Friday with a chuckle. "She's proud of being plain old Cook."

"I like the sound of her," said Miss Branson. "She doesn't put on airs."

"Isn't that what you want to do here?" Lady Opal was still agitated. "Align yourself with a duke so you can go back to America a duchess?"

"Hell, no," said Miss Branson. "I'm never going to marry. I just want to have adventures. And boy, am I having them." She chuckled. "English gentlemen are amusing, I must say, with their big talk and little—"

"Shut *up*." Lady Opal made a face at her.

Miss Branson frowned back. "Why are *you* two here? Do you really think a duke is going to marry a spinster with no money and no prospects from some small village? And even if he did, what would happen to the other sister? One of you is gonna lose, either way."

Lady Rose's face scrunched up. "You're rude, Miss Branson."

"And you're a squatter," she said. "At least I'm paying my way here. Room and board."

"Y-you are?" asked Janice.

"Sure," said Miss Branson. "His Grace might be rich, but he's got a fondness for gambling, among other things." She lofted a brow.

"What other things?" Janice asked her.

"Nothing, I'm sure," Mrs. Friday said quietly, fingering her modest neckline.

Miss Branson grinned at the chaperone. "I'm sorry, but I find this entire setup entertaining. Now you've arrived, and Lady Janice, too. How many more unmarried women are going to play house here?"

"Lady Janice and I are not here to play house." Mrs. Friday's beautiful lips were white. "She's visiting the dowager, and I'm her chaperone. Everything is entirely proper, and while we're in residence, it shall remain that way."

Janice was genuinely touched by how protective the young widow was of her. She felt guilty, too, after what she'd done last night. But she'd do it again.

In a heartbeat.

Beneath her lacy drawers, Janice was a wanton.

On that bench, Mr. Callahan had brought her to a height of pleasure she'd never known. Even now the memory caused a sharp, pleasurable tingle to descend from her belly to the heart of her femininity.

Oh, yes, she would most definitely do it again, as wicked of her as it was to indulge in. From the beginning, Mr. Callahan had been impossible to resist. And now she didn't even want to try.

Though you must.

It was Mama's voice she heard. Mama, who knew that Janice was too full of common sense to let what happened to Marcia happen to her—now that she'd been warned. Only a fool would ignore a good warning.

Janice swallowed and tried to think about the dowager and not Luke Callahan's thighs spread on that bench in the tack room last night, and his fingers, how well they'd played with her . . . making her completely forget all the proprieties that Mama so treasured.

Lady Rose stood. "I want to go with *you,* Lady Janice." Her voice was thinner than usual.

"I'd love to have all of you come," she said, "but this time I'm going alone—to prepare Her Grace for more visitors."

That was true, but she also wanted to check in with the dowager about their little secret. She had no idea if the elderly lady remembered sharing it with her. After all, she'd been the Queen when she had.

When Janice arrived in the dowager's bedchamber a few moments later, she was pleased to see that the old lady's cheeks were a rosy hue and her eyes bright.

The curtains were pulled back, and that bright snow light filled the room. The nurse was stitching a pillow in a small chair, and this time when Janice said hello the servant did more than grunt. She actually said, "Good morning, my lady."

Janice was also pleased to see that the dowager was being herself and not the Queen. "Good morning, Your Grace." She sat next to her and held her withered hand.

"Good morning, Lady Janice." The duchess bestowed a kindly smile upon her. "I hope you're enjoying your stay."

"Yes, Your Grace. In the one day I've been here, I've enjoyed myself very much."

"Excellent. What do you think of Halsey?"

"He's imposing." Janice chuckled. "I think most dukes are."

"Yes, they are." The dowager laughed. "My own duke—Liam, I was privileged to call him—was very much that way. We produced two boys, a bossy one like my husband—that would be Russell. And a sensitive one like me: Everett, the heir."

"But I'm sure you loved them both equally well." Janice sent her an encouraging smile. It was obvious the dowager wanted to talk. "I know that all six siblings in my family are vastly different, but none of us is loved any less than the others."

"That's because love can't be measured." The duchess's smile faded, and her eyes clouded with a tinge of sadness. "It was such a shock when I lost them both— Liam first, and then Everett, one nearly after the other."

"I'm so sorry." Janice gave her hand a little squeeze.

The dowager sighed. "In the midst of crisis, Russell stepped in beautifully. I suppose I wasn't grateful enough that he did. I was too immersed in my own grief to thank him properly."

"I'm sure he understood."

The dowager shook her head. "I don't know if he did. He had a terrible temper. Perhaps it was his own grief, but after Liam and Everett died, he changed. He was unkind to me. And indifferent when I was ill." She swallowed hard.

Janice noticed. "Please don't upset yourself, Your Grace," she begged her gently.

"I brought you here to tell you this," the old woman replied, "before I die."

"Your Grace"—Janice shook her head—"please don't speak that way."

"It's all right." The dowager sighed. "Everyone must go someday. But each of us has a story, don't we?"

"Yes, indeed."

"And those stories should be told." The duchess seemed more content. "And *you*, Lady Janice, are the person I want to tell my story to. There was something in your eyes that day—when you were a little girl. Even then I saw that you had a sensitive soul, like Everett. If I'd had a daughter, I would have wanted her to have your eyes and your grace. Every time I went to your mother for fittings, I always looked for you."

"My goodness, Your Grace. That's such a lovely compliment. Thank you." Janice was overwhelmed again. And so touched.

"As for Russell," the dowager continued, "the boy I knew wasn't there anymore. He'd been replaced by an equally strong-willed man. But the man lacked a heart that I was sure the boy had."

"Sometimes people change because of their circumstances," Janice offered as explanation. "I'm sorry that happened to Russell."

"I am, too." The duchess gave another weary sigh.

The nurse stood up and sent a warning look to Janice.

She understood.

"Your Grace," she began softly, "I'm privileged to hear your story. But perhaps you should rest for a bit."

"I think you're right." The dowager's smile was weak. "These memories agitate me so. And sometimes they disappear—*I* disappear—and I get confused. So very confused."

"I understand." Without asking, Janice leaned over and kissed her cheek. "You're a dear lady. I'm so glad you invited me to stay." She was humbled by the woman's kind interest in her. "And about that special strategy you shared with me, I'd like to thank you." She leaned in closer so Mrs. Poole couldn't hear. "Saying no has been . . . liberating in a way. It's hard to explain."

"Whatever are you talking about?" The dowager's eyes registered real confusion.

Janice scratched her temple and smiled. "Nothing, really." Somehow she thought that the dowager had known what the Queen was doing—but apparently not.

In less than a few seconds, the dowager fell into a light doze.

"I'll come back, of course," Janice told the nurse.

"Just not at three o'clock. That's when His Grace visits."

"All right. What does he do if she's asleep?"

"He simply sits with her."

"That's so kind of him." Janice was surprised somehow to hear how devoted he was.

"He's a good man," replied Mrs. Poole.

He must be, Janice thought as she made her way to the main wing of the house. *He really must.*

Chapter Fifteen

All morning long, the wind blew and the snow fell. Janice's conversation with the dowager had made her rather sad. So she'd wrapped herself up and gone to the stables, presumably to check on the puppies and Oscar. Poor man, he had no idea how feeble the residents of Halsey House supposed him to be.

Of course, she was hoping to see Mr. Callahan as much as she was the puppies and Oscar.

No, *more*.

She felt guilty about that fact when she pulled open the door to the stables and stepped inside, comforted by the familiar smell of horse and hay and the warmth that pervaded the space. Esmeralda was her delightful, wagging self. Her babies, their eyes closed tight, had each managed to roll and scoot at least a foot from their mother. Aaron, the junior groom, and Oscar laughed with Janice over their antics.

"Where's Mr. Callahan?" she asked outright. The question wouldn't draw attention, she was sure, as he was the person who'd found Esmeralda in the first place and arranged her bed.

"He's in Bramblewood," said Oscar. "Stranded with Sir Milo, who refused to be stranded here. He said it wasn't as interesting a place to be as the pub there. So he asked His Grace if he could take Luke to serve as both valet and groom."

"Oh." Janice tried not to be disappointed. But she was, terribly. "When is he coming back?"

"When Sir Milo sends him," said Aaron. "It could be a few days."

"I see." Janice's heart sank. But perhaps it was a good thing. She needed to forget about the groom.

She *must*.

What was she doing seeking him out, other than torturing herself?

Back in the drawing room at Halsey House, she was determined to read—hoping she'd forget about him—while sitting next to Mrs. Friday, who was working on her sampler. It was a verse about love, and at the bottom the assiduous chaperone had stitched her late husband's name entwined with her own.

But gazing at it made Janice remember that the night before she and Luke Callahan had been entwined, too, in their own way.

So she focused on watching the duke, Lord Rowntree, and Lord Yarrow play cards. The other women, who always seemed to be bickering, lingered behind them, making nuisances of themselves by looking over the men's shoulders and making supposedly cryptic comments about the hands the men had been dealt.

"That's quite enough interference, ladies," Halsey eventually said to them in a clipped voice. "Find something else to do."

The women pouted about their dismissal but sat at another table together and began to play whist. A few blessedly quiet moments passed—although for Janice they dragged because she was desperate to see Mr. Callahan—and then the clock on the mantel chimed.

It was half past two.

"That's enough." The duke threw down his cards. "We've played too long."

"But you're ruining this hand," Lord Yarrow protested.

"You'll live," said His Grace. "We're not playing for high stakes anyway."

"Not today, maybe, but it's bad form—," Lord Yarrow began.

Lord Rowntree sent him a threatening look.

"Lady Janice," His Grace called to her, "if I might have a word!"

She noted that his tone was warm, much warmer than it had been to her yesterday or today, to the other women. Not only that, the look he threw her was charming, attentive. He was, in fact, a new man toward her—but he was the same intimidating duke to everyone else.

She was thrilled that her strategy of saying no was working so well.

"Your Grace?" She refused to say the word *yes* to him—ever.

"Would you like to take that tour now—the one you missed yesterday, of the conservatory and the portrait gallery?"

"No, thank you." She was actually at a particularly enjoyable part of her book, but it would be unkind to use that as an excuse.

The room was silent.

"May I ask why you won't go?" He angled his head, and for a moment again . . . he was Pan . . . hot, earthy Pan. His finely tailored clothes did little to disguise his sensual nature.

Oh, dear. She had to think of an excuse fast, and it was most awkward. *For him, not* you, a small portion of her brain reminded her. She was gaining some authority—true power—and with it came the knowledge that it was often uncomfortable to exercise this power.

"Mrs. Friday is in the middle of a difficult stitch." Janice ignored the stares of the other guests. "I don't want to interrupt her."

Mrs. Friday laughed. "Why, Lady Janice, I'll be happy to set it aside for now. If I do, will you go?"

She was such a cheerful woman.

"I suppose I will," said Janice. "There's a particular portrait that intrigues me."

"It's about time," Miss Branson said under her breath.

"Very good." The duke didn't smile, but his mouth angled up the slightest bit.

A few moments later, he showed no signs of resenting Mrs. Friday's presence as they walked through wide, luxurious corridors to the conservatory, a truly splendid room.

"So much glass!" exclaimed Mrs. Friday.

"And the plants are beautiful." Janice looked round in wonder. "To be able to walk among them when there's snow outside is such a gift."

"I'm glad you think so," said the duke. "Wait till you see the stove house at the dower house. The orchids are stunning. But they need constant tending. I spend a small fortune maintaining that hobby for Granny."

"I look forward to touring it." Janice felt genuinely drawn to him for the first time. "Does Her Grace ever go over to see them?"

"No." He plucked a bay leaf and put it in his pocket. "She has a Bath chair, but she much prefers to stay in her room. On occasion, I'll bring her an orchid in a pot."

"I'm sure she loves that." Janice thought his carrying

an orchid to her was such a special gesture. But she also
wondered why he said the dowager preferred to stay in
her room. She'd made it very clear to Janice that she
didn't. "Wouldn't she like to come down here to see the
plants?"

"No." Halsey gave a light shrug. "She gets too agitated. If she tells you otherwise, you mustn't believe her."

"Oh." What he said made sense, but Janice thought
it was terribly sad.

So did Mrs. Friday. She had a sheen of tears in her
eyes.

"I'm sorry." Their host raked a hand through his hair
and sighed. "Granny's situation is painful. It isn't easy
for her or for anyone."

Mrs. Friday bit her lip. "We understand, Your Grace."
She turned to examine an orange tree, no doubt to give
him a moment to recover.

"Of course." Janice turned away, too, to admire the
same tree.

There was a moment's awkward silence.

"But we can cheer her up," he said.

He was trying so hard, wasn't he? That did more to
win Janice's approval than anything he'd done yet. She
and Mrs. Friday exchanged pitying glances.

"When it stops snowing so hard"—he wore an ear-
nest, serious expression—"we'll take that sleigh ride
over to the dower house, and I'll let you pick out the
perfect bloom for her, my lady. Will you do that?"

"No, thank you, Your Grace." Janice winced at
Mrs. Friday. "I can't."

"No?" The duke couldn't disguise his astonishment.

Without even knowing what Janice was about, Mrs.
Friday stepped in. "She only says no because she can't
bear to choose between them, Your Grace." Her tone
was light. "Isn't that right, Lady Janice?"

"I'm terrible at choosing." Janice sent her friend a grateful look, then turned to the duke. "I'll pick out three orchids, Your Grace, and leave the final selection to you."

"Very well." But the warmth in his eyes had slightly cooled.

So they'd taken a step backward. Or was it forward? Janice couldn't be sure. She wished she could go to the dowager right now and speak to her while she was channeling the Queen. Janice wanted to tell Her Majesty that she was having strong second thoughts about her strategy to win her grandson.

But until Janice and her mentor had that conversation, she'd continue saying no to the Duke of Halsey, who from all appearances—ducal quirks aside—was as fine a man as his reputation in London suggested. All he needed was a wife to weed out the hangers-on and to teach him patience.

Janice could do that.

Up in the portrait gallery a few minutes later, she went straight to the portrait of the woman in love. "Who is this woman?" Janice couldn't help smiling when she saw her. "She's such a bright light. A wit, I can tell. And she appears to be madly in love. She has a glow about her."

"She's my grandmother as a young duchess," Halsey said.

"Oh," Janice breathed. "She was remarkable."

"She was. And *is*," he added. "She loved my grandfather very much."

Mrs. Friday was as fascinated by the painting as Janice was.

They strolled by all the other portraits, and the duke was so entertaining that Janice was completely overwhelmed with this new favorable impression of him.

"Thank you," she said at the end of the tour. He'd been such a gentleman.

"It was my pleasure." He gave her a slight bow.

How gratifying, to be bowed to by a duke!

Mrs. Friday descended the wide staircase to the main hall slightly ahead of them. About halfway down, Halsey slowed and Janice slowed with him.

"I just want to tell you," he said, "that the glow you mentioned in my grandmother . . ." He paused, seeming to search for the right words.

She waited patiently.

"You have a glow, too," he said. "I couldn't help but notice it today. When you walked into the drawing room, no one could look away. Including myself."

Janice's face got so hot, she was sure it was red. "Th-thank you, Your Grace," she murmured, embarrassed at the lavishness of his compliment. Yet it was also extremely kind—

Everything an unmarried young woman wanted to hear from a duke.

She took another few steps. His Grace followed at her side. *Future husband*, a wicked voice in her head teased her.

But Janice had to wonder: Was he inventing that impression of her? Or did last night's interlude with Mr. Callahan literally change her appearance?

She recalled Isobel's words from that morning, as well as Mrs. Friday's. Surely her rosy cheeks and lips had dimmed by the time she'd entered the drawing room a few hours later. And she'd been in that terrible funk because a groom named Luke Callahan had left the estate.

It was all very confusing—unless she credited the dowager's secret strategy of saying no for actually working.

Why not?

Mrs. Friday reached the bottom of the stairs and looked up at them expectantly. "I've always been a fast walker," she said with spirit, and laughed.

She was such a delightful person, and she knew just what to say when the moment called for it.

Halscy excused himself when they reached the bottom of the stairs. "It's time to see my grandmother." He held on to the banister, prepared to go right back up again.

"Oh, that's right." It touched Janice, how thoughtful he was. She still felt very flustered by his remarks on the stairs. "Please send Her Grace my best."

"I will." He raised Mrs. Friday's hand to his mouth and kissed it. Then he did the same for Janice. "I'll see you both at dinner." He smiled again.

And when he turned his back and climbed the stairs, Janice and Mrs. Friday exchanged another glance.

He's wonderful, mouthed Mrs. Friday.

Janice smiled, understanding, and looked up at his retreating back. *Fall in love with him*, she told herself. *Fall in love.*

But her heart refused to be stirred.

Chapter Sixteen

It was the following morning, and until Luke Callahan returned to the estate Janice couldn't think. She couldn't eat. She couldn't sleep or care how well her campaign with the duke was going, although it seemed to be going very well.

One thing she could still do while the groom was gone was continue saying no. And she was getting better at it. As she invented creative answers to avoid blatantly insulting His Grace, she realized she was being like Mama, the queen of saying no.

But until she'd come here to Halsey House, Janice had never noticed this trait in her mother. And come to think of it, Marcia said no very easily, too. It seemed that both Mama and Marcia had very strong opinions and, captivating as they were, they adhered to those personal sentiments.

Perhaps saying no was actually the very essence of their charm!

Janice, on the other hand, had always tried to be agreeable. But what was *agreeable,* really? How treasured were smiles and nods that came from a person who didn't know her own feelings—or, if she did, didn't value them enough to protect them?

Was saying no what she had to learn in the country? Janice was beginning to wonder. . . .

She spent the entire morning searching for Emily March's journal on the duke's library bookshelves, but she came up with nothing. Neither did Isobel. Which meant the escritoires were next, and after that Janice wasn't certain. She'd have to do some subtle probing of the occupants of the house, starting with the dowager.

When Janice entered her bedchamber, the Queen was presiding over her own version of Court. The throne of pillows behind her supported her tiny body well. "You again," she drawled, her gaze flinty.

"Yes, Your Majesty." Janice curtsied. "Good morning."

The dowager threw out a lazy finger, indicating that Janice might sit in the chair by the bed.

Janice did as she was told. She was dying to tell her that she loved the duchess's portrait, but she was afraid the comment might confuse her.

"I'll have a song this morning," said the old lady. "I haven't heard one this age."

"A song?" Janice was somehow surprised.

"Can you not hear me? Or is this willful disobedience on your part? Court's been rather dull. Get to it."

Janice was well aware of the presence of the nurse behind her back. "Well, if you don't have a preference—"

"Stop dillydallying," snapped the dowager.

"All right." Janice cleared her throat. "'Good morning, pretty maid,'" she sang, "'Where are you going?'"

Her voice started out thin—it had been a long while since she'd sung a note—but as she continued the ballad, which Daddy sang every morning to Mama as he prepared for the day, the notes grew stronger and stronger. And by the middle of it, she was in full voice and her heart was happy—

Especially when she saw that the dowager was well

pleased. Her eyes brightened and she seemed to follow hungrily every word Janice sang.

When the last note finally drifted away, Her Majesty sighed long and loud. "Now that's singing," she said simply.

Janice smiled. "I'm glad you enjoyed it." She had, too.

She glanced over her shoulder at Mrs. Poole, who for the first time ever managed to smile in return. It was nothing spectacular—it was barely a curve of her lips—but at least it was better than the grim face she usually presented.

"My grandfather used to *s-s-s-sing* that," she said, her whistle particularly pronounced.

"No noise from the minstrels' gallery," barked the dowager. "I can't abide the flute. Such a prissy instrument. Give me a horn any day."

Janice cast a glance at the nurse. Her face was redder than usual. Of course she'd heard the slight. "I'm so sorry," Janice murmured.

The nurse turned her very square back on her.

"Your Majesty"—Janice felt terrible for Mrs. Poole—"you must be kinder. You must be terribly unhappy to pick on your caretaker."

"What do *you* think? I can't do any proper ruling from this bed." The dowager gave a great sigh. "How's your plan going, by the way? Are you listening to my advice?"

"Yes." Janice was glad for the change of subject. "And it's working."

Her Majesty chuckled. "I knew it would. So, what will be the first thing you do as duchess?"

"I don't know" Janice's face heated. "It might not happen. We're only at the beginning stage of the . . . the strategy."

The dowager waved her hand. "It works fast. So prepare yourself. Soon you'll be a powerful woman."

"Like you?" Janice asked her.

"I've had my moments," her hostess said smugly, but then her forehead wrinkled. "Although . . . although I recall not taking advantage of all of them. I should have spoken up. I should have said no. *No*." She slapped the coverlet, the creases around her eyes and mouth deepening.

Janice detected a slight tremble of her lips and took her hand. "It's all right. Please let me sing you another song."

But the dowager seemed to forget she was there. "I stood by. . . . I knew what he'd done."

"Really, Your Majesty. I know a lovely marching song—"

"But I didn't know what to do," Her Majesty insisted, not heeding Janice in the least. "I loved him, you see. He was all—he was all I had left." She lifted her chin and looked off into the distance, the very picture of a noble queen.

Janice felt compelled to take *both* her hands and give them a squeeze. "Really, Your Majesty, you did everything you could. Please don't have any regrets."

"Regrets?" The frail lady made a scornful face. "I can't afford those. Duty won't allow it. We must—" She stopped speaking, and after a long second of inhaling and looking generally uncomfortable she reached out for the handkerchief on her lap and sneezed.

Atchoo!

Janice looked back at Mrs. Poole, who was standing and watching. There was a trace of something in her eye—concern, Janice could see. Genuine concern.

"She doesn't usually talk like this," the nurse said. "You mustn't rile her."

"I'm so sorry." Guilt made Janice shrink up in her chair.

"I'm *fine*," said the patient with a chuckle. Her entire demeanor had changed. She was back to being the sweet elderly Dowager Duchess of Halsey. "Good thing you're here, Lady Janice. I'm ready to leave this room. No one else will let me. Will you?"

She had a charming twinkle in her eye.

Janice breathed a sigh of relief. Yet she couldn't be at ease for long. Both the Queen and the dowager wanted to get out of the bedchamber. And in Janice's heart—no matter how well-intentioned the duke and the doctor were—she believed, too, that some fresh scenery would do the dowager a great deal of good.

But she shouldn't make that decision. Surely not. It wasn't her place.

"Let me . . . let me talk to Mrs. Poole a moment, Your Grace. I'll be right back." She smiled—trying her best to be cheerful in spite of her concerns—and stood.

Mrs. Poole looked at her suspiciously as she approached. "My lady, don't even think about it."

Janice sighed. "It's cruel to keep her in here."

"It's what His Grace demands. And what the doctor ordered."

"Who *is* this doctor?"

"Dr. Nolan."

"When was the last time he was here?"

"About three months ago."

"Three *months*?"

Mrs. Poole nodded.

Janice shook her head. "I'm sorry. I'm taking her out."

"You will *not*—"

Janice strode by the nurse to a door she'd never seen Mrs. Poole open and laid her hand on the knob. "You don't have to help, and I'll tell His Grace you tried your best to stop me."

"No one will assist you. No servant here wants to lose his or her job."

"That's a shame but understandable. I have my own maid and Mrs. Friday, my chaperone, to lend me aid." Janice opened the door and looked into a small room that held a cot and a bureau but nothing else. "Where's Her Grace's Bath chair?"

"I'm not telling," said Mrs. Poole from behind her. "And your own maid and chaperone are in the stables. I saw them walking out there myself."

To see the puppies, of course.

Janice immediately thought of Mr. Callahan and wondered when he'd be back.

"I'll fetch them then." Janice shut the door. "And I'll find that chair. I'll get Her Grace out of here without you, Mrs. Poole. So there."

The nurse crossed her arms. "By the time you get your maid and chaperone, the dowager will be asleep again. So you might as well not bother. Besides, I'll tell His Grace."

"Fine." Janice gave a short laugh. "You do that. And when you fall asleep *there* tonight"—she angled her head at the little room—"you'll know that you've done your duty."

"Exactly." The woman's tone was self-satisfied.

"And when you wake up tomorrow," Janice reminded her, "you'll come right back into this bedchamber and sit all day. Just as you always do. You're as trapped here as the duchess is."

"No, I'm not."

"You're right. You have your own box to retreat to at night."

Mrs. Poole's mouth thinned. "There's nothing wrong with it. At least it's private."

"Right. The rest of the servants are crammed into the attics, aren't they? Poor things. Always seeing each other . . . laughing, joking, having company. It must be awful. Much better to be in here with nothing to do and no one to speak you except your patient—whom you ignore."

Mrs. Poole took a deep breath. "You've *s-s-s-said* enough, my lady."

"I wonder what you're so afraid of?" Janice cocked her head. "Are you nervous about that whistle? Because once you hear it several times, you don't notice it anymore."

"How dare ye speak of that!" A rough accent spilled from the attendant now. "You heard Her Majesty. She don't like it."

Janice shook her head. "She's difficult, isn't she? But I'll wager that when she's herself—the dowager duchess—she's never said a word about it to you."

The nurse hesitated. "No, she hasn't. Only the Queen has."

"I'm so sorry about that," said Janice. "Listen to me, Mrs. Poole. I'm speaking the truth. I find your whistle not imposing at all. And when you smile—as you did today—I completely forget about it anyway."

Mrs. Poole went to the window and looked out. "You're only one person," she said over her shoulder. "I see them snickering, the other servants."

"Perhaps it's because you're always grumpy. I know that my own maid, Isobel, told me that you were so lucky to be able to sing like a bird. And she was sad that you weren't more cheerful."

"Easy for her to say." The nurse's square back was unyielding.

Janice walked slowly up to her. "I'm sure it will require courage. But perhaps you could smile more when you're in the other parts of the house and when you're here with the dowager. I know she'll appreciate it, even if the Queen never does."

Mrs. Poole turned, her mouth grim. "I'll think on it."

"Good." Janice smiled. "Now it will take more courage to direct me to the Bath chair. But I assure you that I won't let the duke fire you. I'll tell him I found it myself and that you protested mightily when I removed the duchess from her bed."

"A scrawny thing like you can't do that on your own." There was no heat or insult in the nurse's voice.

"Certainly I can," Janice assured her. "I grew up with three brothers. I swung from trees often. I can lift a sack of potatoes with ease. I'm sure I can get an elderly woman into a Bath chair."

"I'll help you do that, at least," Mrs. Poole muttered.

"Will you?" Janice's heart sped up.

Mrs. Poole nodded. "I'll be right back. The chair is down the hall. It hasn't been used since we moved here a year ago. I lift her off the bed and directly into the tub to bathe her."

Poor dowager, she'd been trapped in this bedchamber for far too long!

While Mrs. Poole was gone, Janice prepared the elderly lady for their outing. "We're going to take you to a special room," she said, "with a beautiful view. The windows go from the floor to the ceiling, and you'll be able to see the gardens covered in snow and, behind them, the beautiful pasture and trees."

"My old sitting room," said the duchess with a bit of wonder.

Janice's heart lifted. Her elderly friend seemed excited!

But then the duchess hesitated and slowly shook her

head. "No," she said. "I've changed my mind. I'm not ready. I'll never be ready."

"It's all right," Janice assured her. "You belong there, Your Grace."

"I-I can't."

"You just sit back." Janice would be confident for her. "Don't worry. I'll take care of getting you there."

The dowager didn't look at all happy, but she said nothing else.

Janice realized she'd have to coax her little by little to resume a normal life.

When the nurse returned, she insisted on putting the fragile old woman in the chair herself. Janice held her breath, but it went quite well. Mrs. Poole tucked a pretty quilt around Her Grace and stood back.

"There you are." The nurse was as stiff as ever, but she also looked a bit proud of herself.

"Thank you so much," Janice said. "You were very gentle."

Mrs. Poole nodded.

Janice pushed the chair to the door, which Mrs. Poole opened for her.

"See you in an hour or so," Janice told her cheerfully.

Mrs. Poole said nothing as she walked by.

Out in the hall, Janice felt all the importance of the moment. The dowager was free!

"How are you?" She smiled as she looked around the chair at the elderly woman.

But the dowager wouldn't answer. She was obviously frightened at being out of her room, which made Janice furious at the duke.

She resumed pushing the chair. "I promise it will be all right. Remember how anxious you were to get out? Well, now it's happening. You're going to enjoy yourself."

At the turn of the corridor, she suddenly remembered the two flights of stairs she'd have to go down and swallowed back her panic. No doubt she could manage. She was strong as an ox. She'd turn the chair backward and go first, holding the handle in an iron grip. And then she'd gently lower it from step to step. . . .

She hoped she wouldn't jar the duchess too much.

But what if Her Grace's bones were brittle and weak?

Janice paused and swallowed. What if she'd been a complete idiot to ignore the doctor's advice? And the duke's orders?

Breathe, she told herself.

But the panicked thoughts came at her, a relentless onslaught of doubt.

You've involved this poor old woman.

You're prideful.

Stupid.

Mama and Daddy would be furious!

"Lady Janice?" the dowager asked her hopefully. "May we turn around now?"

"There's no need, Your Grace." She did her best to sound merry. "You'll be fine. We'll get there soon enough." Should she simply leave her here, run out to the stables, and get Isobel or Mrs. Friday? Wouldn't that frighten the duchess, to be left all alone? And what if she *did* fall asleep again? "I-I only paused because I needed to adjust my shoe." She said a quick prayer and continued down the hall, the Bath chair rolling smoothly over the carpet.

She'd do it. On her own. But when they came to the stairs, she couldn't help it—her eyes welled up. This was going to be extremely difficult. But she couldn't disappoint the dowager now. Yes, the old lady acted as if she didn't want to go, but she needed to see that she could thrive outside of that bedchamber. She *must* see that. Otherwise, she'd continue begging Janice to help her escape.

Janice's hands trembled on the handles of the chair. What if she dropped her hostess?

She inhaled again, another long, slow breath, and decided that she simply wouldn't drop her. She'd keep Her Grace safe.

With a deliberate air, Janice turned the chair around, looked behind her, and lowered her own feet to the top stair.

That's it.

She lowered her right foot another step and gave a gentle pull on the chair. At the same time, she lifted with all her might so that the wheel wouldn't go *ker-plump.*

There. Her heart pounded furiously. But the duchess was safe on the first step.

Just, um, ten or fifteen more to go. And then another staircase . . .

Refusing to be cowed, Janice gripped the handles, prepared to go one step down again.

"Wait!"

She daren't move, but she glanced upward.

There stood Mrs. Poole at the top of the stairs.

Thank God.

"I'll take the bottom," the nurse said. "But come back up here. We're going to turn the chair sideways and walk down together. Going backward is too difficult."

Janice nodded, unable to speak, she was so grateful.

When all was said and done—and it was a rough few moments descending those stairs—the dowager was safe on the lower floor.

"Thank you," Janice told Mrs. Poole, and continued pushing the chair down the corridor.

"I might as well go with you." The nurse didn't smile.

But on those stairs, they'd formed a partnership.

Maybe not a friendship, but a partnership was nearly as good.

They passed two footmen separately, both of whom were goggle-eyed at the sight of the duchess.

Neither Janice nor Mrs. Poole said a word.

After the second footman passed, Janice murmured for the nurse's ears only, "Do you think they'll say anything to anyone?"

Mrs. Poole nodded. "They would have even if we'd threatened them not to," she whispered back.

"You're right, I'm sure." Janice peeked over the edge of the chair. "Are you all right in there, Your Grace?"

"Yes, my dear," the old woman said softly.

She wasn't saying much, but Janice refused to be worried. This was a very big outing. No doubt Her Grace was overwhelmed.

So it was a triumph—and a relief—when at last Janice and Mrs. Poole turned another corner and rolled the dowager's chair through a door and into the sitting room she so loved.

Who knew that her grandson apparently loved it, too?

Chapter Seventeen

The duke was standing at one of the windows himself, and when he turned around he wore his usual indifferent expression. But when he saw his grandmother in the Bath chair, all of him—from head to toe—became exactly like one of the icicles that hung from the eaves of the house, one of which, a particularly dangerous one, was visible through the pane of glass.

A similar state had overcome His Grace two nights ago at dinner when he'd told Janice not to go to the stables. But this was far worse. Her palms were slippery on the handles of the chair. Next to her Mrs. Poole's breathing became audible—and was clearly labored.

"It's all right, Mrs. Poole," Janice assured her in a calm voice while she kept her gaze on the duke. "I take full responsibility for bringing the dowager here. Go sit down, please."

Mrs. Poole did just that.

"Halsey?" The duchess's voice was weak but hopeful.

The duke smiled at her, but his eyes were still cold. "Hello, Granny." He strode over and stood before her, his hands behind his back. "You're up and about, I see."

"I don't want to be here," his grandmother said. "Take me back. I told her. . . ."

Through the handles of the chair, Janice felt rather

than saw the duchess crane herself forward, then fall back—almost an act of desperation.

"I want to go back to my bedchamber," said Her Grace. "Please."

Suddenly Janice felt as if she were the most horrible person on earth.

Halsey threw her an accusing glance. "You shouldn't have ignored my grandmother's wishes."

"But she's been telling me she wants out of that room," Janice said. "I was only trying to give her a little holiday. If she could see the view, I'm sure she'd change her mind." She paused a beat. "Now if you'll excuse me, please. I'm taking Her Grace to the window."

Janice locked gazes with him, and once more she remembered him greeting her when she'd arrived and she'd sensed he'd explored dark things. . . .

Several seconds went by. She didn't blink. But her heart—it was beating so fast, she almost felt dizzy. She inhaled a discreet breath and released it slowly. How long would they have this standoff?

"You'll take my grandmother back to her bedchamber, Mrs. Poole," the duke said in a casual tone. He kept his eyes on Janice. "And this time there won't be any repercussions. I understand that Lady Janice has her own ideas about what's good for the dowager duchess. But the doctor wouldn't approve."

Mrs. Poole stood. "Very well, Your Grace."

Slowly, she walked over to Janice and reached out a hand to take the chair.

"*No*," Janice told her, but she was looking at the duke. She moved as close as she could to the chair handles to block Mrs. Poole, who, to her credit, didn't try to wrestle the contraption from her.

"Pardon, my lady?" the duke said softly.

"You heard me, Your Grace." Janice couldn't back

down now. Not when they'd come this far. "I'm here as the dowager's guest. She shall see the view, and we'll stay here a good half hour or until she tires, whichever come first."

Halsey stood utterly still. "My uncle Everett drowned in the pond behind that copse of trees," he said quietly, and pointed to his left, to the farthest window.

Janice's heart almost juddered to a stop. "W-what?"

"He *drowned*, Lady Janice." His Grace spoke without any emotion, even as the duchess gave a little whimper. "Will you let Mrs. Poole take my grandmother now?"

Janice nodded her head shakily and stepped aside. "I'm sorry," she whispered to the dowager, who said nothing back. Her eyes were on her lap, her scalp showing through thinning silver hair.

Mrs. Poole came up slowly and quietly, fear emanating from her in waves.

"Take Her Grace to her old bedchamber down the corridor, the third door on the left, please," the duke ordered her. "She used it when she lived here years ago. But keep her away from the windows."

"*Yes-s-s-s, Your Grac-c-c-ce.*" Mrs. Poole's whistle was stronger than ever. "I'm *s-s-s-so s-s-s-sorry.*"

"I never saw any reason to tell you what I've just told Lady Janice about our family history," Halsey told her. "Dr. Nolan's orders—and mine—should have been sufficient for you to obey."

Mrs. Poole hung her head. "I apologize, Your Grace."

"You should be remorseful," he said, "but I'm also at fault. I see now that I should have been more forthcoming with what is a painful, private matter. You're an excellent nurse, otherwise. You'll keep your job."

"Thank you, Your Grace." Mrs. Poole's voice had a little hitch in it.

Janice's cheeks prickled with heat. She'd botched things terribly.

"Ring for tea," the duke said, "and you'll all recover yourselves before my grandmother is returned to her preferred bedchamber."

Mrs. Poole thanked him again and departed the room.

Janice felt no comfort being alone with him. Quite the opposite. She was desperate to get away.

The duke seemed to sense her wish. "No need to fear me, Lady Janice."

"I don't," she insisted. But she knew part of her did.

"Further explanation is in order, I believe."

"All right," she said, "but do you mind if I catch my breath a moment?"

His lips twisted in a cool smile. "I'm not asking *you* to explain. I want to shed more light on this situation for your benefit."

"Oh." She clutched her skirt.

"Granny might be addled," Halsey said, "but even she has her memories. She doesn't like to be here at Halsey House and has avoided coming here since before I was born. When I moved her over last year from the dower house, it was only because her wits were so far gone that I'd no other choice. She requested to stay in that room in the far wing herself. The doctor utterly supported her decision. As do I."

"I had no idea." Janice's throat burned with shame. She was a fool. She should have listened to the dowager.

"I forgive you," the duke said easily. "Your intentions, I know, were good. But now that you see the whole picture, you'll understand, I'm sure, why I was so adamant about Granny's not seeing the view. Or leaving her room."

"I do see," she murmured.

What he said made perfect sense. Surely they should respect the duchess's wishes. No doubt Dr. Nolan wouldn't want her plagued by bad memories, either.

But what about getting past grief? Should the duchess hide until she died? Shouldn't she have an opportunity to experience joy again?

"Your Grace?" Janice swallowed hard.

"Yes?" His voice had an edge of caution to it.

"What if the view from her old bedchamber, as it's on the other side of the house, doesn't conjure bad memories for your grandmother? The view will encompass only the drive, and in the distance, over the treetops, the spire of the village church."

The duke released a sigh. "You don't know when to quit, do you?"

Janice bit her lip. "I only want Her Grace to be happy. I promise, I won't allow her to endure something she can't bear. But . . . what if she can?"

For a moment, all was quiet. Janice waited and wondered if Mama and Daddy would be pleased by her obstinacy—or appalled.

"Very well," the duke said eventually. "You may put her before a window in her old bedchamber."

Janice smiled. "Thank you, Your Grace."

"The only reason I'm saying yes," he said, "is because you'd have tried it anyway, wouldn't you have, my lady?"

She must be truthful. "Yes," she whispered. "I would have."

He gave a short laugh. "You're an interesting sort of woman."

She said nothing, and he strode to the door and turned around. "I'll send two footmen to attend you. Neither you nor Mrs. Poole need lift the chair again."

"Please send *cheerful* footmen, Your Grace," Janice asked on a whim. "We could all use cheering up."

Vague amusement lit his gaze. "As you wish, my lady," he said.

And then he left.

In the bedchamber across the corridor, Janice exchanged a sober glance with Mrs. Poole. "I'm so sorry," she said, a catch in her voice.

"It's all right." Mrs. Poole heaved a sigh. "You meant well."

"Thank you, Mrs. Poole."

"It was frightening there for a moment."

"Yes, it was."

The tea came in right behind Janice, and for a good ten minutes they allowed the ritual of pouring, stirring, and sipping the hot brew to calm their nerves. The stress of their encounter with the duke—and near miss with upsetting the dowager—had rattled both Janice and the nurse. As for Her Grace, she was subdued—almost oblivious, it seemed, to their presence and small talk. But at least she had the appetite to finish two biscuits and a cup of tea.

Finally, Janice set aside her own cup and told Mrs. Poole what the duke had given her permission to do.

"Are you sure?" Mrs. Poole's eyes flooded with doubt. "We've already been through so much."

"I agree," said Janice. "But we can't let this opportunity go by. What if it makes her happy?"

"It might make her *sad*."

"I know." Janice cast a glance at the old woman. "But it's worth the risk. If it works, Her Grace may have a life again."

"Go ahead, then." Mrs. Poole's tone was skeptical.

Even so, Janice steered the dowager to the window, sure that she was doing the right thing. "Look, Your

Grace, beyond the trees . . . it's Bramblewood's church spire."

"*Oh-h!*" Her Grace breathed.

The fragile exclamation made Janice's eyes fill. "It's beautiful, isn't it?"

"Yes," said the dowager. "Oh, *yes.*"

Janice smiled over at Mrs. Poole, who sank into her chair, her eyes blinking. "You did it," she whispered, clearly as moved by the dowager's delight as Janice was.

"The duchess did it," Janice said back to the nurse.

The next half hour passed almost as if in a dream. Mrs. Friday came in to join them, having heard about Janice's bold move in the kitchens. She listened with great sympathy to Janice's story about running into the duke in the other room. And she was equally ecstatic about the dowager's presence in her very own bedchamber from long ago.

From her perch at the window, the dowager didn't sneeze once. And she even nibbled at another biscuit. Words for her were few, but anyone could see in her eyes how happy she was, how content.

Janice remembered that she'd like to ask her about Emily March, Mr. Callahan's mother, but she was afraid that would be too much, too soon.

"Her Grace needs to be moved from that awful, stifling bedchamber and put in here," she said out of the duchess's hearing. "And when the weather is fine, perhaps she could go outside on this side of the house. And who knows? Maybe someday she could bear to look out the windows in the sitting room or even enter the gardens."

"Yes," said Mrs. Friday. "I hope that day comes."

Janice turned to the nurse. "Do you agree, Mrs. Poole, that the duchess should be moved?"

The nurse halted her teacup before her lips. "What I say doesn't matter."

"Of course it does," said Janice. "You're a capable nurse. I'd like your opinion."

Mrs. Poole put her cup on its saucer. "I'm beginning to see your point, Lady Janice, about the dowager's bedchamber being very limiting. If Her Grace is moved to this wing . . . I'd be happy to come, too, if the duke permits it."

"Would you?" Janice asked softly.

The nurse nodded. Her eyes were still guarded, but there was something else there, too—

It looked very much like hope.

And not just for the dowager. It would be good for Mrs. Poole to be in this wing, as well.

"Very good." Janice passed round the plate of biscuits. Out of the debacle of the last hour, she'd reached a perfect moment. She'd *done* something.

She was living—out here in the country. She wasn't hiding at all, as she thought she would. As she'd *wanted* to.

And it was the most splendid feeling.

When the footmen came to assist them with the dowager's return to her bedchamber, Janice knew that she'd have another hurtle to face when she recommended to the duke that his grandmother should be moved permanently to the main wing. Janice wasn't mistress of Halsey House. She'd need the housekeeper's and the maids' cooperation in preparing the new bedchamber, and surely none of them would give it without their master's approval.

"Choose your battles," Daddy always said.

So she'd get His Grace used to his grandmother's visits to her old bedchamber at first. Janice intended them to be daily.

With the footmen in the room, it was as if they were a small traveling party preparing for a long journey—which it was, actually. The dowager seemed to enjoy the attention as one of the young men adjusted her lap quilt.

"You look lovely, Your Grace," he said.

Janice liked him. He had friendly eyes.

"Thank you, lad." The dowager beamed at him.

The other footman was cheeky, asking Her Grace which of them was the more handsome.

"You're *both* handsome," she replied softly.

Janice and Mrs. Friday exchanged pleased glances. The dowager was alert yet calm. And most definitely improved in spirits from when Janice had last seen her.

With the cheeky footman pushing the chair, they'd just begun to wend their way down the corridor when the duke appeared.

Janice's pulse picked up. She was nervous around him, she knew. But should she be anymore? The *no* she'd told him about the dowager had had nothing to do with trying to win him. That *no* was all about trying to do the right thing for Her Grace. Yes, she'd made a hash of things, to some extent. But look at the duchess now!

Janice couldn't regret her decision.

She held her head up high. And for the first time since she'd arrived, she felt as if she had something to offer, so much so that she began to believe her game of saying no—as much as she'd learned from it—was unworthy of her.

She'd say no if she really felt like it. And she'd say yes when she wanted to, as well.

She'd win the Duke of Halsey on her terms—or not at all.

Mr. Callahan's the one you want, her own thoughts betrayed her. But she knew full well she couldn't have him. He was a groom. She was a lady. Was she going to be an adult about it?

Or wallow?

She had no choice.

The knowledge pierced her heart.

But she couldn't wallow. Members of the House of Brady didn't.

"Hello, Your Grace," she said purposefully. "Will you be accompanying us upstairs?"

"No," he said. "In fact, I'd like a word with you, Lady Janice."

"Oh . . . I see." *What about?* He looked so serious. She had to swallow her panic again. There was nothing easy about the duke. She must always be ready for him.

But she *was* ready, that new inner voice reminded her. She'd already done wonders standing up to him. No one else had. That should say something, shouldn't it? It also said something about him that in the end he'd chosen to be reasonable about his grandmother's visit to the sitting room. Janice must give him credit for that.

"Mrs. Friday, of course, can join us." The duke looked at Mrs. Poole. "I trust you can see Her Grace safely back to her room with the footmen assisting you."

"Yes, Your Grace," Mrs. Poole said quietly.

Mrs. Friday exchanged a glance with Janice. The widow, too, appeared slightly concerned.

"Shall we return to the sitting room?" the duke asked Janice.

"Yes." She felt such relief at saying what she really wanted to say.

The duke didn't appear to notice the change—yet. He had a rather brooding expression on his face. When he opened the door and allowed the women to pass ahead of him, Janice got the feeling that he was feeling genuine stress. He was silent, his back straighter than ever. But in his eyes she glimpsed the slightest amount of indecision, which was unlike him.

She didn't know what to do, so she sat down on an inviting but overly firm gold silk sofa. Mrs. Friday sat next to her. The duke shut the door behind him and came and sat opposite, on a plush burgundy velvet chair. A low table strewn with books separated them.

"Well," he began briskly, "I simply want to let you know that I'm writing your parents, Lady Janice. As soon as the roads clear, I'll post the letter."

Janice felt her face blanch. Beside her, Mrs. Friday shifted her weight on the spartan cushion.

"But Your Grace." Janice curled her hands in her lap. "I don't want to leave. I know today was a bit of a shock. But it was such a success. The dowager is happy. Please don't send me away."

And she wasn't even asking to stay because she wanted to hide. The truth was, she wanted to be here. For the dowager. Because she enjoyed Mrs. Friday's friendship, the puppies, and Esmeralda. There was the beautiful winter landscape and of course—

Luke Callahan.

The man she must forget . . . but couldn't seem to manage to, however hard she tried not to wallow but to put on a brave face, to make her parents proud.

The duke rested his palms on his thighs and leaned forward. "I'm not trying to send you *away*."

"You're not?" Janice's throat felt tremendously dry.

"No." He leaned back into a plump pillow. "I want to marry you." His cool, ducal gaze never faltered.

Janice blinked several times. "Excuse me?"

"I've made my decision." He crossed one leg over the other. "You're to be my duchess."

Janice simply stared at him. She must be fatigued.

Or *something.* There was no way that the duke was proposing to her.

"My goodness," said Mrs. Friday softly, and put her arm around Janice's shoulders. "This is wonderful news."

"This isn't the official proposal, of course. I'll do that in private." Halsey glanced at Mrs. Friday.

"Of course." The chaperone smiled back at him.

"That audience won't occur until your parents arrive," he told Janice. "We'll plan our engagement ball while your mother's here."

"Ball?"

"Yes, a ball." His tone suggested that she should know such things happened when one got engaged.

And perhaps she should.

"Meanwhile," he said, "I'll select a ring from among my grandmother's."

"It all sounds quite splendid," Mrs. Friday assured him. "Congratulations, Your Grace."

Janice didn't know what to say. She was still in shock. And she was terribly glad that Mrs. Friday hadn't congratulated *her*—because she was far from being ready to be toasted, acknowledged, cheered, or feted in any way, shape, or form.

"Lady Janice?" the duke asked. "Are you all right?"

No, she wasn't all right. She wasn't nearly all right. And part of her not being all right was wondering why she wasn't: Should she be the happiest woman on earth at the moment?

She cleared her throat. "Forgive me, but I feel a bit . . . a bit overwhelmed."

It was a raging understatement.

Mrs. Friday squeezed Janice's shoulder, which did help her focus. At least a quarter of her brain did. But another quarter of her mind envisioned her running to the stable block right now, screaming, *Luke! Luke*

Callahan! Where are you? And yet another quarter was reading in her bedchamber on Grosvenor Square while Isobel prattled on unheeded about one thing or the other. And the last quarter was curled up in the straw with Esmeralda and her puppies—just being with them while they were cozy, happy, their tiny pink mouths and wriggling bodies the most adorable things Janice had ever seen.

But she forced herself to focus on that first quarter—the one still in the sitting room, planted on an unforgiving sofa and facing a duke.

"Your Grace," she asked, "might I ask what inspired you to offer for me so quickly?"

"There was nothing quick about this." He leaned back on the sofa and crossed one leg over the other.

"How can you say so?" Janice asked. "I only just arrived."

"I've waited years to make this decision," he said. "No woman, and I've met many, has ever inspired me to offer my hand in marriage—until I met you. You're the duchess I've been seeking, Lady Janice."

He stood in his impeccably tailored clothes and looked down at her, that one brown, wavy lock of hair nearly but not quite in his eye.

Janice stood as well and felt frumpy by comparison. She was sweaty from trying to carry that Bath chair. And wrinkled from pressing on the rungs on the ladder in the library while she opened any book that had no title on the binding as she searched for a journal that had belonged to Emily March.

"I'm gratified by the offer, Your Grace." She truly was. "But you speak as if it's assumed I'll say yes when you do propose. The truth is"—she clasped her hands in front of her bodice—"I need more time to think about this."

She could see in the flicker of his gaze that once more she'd surprised him.

"I see," he said. "Are you suggesting I delay writing your parents?"

The moment was so awkward that she knew when she got back to her room she'd need Isobel to brush her hair a long while.

"Yes, Your Grace." She'd need more tea, too. Several cups, with extra sugar. "I'd appreciate a few days to consider it."

She wondered what Mrs. Friday thought. Was the good lady shocked that Janice hadn't immediately said yes? She knew Ladies Opal and Rose—the women without options—would think her completely mad.

Even *she* was astonished that she wasn't agreeing right away to the duke's offer. It would solve all her woes to become the Duchess of Halsey—all but one.

She couldn't love him.

Because she was most definitely preoccupied with someone else, a man she couldn't have. No one ever said, *If you fall in love, it might as well be with a groom*, did they?

Which was why when His Grace lifted her hand and kissed it, she prayed that she *could* fall in love with a duke.

And soon.

Chapter Eighteen

Luke was in a very bad mood. He'd spent the last thirty-six hours in Bramblewood with a small rat by the name of Sir Milo, a man Luke wanted to pummel for spreading a vile rumor about Lady Janice that Luke knew wasn't true. As hot as Lady Janice's kisses had been, however sensual her nature, she was an innocent. He'd known from the very first kiss they'd shared. He'd needed no proof two nights ago when she'd joined him in the tack room. And he'd never received it, as he'd chosen to go lightly. It had obviously been her first time being pleasured so intimately by a man.

Even if the rumor *had* been true, his regard for her wouldn't have changed. He knew how skilled scoundrels were at seducing young women. There were many virgins in his past whom he could have taken advantage of himself but hadn't.

He was furious that he'd been forced to leave the estate without getting word to Lady Janice of Grayson's plan to seduce her. While Luke tended to Sir Milo's drunken self the previous afternoon, he'd made plans to escape the village and go back that night to the estate while Sir Milo slept—and return to Bramblewood in the morning. But instead, Luke had spent the night cleaning up the shambles Sir Milo had made of the tap-room owned by a good-hearted couple who knew Luke

well. He couldn't abandon them. And by morning Sir
Milo was up and about, his head aching, and he began
his drinking once more.

Finally, finally, the man had fallen into a drunken
slumber this evening, and Luke was able to make his
escape.

All the way back, he had to hope that Janice had re-
lied on his earlier warnings about Grayson, as well as
her own wits. The idea of that scum making eyes at
her—pulling out her chair, leaning close, compliment-
ing her hair—made Luke physically ill. At this point,
he didn't even care if she'd been able to find the journal.
It was more important that he knew she was safe.

And without a doubt, as soon as the roads cleared she
must depart Halsey House.

He hated to think of her leaving.

So he simply wouldn't.

It was slow going in the snow. But after forty-five
minutes Luke found himself on the drive to Halsey
House, the stable block off to the right. He looked at the
moon and guessed it was somewhere close to midnight.

Was Lady Janice awake? And if so, what was she
doing?

For that matter, what was Grayson doing?

Luke prayed that they were separated by many
rooms, floors, and doors—doors that could lock Grayson out and Lady Janice in.

In the stable block Luke said hello to the last man
awake and told him to go to bed. He'd close everything
down for the night. And then as swiftly as he could, he
lit the lantern and set it in the south window.

It had been a very long day.

But now . . . *now* he must speak to Lady Janice.

Be awake, he thought. *Look out your window.*

She came more swiftly than he thought possible. Was

she already dressed in her coat and boots and sitting at her bedchamber window waiting for his signal? She practically flew through the door, without a bonnet, too. Her hair swung in that braid, and her boots and the bottom half of her coat were splattered with snow and even a bit of mud. The path between the house and the stables had been well traveled, so it was wearing down to the icy earth.

"You were gone so long," she said, her face white and her cheeks pink.

"It did seem a stretch." He wouldn't let himself be pulled in by her obvious dismay at his absence.

He picked up the lantern, and they both immediately began to walk back toward Esmeralda and the puppies.

"How was everything here?" he asked.

Janice pushed her hair back. "Eventful. And you?"

"Endless." Because he couldn't see her, that was why.

They stopped outside the stall, and he hung up the lantern as he had before. The puppies were even more active, and Esmeralda, poor thing, was having a fine time of it trying to keep up with them.

Lady Janice leaned her arms on the gate and laughed. "Oh, it's so good to see them."

"Didn't you today?"

She shook her head. "No, actually. I spent some time looking for the journal. By the way"—she looked up at him—"I confided in my maid. She might appear eccentric, but she's quite trustworthy, and she may be able to look some places I can't. Plus, she can talk to the other servants."

"I sincerely hope she'll be more subtle with them than she appeared to be in your carriage."

"She will." The lady seemed quite sure on that point. "But back to my busy day—after I looked on every bookshelf in the duke's library, to no avail, I visited the dowager. She was channeling the Queen, and when she's like that she doesn't seem to know who anyone is. Later, she reverted to the dowager's friendly self, but I felt it was too soon to speak to her about your mother. I realize you're giving me only this week to find it. But I need to tread carefully."

Her nearness was making it very hard to focus again. "You seem more quiet than usual. That is, you're speaking as much as you ever do, which is quite a lot." She made a disparaging face at him. "But was there more to your eventful day than what you've revealed so far?"

She sighed. "Yes, actually."

She told him the story about taking Her Grace to the sitting room and the drama that ensued afterward—at least the part about how the duke had told Janice to turn around and take the dowager back to her bedchamber.

"You told him to get out of your way?" Luke couldn't believe it.

Or perhaps he could.

"Essentially," she said. "There was no way I'd let the duchess leave the room without her looking out those massive windows. But then . . ."

"Then what?" Luke asked.

Her lips thinned. "He told me his uncle Everett drowned in the pond behind the copse. It would've traumatized Her Grace to be reminded when she looked out the windows."

Luke's father.

It was like a punch to the stomach to hear how he'd died.

Janice's face flushed. "I felt so foolish then. Here I'd been trying to help."

"No," said Luke, trying to focus back on her. "You shouldn't feel that way. You were thinking about the dowager's comfort."

Luke had to admire Janice's courage. She was truly a woman of action. And principle. But he didn't have to tell her any such thing. "So you plan to inform Halsey that she needs to be moved to the newer wing?"

"Yes. But I need to work up to that."

Luke felt a twinge of regret that he pushed aside. She had no idea yet that she'd have no time. She'd want to pack her bags and leave when she learned what he had to tell her about the duke's perfidy. Luke was working up to that himself.

"Tell me about your day," she said. "And yesterday, for that matter."

Part of him was incredulous that anyone would care enough to ask how his day went. It had never happened in his life. The nuns had been generous in their love, but they'd been run off their feet. They hadn't had time to ask a boy about his day.

"Sir Milo," he said, "the duke's visitor who arrived yesterday morning and who demanded I go back with him to Bramblewood, has drunk himself into such a stupor that I left him without permission. I'm not going back, either. If he complains to the duke, I'll simply tell His Grace that Sir Milo sent me home. He won't recall either way."

Lady Janice clamped a hand over her mouth, but Luke could hear her giggle. When she subsided, she took her hand off her mouth. "Sorry." She grinned. "We've both had a difficult time of it."

"Yes, we have. It's been quite frustrating."

"You want to be here—so you can find out about your mother."

And kiss Janice. Didn't she know that reason compelled him more than anything to come back? "That's true," he said. "But it's more complicated than that."

"Is it?"

He shrugged. "There are people relying on me."

"Who?"

He shook his head. "It doesn't involve you."

"But I want to *know*." Her chin jutted out at a stubborn angle.

"Why?"

She stared at him a moment. "I don't know. I simply do."

There was a long silence. They watched Esmeralda cleaning her brood. Her tongue never quit going from one pup to the next.

Lady Janice chuckled. He said nothing.

"Who's going to take all these puppies?" Her chin was in her hand now.

It was his turn to say he didn't know.

"You'll have to help me find people to adopt them," she said.

"They have to stay with their mother about eight weeks." She'd be gone long before that, he was sorry to realize.

"Oh." Her brow furrowed. "At least I can extract promises from people."

She wouldn't be able to do that, either. It was a shame. But he couldn't dwell on that. He had a job to do.

Esmeralda settled in for the night with her pups a moment later, and Luke and Janice were back to a sort of diffused sadness that hung between them both.

"What about you?" he asked the braided temptress beside him. "Is there something beyond the dowager's suffering that has brought you low?"

She shrugged.

"Hey." He pulled lightly on her arm, forcing her to stand up straight and look at him.

And then he did what came naturally. He took her

around the waist—she in that blasted winter coat—
bent low, and kissed her.

The kiss didn't take away any of the strain. But like
a brilliant sunset at the end of a hard working day, it
made him suddenly glad, despite everything else that
was wrong.

And much was.

Sister Brigid was running out of time. Every week
someone stopped helping the orphanage—a vendor here,
a farmer there. The local priest made all sorts of excuses
to Luke about why the orphanage was constantly short
of food, supplies, and families looking to adopt a child.

Luke recognized fear when he saw it.

Soon no one would dare to help Sister Brigid. And
he knew it was all Grayson's doing.

Luke sensed Janice was as glad as he was, that she
needed this sensual respite. He cradled her head and
kissed her handily, the way a laborer or a soldier or a
boxer—he'd been all three—would kiss his woman.

She wasn't his and never could be. But for a few minutes, he could pretend that she was.

She moaned against his mouth, and he kissed her as
he undid the top of her coat. And then she pulled
away—a bit wildly—and unbuttoned the rest while she
watched him silently, her lips pressed in that serious
way he knew meant she was holding something back.

When she took his hand, he understood what she was
asking. He picked up the lantern and allowed her to
lead him this time to the tack room. There wasn't much
there but the bench. And the floor.

But it was warm, and both of them could shed their
coats, which they did.

He sat cross-legged on their coats and drew her down
on his lap. They kissed for a long, cozy minute, her
body curved into his, the weight of her hip and thigh a

heady pressure on his erection. Again she took the lead when she bracketed his face between her hands and kissed him deeply, then dropped one hand to stroke his hard length through his pants.

He pulled back. "You don't know what you're doing."

"Why do I need to? All I know is that I want to touch this. Badly."

"It's dangerous territory," he said, feeling more dangerous by the second.

"I'm aware of that. I want you to be dangerous with me, Mr. Callahan."

"Luke."

"Luke," she said softly. "Will you call me Janice?"

"No," he said. "You're 'my lady.' And that's that."

She chuckled. "Surely not when we're like this." She looked down at her night rail. And then she traced a finger down his throat to his open shirt.

"Always you shall be 'my lady.'" He spoke sternly.

But his body would have nothing to do with restraint. His body craved completion—total union with her. And no words, no thoughts, would stand in its way.

Before he knew it, she was beneath him, her arms spread out on either side of her head, his hands clenched around her fists. He was kissing her openmouthed, her legs were spread wide, and he pressed his pelvis into hers with all the abandon of a rutting buck. She wrapped her legs around his hips and clung to him, her breasts in her night rail pressed sweetly against his shirt.

It was too much.

Yet it wasn't enough.

He pulled back and looked down at her open mouth, prettily pink, like a rosebud. She was breathing hard— and he saw in her eyes that she felt the same way: frustrated.

Yet who could stop?

He kissed her again. She laid a hand on his crotch and probed the tautly stretched fabric. He rolled over and pulled her with him to lie side by side. They were desperate. Both of them.

"It's not enough," she whispered. Her eyes were huge, her pupils dilated.

He ran a hand over her forehead. "We can't do all a man and woman are meant to do together."

"I know that leads to children," she said. "But does it have to? I hear snippets from married women when they don't think I'm listening. And once—once I saw a picture. It was in a shop, in a book I suppose I wasn't meant to see."

"Hm-m-m."

"You're not very helpful."

"I'm trying my best not to be." He allowed himself a small grin.

"What I want to know is . . ."

"What?"

"What exactly are the ladies at Halsey House doing here? Please be honest with me. You spoke of strumpets when my carriage came up the drive. These houseguests clearly can't be that. But are they something else? Lady Rose mentioned going north to find other men. And Miss Branson—well, I don't know what she's doing here. She *paid* to come. Please be honest with me."

"Very well." He brushed her hair out of her eyes. "The two sisters are here in the hopes that they'll become someone's mistress. Perhaps Lord Yarrow or Lord Rowntree will take a fancy to one of them and set her up in her own house. I somehow doubt they believe they can capture the duke's interest."

"Oh, no," Janice murmured. "That makes me so sad."

Luke was silent a moment. "Women do what they

have to do. Perhaps Ladies Rose and Opal believe it's their only option."

"I know they do." Her eyes registered concern. "I heard them. They wanted to get married. . . ."

Luke shrugged. "Life doesn't always turn out the way we plan it to."

"What about Miss Branson then?"

"It could be that she's paying the men for their, um, services."

"No!"

"It's not unheard of. If a man has gambling debts and a rich heiress offers him a way out, who's he to say no?"

Janice gasped. "She said the duke had gambling debts."

"He's rich enough to pay them all off. He has multiple properties. But he's probably flattered. And she might be into some unusual practices that he rather enjoys, too."

Lady Janice's face fell. "I-I'm appalled thinking of the duke getting involved in that sort of thing."

"Most men aren't saints."

"But if he were married . . ."

"Even then, you must know that many gentlemen in your rarefied stratum of society think nothing of being unfaithful. Marriage among the members of the ton is much more a business contract than anything else."

"Not between *my* parents."

"Then I'd say they're the exception to the rule."

"I can't believe it of Marcia and Duncan, either. Or Gregory and Pippa."

"You're a good sister. And perhaps you're right."

"I know I am. They married for love."

Luke wouldn't disabuse her of that notion.

She put her palm on his face. "Show me something else that men and women do that won't lead to babies."

"I did show you. Don't you remember?"

Even in the low light, he could see her blush. "Of course. I can't forget."

"I can't, either."

They looked at each other a long moment. She reached over and kissed him softly. And then she moved her mouth beneath his chin and kissed him there at the soft junction between his jaw and his throat.

"You're not going to stop until you get your way, are you?"

She laughed. "No."

"Very well," he said. "Just know that what we do here is nothing more than a lesson in the sensual arts."

"It has to be that," she said. "You're a groom. And I'm a lady."

"Exactly."

When he lowered her night rail and saw her breasts in the lantern light, he had to suck in a breath. She was stunning—two globes of milky white skin topped with rosy nipples.

"Someone should paint you," he said.

She smiled and peeled off his shirt. "Ah," she whispered, and rubbed her breasts against his skin. "Mm-m-m," she said next, and reached for his breeches.

He helped her open them but let her slide them down his hips. She gave several tugs and made noises that somehow reminded him of the puppies—frustrated sounds that warmed him, made him grin.

"Oh," she said when he stood in his naked glory.

He said nothing, but he enjoyed her staring.

She looked up at him, her eyes wide. "I'm rather

scared now," she whispered. "Not to hurt your feelings, but"—she swallowed—"it's very imposing."

He chuckled. "There's nothing to fear. I promise you."

"Really?"

"Yes." He pulled her close against him and reveled in the silken feel of her. "You're safe with me. Tonight your lesson only goes so far as a look."

She snuggled closer.

"We're not done with you, though," he said.

"No." Her entire body was taut with anxiety.

He put his hands on her waist. "I promise," he said, "you're going to be beautiful naked. You already are."

She bit her lip. "I-I do like my body. That is, when I bathe, I think it's rather pretty when I hold up my leg and soap it. And I even like the curve of my breast."

"And your belly," he said, and ran his hand over it. "It's perfect. All of you is."

Her eyes grew luminous. "You think so?"

"I'm sure of it."

She took his hands at her waist and pushed them downward. He took over then, removing her drawers slowly, crouching down and kissing her, inch by inch of exposed flesh, as the delicate fabric came off.

When her drawers were at her feet, he got her to step out of them. But before he stood, he nuzzled her feminine curls, spread her legs, and kissed the sweet pearl of flesh between her thighs.

"Oh-h-h," she said, leaning on his shoulder. "That's exquisite." She moaned her pleasure as softly as she could. "Is this what they're doing at Halsey House?"

He thrust his tongue inside her once, for good measure, then pulled back to look up at her.

The shock on her face made him laugh out loud. "It could be."

"If—if they are, I don't know why they'd ever leave their bedchambers."

He wrapped one of her legs around his shoulder and held on to her derriere, and he licked and stroked and thrust his tongue in her most intimate place until she writhed against him and cried out, over and over, softly.

She collapsed onto the coats, and he held her there, shocked that he never wanted to let her go.

Chapter Nineteen

Lady Janice's face was flush with pleasure. "I understand now why Miss Branson would pay for that. Although . . . it can't be good with anyone else but you, Luke. I can't think of a single other man with whom I'd want to be this private."

She was such an innocent.

"Thank you for the compliment." He kissed the back of her hand. "There's something I have to tell you."

She became very quiet and still. "What is it? There's something I have to tell you, too."

"I thought so," he said. "You go first."

"Very well. She looked suddenly shy. "The duke asked me to marry him."

Luke's entire body tensed. "You're jesting."

She shook her head.

"Not that you're not worthy of him." Luke raked a hand through his hair. "You're much too good for him, actually."

She sighed. "I admit that when he's acting the duke he can be quite intimidating. I get this fleeting feeling that something is terribly wrong. But I think I'm imagining that. The truth is, he's been very courteous. And I have to say, even when I challenged him about his grandmother, he came round."

"So do you want to marry him?" Luke had to know.

She bit her lip. "A lingering part of me does. Long ago, I was sure that dukes and duchesses don't have any worries. But that's foolish, of course. Here my father's a marquess and my mother a marchioness—and they certainly have their share of problems. Becoming Duchess of Halsey would mean that—well, only a day ago I thought it would mean that I'd be happy." She sighed. "But I don't think so anymore."

"So did you say yes?"

"Not yet."

"Has he kissed you?"

"No."

"Do you want him to?"

"No."

Something primitive inside Luke was very satisfied with that answer.

She brushed her hand over his hair. "Every time I think of marrying him, your face comes to my mind. It's an awful feeling. How—how would you feel if I married him?"

As if my world would fall apart.

"You can't worry about me." He held her hand.

"I want to know." She squeezed his hand back.

He looked away. "I told you, and you've told me. I'm fit only to lift you into the saddle and put up your horse after a ride."

He looked back at her and saw how stricken her gaze was. But he'd had to say it. To remind her. And although he was at fault for walking willingly with her into intimacy, there was a line to draw, reality to face: whether he was a groom or heir to a dukedom, he'd never be worthy of her.

And while they were speaking harsh truths, it was time to say what he must about Halsey. "I don't want to delve into details." Their hands were still joined. "But I

have some bad news about the duke that will be difficult to hear."

"Tell me." Her palm was smooth and cold, but he
could feel a tinge of sweat slicking its surface.

"I heard him make a hundred-pound wager with the
other men—Sir Milo included—that he'd be able to
bed you outside the confines of marriage."

She blinked. "They *bet* on me? That he'd be able
to . . . to seduce me?"

Luke hated seeing her eyes so anguished. He lifted
her onto his lap again, her back to him, making it easy
for him to wrap his hands around her waist and rest his
chin on her shoulder. Her cheek was soft as down against
his. "I wanted to tell you before I left with Sir Milo. But
I couldn't get a message to you. I had to hope that you'd
keep your wits about you."

She grabbed his hands and held them tight. "If he
thinks I'm of so little worth that he'd wager on me with
his equally despicable friends, he can't possibly mean
to marry me."

"I think you're wrong there." Luke gave her belly a
little squeeze. "Halsey believes he's invincible. He's a
duke, after all. He could make a tavern wench his duchess, and no one would say a word."

Luke couldn't tell Janice this, but he saw exactly
why Grayson would want to marry her. She reminded a
man that amid the rubbish of life there were puppies.

And sweet kisses.

Acceptance and laughter.

It was as simple as that.

She sighed. "Are we done yet with the revelations?"

"I've nothing left to say." Except that he wanted her
and the fact that he couldn't have her hurt more than
anything else ever had.

She wriggled in his lap. "I've one thing left."

"And it is?"

She looked at him over her shoulder at the same time that she snaked her hand between his legs and cupped his privates. "I want to make you as happy as you've made me."

He wished he could tell her the truth—that she already had.

Janice was amazed at how quickly Luke's erection sprang to life beneath her fingers. She turned completely around to straddle him and stroked the hot, hard length of him while he held on to her back.

"Steel sheathed in satin," she whispered. "Am I pleasing you?"

"Yes." He reached up a hand to cup her head and drew her close for a deep kiss that filled her with a sense of utter rightness.

She belonged here, with him.

Groom or no, he was her man like no other.

Now she understood what Mama and Marcia were talking about. The knowing was a mystery. What was between her and Luke was whole and perfect, as if it had been there all along and always would be. It had only taken special eyes to see.

This was what love was.

And she didn't know how she would ever leave him.

When he found his release, his seed spilled over her hands and onto her lower belly and she marveled at the strength of him even at his most vulnerable. As his pleasure receded, his head lolled to the left and he opened one eye to peek at her.

She laughed. "Satisfied?"

He grabbed her close. "Never completely. As long as you're around, I want more. But yes, for a moment there, it was sheer heaven."

They kissed, but it was more a conversation without words. There were pauses, questions, affirmations, denials. Afterward he wiped evidence of their intimacy off of her belly and hands with a piece of clean flannel from the stack on the table.

"You should go," he said.

Was that regret she heard in his voice?

Of course it was. She was beyond wondering. He cared for her. That much was clear. But what did it matter?

Whatever happens, it does, she thought.

She did have to go, so she picked up her night rail and he helped her don the yards of soft muslin and lace.

"I have much to accomplish tomorrow," she said, adjusting her sleeves.

He pulled her braid out of the back. "What will you tell the duke?"

"That I can't marry him." Never in a million years would she consider it. And not simply because of his vile wager. She wanted to tell Luke that even had the duke been a good man, her heart belonged to another.

To him.

For a moment, they did nothing but look into each other's eyes.

"That's the right decision," he eventually said, fingering the tendrils of hair at her temple.

She wished he would tell her that his heart would break the day she married another man—any man.

But he didn't.

And she shouldn't expect it.

Just as he should expect nothing from her.

Her eyes stung as he buttoned her into her coat, but by the time he was finished she had herself under control. They spent a few more seconds together at Esmeralda's stall.

"I'll be in the duke's bad books as of tomorrow," Janice said, "so I don't know how much time I'll have left here. I assume he'll want to send me packing as soon as the snow melts."

"I think so," Luke said softly.

"I don't want to go," she whispered. "I should, of course. After hearing about this bet, I should pack my bags and leave as fast as I can. But there are the puppies. The dowager. And *you*."

Luke put a hand on her shoulder and squeezed. "I don't like to see you go, either."

It was the most he'd ever said to her about his feelings. But she hoped he meant it. Oh, how she hoped! Even if it was futile.

She buried her face in his coat. "I can't marry him. I never thought I'd be horrified at the idea of marrying a duke." Her voice was a little muffled, but she didn't care. She wished she could scream into Luke's coat—scream at the world, which was so unfair.

"You *are* unusual," he said with a tinge of amusement. "But no one who knows the truth could blame you for turning him down."

She gave a little chuckle. "Life is strange sometimes."

"Very surprising." Luke smoothed her hair again, and she preened like a cat. "Did you ever think as you were traveling here that you'd spend more time in the tack room than the drawing room, for instance?"

She looked up, smiling. "I can never tell anyone. And I wouldn't want to. That's between us." Their own special memory. One that she'd carry with her all her life.

"Now that it's apparent you won't be staying," he said, "I can't force you anymore to look for my mother's journal. So consider yourself free of that obligation, at least."

"You're not getting rid of me so easily," she said. "I plan to continue looking for it anyway—at least until the duke forces me out of here. Until that time, expect to see me every night with a full report of the day's search. On one condition."

"And that is?"

"You said you had other people relying on you. I want to know more. What do you know of your mother?"

"She lived at the orphanage with me, until I was almost four. I thought she was a nun. She took care of me, sang me to sleep, held my hand. But she was dressed in a habit. I didn't know, but she was hiding."

"Why?"

"The nuns don't probe. They simply accept. And they accepted that my mother was afraid, and that she needed a place of refuge. It wasn't until right before her death that she told Sister Brigid about the journal."

"Sister Brigid?"

"She runs the orphanage."

"I'm glad you told me," Janice said, "This makes my search even more imperative. It seems as if this mistreatment must have been severe. Emily was afraid. But of whom? And why? I wish you'd told me earlier. Is there anything else?"

"No." He was too detached when he said it—his *old* self.

She saw it in his eyes, the shutter that came down when he didn't want to connect. "There *is* something," she said. "I'm sure of it."

"There isn't."

"You're lying." She laid a hand on his forearm.

"And you're much too nosy." He pulled away.

"Fine. Don't tell me anything, Mr. Callahan. But know this"—she spoke an inch from his face, up on her toes—"the truth always comes out." She thought about how it had in her own family: for Marcia and, most recently, for Gregory. "And I, for one, believe that standing in that truth is better than running away from it. Nothing good can come of running. Ever."

She left the stable door wide open. Luke stood in its frame and watched her stride back to the darkened house, her arms swinging, her braid swaying on her back. She slipped once on the icy path but regained her footing and kept going, not missing a beat.

Overhead, the moon was like a silver platter laid on an ink black tablecloth. *Remember this,* he thought, and basked in the sight of her. *Janice.* He allowed himself to call her that.

Come morning, he'd be one day closer to never seeing her again.

Chapter Twenty

Janice began to walk as quietly as possible up the main staircase at Halsey House, her stomach roiling at the memory of how kind the duke had been just the evening before on the same set of stairs. He'd told her she had a glow about her.

How despicable of him to flatter her to her face and work against her behind her back.

The only light tonight came from the glare of the moon through the transom above the front door, but it was brilliant enough that she saw from the case clock below that it was half past two. All was still. Her stomach was tied in knots, and she wondered if she'd ever get sleep. She needed to. Tomorrow was going to be a momentous day—in an uncomfortable way   what with her turning down Halsey's offer.

She'd been so excited, thinking that perhaps she could fall in love with him. He'd been attentive on their tour of the conservatory and portrait gallery. He'd been kind to his grandmother. He'd had the intellectual curiosity Janice desired in a mate, along with good looks. She could even be enchanted by the fact that he had a premium title and gobs of wealth—enough to rescue her from her precarious social position and make her parents proud of her.

Everything was in place, or so she'd thought.

Except for the fact that she preferred a groom to him—and, unbeknownst to her, the duke had made a lecherous bet about her.

She paused halfway up the stairs, the base of her spine tingling from a sense that someone was watching her.

She prayed that if it had to be anyone it would be one of the women. Janice understood them better now and would plead with them to keep her nighttime wanderings secret.

But her stomach clenched when she looked over her shoulder and saw a man's form at the base of the staircase. The moon made it very clear that it was the Duke of Halsey himself.

"Don't bother wishing you hadn't turned to see me," he said quietly. "I would have recognized you by that braid alone. No other woman here has hair that reflects the moon so well."

Her heart was out of control, but she gripped the railing hard in an effort to master her panic. "Good evening, Your Grace."

He gave a low laugh. "Come down, Lady Janice. We'll talk about where you've been. Although I already know." He bent down and picked up a piece of straw from the tile floor. "The stables. Yet again."

She took a few steps down. "I have been there. But I was with—"

"The dog and her puppies?"

"You know about those?"

He crossed his arms over his chest. "Of course. I'm master here, my lady. I know everything that goes on. As I told you when you arrived."

"But you didn't, Your Grace. You didn't know that I was coming here at all."

"Why are you being so obstreperous, my dear?" He

gave a short laugh. "You know I find it mesmerizing—is that it? You say no to me, but you say yes to everyone else. To Mrs. Friday, my grandmother, to my other guests. And don't think I don't know about that groom. Have you said yes to him, Lady Janice?"

His tone was silky, almost as if he'd like it were she to admit that she'd done scandalous things with another man.

Her legs began to shake so hard, she sank down to the steps. "What do you want from me, Your Grace?" She placed her palm on her coat, above her heart, and had a sudden flash of longing for Luke.

"I want you to come down here. *Now*. We're going to finish this conversation in the library."

"There's nothing to speak about," she said. "You may rescind your offer. I won't marry you. I know about your wager."

There was the slightest pause.

He put the edge of a boot on the stairs and his hand around the finial at the bottom of the banister. "So the groom told you?"

"I don't know what groom you're referring to. My own driver told me." She could use Oscar's name. His job wouldn't be in jeopardy. "And it was despicable of you."

He didn't deserve being called Your Grace, and she wouldn't do it anymore. Her nerves were shot, and she felt tears building behind her eyes.

"I'm sure it was very upsetting to hear," he said softly.

His tone set her even more off balance.

He pushed off the step. "Come with me to the library. I'm going to pour you a brandy. You could use one. So could I."

For the first time, she considered going. She did need

something. She'd been here only a few days, and nothing had been simple. Nothing.

She stood and walked down the stairs, wondering if she was making a huge mistake. But if she went to bed now, she'd never sleep. She might as well finish the conversation.

He waited for her, but he didn't offer his arm. *Thank goodness.* Because she wouldn't have taken it. They walked side by side down the main corridor, and as they went it grew darker as they left the bright moonlight behind.

Once inside the elegant room, a tribute to leading a civilized life, she stood quietly while he lit a lamp and poured two brandies. When he handed her one, their fingers touched and she felt instantly repelled, although she did her best not to show it. It would bring her as low as he was.

"So you dislike me more than ever, I see." He indicated a chair for her to sit on.

Oh, well. So much for disguising her feelings.

She lowered herself onto an Egyptian-style chair and took a large sip from her glass. *Ugh.* It burned. But it was also what she needed. "You can't expect me to have any sort of respect or affection for you after finding out what you've done."

He leaned on the edge of his desk. "Am I supposed to have any of the same for you? The woman who claimed she'd consider my proposal—while staying out until the middle of the night in my stables?"

He had her there.

She swallowed more of the brandy, and this time she began to appreciate the flavor as well as the fiery sensation it produced. "I was going to tell you in the morning that I couldn't accept your proposal."

"Have you considered that it was extraordinary that I offered in the first place?"

"Oh, I know it was." She nodded. The brandy was beginning to relax her. "I never expected you, a duke, to offer for me."

"Yet you're saying no."

"Correct."

He stood and paced before the fire. "This is how I see it, my lady. You've not had a very successful run in London. Your older sister's reputation seems to overshadow you. You've now been found by me—a peer of the realm with great influence and a sterling reputation—wandering about after midnight, unchaperoned, up to who-knows-what." He stopped and stared at her, and she couldn't help blushing. "And you also have a terrible scandal following at your heels, waiting to trip you up."

"What scandal?" she whispered.

"Must I repeat it?"

"Yes. Let me hear from your lips what it's about." She hoped he felt vile and guilty and slimy as he recounted it.

"It seems that a young man named Finnian Lattimore might have ruined you." He eyed her speculatively. "Or he might not have. But there's been talk."

She sighed. "It's a lie."

He stopped pacing. "The wager I embarked upon was to determine if the rumor was true."

"How loathsome of you to take ridiculous gossip and use it as fodder for your own entertainment!" She stood, her breath coming in shallow bursts.

"True or not, the rumor is there. And I admit that you're right. My participating in such a bet was a heinous act of cruelty. Shallow. Disgusting."

"Yes, and if anyone in London knew—"

"But they won't. Because then you'd have to reveal the rumor, which not everyone has heard, have they? Probably including your own parents."

"No." She gripped her glass hard. "They can't have. At least, I pray they haven't." She watched him pour himself another brandy. "So why am I here? I won't apologize for turning down your offer. And I rescind being grateful for it. That's all I can do at this point, because you're right. I can't bring down the Duke of Halsey, and I'm not interested even if I could. I simply want to be left alone. But what will *you* do?"

He came close to her and took the fingertips of her free hand. She wouldn't let him see her flinch, but she wanted to pull away.

Desperately.

His knowing brown eyes looked into hers. "Even now you captivate me, Lady Janice. You act as if this rumor can't be true, yet you're spending time in the hay in my stables. You turn down my proposal of marriage, yet your good reputation is seriously in danger of being lost forever."

"And you acted as if you had genuine respect for me," she retorted, "yet you were a snake in the grass waiting to strike. Is that why you suggested that near proposal? So you could talk me into your bed this week—only to rescind the offer when the snow melts and you can be rid of me?"

She did pull away from him. She walked to the other end of the room to get as far away from him as she could.

He followed her and sprawled in a chair a few feet away. "My offer was sincere. And still stands. I told you in my grandmother's sitting room that every day I've had opportunities to marry and not one woman has stirred me to even consider it until you arrived. I'll admit that I was thrown off by your blunt rebuttals of nearly everything I said. No woman has ever spoken to me quite that way. Nor any man. But the truth is, Lady Janice, your opposition is the very reason I must have you as my duchess."

Her opposition . . .

Good Lord, the dowager's advice had been right on target! And now Janice wished with all her heart she'd never followed it. She'd done so out of fear. She hadn't believed in herself. She'd needed something outside to prop her up—

But it was wrong.

Wrong.

She had plenty to offer the world.

"I want you because you don't want me." He took a sip of brandy and shrugged.

"But I was playing a game," she said. "A stupid game. I told you no simply to get your attention, and now I rue that I ever did."

He gave a short laugh. "I knew you loved Paris. And I could tell you adored Shakespeare. I also knew that you wished to look at the stars through my telescope. And I happen to believe you like strawberries and sparkling wine."

She sighed. "I do. Very much. I was being foolish. And false. I was desperate for approval, and I believed that by standing out from the others, I might get it."

She remembered the dowager as the Queen—how driven she'd seemed. Yet desperate, too. She'd struck a chord with Janice, who'd been just as insecure. Nothing mattered to her more than being that successful woman everyone expected her to be. But she became the wrong kind of ambitious as a result.

"You think I've never had experience with that sort of thing?" The duke gave a light laugh. "Clever women know men love a good hunt. You're not the first female who's acted standoffish to capture my attention. But as I watched you fumble your way through it—and you improved as you went along, I might add—I saw something you didn't even see yourself. You truly had no interest in me whatsoever. You never have. From the moment I met you outside the house. And even when I tried to woo you with a sleigh ride, interesting conversation in the conservatory, and a declaration of admiration on the stairs, your attention wasn't really on me. That glow . . . it came from another source."

She knew very well it came from being with Luke.

"And damned if it didn't frustrate me," Grayson said. "But your game ended when you brought Granny to the sitting room. You'd have fought me tooth and nail to keep her there. Isn't that true?"

"Yes. In fact, your grandmother needs to be moved to that wing. The sooner the better."

"Which is why I still want you as my duchess. You do oppose me, at a much deeper level than your silly games implied, and I find that . . . excruciatingly interesting—to the point that I must have you."

"There's something terribly wrong with your reasoning. Don't you see?"

He shrugged. "I am who I am. And quite frankly, you are who you are—virgin or no. Yet I'm still willing to take you as my wife. Consider that, my lady. Consider that very carefully."

"I don't need to. I'm not interested in being your trophy. You don't love me. You don't even like me. I'm not sure you like anyone."

He didn't deny it.

"Do with my reputation what you will," she said quietly, "but my answer is still no."

His eyes flared with heat.

She couldn't win, could she?

"As soon as the roads clear," she said "I'm leaving, whether my carriage wheel is fixed or not. I anticipate that my departure won't be for several days, so until then, please stay out of my way, as I will stay out of yours. I'll take meals in my bedchamber."

She tried to stride past him, but he reached out and grabbed her arm.

"Oh, Lady Janice."

She swallowed hard. His voice was smooth but vastly unsettling. When she looked down at him, his face wore that same icy expression she'd caught a fleeting glimpse of twice before.

"What is it?" She dearly wished for her bed. And Luke. Being here with the duke was becoming an absolute nightmare. Hadn't Luke warned her when she'd first arrived?

"I appreciate your saying no so vehemently," Halsey said. "But now, I'm afraid, you must accept my proposal."

"I told you," she said evenly, "I won't. And if you don't like it, that's unfortunate. I don't care what you say about me or to whom. Just *leave me alone*."

He released her arm and stood. He wasn't as tall as Luke, but he was strong. And athletic. Luke's warnings came back to her. His very strongly worded warnings . . .

The ones she'd ignored.

She had the sudden thought that if she ran, Halsey could chase her down easily and physically force her to his will. Not that he'd ever do such a thing. He was a prideful man, yes.

But not a dangerous one.

Surely.

"You *will* accept my proposal," he said in that soft,

understanding voice that made her ill. "You're a very caring young lady. So caring that you're willing to wear hay in your hair and risk your reputation if it means you can be with the lowlife friend you've made in the stables. Wouldn't it be a shame if he got into trouble? It's very easy to make mistakes as a groom. Tack goes missing; horses are stolen. Not to mention that puppies can disappear. Quite easily." He shrugged. "Why, even young widows can succumb to masterful seduction."

Their gazes locked.

"You can't mean—" Janice's heart beat wildly.

"I know about your little canine family. And Mrs. Friday *is* a luscious morsel. But I'm happy to leave them alone if you cooperate."

"I knew you had an excess of pride," Janice said, "but I didn't know you were capable of . . . of *this*."

"I don't know what you mean." The duke brushed a tendril of hair off her cheek. "Everyone loves me, Lady Janice. They respect me, too. As will you. It would behoove you, my dear, to stay away from your handsome groom from this moment on. And if you attempt to pass messages to him through any of your friends, they'll have to answer to me when I find out—and I will. Your father would appreciate my concern, I'm sure, even if you don't."

He smiled at her, and bile rose in her throat.

"So," he said. "Will you marry me?"

She said nothing. How could she get out of this? *How?*

"Lady Janice," he said, "I'll ask again: will you marry me?"

"What do you think, *Your Grace*?" She stared at him for a pointed moment, and in his eyes she saw no warmth, no generosity. No genuine interest in the world. His focus was inward. And small. Very *small*.

She walked around him, giving herself a good few

feet of space, and as she exited the library she thought what a difference a day made. She'd no idea when she was searching for that journal in this very room that she and Emily March would ever have anything in common.

But they did. In more ways than one.

"I'll get a special license!" he called after her.

She didn't answer.

Chapter Twenty-one

Oh, the irony. Grayson chuckled early the next morning, knowing full well that the groom his informants in the stables had reported on was the same one who'd promised to protect the estate. He'd guessed, even before the snitch—one of the older stable hands, a lazy one—described the man as having waited for Lady Janice the evening previous with a glowing lantern in the window.

They'd had a secret assignation.

Grayson knew it had to have been the quietly defiant groom. That man would turn any woman's head.

He'd certainly turned Lady Janice's.

At the request of Grayson's secretary, the man appeared at the library door while Grayson was reading the week-old London newspaper. Rowntree sat in a chair by the fire, looking into it drearily. He'd drunk too much the night before, as usual, and was bored and ready for a nap already, like the hounds who lay sprawled on the floor beside him. Yarrow, the idiot, was absent, probably still asleep himself.

"Good morning, Your Grace," said the groom.

His name was Luke Callahan, according to the tattling stable hand.

Grayson raked him with an indifferent glance, but inside he felt far from indifferent. He was supremely jealous of him. "Why did you leave Sir Milo in Bramblewood? Weren't you supposed to stay with him?"

"He told me to come back," the servant said. "So I obeyed."

"Really?" Grayson rested his jaw on his hand and observed the Callahan fellow speculatively. "Why would he do that?"

"I've no idea." The groom shrugged, his shoulders so broad, he looked like Atlas.

He was a cool one.

"I don't suppose you came back because you missed the horses and the other groomsmen so much that you disobeyed orders. Perhaps you were in the midst of an enthralling card game." Grayson chuckled.

"Of course not, Your Grace."

Grayson arched one eyebrow. "I wonder who else you might have missed here?"

The man looked at him without blinking.

"No answer?"

"None," Luke Callahan said. "As I said earlier, I came back because Sir Milo told me to."

Grayson yawned. "How long have you been working here, groom?"

"About six weeks, Your Grace."

"Not very long." Grayson shook his head. "Not long at all."

"No, Your Grace."

Grayson stood. "Yet you believe you can protect the estate."

"I know I can, Your Grace." Luke Callahan spread his legs a little wide, like a soldier.

"Interesting," Grayson said. It took everything in him not to say that he knew the groom had lain in the hay with a young lady in his charge. "This afternoon I'll be taking my future wife and the rest of my guests to see the orchids at the dower house. Prepare two sleighs. There will be eight of us in all. We'll leave at half past two."

"Yes, Your Grace."

Grayson watched him closely but saw no change in his expression. "You'll drive my sleigh. I take it you do well with the reins?"

"Yes, Your Grace."

Was that a clenching of the man's jaw he saw? Grayson had a wild hope that it was. "Off with you." He waved him out.

But he wasn't done with him. Not by far.

Back at the stables Luke and Aaron were busy cleaning out two adjacent stalls. Luke had never worked so hard in his life. It couldn't be true. Not possibly. Janice had told him herself she'd never marry Grayson. Ever.

"Did you hear?" Aaron called over to him.

"No," said Luke. "What?

"Lady Janice is going to marry the duke."

It smarted to hear it confirmed, like a cut exposed to salt. Luke leaned on the handle of his pitchfork. "Where did you hear that?"

"From Mr. Camp," Aaron said. "He likes to visit the maids in the main kitchen. He heard it from one of them. The duke already told the butler and the housekeeper that there's to be an engagement ball in London at his town house."

"Any idea when?" Luke asked carelessly.

"Soon, Mr. Camp says. The duke wants to get a special license and marry her at St. Paul's."

"So he's impatient." Luke went back to pitching hay. "I suppose he must be."

It made no sense. Lady Janice did *not* want to marry Grayson. Luke wouldn't believe that she'd lied to him.

Nor would he believe that the agitation she'd felt when she'd left him in the stables had anything to do with it. She'd been frustrated with him, yes, because he wasn't very open about talking about his past. But that wouldn't drive her into his cousin's arms.

There had to be a reason, and all Luke could think was that Grayson had given her no choice.

He had to see her. Speak to her. He had to know what had occurred.

"I don't know how it happened so fast," Oscar told him near the coal stove, where he sat polishing his gold coat buttons with the House of Brady seal, "unless the marquess had an arrangement with the duke that none of us knew about."

"How do you feel about it?" Luke was curious to know.

Oscar raised one eyebrow. "A few days ago, I would have thought it was a fine thing. But now that I've been here and I see how this place is run, I'm not so sure."

"What do you mean?"

"No servant appears very happy. And that tells me a great deal about the master." He sighed. "I've heard no bad tales against him, but I wish I had the marquess's ear. As soon as the roads clear, I'll get a letter out."

"What will you tell him?"

Oscar's brow furrowed. "That he should withhold permission until he stays at this place."

"Do you have that much sway in your household?" Luke asked him.

"My opinion, kind sir, holds a great deal of sway. I've been with Lord Brady's family since he was ten years old." Oscar eyed Luke with wry amusement—as if he couldn't believe he didn't know—then went back to his coat buttons.

Luke would love to have told Janice's driver the whole

truth—he was sure the man was trustworthy, and there might come a time when he needed to confide in him. But if Luke said anything now, Oscar could do nothing to help. In a few days, the roads would be open for travel. Things would be different then. Letters could go out, for one. Beleaguered women could be whisked away from rotten cousins. . . .

Not that Luke would consider such an extreme possibility yet. He needed to know more.

At the appointed time, Grayson and Janice came out together leading the party. Luke felt burning fury upon seeing Grayson possessively holding Janice's arm. *Steady,* he told himself. *Stay the course.*

Luke caught her eye, but she looked away immediately. Clearly, she was unhappy. There was a pall to her skin. And she looked as if she'd gotten very little sleep.

Everything in him cried to save her. To punch Grayson to the ground. To scatter his questionable houseguests—leaving Mrs. Friday alone, of course—and go roaring into Halsey House in search of his mother's diary.

Instead, he held out his hand. "May I help you, my lady?" he asked Janice.

She said nothing—and still wouldn't look at him—but when their hands clasped, even through her glove he thought he felt it: Her fear. Her need of him. Her determination to be brave.

He couldn't be sure. How could he be sure of anything with her, especially now? Even so, he had difficulty letting go of her fine fingers. Only last evening, they'd clasped his neck, caressed him, and brought him to a state of utter bliss.

The duke got in on the other side and sat next to Janice, facing the front. Opposite them were Lord Rowntree and Miss Branson. Lord Yarrow rode in the other sleigh with Mrs. Friday, Lady Opal, and Lady Rose.

"All ready, then?" Luke called to the other driver, who nodded.

The sleigh bells jingled. It was too early to think about Christmas, but to Luke's ear the merry sound was usually welcome, especially when winter was unrelenting, as it had been this year. Today, however, the ringing sounded false. Jarring. His back was to Janice, but he could sense her there next to Grayson. And it killed him a moment later to listen to them speak to each other as if the world hadn't just turned upside down, which for Luke it had.

The sleigh was a beauty and the ride smooth. The two horses pranced, their ears twitching in enjoyment, as they pulled their load to the dower house. The air was cold and dry, relentless, like the conversation behind him, which exposed more of Luke's misery with every passing second.

"We'll go to Paris on our honeymoon," Grayson was saying. "And then Rome. Which is your favorite, my dear?"

Luke's hands tightened on the reins. *My dear.* Hah!

But before Janice could answer, Miss Branson spoke up. "What about Boston? I can set you up in a cozy thirty-room cottage facing Boston Harbor."

"Next year," Grayson said. "I plan on taking my bride all over the world and lavishing her with anything she wants. America is on the list of destinations."

"You're a fortunate lady," Lord Rowntree said. "To be a duchess and so adored. How many women in London would like to take your place?"

There was silence. A long silence that made Grayson's heart soar. Good for Janice for ignoring the blathering of Grayson and his friends!

"My lady?" Grayson's phony cultured voice was more annoying than ever. "Lord Rowntree asked you a question."

Luke detected some pique there—and loved it.

"Did he?" Janice sounded surprised. "I was admiring the view. I didn't hear. What was that, Lord Rowntree?"

Luke's spirits plummeted. Deuce take it, maybe she really *hadn't* heard the question! The sleigh bells were jangling so loud, they were giving him a headache.

"He wants to know how many women in London would like to be the next Duchess of Halsey," Grayson said.

Smug bastard. Luke urged the horses to go a little faster. He couldn't wait to get to the dower house.

"All my London friends will be envious, I'm sure," Janice said.

God, Luke hated that answer. And he hated that voice. It was the same lofty London one she'd used on him when they'd first met and she'd been so defensive. Which meant either she was scared at the moment—which wasn't good but gave him hope—or she'd given up.

Surrendered to the life that she was meant to lead, according to her class.

He knew that was the right choice for her. But even so, his stomach roiled at the thought that perhaps she *had* decided to take on a leading role in the ton. Her parents would be pleased. She'd never want for any material thing. Her life would be colorful. Adventurous. She'd become that world traveler and meet important people wherever she went.

The temptation of becoming a duchess might have proved too strong for her to resist.

And if that was the case, well, Luke was relieved to be done with her. And on the heels of that thought, he swiftly admonished himself not to be angry. She'd proved herself just like the rest of the world by looking out for herself.

It was his own motto, wasn't it?

He shouldn't be angry. No. He really shouldn't. He focused on the sleigh hissing across the snow. Around the next tall hedge the Oriental-style gazebo would come into view, and around the bend from that the dower house. But—

Dammit, he *was* angry. And he well knew why.

Forget her. He inhaled a deep, cleansing breath. What had he been thinking getting all soft and caring? *Get yourself back on track, Callahan.*

"Damn tootin' she's a lucky woman," Miss Branson was saying. "What do you think, Lady Janice? Boston next year? Lobster? Clam chowder?"

"Whatever His Grace decides is best," Janice answered.

Luke made a face at that comment and sat up a little taller so no one would guess that he was dying to get away. He'd begun to hunch over, he noticed, as if that would help him hide.

But no, he determined as the sleigh slid past the snow-laden gazebo. He would endure this ridiculous conversation.

"Boy, she's obedient," Miss Branson said with a chuckle, presumably to Grayson. "I know you men like that kind of woman." She sighed. "Just don't get all namby-pamby on us, Lady Janice. When you come to America, you'll need a backbone."

Miss Branson obviously didn't know Janice. She had a backbone, all right. Luke prayed she still knew how to use it.

At the dower house, he jumped down to help the ladies out.

Once on the ground, Miss Branson gave him the once-over. "You're a fine specimen of manhood," she said, not bothering to lower her voice.

But Janice never looked at him. She simply held out her gloved hand and he helped her alight.

"Are you all right, my lady?" he murmured for her ears only.

It was all he wanted to know. It had been growing inside him from the moment he'd heard about her engagement. Waiting through the sleigh ride had taxed his patience more than anything else he'd ever done. He needed to know: was she all right?

But she didn't say a word.

She walked right past him to the front of the horses, where she waited for Grayson to join her, never once looking back at Luke.

The knowledge sat like a great stone on his chest. She was a lady, and he was a groom. Even if he proved to be a duke, he was still a groom at heart. A boxer. A soldier. A man who'd made money throwing trouble-makers out of pubs.

Face it, Callahan. She's beyond you. He watched her take Grayson's arm. *And you don't need her anyway.*

Chapter Twenty-two

Janice was desperate to talk to Luke. But she couldn't. Grayson was like a hawk, watching her every move. When Luke had asked her if she was all right when he helped her down from the carriage, she could hardly bear it. She wanted to say, *No. I'm not. And there's nothing I can do about it. If I do, you'll be in danger.*

She'd gone round and round in her mind, looking for a way out, but she hadn't been able to find it. Her best idea had been to run to Mama and Daddy and tell them what had happened. She'd have to let them know the whole truth, and they'd be devastated at the choices she'd made, but they wouldn't make her marry the duke, surely. And somehow Daddy would make sure that Halsey couldn't hurt Luke.

But could her father really protect him?

Daddy was an Irish marquess. As a duke Halsey outranked him. And if Halsey wanted to see something done to Luke, he could do it.

Janice also had to consider the awful possibility that Daddy would *agree* with the duke. Halsey would tell him how the groom had taken advantage of her, and Daddy would—God forbid—want to hurt Luke, too.

So why get her family involved at all?

For now, at least, Janice was trapped.

"We'll see the house first, and we'll finish our tour

in the stove house, where the orchids are kept," His Grace told the company, and held tight to Janice's arm.

Out of the corner of her eye, she saw Luke tending to the horses.

How could she get over there to see him? She had no idea. She wished now she'd accidentally left something in the sleigh, but she hadn't, except for her muffler.

As they walked through the house—which was charming—her frustration grew. She looked discreetly out of every window on the north side, which faced the stove house and the small stable, to keep an eye on Luke. As a consequence, she wound up missing some of what the housekeeper told them about each room, lovely though they were. Janice did learn that the dowager had moved there long ago, when Halsey's father had been duke and had brought his own duchess home, the current duke's mother. That was the usual way of things, of course. Old duchesses must make way for new.

Over strawberries and sparkling wine in the front drawing room—which she was required to thank the duke for—Janice truly felt that coming to live here wouldn't seem like a step down for any dowager. She liked the house very much.

The dower house was populated with caring servants. It was sunny. And beautiful. Yet Halsey had moved the dowager to a dark room with no company in a house in which the duke's questionable guests got far more attention than she did.

"Are you enjoying the strawberries?" He leaned closer to Janice.

Because he'd provided them, she loathed eating the precious fruit and drinking the fine sparkling wine. But she must make a pretense to or risk his wrath, which was subtle, cold, and struck one unaware.

"Delicious." She quickly bit into another strawberry so she wouldn't have to talk to him.

He looked mildly satisfied. But now that she knew how perceptive he was, she had no idea how well she was hiding her utter misery.

And then she saw a beautiful painting of an Irish cottage.

Her heart nearly burst with homesickness. She was a grown woman, but how she wished she were at Bally-brook right now, in the bosom of the family who loved her! She drained her glass of sparkling wine so she wouldn't think too hard about how lonely she felt. And she determined that as soon as she got back to Halsey House she'd have a tea break with Isobel and talk about silly little things.

Only Isobel knew the truth about Janice's engagement and the fact that she had spent private time with Luke. The maid was ecstatic about the latter development and clever enough not to ask Janice for details. But about the duke—Izzy felt as wretched as Janice did.

"I don't want you to be the Duchess of Halsey," Izzy had said this morning, "if it means you have to be married to such a wicked man. I wish I could do something to help. But I don't know what."

"You can help by staying out of it," Janice told her. "He means what he says. And I'd never forgive myself if Mr. Callahan got sent to jail on trumped-up charges."

"He could even be shipped out of the country"— Isobel winced—"or . . . or hanged, if the crime he might be accused of is particularly loathsome."

"God forbid." Janice's pulse raced at the thought.

They shared a worried look.

Isobel sighed. "I suppose we're here for a while then."

"Yes," Janice said. "I suppose."

"Perhaps your whole life." Isobel looked pityingly at her.

"I should hope not." Janice plucked at the bedcover. "The duke does have a house in Town and other properties scattered about southern England."

Isobel sank onto the bed beside her and patted her arm. "That's good. You'll be able to see your family. Let's look on the bright side. At least now we can keep looking for that diary."

Isobel was searching for it at that very moment, and Janice desperately hoped she'd find it, because then Luke could learn about his mother. That would make her very happy. If she couldn't *talk* to him, at least she could find him that journal.

She imagined sort of secretly throwing it at him as she walked by and began to get that lump in her throat again, thinking about how she couldn't talk to him or kiss him—good Lord, she couldn't hold the puppies, either! or laugh with Aaron!—when the duke stood and held out his hand.

"We'll go to the stove house now," he said.

Of course they would. They'd do whatever he wanted. Janice placed her hand in his and stood, a slow-boiling fury starting to replace her self-pity.

Miss Branson wasn't yet done with her sparkling wine, and Lord Rowntree had requested tea, which had only just arrived. Mrs. Friday, the dear, was opening her mouth to bite into a strawberry.

But Halsey had to have his way.

Everyone else stood, too, and no one complained.

Janice inhaled a deep breath through her nose and wondered how long it would take her to get used to being the Duchess of Halsey. How many years would she spend with this intimidating man with no heart? Would they grow old together? And what about . . . children?

Dear God, of course she'd have to produce at least an heir and a spare!

She hadn't thought that far. The idea of getting into a bed with Halsey and having him touch her that way was *awful*. She prayed he'd tire of her quickly and that they could live separately.

The walk to the stove house was an easy one, down a stone path that had been cleared of snow. Janice looked swiftly about to see where Luke was—

"He's in the kitchen, having tea," said the duke.

How on earth did he know what she was thinking? And how did he know where Luke was?

The man never rested, did he? Janice felt positively suffocated, knowing she was being watched so closely. And he had minions everywhere, it seemed. The members of the sleigh party certainly hadn't dipped into the kitchen on their tour—a servant must have come to tell Halsey where Luke was.

Either that or the duke was lying, just to keep her in her place. She wouldn't put it past him.

She could lie, too. "I don't know who you're talking about," she told him.

He chuckled. If one didn't know him, one would think him a pleasant man, judging from that chuckle. But Janice recognized that it wasn't a nice sound. It was horrid. It promised retribution of an unknown sort to anyone who crossed him.

And she realized at that moment that she was a

prisoner forever. If she ran away, Halsey would hurt someone she cared about. Even if she tattled on him to her parents, they couldn't protect Luke. And Aaron. And Mrs. Friday.

The only way out was if Halsey died. And Janice couldn't kill him. She felt so guilty even thinking in that direction, she said a quick prayer just as they ducked into the stove house.

It was such an interesting place.

In the warm, moist air, she immediately forgot about the duke. The orchids were so exotic. Many appeared fragile, their stems and petals stark in a hauntingly lovely way. Others were wildly beautiful: the bold pinks and oranges were Janice's favorites. She'd seen orchids in London and heard how different they were from other flowers. But walking up and down the rows of them, she got to learn from the elderly gardener who watched over them exactly how much work went into producing them. And there was no guarantee that work would pay off.

"Sometimes it do; sometimes it don't," he said in that simple way that good country folk often did.

"Keeping the fire stoked appears to be a full-time job." Janice admired his stamina.

"It's my privilege to do it," he replied.

He was such a nice, hardworking man who seemed to genuinely love the orchids. He must have liked how interested she was, because he drew her aside, almost as if she were his special guest, and showed her some remarkable drawings he'd made of the orchids using a stick of coal.

"You're a true artist," she said, marveling at the pictures.

"Thank you." He beamed. "I like to pass the time

while the fire's heating up by sketching my favorite ones. My fingers don't work like they used to, but I think the drawing helps keep them limber."

As he flipped through the book, he explained what he liked about each different orchid. And then he'd say, "This one didn't last long" or "This one's over in the corner" or "The dowager's favorite is this one here."

Janice was intrigued, to be sure, and so grateful to be able to relax for a moment and enjoy his company.

"Do you have any more?" she asked him when they were through perusing the sketches.

"I have an entire collection on that shelf." He angled his chin at a small buckled shelf that held a few clay pots and a stack of simply bound sketchbooks.

"My goodness," she said, "I'd love to see them!"

But she sensed that she was missed. Indeed, when she looked over her shoulder the duke was gazing their way, his pocket watch in his hand.

"Perhaps another time," she said to the gardener. "I believe we're leaving now."

He nodded, and she could tell he was disappointed.

"I promise," she said. "I'll be back."

"You are the duke's intended bride, are you not?" he asked.

She smiled. "Word travels fast, doesn't it? It's not official yet, but yes, we're to marry."

The gardener's face lit up. "Good. Because I hope to make some improvements here." He lowered his voice. "Her Grace's greatest joy when she lived at the dower house was coming out to see the orchids every day, but His Grace is adamantly opposed. He thinks this entire operation is a waste of money. But with a missus in the house, perhaps he'll think differently." He winked at her.

A wave of guilt rushed over Janice. She was about to lie to this wonderful man. "I'll do what I can," she said with a nervous smile.

But she knew she wouldn't be able to help him. If Halsey didn't want something, it didn't happen.

The gardener must have sensed her fretting. "Don't you worry, my lady." He shut the little sketchbook with fingers stiff and bent with age. "If you can't do anything, we'll get by. We always have in these parts."

He smiled as if to reassure *her,* she who had wealth and status and privilege—and she was so touched by his simple courage and good cheer that she took his hand and squeezed it. "I like you," she said, feeling inspired by him.

"And I like *you,*" he said back. "But I'd better let you go. The duke is waiting."

"All right." She winked at him and felt miles better.

She couldn't wait to see Luke again. She wished she could tell him about the orchids. He was such a good listener. And this time, when he helped her to her seat, she hoped somehow to convey to him (without the duke being aware) that she didn't want to be this way: cold, removed, and seemingly oblivious to his existence. She didn't know how she'd manage it, but she wanted to try.

But she never got the chance. She was holding Halsey's arm when she walked up to the sleigh, and he helped her into it. This time Lord Yarrow and Mrs. Friday joined them.

When Luke climbed up to his seat, he didn't even look at her.

Janice struggled not to let her disappointment show. It helped that Lord Yarrow kept asking her questions about her family's Irish estate, but she felt the duke's eye on her as she answered and wondered if he saw through her contrived amiability.

The sleigh took off smoothly—theirs was in the lead—when the duke called out sharply, "Driver!"

Janice's heart jumped. What could Halsey mean, calling out so sharply? Nothing appeared wrong with the sleigh or the horses.

Luke looked over his shoulder. "Yes, Your Grace?"

The horses pranced merrily along.

"Stop by the gazebo," the duke commanded him.

The gazebo was looming, so Luke pulled gently up on the reins, and the sleigh came to a graceful stop. The other sleigh, too, stopped behind them.

Janice couldn't help feeling nervous, and she knew her eyes were wide as she gazed across at Mrs. Friday. The widow's face, as always, was reassuringly calm and kind. But how would she look if she knew that the duke had threatened harm to her?

The very idea made Janice's stomach burn with anxiety.

Halsey jumped down from the sleigh and held out his hand. "Lady Janice, you will join me in the snow." It was no request. It was an order.

What choice did she have?

"Very well," she said, and took the duke's hand.

It was an awkward descent from her seat. All eyes were upon her. She could feel Luke's, especially.

When she stood before Halsey, he looked down at her with that cool smile of his. "We're off to the gazebo."

"Are we?" Everyone was watching. She had no idea what was going on, and judging by the silence, no one else knew, either.

The duke held out his arm and, of course, she took it. Together they walked through the slushy snow to the gazebo, which since they'd arrived must have been swept clean of the snow that had blown into the interior. No snow graced the railings, either.

The duke turned to face the occupants of the sleighs. "It's early days yet. But all of you know that our engagement to be married will soon be official. As a token of my esteem for my future duchess, I'm presenting her with a gift. And I do it here, in this gazebo, because this is where my own grandmother received this same token from my grandfather, the fifth Duke of Halsey."

It would have been a lovely gesture in any other courtship. But theirs? An alliance based on threats on his part and fear on hers?

No.

Janice's temples and hands were damp from nerves. Luke was looking directly at her. Could this be her moment of communication with him? In front of all these people? What could she do to let him know that none of this was her choice?

Before she could manage anything, the duke took her elbow and spun her slowly around. She felt his arms lift over her head and then move to the back of her neck. When she looked down, atop her coat was a magnificent ruby necklace, so large that she gave a little gasp.

"Do you like it?" Halsey murmured in her ear.

"It's impressive," she said back. Never would she say that she liked it.

He turned her around to face him again. He raised her gloved hand to his lips and kissed the back of her hand, after which he held her hand aloft in his. "It is done!" he called to the crowd. "The lady is well pleased!"

Janice's cheeks burned with mortification.

Everyone began to clap—everyone, that is, except Luke, who sat with the reins loose in his hands, his face an inscrutable mask. And then before the clapping even ceased, he turned to face the front of the sleigh.

His neutral profile said it all. That brief, idyllic time with him in the stables might as well never have happened. Her love for him—because that was what it was, she realized—was for naught.

They were strangers again.

Chapter Twenty-three

As the sun hid behind the clouds and the day was laden with gray, the ruby necklace seemed to glow with its own light on the rest of the sleigh ride home. In Janice, too, an idea blazed, fueled by fury and a broken heart.

If she couldn't speak to Luke—if she must consign herself to being Halsey's wife—then she would *be* the future Duchess of Halsey. Starting now.

Lord Yarrow had just finished discussing—in his pompous way—the exhibit of the Elgin Marbles at the British Museum with Mrs. Friday, who'd never seen them.

"A travesty that you haven't," he said, not even bothering to look at her.

"I don't live in London," she replied, "and I was recently widowed. I don't know when I'll get there."

He waved a hand. "See that you do."

Really? Was that how one spoke to a kind widow? Treat her as if she was less than nothing? Dismiss her with a hand?

Janice glared at him. "I suppose if Mrs. Friday had been wealthy and titled, you might have given her a more tolerable answer, Lord Yarrow. In future, if you expect to be invited to Halsey House, you'll conduct yourself with true civility. Pompous airs aren't welcome."

The sleigh bells jingled, the snow hissed by, and within the sleigh there was utter silence.

"Halsey?" Lord Yarrow begged hoarsely, and pulled at his cravat.

Janice turned to her future husband and looked so coldly at him, she shocked even herself. But she *was* cold, down to her very soul. She saw no hope for happiness in her future.

"You'll do as Lady Janice asks, Yarrow," he said, his eyes still on hers.

Hah, Janice thought. Maybe something good could come out of this "duchess" business, after all.

When they reached the estate, Luke once again pulled the sleigh directly in front of the house. This time several footmen swarmed it, but Janice leapt out with no assistance at all. Without looking at anyone—Luke, she knew, was expressly avoiding eye contact with her, as well—she walked directly to the house. Once inside, she instructed the butler to bring tea for the entire sleigh party to the drawing room and to send the housekeeper in when the tea was served.

"Yes, my lady," he said.

"Thank you." She gave him her coat. "And do see that a spare room is prepared near the kitchens for a dog and her pups. When it's ready for inspection, send for me."

"*Yes*, my lady."

The rest of the sleigh's occupants trailed in and joined her in the drawing room.

She poured out for everyone, serving Halsey last. "Esmeralda and her pups are moving into the house," she told him when she handed him his cup.

His hand froze. "Are you jesting?"

"No. I'll make a bed for them in a spare room off the kitchen. And every day until we leave for London, I'll walk Esmeralda, the mother. I'll also be making the rounds of the tenant farmers to see who would like to adopt a pup. Do you think I'll have to extend the search to Bramblewood?"

The duke stared at her a long moment. Janice stared right back. She'd already practiced defying him when she didn't mean it—merely to capture his attention. Now she was going to do what she wanted when she wanted to—she was going to be herself if she had to be a duchess—and not give a fig what he thought.

And she would enjoy every minute of it.

"On second thought," she said, "I have a craving to keep all of them. We certainly have room enough here to do so. Why separate a family unnecessarily?"

Lady Opal set down her own cup. "But Halsey doesn't care for dogs that aren't his hounds."

One of them looked up at them from the rug, its ears twitching.

"Please don't speak for the duke," Janice told Lady Opal. "He can do that for himself." Janice glanced at him, but he didn't appear inclined to talk at the moment. He was no doubt trying to adjust to the new duchess in her—because she'd given him no choice in the matter.

"But Opal's right," Lady Rose broke in, staring aghast at Janice. "Halsey's hounds have a special place in his heart."

"The pups are coming inside," Janice told both sisters quietly. "And as you're so well able to defend the duke, you're clearly ready to stand up for yourselves. You make a formidable team. As soon as the snow melts, I must ask you to leave Halsey House so you can get started."

"What?" whispered Lady Rose.

Her sister glowered.

"You know what I said about you being namby-pamby, Lady Janice?" Miss Branson grinned. "I take it back."

"Thank you, Miss Branson." Janice smiled. "Your observations are always refreshing. But you must agree it's time to stop paying room and board here and take your holiday elsewhere when the roads clear. Why deny the rest of England the pleasure of meeting you?"

"Ah . . ." Miss Branson winced and scratched her head. "That's an idea."

"A good one," Lady Opal said.

Lady Rose giggled.

"Perhaps all three of you can travel together," Janice suggested.

The two sisters' amusement faded instantly.

"You've gotten to know each other well," Janice said. "I think—" Something was coming to her. "*I* think that what with Miss Branson desiring adventure and having a full pocketbook and needing company—because travel is always better with company—you two sisters can comb England, Scotland, and Wales with her for an ideal place to locate your business."

"Business?" Lady Opal drew in her chin.

"Yes," said Janice. "You're an excellent cook, Lady Opal. And Lady Rose, you'd make an exceptional innkeeper. I propose that with Miss Branson's money, you find yourself a small castle and renovate it. Convert it to an inn."

"Good Lord, that's a brilliant idea," said Miss Branson. "I've always wanted a real castle. And they're a dime a dozen over here."

Lady Rose and Lady Opal stared openmouthed at each other.

"It is a wonderful notion," whispered Lady Rose.

"I agree," said Lady Opal. "All we need is money."

"And I have that," said Miss Branson. "Girls, as soon as those roads clear, we're on our way."

"Splendid," said Janice.

But Lord Yarrow and Lord Rowntree wore uncertain expressions. Were they afraid of being thrown out? She hoped so. They'd probably been getting free entertainment from the ladies, however, so if the women went, then the men might be more amenable to leaving, too.

She didn't care to think about whether Halsey would miss the women's favors. She suspected so. But it didn't matter anymore. All these questionable guests would soon be on their way. And it was because she'd insist, as the future Duchess of Halsey, that they go.

The housekeeper walked in. "You wanted to see me, Lady Janice?"

"Yes, I did." Everyone but the duke looked at Janice with some trepidation. His Grace kept his usual cool expression in place. "I'd like you to move Lord Rowntree's things out of his bedchamber and make the one next to it over as the dowager's. She'll be moving there tomorrow. Meanwhile, Lord Rowntree will need another room farther away. Smaller will do as he won't be staying past the snow."

"Yes, my lady." The housekeeper curtsied and left the room.

Lord Rowntree put down his cup with a clatter. "I think not, young lady," he said to Janice, his voice booming. "You're not duchess here yet. Halsey? Are you going to let her get away with this? And I thought that the doctor ordered your grandmother to stay in seclusion."

The duke lifted his cup to his lips and watched Janice over the rim.

Don't give an inch, she told herself as she stared back. The dowager duchess deserved better. And Rowntree, the mushroom, needed to depart.

"You'll take the smaller room, Rowntree," the duke said. "And as for my grandmother, that's none of your business."

There were audible intakes of breath from the women, and Lord Rowntree stood. "This is preposterous. Forget giving me the smaller room. I'm packing up and leaving now. At least I can get as far as Bramblewood."

Janice didn't say a word. She busied herself adding milk to her second cup of tea. The dowager would be moving, and it was a great triumph!

What else could she do?

Drink her tea, that was what. She was exhausted from doing exactly what she wanted. But it was exhilarating, and dare she say it? She had excellent ideas.

Which reminded her: she had one more.

"Lord Rowntree, " she said, "while you're in Bramblewood, you'll kindly ask the vicar to attend me as soon as possible. I want to make a massive contribution to the parish fund, payable only if it is split with St. Mungo's Orphanage, a couple of hours' ride away. You'll preface my donation by making a substantial one of your own to both the parish and the orphanage, if you wouldn't mind. Consider that your way of repaying the duke for his unceasing hospitality, of which you took full advantage."

"I'll do no such thing." Lord Rowntree's face was bright red. "You can't promise Halsey's money when you're not even his bride. And you certainly can't demand that I empty my own pockets for people I don't know or care about."

"Very well, my lord," she said serenely. "I see many similarities between His Grace's friends: mainly a desire to wring every bit of influence you can from the duke, as you have little to none of your own."

"How dare you." Lord Rowntree's eyes narrowed dangerously.

Janice maintained her aplomb. She'd already dealt with Halsey's nastiness. She could handle this man's. "When I join the duke's household," she told him, "friends will be true friends. I won't tolerate sycophants or charlatans. If you're so miserly and selfish that you won't do me this small favor, don't expect to be received by His Grace ever again, either here or in London or at any of his properties."

Lord Rowntree's lips thinned. "You're a bloody nightmare, Lady Janice." He stormed to the door without looking at the duke or anyone else along the way. And then he paused and turned to her. "But I'll do as you ask—*my lady*."

He left without another word.

"Damn, Lady Janice," said Miss Branson. "You were born to be a duchess."

Lady Opal nodded her assent. Lady Rose's mouth softly gaped.

Lord Yarrow stood up and glanced at the duke, who sat with his hands steepled before his face, quite as if he was enjoying the spectacle. "I believe I'll depart today as well," Yarrow said with a nervous smile, and yanked his thumb to the door.

"But the snow, my lord," Janice said. "It will be rough going."

"What's a little snow? I've never stayed in Bramblewood. Perhaps it's time."

"I think that's a wonderful idea," she said. "And—"

"Oh, yes," he interrupted her. "I plan to make a substantial donation to the parish and St. Mungo's, too."

"Very good, sir." She smiled at him. "But I must also ask your help in getting Sir Milo involved. When we get back to London, you and Lord Rowntree will go with the duke and me to deliver the news to the baronet: he's now a benefactor of Bramblewood Parish and the orphanage."

Lord Yarrow winced. "Very well, my lady."

"Good-bye, my lord." She sent him a little wave and thought, *Mission accomplished*.

But she had many more as Halsey's future wife. Her job as duchess would keep her busy, busy enough, she hoped, that she could bear not leading the fantasy life she longed for—

A life that centered around her love for a workingman named Luke Callahan.

She remembered how he'd cradled her in his lap and kissed her so tenderly, and her longing for him nearly made her double over.

But it was not to be, she reminded herself dully.

It *couldn't* be.

She caught the duke's gaze. The soft smile playing about his lips appeared benign to the casual observer. But she knew him better than that and suddenly realized why he'd not stood in her way that morning. No matter how much she asserted herself, there was one thing she could never have: Luke.

And as long as Halsey could taunt her with that fact, he was happy.

Chapter Twenty-four

"There has to be a bright side to being the Duchess of Halsey," Isobel said. "Other than the fact that you'll wear exquisite ball gowns, travel the world, and be rich."

They were in Janice's bedchamber writing letters to their loved ones in London. Surely the snow would melt soon and the missives could go out.

Janice laid down her quill. "I'm determined to find one," she agreed. "This morning was a good start."

"The dowager's situation is sure to improve," Isobel said. "And you won't have to worry about having ramshackle guests lounging about."

"True, and now that I think about it, Mrs. Friday can also stay my companion as long as she wishes."

"You can find her a husband, too."

"Good point. And I can be glad that Esmeralda and the puppies will be close by."

"They're already adored by Cook." Isobel chuckled. "She gave Esmeralda a massive bone and a talking-to to the pups. They're running their mother ragged, rolling about as they are and squeaking so loudly. Cook won't put up with it."

Janice chuckled. "Then there are all the roles I'll play as a new duchess. I'll get to know the tenants at all Halsey's estates, and I'll participate in village life."

"I've already heard the vicar in Bramblewood is gorgeous," said Isobel.

"And in London, I'll have so many parties to attend and give myself that I'll probably never sleep."

"Don't forget children," Isobel said.

"Right," Janice said faintly.

Isobel leaned closer. "You know how they say to think of the Queen when you're in bed with your husband doing your duty?" she whispered. "I've heard something else entirely."

"What?"

"Think of the handsomest man you've ever seen." Isobel gave one nod of her head. "That would be Mr. Groom-in-the-stables. I know *I* will."

"But I can't!" Janice cried. "That would be too . . . too much torture. And *you* can't because he's—he's mine."

Isobel bit her lip. "You really care about him, don't you?"

Janice nodded. "I do, Izzy. This isn't some fling to learn how to kiss better. Or to satisfy some curiosity about what men's bodies look like."

"Oh, God. Do you know?"

Janice nodded.

Isobel fell flat back on the bed. "You've seen . . . *him*."

"You *are* supposed to be a maid, you know." Janice said, looking down at her.

Izzy sat up on her elbows. "My lady, you are the luckiest—"

"But surely all these things," Janice interrupted her with a steely glance, "will serve to distract me."

"From him?" Isobel asked tentatively.

"Yes." Janice sighed. The plain fact was that she

couldn't be with her own man like no other. "Please move over, Izzy. I want to fall back on the bed now."

"Yes, my lady." Isobel looked most concerned.

But instead of falling, Janice merely crawled onto the bed and held on to a pillow. "Oh, Marcia and Mama," she whispered.

"What is it, my lady?" Isobel reached out and patted her back.

"They told me that true love would be mine."

But instead she faced the prospect of bringing children into the world when she didn't love their father. How painful would that be? Always she'd have to hide the truth from them—and from her own siblings and her parents—that she and Halsey were not a love match.

Lies. She hated telling lies. She'd never be able to be herself again. . . .

Misery loomed before her.

But she wouldn't succumb to it.

She sat up. "I'm of the House of Brady, Isobel. And although I'll be the first of us to marry without love, I'll forge on."

"You will, my lady."

"I can't have Luke, but I can still help him."

"Yes," said Isobel. "You will. I'm sorry to say that I've had no luck with the other servants. At dinner I told them my mum knew someone named Emily March who once worked here, but no one's been here long enough to know of her, except the butler, and he said he can't remember lady's maids from thirty years ago."

"That's all the more reason for me to get up and go see the dowager."

Isobel brushed Janice's hair an extra hundred strokes for good luck, then sent her on her way.

In the dark bedchamber, Janice sat in her usual chair. "Your Grace, do you remember a lady's maid called Emily March?"

The dowager squinted into the distance. "Oh, yes. She worked for me." She rested the butt of her palm on her forehead. "I can't remember. There was something about her. Something important."

Janice's temples pounded. What if she could find the journal for Luke? "Was she . . . a good lady's maid?"

The dowager nodded. "The best. I didn't have her long, though, and I can't remember *why*. Mrs. Poole!"

Mrs. Poole looked up from her sewing.

"Do you remember Emily March?"

"No, my lady. I've only been working for you the past year. Did she work for you long ago, when you lived at Halsey House before?"

"Yes," said the dowager with some excitement. "She was my lady's maid when my husband, Liam, was still alive."

"Anything else you can remember about her?" Janice asked.

"No, no." The dowager shifted on her pillows. "And I want to remember her. Desperately. Something happened to her."

"Really?"

The dowager nodded. "But I'm drawing a blank."

Janice withheld a sigh. "That's all right."

The dowager held her hand. "Mrs. Poole tells me you and Halsey will be married."

"Yes," said Janice.

The elderly woman smiled. "Are you happy?"

Janice nodded. "Everything's wonderful."

The dowager stared at her a moment as if seeing her for the first time. "There's something not right," she said. "Which grandson are you marrying, my dear?"

Janice patted her hand. "Halsey, of course."

"Yes, Halsey." The dowager blinked. "I want you to marry the duke. Please—don't marry anyone else. I'm sure he's a good man. I feel it in my bones. He'll make you a fine husband, and I want *you,* Lady Janice—only you—as my granddaughter."

"I plan to marry him, Your Grace, so you don't have to worry on that count."

The dowager smiled sadly. "If only I could see him before I die."

"But you do, Your Grace." Janice went along with her. "You see him every day at three o'clock."

The dowager's forehead furrowed. "Yes," she said, "I-I do, don't I? You mean Grayson, of course. He was such a sweet little boy. I remember when his mother was alive. She was a darling girl, and I'm sorry to say she wasn't here long. He was ten when she died of the influenza—but she loved him. Oh, how she did."

"I'm so glad he knew a mother's love," whispered Janice, and wondered how Grayson could have gone so wrong.

The dowager sighed. "Russell never remarried, and I always wished that he had." She sucked in a breath. "Little Grayson needed a mother. I tried to move back in here to be that mother figure to him, but Russell wouldn't let me. I begged him. I even offered to take Grayson to the dower house, but Russell said no. And so . . . I failed my grandson. It was the greatest opportunity of my life, to nurture that boy. But Russell won. He seemed to delight in keeping Grayson and me apart."

Her eyes were filled with such remorse, Janice leaned over and embraced her as best she could with all the pillows surrounding her. Her heart broke at the little sob the duchess emitted. "You can't have failed him,

Your Grace, if he loves you so much that he comes to see you every day at three o'clock."

Janice took a moment to wipe the one tear that clung to the dowager's paper-thin cheek with the lacy handkerchief she always had in her lap.

"His mother died at three o'clock," the duchess said. "And he was there at her bedside when she did. The doctor told everyone to keep him away. But he was as strong willed as his father. He sneaked in to be with her. Russell was nowhere near, of course. He was out carousing."

"Poor Grayson," Janice murmured. She hated him. Truly hated him. But she somehow couldn't help feeling sorry for the little boy he'd been.

The dowager dabbed at her eyes with her handkerchief. "I think he comes to see me at three because I'm a link to her. I should have taken her place when she died, and I didn't. I'm not sure if he's here every day to punish me for neglecting him—or if he needs me still."

"People are complicated," Janice said. "Perhaps it's both. Have you told him how hard you fought for him?"

"Yes, but he doesn't seem to believe me."

"Why not latch on to the positive then? Let's assume he craves your interest in him. What do you talk about when he's here?"

"I-I pretend to sleep most of the time." The duchess blushed. "My guilt is so deep, and his scorn so great. He tries not to show it, but I see it in his mouth, how it's never soft and relaxed. And in his eyes. They're full of smoldering anger."

Janice knew exactly what the dowager was talking about.

"Other times," the dowager said, "I simply don't remember his visits at all."

Those must have been the times she channeled the

Queen, Janice realized. And the ambitious, Machiavellian Queen was very fond of Halsey—she'd wanted to see him married, after all, and told Janice the secret to winning him. Maybe the Queen and Grayson had discussed that very thing and the dowager simply wasn't aware of that.

"I have an idea," said Janice. "Speak to him about what kind of qualities you valued in your own husband. And remind him of all the hopes you have for him as my future husband. I could use the help, Your Grace." She smiled wryly.

"I like that idea," said the dowager. "My husband was a very good man and a wonderful husband. Grayson should know more about him."

Janice was glad to see her smile. "On a new subject, I have to tell you—your orchids at the dower house are lovely."

"Oh, yes. I'm obsessed with them."

"I know you'd like to see them again."

The dowager nodded. "Will I ever?"

"Yes." Janice smiled. "You will. We're going to start slowly. First, we'll move you downstairs to your old bedchamber here at Halsey House, the one you shared with your duke."

"Really? I'll get to see the seasons change." The dowager couldn't look any happier.

"After a while, we'll start moving you around to other parts of the house—the library, the drawing room, and the conservatory."

The dowager's eyes lit up.

"And then," Janice said, "on your next birthday, which I understand is in June, we'll take you to the stove house again. How does that sound?"

"Perfect," said the dowager. "A little bit at a time."

"Exactly," said Janice.

"Because I can't—I can't go too fast. No, if I do, I

forget things." She grabbed Janice's arm. "I-I don't want to forget about my grandson. I want to see him."

She sounded so distressed!

"It's all right, Your Grace. I won't let you forget him. And you will see him, many times."

The dowager's nose puckered up, and then she sneezed into her handkerchief. Janice held her breath while she dabbed at her nose and opened her eyes. The Queen looked back at her with her usual scornful expression.

"Good afternoon, Your Majesty," Janice said with a smile. "How can I help you?"

The old lady scowled. "You've won Halsey, have you not?"

Janice nodded.

"Very good."

"But I-I wish I hadn't, quite frankly."

The Queen drew in her chin. "How can you say that?"

Janice hesitated. "He's . . . he's wicked, I'm afraid." She felt the Queen should know, but she hoped speaking honestly wouldn't upset her too much.

The Queen merely swatted her with her handkerchief. The spirited lady reveled in conflict, after all. "He's cut from his father's cloth, you idiot. What do you expect?"

"No," Janice said, "*you've* told him that he's like his father, but he doesn't have to be. Next time he comes up here, I demand you tell him to improve his behavior. You let him know that it's not all right to act like his father. Or I'll . . . I'll stage a coup."

"You wouldn't."

"Oh, yes, I would."

The Queen sat quietly for a few moments, and Janice could swear she was scheming.

"What do you know of Halsey's father?"

"Russell?" Janice shrugged. "Not much. Just that he wasn't a good husband. And he wouldn't let you see his son—"

"Who said that?" The Queen leaned toward her in a threatening manner.

"A little bird told me." Janice backed away an inch. "You know how that goes." She waved a hand. "At Court, there's always a tattle."

"Yes." The Queen curled her lip. "It makes me ill."

"Why do you ask what I know about Russell?" Janice queried her.

The Queen gave a short laugh. "I don't like state secrets to get out. That's why. So if I find this little bird of whom you speak, he or she will have to answer to *me*."

"Is there a secret about Russell?" Janice asked her.

"Is this a joke?" The Queen stared at her. "Do you think that if there were, I'd share it with *you*? Don't you know intrigue is carried out behind closed doors? You'd make a terrible spy."

"But we *are* behind a closed door, Your Majesty. And I'm to marry Halsey. Shouldn't I know everything there is to know about His Grace's family?"

The Queen bit her lower lip. "No. No one shall know."

Janice sighed. "All right then. But may I ask you a question?"

The Queen cackled. "I don't have to answer it."

"Very well." Janice cleared her throat. "Do you know someone named Emily March?"

"Why, you wily thing." The Queen's eyes narrowed, and then she looked over Janice's head to Mrs. Poole, who was conveniently snoring in her chair. "How much must I pay you for your silence?" she whispered to Janice.

She gulped. "Nothing, Your Majesty. I-I'm a loyal

subject. But can't we at least discuss the . . . the situation involving Miss March?"

"I've nothing to add to the subject." The would-be monarch sounded much more sober than her usual self. "It's a pity. A vast pity."

"What is, Your Majesty?"

"That he's missing." She twisted her handkerchief. "But it must remain that way. I know what's best. Don't question me."

"But who's missing?" Janice wished *she* had a handkerchief to twist, too.

"Him." The Queen lofted one magnificent brow.

"Do you mean Russell?"

"*No.* Russell died. Nincompoop."

Janice brushed off the insult. Somehow this story involved Luke's mother, and she must get to the bottom of it. "Perhaps you mean Liam."

The Queen shook her head sadly. "He was a good subject. One of my best." She got a naughty look in her eyes. "He was a man's man, and he knew how to make a woman feel like a woman."

"I see." Janice bit back a smile. She felt the same way about Luke. He'd made her feel adored. The memory of his caresses—his face as he looked at her—made her shift in her chair.

"You know what I'm talking about, don't you?" the Queen asked archly. "You have a lover."

"Had one," said Janice. "Yes."

"But it wasn't Halsey."

Janice shook her head. "Sorry."

Her Majesty shrugged. "It's the story of most marriages in the ton."

Janice tried to focus again. "Let's get back to the person who's missing. Are you possibly referring to Everett?"

"No. Not Everett." The Queen winced and put a hand on her heart. "Oh, dear Everett. I miss him, too."

There were traces of the dowager in the Queen, and Janice felt sorry for her. "Then who, Your Majesty? Who else is missing?"

"The boy," she said plainly. "But he must stay gone. Halsey needs his position. And as you're marrying him"—she wagged a finger at Janice—"you'd do well to help him keep it. So, *ss-s-sh-h-h*." She put her fingers to her mouth and made a gesture as if she were turning a key in a lock.

Janice's head was dizzy with this new revelation. There was a boy. Missing. Perhaps the dowager meant Halsey. But did she mean someone else? Could Emily and Luke's story be tied into this one?

"Do you know where the boy is?" Janice asked her.

"You ask too many questions." The Queen looked down her nose at her. "Go away now. Don't you know when an audience is over?"

Chapter Twenty-five

It had been the week from hell. He loved her. Deuce it all, Luke loved Janice. He'd figured it out on that debacle of a sleigh ride back to Halsey House, in the middle of enduring Grayson's stupid posturing as he presented her with what looked like a dog collar to claim her as his own.

Apart from the fact that Luke's beloved apparently didn't know him anymore, had embraced her new role as Grayson's fiancée, and had made no effort to contact him about his mother's missing journal, the low point had come when Aaron and Oscar carried the puppies and Esmeralda to the house. Luke was disgusted with himself for feeling a huge jolt of pain when he saw Esmeralda's furry head peering back at him over Aaron's shoulder. Oscar carried away the basket of puppies.

Luke cursed, rolled up his sleeves, and punched a bag of oats for an entire hour. That dog and her pups reminded him of Janice. He'd miss them. He missed *her*. He missed how she chatted with him about little things. How she watched him speak as if what he had to say mattered. And he missed running his hands down her bare back and tugging her close.

He was a fool. Every night he put the lantern in the window.

But she never came.

And each time he extinguished that lantern, he realized it was getting harder to be the solitary man he knew he should be. With her gone, he was back to keeping to himself, except when he taught the other lads to knuckle box, which he admitted to himself now he thoroughly enjoyed.

Outside of that, he found himself hoping for some conversation. A joke here. A chat there. But everyone was so used to his silence, they didn't speak to him much.

With Janice gone, each day was routine to the point of utter dullness. He almost wished there were more drunken baronets to look after—well, no, that wasn't very kind of him. But he could stand to see the two peers again—the prig, Rowntree, and the dunce, Yarrow, who'd left in a hurry the same day they'd made that excursion to the dower house. At least when they were here, Luke could make fun of them behind their backs with the other stablemen.

The female houseguests had gone as well. The roads were passable but difficult, so Lady Janice told them to take their time before they left. But according to Aaron, Miss Branson had said Americans waited for nothing and were afraid of nothing, so they'd ventured forth, too. Janice, Mrs. Friday, and Isobel had waved them off with handkerchiefs and smiles and wishes for good luck.

And in the stable block nothing of any significance was happening: no new stallions, and foaling season wasn't for a while. Aaron and some other stable hands were inspired by Luke's frustration and, along with him, punched bags of oats every night to build up their stamina while Oscar sat back and watched. He'd knuckle boxed himself as a young man and had his own tips to offer to the boys.

The only noticeable change of pace occurred when

the snow melted enough that the vicar, of all people, came to visit Halsey House. Luke caught a glimpse of Lady Janice on the front steps, there to greet the esteemed visitor. And Luke remembered the day he'd cleaned those front steps for her.

How things could change in less than a fortnight!

"The vicar's never been here before," Aaron said over a juicy drumstick at their dinner. "What the devil is going on?"

"Watch it with the language." Luke drank his glass of ale in one giant swallow.

Aaron made a face. "You tell me to watch my language, when you've been cursing like a sailor all week?"

"Do as I say, not as I do."

"Not only that, you've been drinking more lately," Aaron accused him. "Watch out yourself—it'll ruin your flat belly."

"Are you telling me what to do?" Luke gave him his most lethal stare.

Aaron's eyes widened, and he jumped up from the table. "No-o-o," he said. "Not me!"

He ran away before Luke could grab him by the tail of his shirt and put him in a headlock right there.

Out of reach, Aaron said, "Don't forget the meeting downstairs about the special visit coming up."

"A meeting?" Luke asked. "Who's coming this time? The King?"

"*No.*" Aaron chuckled at his ignorance. "The Marquess and Marchioness of Brady are arriving two days from now."

Luke hid his dismay. "So soon?" He looked at Oscar.

"The mail coach started up again," Oscar said, "slightly slower than usual because of the roads. His Grace just heard back this afternoon."

Aaron's cheeks were two bright red circles of

excitement. "The butler said he heard from the secretary that Lord Brady's withholding his consent until he meets with the duke in person and speaks to his daughter. And he's bringing almost his entire family."

"Good Lord, there are a lot of them, aren't there?" Luke looked to Oscar.

"Indeed, there are."

"So we all have to make a tremendous impression." Aaron grinned. "That's why we're to have the meeting."

Oscar shook his head. "It won't sit well with the marquess and marchioness that Halsey gave Lady Janice that fine ruby necklace already."

It didn't sit well with Luke, either. Not that anyone cared.

When Aaron went downstairs, Oscar and Luke were the only two left at the table. The older man tipped back in his chair and threw his own drumstick on his plate. "You like her, don't you?"

"Who?" Luke said, and couldn't help feeling testy.

"Oh, you know who. Lady Janice. You're always asking about her. In subtle ways."

"And you never tell me anything." Luke crossed his arms and looked out the window at the patches of brown appearing all over the meadow.

"It's my way of trying to get you thinking of other things, lad," Oscar said. "But you have good taste. High-falutin taste." He chuckled.

Luke looked back at him. "This isn't helping."

The driver shrugged. "A long time ago, I was in love with Lady Brady."

"Lady Brady?"

"See? You know how impossible that would be."

"If you think I need reminding that I can't have Lady Janice—"

"No, you're a clever man. But let me tell you my story. When I saw Lady Brady the first time, in her sewing shop, she was a sweet little miss with a smile that made you thank God to be alive. I fell hard. Right along with Lord Brady." Oscar shook his head and chuckled. "Just because we're workingmen doesn't mean we don't have hearts."

"Did Lord Brady know?"

"Of course he did! He patted me on the back and said he understood. And he wasn't at all cocky about it. He truly felt sorry for me, because he loved her, too, and he said that he didn't know how he'd live if she didn't love him back." Oscar was silent, remembering. A flash of pain on his face told Luke that this story was no idle tale. "He gave me forty pounds that Christmas. A whole two years' wages. And he offered me unfettered access to his favorite fishing cottage at Ballybrook for life."

"You were lucky."

Oscar laughed. "And then he told me I was a dirty old man. Lady Brady was a good twenty years younger than I."

"You *are* a dirty old man." A grin slipped out, and Luke leaned forward. "So do you have any advice? And by the way, don't say a word. I'm appalled at myself for letting this happen. I never thought it would."

"Don't be so surprised." Oscar took his measure. "You're a red-blooded man. Just move on. Build a life for yourself. I did, and it's a good one."

"You're not married," Luke noted.

Oscar lifted a shoulder and let it drop. "I was never the marrying type. My love for Lady Brady wasn't as true as Lord Brady's. I came to see it was more an infatuation. Even had I been her equal in station, I never would have pursued her. I like my freedom."

"Obviously."

"You do, too, I take it."

Luke took a minute to answer. "I thought I did."

Oscar pointed at him. "Here's the test—if you felt you had a fighting chance, would you offer for her?"

Luke pushed back from the table. "Don't ask me things like that."

"Ah." Oscar stood, too. "So your temper's up. That's a dead giveaway. You *would* offer for her."

"No, I wouldn't."

"Are you certain?"

"Of course," he lied.

"Then you've got a lovely case of infatuation." There was a new twinkle in Oscar's eye. "True love takes you to the edge of the cliff and right on over. You should be relieved, lad. I know I am. I was beginning to pity you."

"I don't need pity from anyone." Luke sent him a warning look, although he tried to keep it light, out of respect for the older man. At the moment, Luke wanted nothing more than to be left alone.

"I know you're ready to be rid of me." Oscar's voice was softer now. "But I want you to know that even mere crushes die hard, so give yourself some time." He slapped Luke's back. "Who knows? Before you know it, another girl might come along, one of your own station. A girl you'll truly love."

"I don't want to hear that."

"I know. Get angry at me. I'd rather you do that than mope." The driver winked at him and clattered down the stairs like a kid.

Luke watched him go. He was more uneasy than ever after that conversation. He'd outright lied to Oscar—and Oscar probably knew it, too. Of course Luke would offer for her. But what could he do?

Truly?

How could a man in love with the wrong woman ever make it right?

He couldn't. The knowledge burned, but it cleared a spot in his muddled thinking. His feelings for Janice had jeopardized his mission to help St. Mungo's, but it wasn't too late to fulfill it.

And she might think marriage to his cousin was endurable, but if she found that journal she'd be wrecking her own wedding plans.

The lantern hadn't worked to summon her, so he'd write her a note instead and send it with Aaron.

Chapter Twenty-six

If Janice could never be happy, at least she could learn to be content. She'd become expert at avoiding the duke: never taking her breakfast at the same time and spending most of her day working with the housekeeper, the occasional footman, and Mrs. Poole to improve the dowager's circumstances. When Janice wasn't with them, she was often visiting the puppies in the room by the kitchen, where a small crowd could usually be found, including Mrs. Friday, Isobel, Aaron, and Oscar, for starters.

This morning, the duchess's move to the light, spacious bedchamber in the main wing of the house was now complete. Janice and Mrs. Poole fussed about like excited hens putting everything in the new nest in order. The dowager herself sat by the window in her Bath chair, gazing outside as if she couldn't believe her good fortune.

"I haven't seen this view in so long," Her Grace said. "Every day I'd look out at the trees when my maid dressed me in the morning. My children used to play out front, too. I'd laugh from this very window at their antics and call Liam over. He'd put his arms around me from behind and watch over my shoulder."

Janice felt a twinge of sadness. She remembered

Luke holding her just that way, but instead of standing, she'd been sitting on his naked lap.

"Every night," the duchess went on, "we'd both stand here to gaze at the stars and the moon." She paused. "It was a good life."

"And I'm glad you can tell us stories about it," Janice said.

She and Mrs. Poole exchanged a satisfied glance.

"Your Grace," Mrs. Poole said in an airy manner that suggested she was now happily oblivious to her whistling *s*'s. "Do you want me to remove these books from this shelf? Is there something else you'd like here?"

The dowager winced. "Books? What books?"

"These ones over here." Mrs. Poole pointed to a row of them.

"They're mythology and history books, most of them," Janice explained. She already knew because she'd looked through them as she searched for Emily March's journal.

The dowager put her hand to her forehead. "I-I don't know. Books? Here? This is too much. This is all too much."

Mrs. Poole sped over to her and began to push the chair to the bed. "It's time to lie down," she said calmly.

Janice went to the bed and threw down the covers. "Everything will be fine, Your Grace."

But before they could get her onto the sheets, she sneezed into her handkerchief.

Oh, dear. Janice and Mrs. Poole knew what this meant. The Queen was much more difficult to deal with than the dowager.

Sure enough, the elderly lady looked at Mrs. Poole

with a haughty stare. "I thought I'd gotten rid of the notebook."

Notebook? Janice's heart began to thump hard against her chest.

Mrs. Poole's brows flew up. "What notebook, Your Majesty?"

"*Ss-s-sh!*" She put her finger on her mouth. "We don't want *her* to know." She tilted her head at Janice.

"I'll—I'll walk away." Janice retreated a few steps and silently indicated to Mrs. Poole that they needed their own little conference.

Mrs. Poole came over, her eyes rimmed with worry lines.

"I know we don't want to upset her," Janice whispered, "but please encourage her to talk about the notebook."

"Why?"

"Remember I asked you about Emily March?"

"Yes, and I told you I wasn't here when she worked here."

"I know, but my friend said she left a diary."

Mrs. Poole scratched her temple. "This is all very odd."

Janice hesitated, not sure how much to say, but she needed the woman's help, didn't she? "It's really not," she said. "I have a friend who never knew his mother and would like to find out more about her. This was her diary. He was told that she might have spoken of being mistreated here."

"Really? By the dowager?"

"No, I'm sure it was somebody else."

"I see." Mrs. Poole didn't look very comfortable.

Janice laid a hand on her arm. "Miss March is dead now, but if we could find her notebook, at least my friend would have some peace. I need your help, Mrs. Poole. The Queen won't talk to me. Please."

"All right." Mrs. Poole nodded. "I'll do my best."

"Thank you." Janice threw her a grateful smile.

She walked away but she didn't go far, only over to the window. But Her Majesty's Bath chair, faced as it was toward the bed, prevented the grande dame from seeing her.

"Now, Your Majesty"—Mrs. Poole picked up her hand and held it—"please calm yourself so that you can tell me about this notebook."

"What notebook?" the Queen snapped.

She'd already forgotten about it.

Janice put her hands to her temples and shut her eyes to calm herself. They'd been *so* close.

Five minutes later, Her Majesty was in bed, propped up on her pillows.

If only there was a way to get her thinking about the notebook again . . .

"Would you like me to read you a *book*?" Janice asked her. "There are so many books on that shelf. We should look through them. Unless you want me to find a *notebook* for you."

The Queen eyed her askance. "What nonsense you spout. Get out the cards. We'll play."

Terribly disappointed, Janice dutifully opened the escritoire to look for them. "I don't see them, Your Majesty. Mrs. Poole, would you know where the cards are?"

"I don't think we have any," Mrs. Poole said. "Her Majesty never asked for them upstairs."

That was because upstairs had been like a gloomy dungeon.

The dowager was coming to life again, and it was

good to see. Janice decided to focus on that rather than
the fact that she was getting nowhere with the search
for the diary.

"I'll be right back," she said. "I have some cards in
my room. I keep them in a hatbox. My maid and I often
play."

"Hatbox?" Her Majesty sat up taller on her pillows.
"*You* have my hatbox?"

"No, Your Majesty." Janice looked to Mrs. Poole,
who discreetly lifted her palms and shrugged. "It's my
own."

"I knew you were up to something." The Queen's
eyes narrowed. "The problem with having clever subjects is that they're often nosy, too."

"I'll show you my hatbox," Janice said. "I promise
it's not yours. I'll get it right now." She walked briskly
to the door.

"Don't bother," the Queen said with a sly chuckle.
"You're too late. I moved it."

"Moved my hatbox?" Janice asked her carelessly,
hoping not to overexcite her.

"No. The *notebook*."

Oh, thank heaven. She was on to the notebook again!

Janice's entire body tensed, but to appear nonchalant
she leaned against the doorjamb. "What do you know
about this notebook?"

"She put it in the hatbox," the Queen said as if Janice
were a small child. "And it was in this very room that I
found it years after she'd left, when I'd already moved
to the dower house."

"After who left?" asked Mrs. Poole.

"The girl. Emily." The dowager folded her hands
together.

Emily!

Janice's mouth felt exceedingly dry as she walked to

the bed and tucked the old lady's quilt around her. "What about Emily, Your Majesty?"

She slapped away Janice's hand. "I sneaked over to visit one day when Russell wasn't here. No one tells *me* I can't visit my grandson. I was going to be in a skit with Grayson and he needed me to wear a silly bonnet. I hoped to procure one that was out of vogue from one of the hatboxes in this room. And there it was—the notebook—in the box containing my favorite emerald silk bonnet hat from years before."

"Really?" Janice was so excited, she could hardly keep from doing a little dance. "Why do you think it was there?"

"I think Emily meant for me to find it. But the day after she went missing, I moved to the dower house without taking anything except one bag. Russell was in high dudgeon. I refused to linger, especially as he . . ." She hesitated.

"He what, Your Majesty?"

"He was rude," the old lady said gruffly. "The only reason I didn't send him to the Tower was because he was such a pathetic creature. I should have." She raised a finger. "Remind me next time not to be so merciful."

"Very well, Your Majesty," said Janice. "So . . . the notebook was left, forgotten, all those years?"

"Yes." The old lady shrugged. "It moldered away with all those lovely bonnets."

"Where is it now, Your Majesty?" Janice held her breath. This was it, the moment she'd been waiting for.

"Destroyed," the Queen said proudly.

No.

Janice's chest felt hollow with disappointment.

"I asked my gardener to throw it into the stove in the orchid house." The old lady chuckled. "It's got the biggest fire I've ever seen. I knew it would become ashes in seconds."

"So it's gone then," practical Mrs. Poole said.

The Queen nodded. "And good riddance."

Janice's eyes were stinging and hot. She was upset— much more upset than she'd imagined she'd be. "What happened to Emily March, Your Majesty?"

The Queen stared at her.

"What *happened*?" Janice asked again. "Did someone here mistreat her? Why did she leave? For that matter, why did you, the very next day?"

"Lady Janice," warned Mrs. Poole.

The Queen opened her mouth as if to speak. Her eyes grew confused. Fearful. "No," she whispered. "It's a state secret. You're not privy. It's my responsibility. *Mine*. I should have called the guards. I should have stood up to him."

Janice sat next to her and held her hand to her bosom. "The guards were busy elsewhere," she soothed her. "It wasn't your fault. And whatever the secret was, it's over and done."

"What do you know?" Her Majesty's scorn was palpable. "It's never over. The pain goes on."

"I'm sorry, Your Majesty." Janice held firm to her hand. "If you can't talk about it now, I understand. But I'm here to listen if you change your mind. It can't be easy to keep secrets. In my own family, we've had several that have come out recently. And we've discovered we're much better off sharing them than not."

Mrs. Poole's eyes filled with worry. "Let's get some sleep, shall we?"

The Queen sighed and shook her head. "He left him," she croaked. Her fingers curled tighter around Janice's. "The traitor . . . left him."

There was a beat of silence.

"Who, Your Majesty?" Janice asked gently. She'd hoped they'd talk about Emily, but the dowager's mind flitted about like a butterfly. "Who left whom?"

The elderly woman's rheumy blue eyes were shiny with tears, but her mouth was bitter and unforgiving. "Russell left Everett in the pond to drown. His own brother."

Chapter Twenty-seven

Janice and Mrs. Poole stared at each other.

The last words that Her Majesty—or was it the Dowager Duchess of Halsey?—had spoken were so chilling, the temperature of the room seemed to drop ten degrees. The old lady began to tremble.

"I'll get her a cup of tea," Mrs. Poole said quietly. "I'll get all of us a cup of tea."

But by the time she'd rung the bell rope, the matriarch of the House of Halsey had fallen into a doze. Or was it a faint? Janice wasn't sure. But the old lady's color was good, which was a great relief.

"I'm sorry." Janice backed away from the bed and looked at Mrs. Poole. "I'm so sorry I questioned her."

Mrs. Poole sighed. "Let's let her sleep." She paused. "Perhaps it was good for her to confess such a heinous secret."

As sunny and cheerful as the room was, the atmosphere had changed. It felt as though there were secrets hiding in corners. The disjointed observations of the woman in the bed weren't as easy to shrug off anymore.

Her pain had been real.

"Do you think it happened?" Janice asked Mrs. Poole. "If so, it must be the worst burden a mother could ever bear."

And the worst for a child, too. Russell was the current duke's father. Janice had to wonder if Grayson had heard of any of this.

"I have no idea." The nurse was somber. "As both men involved have passed away, perhaps it's best to let this go. Let's not ask her any more questions about it."

"All right," Janice said. "Although—"

"Although what?" Mrs. Poole seemed prepared to be skeptical.

"If she insists on speaking of it again, I won't refuse to listen. You said it yourself—it might have been good for her to talk about it."

"Very well," said Mrs. Poole gravely. "But we're not going to be Scotland Yard."

"No," Janice reassured her.

Janice left then, and as she walked down the corridor her whole body felt as if it were whirring with extra tension.

What other secrets did the house hold?

And who knew of them?

Fifteen minutes later, she and Isobel were behind the kitchen garden walking with Esmeralda. The dog sniffed the air and trotted happily through the melting snow, her teats swinging from her sagging belly.

"She's enjoying this break from the puppies," Isobel said.

"Isn't she, though?" But Janice was distracted. She couldn't stop thinking of what the dowager had said when she'd been channeling the Queen. "Do you know where the pond is?"

"Over there." Isobel pointed to a distant copse of trees behind the house. "On the other side. What's wrong, my lady? I know you're dreading having to marry the duke, but is there something else?"

"Yes, as a matter of fact. I told you of the long-ago drowning. But I just found out that Everett's brother, Russell, made no attempt to save him."

"That's ghastly." Isobel shivered. "I-I wish I didn't know that."

"Me, too," said Janice. "I don't think that's the story that's told about Everett's death in Town. I seem to recollect my father suggesting he died of a fever."

"So many people do die that way."

"Sadly, you're right. A drowning is something people would recall, however, especially one in which a brother didn't attempt to rescue the victim."

"Why would an entire household stay quiet about that?" Isobel asked. "And how could such a secret be kept all these years? Surely the people of Bramblewood know."

Janice shrugged. "It's a painful memory, I'm sure. Perhaps the family asked the staff not to talk about it. And who knows? The family influence might extend to Bramblewood. Mr. Callahan told me that the duke supports the town very nicely."

"It's such old news now." Isobel bent down to pet Esmeralda, who'd come running back to them after sniffing a nearby holly bush. "I can't imagine it comes up very much."

"Yes. Nearly thirty years have passed." Janice sent the maid a warning look. "I have another unsettling thing to tell you."

"No," said Izzy, who was always prepared for drama.

"Yes," said Janice. "The duchess, when she was very much Her Majesty, told me she'd found Emily March's diary."

Isobel gasped. "That's good news, isn't it?"

"I wish it were." Janice was gripped with intense regret that their search had come to such an unproductive end. "Years after Emily left, the duchess found it here at Halsey House and took it with her to the dower house. I presume she read it, but she gave it to her gardener to throw into the orchid house stove."

"Oh, no!" Isobel's face twisted in disappointment. "Perhaps she can tell you what was in the journal."

Janice shrugged. "It's so difficult getting straight answers from Her Majesty—or the more gentle dowager—that I don't know if we'll ever know anything about Emily March."

Isobel kicked at a snowdrift. "That's a terrible shame. And now"—she looked at her gravely—"you'll have to tell Mr. Callahan the bad news."

Janice's heart ached at the mention of his name. "I can't. And I've already told you that the duke is watching all of us. He told me that if any of my friends get a message to him he'll know, and he'll punish Mr. Callahan accordingly. So please don't attempt to on my behalf."

"I promise I won't. But if the duke hates him so much, why doesn't he simply fire him?"

"I think it's a game for His Grace, that's why. He's hoping I'm pining after Mr. Callahan, and that Mr. Callahan is mooning over me in the stables."

"That's so romantic if you are!" Isobel sighed.

"It's *not*," said Janice. "It's torture. At least for me. I seriously doubt Mr. Callahan thinks about me at all."

"What do you mean? Every night he puts that lantern in the window. That's his way of telling you he's thinking of you."

"That's true," Janice conceded. "But perhaps he's being ironic. He might hope I'll run out to the stables so that he can say he was fooling me and turn me right back around. It would be so humiliating."

Isobel stopped walking. "*Lady Janice.* You mustn't

let your experience with Finnian Lattimore turn you bitter."

Isobel had been privy to that story—at least Janice's part of it, not Marcia's.

"Mr. Callahan isn't like Finnian Lattimore at all," Izzy went on. "He's strong and quiet and sincere. If he didn't like you, he'd take that lantern down. He doesn't play games."

"Perhaps you're right." It was Janice's turn to stop walking now. Esmeralda looked up at her quizzically, and she bent down to scratch her ear. "But the truth is, my dear Izzy, I was playing games with *him*. I can't be with a groom. We both know that."

Isobel's face drooped. "I know," she whispered.

Janice linked arms with her. "I can get away with being close to you because a lady and her maid are together so often and it's natural to feel affection for each other."

Isobel smiled.

Janice smiled back. "Yes, I'm more familiar with you than some of my friends are with their maids, but who's to know? And if anyone did know and objected, I'd tell them to mind their own business. But I could never consort with a man not of my station. It's not done. And for a very practical reason—money and prestige. One would always wonder if he's after those. And as you well know, I want to marry for love, if I marry at all."

"I've heard of some fine ladies running away with their footmen," Isobel said.

"And that causes great scandal. I don't want to bring that upon my family."

"Of course not."

Janice gave a little laugh. "We're getting ahead of ourselves, aren't we? I'm banned from seeing him. So carrying on a torrid romance would require some sort of miracle."

They'd come to the corner of the house, the side facing the stable block. Janice rued that they had. She usually stuck to the other side of the garden, but she'd been so immersed in her chat with Isobel.

And then the worst possible thing happened. Mr. Callahan—*Luke*—walked out of one of the massive arched stable doors.

Esmeralda's ears perked up.

"No!" Janice cried.

But it was too late. Esmeralda took off like a ball fired from a pistol. She knew that groom. Oh, yes, she did. And she was determined to get to him.

Chapter Twenty-eight

"Go, Izzy." Janice pushed the maid in the direction of the kitchens.

"But Esmeralda!"

"She'll find her way back to the house, or someone will carry her back. We can't be seen with Mr. Callahan."

"Oh, that makes me so angry," said Isobel.

"It's how things have to be."

Inside, they were passing through the corridor on their way to the front hall and up the stairs when they stumbled upon the Duke of Halsey. He was opening the door to the library. "Ah, there you are." He always looked at Janice as if he could see that she was a bad girl, even if no one else could.

"Hello, Halsey." She wished she didn't have to be polite. But the man *was* going to be her husband.

He raked her with a too-brazen glance. She'd worn her prettiest day dress—a white muslin with cherry red accents—simply to cheer herself up.

"You look lovely today," he said. "I look forward to outfitting you as my duchess."

She didn't like how possessive he sounded already. "Thank you. I'm sure you know that my mother was a seamstress before she married my stepfather. She'll want to make my trousseau."

"Will she? I hope she's accustomed to dealing with demanding husbands. I insist on approving every gown, especially the ball gowns. You must outshine every woman in the room."

She saw a spark of lust in his eye that made her rather ill.

"I'm sure Mama will enjoy your opinions," she said, folding her hands together. "If you don't mind, I'm going upstairs"—Isobel cowered behind her—"to rest for a while."

"Of course. But I've a note here for you." He pulled a square, folded sheet of paper from his coat pocket. "One of the junior grooms brought it to Cook last night. She was supposed to give it to your maid, who was then supposed to give it to you. But I managed to intercept it."

He didn't explain how, which she found disconcerting.

"A note?" she asked faintly.

He was about to hand it to her—she put out her fingers to grasp it—when he drew the missive back and chuckled like a rude schoolboy.

"Fine," she said, utterly frustrated with him. She wouldn't enter into his games. She'd learned that indifference was the best way to annoy her brothers when they attempted to tease her.

"I was only jesting, my lady." He relented and gave her the folded piece of paper. "You must know that."

Her heart sped up when she saw her name written in a familiar handwriting on the front. It was from Luke. She immediately thrust it back at the duke. "I don't want it."

She brushed past him, Izzy staying close beside her.

"Are you sure?" Halsey taunted her.

Her face burned. "Yes, I'm sure!" she called over her shoulder.

She heard him laughing, and then there was the shutting of the library door.

What had the letter said? She was dying to know. And had Halsey read it yet? No doubt he had. He was probably gloating over it at that very moment.

She was so upset that she didn't notice the butler opening the front door.

There stood Luke, holding Esmeralda in his arms.

Dear heaven. His nearness made Janice stop in her tracks. Isobel actually bumped into her from behind.

"What are you doing coming up the front steps?" the butler scolded the groom.

Luke.

Janice's heart nearly burst with wanting him.

"Ask the dog," the groom told the butler, but his eyes bored into Janice's. "She scampered up here and put her paws on the front door, and I went after her. It seemed rather silly to scoop her up and walk all the way around the house."

"All right, then," the butler conceded. "On your way."

Luke dropped Esmeralda gently to the threshold, and she scampered over it, straight to Janice.

But Isobel scooped her up. "I'll take her to her pups," she said, and she hastened away.

Thank goodness. Janice didn't want to leave the black marble tile she stood upon at that moment, and no doubt Isobel knew that.

Luke put his hand on the doorjamb. "I'm going," he told the butler, "but can you tell me why the cellar door is never locked on the east side of the house? Shouldn't it be?"

"Why does it matter to you?" the crotchety old man answered him. "We've got nothing worth stealing in there. We use the cellar on the south side and always lock it. What were you doing there anyway?"

Oh, dear. Janice had to move, in case Halsey emerged from the library—or the butler was one of his spies. She couldn't simply stand there gaping at a groom.

She walked to the stairs and started up them.

"I wasn't there," Luke said in that imperturbable way he had. "A junior groom told me he'd seen His Grace's hounds nosing at it. Two of them managed to lift one of the doors an inch, but it slammed back down before they could get in. It wouldn't please the duke to lose one or more of his hounds down there."

"Hm-m-m," the butler said. "You've got a point. I'll get someone to secure it tomorrow."

And then Luke disappeared.

The butler started to shut the door, and raw misery washed over Janice.

"Wait."

Luke again! Janice's heart lifted at hearing him speak.

The butler heaved a heavy sigh. "What is it?"

"I might as well tell you," Luke said, "that there's a card game tonight in the stables. We start at midnight and end at three in the morning. Want to join us?"

"Of course not." The butler huffed. "No decent person is awake at three in the morning. You'd better watch yourselves out there. The duke wouldn't approve."

Janice did think it rather odd that Luke would ask the butler to play cards. He simply wasn't the type.

"Three in the morning *is* awfully late for most people," said Luke. "You know the superstition, don't you?"

"No, and I'm not interested in hearing it." The butler's testiness would have made Janice laugh under other, less stressful circumstances.

"Oh, but it's fascinating," Luke said anyway. "You can't lie in the dead of night. Ask someone anything at three in the morning, and they're compelled to give you an honest answer—if they're brave enough to be awake then, that is."

"Or stupid enough," added the butler.

Luke chuckled. "Be careful what you say—I hear the duke is often awake at three in the morning."

"Not lately he's not. His friends have left, so he has no reason to be."

Janice scampered on silent feet up the rest of the staircase and stood back in the shadows.

"Right," Luke said cheerfully. "Don't forget about that cellar."

"I won't," snapped the butler, and slammed the door shut.

Janice took off down the corridor, her mind racing. What had taken her so long? Of course Luke wasn't interested in playing cards with the butler—and he knew that the man would decline the offer.

Luke had been speaking to *her*.

The cellar. At three in the morning.

It was an extremely crude way to communicate. But she understood.

And terrified as she was to risk Halsey's finding out— not to mention that cellars weren't her favorite places— she'd be there.

Chapter Twenty-nine

Would Janice understand? Would she know to meet him here?

Luke wrapped the blanket closer about his shoulders. He'd stolen over a whole half hour early to be certain that he'd have the place ready—which meant he had a lantern burning very low and another blanket for her.

That desperate babbling he'd done with the butler . . .

It was because Janice's blue eyes, wide with the shock of seeing Luke, drove him to come up with a crazy plan to see her. He'd tried not to care that she'd ignored his note, but of course he had. He cared very much—to the point that every step he took, every word he spoke to the other stablemen, even his usual chores, was agony. At the very least, he wanted to know why she'd completely cut him off. It had taken everything in him when he saw her not to storm into the house, throw her over his shoulder, and carry her back to the tack room, their trysting place, to get some answers.

Now he listened—and hoped—through the deep silence, which was broken by the occasional creak of some unknown beam above his head and the sough of the wind. It was utter madness, he knew, to expect her to understand that he wanted her to come to the cellar at three in the morning. But at some point after the sun rose that day, the butler would see that a lock was put on it.

If they were to meet there, this was their last opportunity.

He pulled out his pocket watch. It was three o'clock. His heart rose, then sank.

As the next ten minutes passed, he vacillated between frustration that she hadn't understood his covert message, depression that she might have understood it but *ignored* it, and fear that she'd tried to come to him but been caught.

The last possibility drew beads of sweat to his temples.

However, he didn't hear anything. That was a good sign. Of course, the house was vast, but surely he would have heard something if there had been a conflict.

One of the doors shifted. Every fiber of his being tensed. *Let it be she.*

He moved to the corner nearest the entrance and waited. Contrary to what he'd told the butler, the doors were tightly fitted. No way a dog could have nosed one of them open. Neither could a beam of light from within the cellar escape. But what if Janice had been nabbed, after all, and this was a footman come to drag him away to be beaten? Or jailed?

What if it was Grayson himself?

Luke had no weapon but his fists, and now they clenched, prepared to slam into the face of anyone who meant him—or Janice—harm.

"Luke!" came the soft whisper.

It was as if a knot of rope in his chest came undone. He rushed to the door and held it up.

"Come in," he said, his voice warm with welcome.

All fear of discovery took a backseat for that one, incredible moment.

She'd understood. And she'd risked everything to see him. She either had not gotten the note or been afraid to answer it.

Clad only in a night rail and a shawl, she pushed her way through the small crack she'd allowed herself at the door and shut it gently behind her. When she descended the steps, he lifted her at the waist, brought her down snug in front of him, and kissed her.

Here, he said to himself. *This is it.* Finally.

The place where he felt safe and loved.

If his life were a song, that moment was its glory note.

"Oh, Luke," she whispered again, in between the kisses he rained all over her mouth, her eyes, her nose, her jaw. . . .

"You're here," he said.

"Of course I am," she said softly, and drew his head down for another long, passionate kiss. "I've been utterly miserable. Halsey is forcing me to marry him. He says he'll hurt you badly if I don't."

Everything in Luke froze. "So he knows about us?"

She nodded. "He discovered me coming back in with hay in my hair."

It wracked Luke, knowing he'd put her in danger. He gripped her shoulders gently. "Are you all right? Has he tried to punish you in any way? Because if he has, I'll—"

"I can take care of myself," she interrupted him firmly. "But I'll admit I can't seem to get out of this. My parents and various and sundry siblings are coming this afternoon to first inspect him at close range and then give their blessing to the union."

"Then you must say no," said Luke. "When your father arrives, you'll be well protected from Halsey's wrath. Tell your parents you're being coerced."

"No." She smiled tenderly and pushed a lock of hair

off his forehead. "I wouldn't dare. I can't put you a risk."

"I'm not." Luke tilted up her chin. "I've been on my own since I was eleven. I've endured countless threats to my person."

She chuckled. "Your nose—handsome as it is—attests to that fact."

"So it does." He pulled her closer and kissed her thoroughly again, this time skimming up her night rail to caress her shapely leg.

She grinned and shook her gown down. "Your seduction skills, excellent as they are, won't make me stop talking sense to you. Luke, he's a duke. He can do anything he wants—have you arrested on false charges, deport you, even kill you, and get away with it."

"It won't happen." He attempted to assure her more by kneading her shoulders. The cleft between her breasts was just visible, making him hungry to worship her body more thoroughly. "As of later today, consider yourself a free woman."

"No," she protested.

"Yes," he insisted. "You can celebrate returning to London with your parents. You can't be with Halsey and be happy."

"I don't care about my own happiness. I only want you to be safe."

"But I'll slip away, too. And it will be as if this whole sorry episode with the Duke of Halsey had never happened."

At those words, she pushed off his chest, her eyes stricken. "How can you speak so easily of my leaving?"

"You know I don't want you to go." But what choice did he have but to let her?

"Well, I'm *not* going. I don't care what you say—I can't put you at risk. I would be terribly unhappy in

London not knowing what happened to you. Every day I'd wake up and wonder if you were in jail or, God forbid, dead in a ditch somewhere."

Her voice cracked, and she sank to her knees. Her eyes shone with unshed tears.

Blast it all, he hated to see her so low. And all because of him. He knelt beside her and took her hands. "You *have* to go," he told her softly. "You can't marry the duke. I can't see you throw your life away on him."

Her breath hitched. "Whether I'm in London or here, I'll have a life without you. So what does it matter?"

She shut her eyes, and a single tear fell out, which he brushed away with the pad of his thumb.

Ah, his heart was sore. "You have a chance for happiness in London," he said huskily. "It's better for you to go."

Better for her.

Not for him.

But he must say it.

"You're wrong." She had a stubborn light in her eye. "I'll be happy nowhere. So I choose to stay here and marry the duke. At least I'll have his word that he won't come after you. That will be my solace."

Luke sighed. "You can't trust anything he says."

She shook her head. "You're only making things worse."

"And I mean to." He stood and pulled her to her feet. "Go back to London with your parents. I want *you,* at least, to have a life again. And you will. It may take time, but you will."

She looked up at him from under long, damp lashes. "You mean, you won't?"

Damn his own hide for revealing too much. It wouldn't help her to know that he'd suffer.

"Will you miss me that much, Luke Callahan, that you won't have a life without me?" she persisted.

There was a long beat of silence while he considered what to tell her. He looked into her eyes and saw all his hope for happiness there. When she was gone, that hope would turn to dust.

How he wished she'd never inspired it in him in the first place!

"You're afraid to say it, aren't you?" Her voice was almost triumphant. "But it's too late. You said it. You admitted that you'd have no life without me. You care about me that much."

He glowered at her. He'd nothing left with which to defend himself. She'd taken it all.

All.

His entire life was in her hands, and he was suddenly angry. "I was fine before you came, do you understand?"

"I-I know, and I'm sorry—"

"You wrecked all the notions I had about how to live." His wall was in pieces now, crumbled all around him.

"Truly, I'm sorry."

"Do you think I can go on, knowing you've given yourself to a scoundrel?"

"You don't have to." She grabbed his arm. "You haven't considered another option. I'll run away with you. I don't care about my title and wealth. I don't care that you're a groom and I'm a lady. Let's run away. Let's go *now*. I love you. And even though you haven't said it outright, I know you love me."

He pulled away from her. "We can't do that." It was the most ridiculous notion he'd ever heard, and it riled him that she was playing so free and easy with her life.

"Why not?" Her face was still alight with that damned hope. "Of course we can!"

"No." He knew it down to his very bones. "*No,* we can't."

"Why not?"

Because he wasn't worthy of her, that was why. Because he didn't deserve the privilege of even being near such an angel, a tender young woman with so much love in her heart that she was willing to throw away the grand life she was meant to live to be with an ex-boxer, a soldier, and a stableman.

She didn't know it, but he'd crush her. He was a man with no understanding of how to love. He didn't know how to live among people and give them what they needed. He was a walking disaster who'd only bring her pain.

He swallowed. "You're not going to throw away your life on me."

"I won't be; I'd be gaining it," she said with such fervor it seared his soul.

"You'd be throwing it away," he insisted. "And as such, I won't consider running away with you. Do you understand?"

She stared at him, her face white.

Good. Let her hate him. "And I won't let you marry Halsey," he added roughly.

She shook her head. "You can't stop me. I will marry him, damn you! I will!" She pushed on his chest. "If you won't run away with me, that's what I'll do."

"Janice—"

"So which will it be? You and me, together as husband and wife? Or me . . . the wife of the man sleeping above us right now?"

"Neither," he said. "You'll go back to London an unmarried lady. And you'll wait for a husband who can treat you the way you deserve to be treated: with respect and love."

She gave a short laugh. "You're not that powerful, Luke. You may be able to crush my love under your feet—for that's what it is, *love*—but you can't make me do anything I don't want to do."

"I can talk to your father about Halsey—"

"Yes, and I'll tell him you're a highly unreliable source of information. You're a groom in the stables. A disgruntled one."

Frustration made him furious. "Listen to me," he said, holding her tight. "Trust me when I say you're not safe married to Halsey. Not only is he a danger to you; I plan to bring him down. And I don't want you suffering with him."

"Bring *him* down?" Janice gave a short laugh. "How do you propose to do that? And why? What has he ever done to you? Does this have anything to do with your mother and her mistreatment? Because I'm sorry to tell you—truly I am—but that diary was destroyed. The dowager gave it to the gardener to throw into the stove house oven. I wanted to tell you, but I couldn't get you a message."

It took everything in him not to react.

His mission . . . gone.

The nuns.

Still vulnerable.

His mother and father . . .

Unavenged.

Janice must have sensed his devastation. "Look," she said softly. "Even if you did find evidence of your mother's mistreatment in the journal, the current duke isn't responsible." He stared at her, unseeing. "Listen to me, Luke!"

He focused back in, reluctantly.

"The one responsible would be someone else," Janice said, "and except for the dowager, the other mem-

)ers of the family are dead." She took a deep breath. "I
lid learn something of interest about this family's past.
Something huge. But it appears to have nothing to do
with your mother."

"What?"

"About that drowning . . . the dowager said that
Halsey's father, Russell, left his brother, Everett, to die."

Luke's entire body was blindsided by a new wave of
shock at hearing actual details of a family picture he'd
been barely able to piece together.

"I get the impression Everett's death was by ne-
glect," Janice said. "Russell simply walked away from
the pond as his brother struggled. It was all I could get
out of the dowager."

Luke shook his head. What a family he came from.
Such evil. Such cruelty. And his two parents both appeared to have been victims of it.

"I know it will be difficult to move on considering
that your mother's history here apparently wasn't pleasant," Janice said, "but I must remind you of a simple
fact: Halsey's a powerful duke who can't be held responsible for what happened to her. You're a groom
with no influence whatsoever."

"Am I?" He held her close. "Have I no influence over
you?" She turned her face aside, but he turned her back.
"You know I do."

She said nothing, but her eyes were stormy.

"And I plan to use it," he said. "You're going to say
yes to me right now. And later today, you'll say no to
the blackguard upstairs when he delivers his official
marriage proposal. You'll remember what I told you—
that you can never be his. And it's because you're mine.
You've made me admit it. Now face the consequences."

Chapter Thirty

Luke slanted his mouth over Janice's and kissed her fiercely.

She wanted to resist him. She did. She was furious a him. "I hate you for not running away with me," she whispered.

"But you love this," he said, caressing her breast "You love what I can do to you. Admit it."

"Never."

It was cold in the cellar, but heat emanated from both of them. The lantern light threw the shadow of their bodies in profile on the cellar wall, and the dusky odor of earth reminded Janice how primal was her attraction to this workingman. According to society, he wasn't fit to look her in the eye.

But he did now. And he did it as if he was not only her equal. For this moment, he was her master.

"Take off your night rail," he told her.

He was clearly giving her no other choice.

She stared at him a long moment. His eyes held so much in their sapphire blue depths. But he refused to let her see.

"I'll agree to your game." She took a step back. "But beware. I'm playing my own." She pulled her gown over her head. "This is what you'll be missing," she taunted him, "as you won't run away with me."

The chill air hit her nakedness like a bucket of cold water, but the look in his eye made her hot with wanting him.

"Damned right I won't run away with you," he murmured. Slowly, he came up to her and laid a kiss on her shoulder. Then he cupped her bottom, none too gently, and rubbed his rough man's hand over it. "Those lacy drawers . . . where are they?"

"I left them off," she said, "for you." She paused a beat. "Idiot. You could have this every night. Every day."

"You're the fool, young lady," he said into her ear, "if you even consider for one second marrying that excuse for a human being upstairs." He teased open her lips with his tongue and explored her mouth with rakish abandon, the way he had the very first day they'd met. And then he moved a hand to her breast, rolling his palm in a circle over the taut tip.

More! her body shouted.

Her back arched, bringing her bare belly into contact with his male hardness, frustratingly concealed by his breeches. When he leaned down and suckled her nipple with his supple mouth, a shot of pure pleasure raced to her feminine core like lightning. And when he put a hand between her legs, inserted two fingers inside her, and rubbed her hidden pearl with the pad of the same thumb that had wiped away one of her tears, she sucked in a breath and moaned, her pelvis rolling over his fingers again and again.

"Luke," she whispered, "you know you have me. You can have all of me. Why are you torturing me so?"

But he wouldn't answer. Instead, he picked her up, laid her on the blanket, and knelt before her. The ground was hard beneath her back, but she felt no pain, only an exquisite sort of agony. She'd go through anything for him.

Anything.

He tore his shirt over his head, and she basked in the sight of his muscles—they bulged enticingly on his upper arms, made armor out of his chest, and rippled over his taut belly. She reached up to touch him, but with barely the touch of his finger to her breastbone he signaled that she must lie back down again. She did, the place between her legs moist and aching for his touch. But he rolled to his feet and, with total control and confidence, undid his breeches and stepped out of them.

"Luke!" she cried. "Please. Come here, and let me touch you."

"Talk is cheap." His chiseled mouth tilted on one side. "Show me that you want me to."

She was afraid. But she lifted her hand to her own breast and cupped it. "Here," she murmured. "I want your mouth here."

The cool air pebbled her nipple, but Luke didn't move.

"Is that all?" He crossed his arms over his chest. "You're very much a lady. We don't belong together, you and I. I'm not a gentleman, and never will be. Too many nights I've slept outside, beneath trees, in back alleys. I've heard people rutting in dark corners, and I've seen people knifed. Pretty pretending is for people like you, people who can afford to pay off the rest of the world to conceal its ills from you. I don't want to be a part of that world. Where I am—as lonely as it is—is real. This is who I am, my lady." He slid his hand once up and down his erection. "A man of simple pleasures. A man who wants to take you deep into the heart of carnal pleasure, so deep you'll lose that mask you wear when you're afraid."

She couldn't look away. "But I told you I'd run away with you!"

"You want to run away with me so you can hide."

"*No.*"

"But it's why you came here. You're not willing to stand up to the world you already know and claim your rightful place in it. I won't have any part of hiding who you are. Ever."

"You're wrong," she said. "I might have been afraid, but that was before I met you. Let me show you who I am." She spread her legs wide and reached down a hand to touch that smooth cleft between her thighs. "I'm a woman who wants you. Who craves you inside me." She swirled her finger over the center of her pleasure, and the small of her back lifted off the ground. "I'm not a simpering miss. I'm bold. I have a voice."

"Let me hear it then," he said. "Unfettered."

She stared into his eyes and fondled her breast with one hand. With the other, she ran her own finger into her slick core. "See?" she said, her breath coming in shorter gasps.

He squatted next to her. "All the way," he said. "On your own. Do you have the fierceness to stand up today against the duke?"

"Yes." She closed her eyes and thought only of Luke and his glorious body, the epitome of male beauty.

"What about your family?" he asked her. "They want you well settled. A duke will do nicely."

"No," she whispered. "I want *you.*"

A moan came from her throat, and her pelvis lifted into the air. She was on the sweet, slow precipice of a great release when she felt his teeth graze her nipple and then gently bite it. The crude, possessive action send her crashing over the edge into wave after wave of bliss.

She whimpered when she fell back to the blanket, and Luke moved his mouth from her breast to her lips, kissing her hard and hungrily. "You were made for this. Made for me."

She knew that was true and luxuriated in his posses-sion of her. With him, she could let go—she could stop being the lady—and still be safe and adored. "We're not finished," she said. "I need you inside me."

"No." He ran a hand down her belly and back up again. "That can't be."

"I hate your stubbornness," she said. "But I'll have you. I'll have you now, in my mouth. And I'll not take no for an answer."

"You're a stern taskmaster yourself." He grinned and lifted her up beneath her arms—she still felt rather like a limp rag doll—and scooted beneath her.

She was thrilled to be seated on his lap, his erection pressing against her bottom.

"I'll allow it," he said into her ear. "On one condi-tion. This sensual act, while highly pleasurable, is rather unpolished. I'm not sure a lady like you will go along with it."

"Your challenges don't faze me," she said. "See what you're forsaking, Mr. Callahan?"

"I know very well, but enough of that sort of talk. Now follow along. I'm going to put you on top so you have more control."

"Me in control? I thought you said you weren't a gentleman."

He lay on his back and turned her around so that her thighs were spread over his face and her mouth was above his erection, which stood at full attention.

"It's not gentlemanly at all to put you on top," he said, looking down at her. "It's very self-serving, I as-sure you."

"Goodness." She giggled. "You're upside-down. This *is* rather unpolished. I can't possibly look like a lady to you from that end."

"You're right. You look every inch the delicious heathen." And to encourage her along those lines, he drew her waiting, wanting feminine sheath to his mouth and twirled his tongue inside her.

"Oh!" she cried, her elbows collapsing beneath her. Her face lolled mere inches above his manhood. "How convenient," she murmured, and, while she was wracked with her own pleasure, encircled the tip of his erection with her mouth.

Luke groaned—right over that small button of flesh that craved his touch—and sent even more luscious vibrations through her.

For several minutes, they teased each other this way. Janice was determined to bring Luke to pleasure first, but she couldn't last—his skills as a lover were so great, she was on the brink of falling into another piece of heaven before she knew it.

Then, out of nowhere, he stopped loving her with his mouth. "Tell me you won't marry him," he said.

"I can't promise," she whispered, the juncture of her thighs throbbing with need of release. "What if he threatens to kill you otherwise?"

"I told you I can take care of myself. Tell me *now* that you won't marry him."

"I won't marry him," she said, and meant it. "I'd rather live alone the rest of my life on this memory with you than marry him."

Luke chuckled deep in his chest. "Good." He paused a beat. "I mean the part about your not marrying him. But you shouldn't be alone, Janice. Promise me you won't let that happen."

"No," she whispered. "If I can't have you, I want no one else. And this time, Mr. Callahan, I won't budge. Now let's get back to what we were doing."

He sighed against her thigh. "You'll change your mind about that being alone. You'll get over me, my lady."

"No, I won't," she said.

He grabbed her thighs and pulled her close, and in seconds she was climaxing against his mouth while her own tongue swirled in mad abandon about the smooth granite of his erection.

He came then, too, strong and true, and she was with him the entire way, never abandoning him once as he pulsed and bucked and groaned his satisfaction.

She rolled off him onto her back, her arms and legs like rubber and spread wide. "If that's not proof that I'm not always a lady . . ."

He reached over and caressed her leg. "You're perfection."

Her heart soared with happiness. She was with her man like no other.

Luke.

And then her beloved sat up on his elbows. "When we go our separate ways," he said soberly, "know this: you have my heart."

The very words filled her like nothing else could.

"But in the world we live in, my love"—still he caressed her—"a heart is not enough. You need security. Companionship."

"You're wrong!" She sat upright and pulled away from him. "You're so wrong, Luke Callahan. But it's not your fault. You never learned about love—yes, you had the nuns, but you never learned about love close-up."

She leapt to her feet and pulled on her night rail.

He stood, too. "I know I didn't. Don't you see? This is why we don't belong together. We believe two totally different things. You believe in hope. I believe in seeing the worst-case scenario right away and preparing for it. You don't believe me now, but the further you get away from me, you'll realize how ill-matched we are. And when you do, you'll look back at this moment and be glad I didn't hold you to your plan for us to run away."

"I beg to differ," she said. "You'll look back and rue the fact that you turned me down."

She went to the door and looked back at him. "It's not too late," she said. "I'll be waiting for you. Every night, for the rest of my life if I have to."

But he didn't understand. He was still too worried about her. His gaze was almost pitying.

"You're the one who needs pity," she said, "because as you reminded me tonight—and have every time we've been together—people are bigger than their circumstances. But you don't apply that same lesson to yourself. You're a coward, Luke Callahan, as strong as you are, as clever as you are. True survivors open themselves up to the world, pains and ills and all—and let it in anyway. They live, in other words. They don't merely exist, as you do."

She pushed open the door to the cellar, hoping he'd come behind her and pull her down and say, *Let's go, right now. Let's run away!*

But he didn't.

No. He didn't.

Her eyes stung with tears. Her throat tightened as she tried to hold back the grief and, yes, her fury at him. Quietly she shut the door behind her.

Not a peep of lantern light shone through. She could no longer smell his skin, the salty aroma of his sweat and his seed. She couldn't see his eyes, touch his face.

They were over, she and Luke, by his choice.

It was a foolish one.

But she loved him all the same. She loved her broken man like no other—

All the same.

Chapter Thirty-one

When the four glossy, unmarked carriages came rolling up the drive in the early afternoon, Janice's heart—which was so bruised after her middle-of-the-night encounter with Luke—swelled with relief at the sight, and her eyes welled up.

Her family!

She could survive anything with them nearby.

"There's an awful lot of them, isn't there?" Halsey said in his cool, ducal manner.

But she sensed his unease. "Yes, there are." They were standing next to each other in front of a large drawing-room window. Mrs. Friday sat on the other side of the room, and as usual, she was peacefully sewing. The hounds had taken to her. One rested its face on her slipper. "They're like ants, my family is," said Janice, "always multiplying, it seems. But I like it that way."

"Right," he said dryly.

"I intend to have eight children," she told him, just to be wicked.

"Eight?" His beautiful brow puckered.

"At least," she said blithely, and thought, *But not with you.*

It would be with Luke or with no one.

She might as well tell Halsey now so that he could prepare himself. It would hardly be fair to wait. Of course, he'd never been fair to her, had he? Coercing her into agreeing to his unofficial proposal?

But she wasn't he. She had more integrity and kindness than he ever would, and she wouldn't be brought down to his level.

"We'll wait outside," he told her.

"Not yet," she answered. "There's something I must tell you first."

"Yes?" He put his hands behind his back and lowered his brow at her.

His fondness for her defying him obviously had worn thin. He wanted control now. Nothing more. It just went to show how cheap were his thrills, how little there was beneath the surface.

She peeked over his shoulder at Mrs. Friday, who didn't seem to notice their tension, which was a good thing. Janice didn't want to embarrass Halsey any more than she had to. "No matter how you threaten me," she said low, "I won't marry you, Halsey. And I intend to go home with my family tomorrow."

It would break her heart to leave Luke. But what could she do? He'd have nothing to do with her.

Halsey's expression didn't change, but his gaze was flinty. "You *will* marry me. If you won't see reason, your father will."

"He cares more about my happiness than reason." It was what she loved best about him.

The duke scoffed. "Those Irish."

She nearly kicked him in the shins. "You'd be lucky, sir, to have a little Irish in you. Perhaps it would make your heart softer. How you could ever wish to coerce a woman into marriage is beyond me."

His eyes flashed with irritation. "Outside, madam. We'll see what's what."

She stood on tiptoe to see her friend. "Mrs. Friday?"

Janice's chaperone looked up, her face alight with interest. "Are we ready? I can't wait to meet the family."

"Yes," said Janice. "And you'll love them, I'm sure. Please don't be intimidated by them, even when they talk over one another. They mean well."

Mrs. Friday laughed. "I'll be sure to give everyone the benefit of the doubt."

The duke was pouting. He still appeared regal and commanding, but there was a noticeable crease on either side of his mouth as they walked outside. Janice didn't care. He'd been warned.

In the hall, she remembered that Isobel would like to be there greeting the family, and she assumed Oscar already knew out in the stables. So the butler sent a maid to the room off the kitchen to retrieve Isobel, where she was keeping the puppies and Esmeralda company.

Janice, Mrs. Friday, and Halsey made it to the bottom of the front steps just as the carriages rolled up to the door. Thankfully, numerous footmen had already stationed themselves outside to greet them. The ubiquitous hounds poured out the front door, baying, but with one snap of the duke's fingers they sat quietly near him, their haunches quivering in excitement.

Janice refused to wonder what Luke was doing. No doubt he'd help with the horses. But it was his own fault if he came over to assist and she didn't look at him. Let him wonder what he was giving up.

Once again, she was overcome with relief from her anxiety when she saw everyone getting out of their vehicles. Much of her family were here: Mama and Daddy; Marcia and Duncan and their three children, Joe, Caroline, and Suzanne, all of whom must have been in London visiting; and Janice's siblings Peter,

Robert, and Cynthia. Gregory was still living in Paris with his Pippa and their darling Bertie, but that was all right. They were due to arrive back in London in a few days for a visit.

Janice was glad to see that Marcia and Duncan had brought a special guest with them, too, the Duke of Beauchamp, who was practically a member of the family. His ruddy, expressive face looked up with such delight at seeing Janice, she laughed out loud. One never knew if Beauchamp was going to be in a good mood or bad, but he never hid his emotions and even when he was in a bad mood he was somehow charming.

One always knew where one stood with him. Perhaps that was one reason he was a compelling figure—that and the fact that his own brand of ducal authority was so much more substantial than Halsey's, Janice realized now. It was because Beauchamp had a heart—a loving, big heart—whereas Halsey appeared to have none.

Funny, Halsey and Luke were alike in some ways: neither had grown up with much love, it appeared. Halsey had had his grandmother and mother to a limited extent. And Luke had had his mother for a short time and the nuns. But Luke, although he shied from relationships, was capable of tender feelings.

Why wasn't Halsey? Was it born in him to be so hard? Or was it a choice he'd made?

Of course it was a choice, she told herself. He didn't deserve pity. And she wouldn't give it to him. Neither, of course, did Luke, although she'd told him she'd pitied him today to rile him. He would hate that she did.

She hoped her so-called pity would give him pause.

Janice, of course, had eyes only for her parents as the crowd merged together and came toward her.

Mama threw open her arms, and Janice ran to embrace her.

"Mama." She squeezed her hard. "I'm so glad you're here."

Janice's sweet-smelling mother pulled back and smiled at her broadly. "Darling, how fast things have changed!" She looked Janice up and down. "You've become a woman in love! I can see it in your eyes, dearest." She gave her a kiss on the cheek.

Janice's heart broke once more hearing Mama say that. She *was* in love—with a man she couldn't have.

"Mama, there's so much I need to explain. Look for Mrs. Friday—she's my chaperone."

"So the duke told us in his letter. The dowager was unable to serve in that role?"

Janice nodded.

Mama's eyes grew large. "Whyever not?"

"She—she's addled," Janice said. "She thinks she's the Queen."

"My goodness." Mama's face paled. "The duke didn't mention that."

"But it's not all the time," Janice assured her. "And she's quite all right, once you get to understand her."

Mama regained her usual brisk manner. "Well, I'm sure you did a beautiful job sorting it all out, and I can't wait to hear all the details."

Daddy, too, hugged Janice as if she'd been gone for ages rather than a few weeks. "We'll need to talk," he murmured in her ear. "I won't give a word of consent unless this is what you truly want. I don't give a rabbit's foot that he's a duke."

"But I thought you and Mama were anxious for me to marry him if I could," she said back.

The hubbub was making it easy for them to speak up without really having to whisper.

"Oh, parents can get a little too set in their expectations, sometimes," Daddy said. "You know we only want what's best for you, darling girl."

He looked straight into her heart with those big Irish eyes. She hadn't planned to tell him until later, when they could be alone.

"Janice?" he asked with such love, she swallowed hard.

"I don't want this, Daddy," she said in a ragged whisper. "Help me get out of it. Please."

"I suspected as much," he said.

"How?"

"You could have gotten a letter to us, too, but you didn't." He squeezed her arm. "Consider it done. We'll talk after it's all over."

"I love you," she managed to say before she was pulled away by her younger siblings, Cynthia and Robert, who insisted on showing her Robert's black eye, which he'd received in a terrible fight he'd gotten into at Tattersalls with another young man who'd accused him of poor taste in horses.

"Robert," Janice chided him, although in the back of her mind she was still back there with Daddy, "you believed him?"

"No," Robert said in his light Irish accent, "but I was looking for a good excuse to fight. So was he. It was a grand one, too."

Cynthia rolled her eyes. "Men are so uncivilized."

Janice couldn't help thinking of Luke and his knuckle boxing. She'd heard him discussing it with Aaron. "I hope you kept your shoulders down," she told Robert. "That way you have greater power behind each punch. If you hunch up, you're going to lose."

She showed him how when he pivoted from the waist with his punching arm at the ready the leverage behind his punch was far greater when he kept his shoulders down.

His eyes widened. "What's happened to you?"

Cynthia asked the same thing.

"Nothing." Janice shrugged, and with an inward smile went to greet the rest of the family.

No one mentioned anything about her unofficial engagement. Not even Cynthia and Robert. They knew that Daddy had yet to have a private meeting first with Janice and then with the Duke of Halsey.

The small children were hugged and fussed over by Janice and then taken upstairs for their own tea with Isobel. Oscar, who'd come jogging over to greet Janice's parents and the rest of the family he called his own, returned to the stables, well satisfied that all had arrived without mishap, including the horses.

Janice, of course, noticed with a heavy heart that Luke never appeared in front of the house to take any horses with the other stablemen, three of whom she'd seen assisting Oscar.

But she wouldn't think of Luke. She simply wouldn't, although her back was sore, her breasts tender, and the V between her thighs still tingled at the memory of what they'd done together in the cellar.

For the rest of the party, tea was served immediately in the drawing room, along with thin slices of buttered bread, tender roast beef, and fine cheese. Beautiful iced cakes were available, too, along with strawberries, grapes, and sparkling wine. Halsey was at his best, Janice noticed: formal but polite, witty on occasion, and even slightly warm. He was well able to carry his own with Daddy and the Duke of Beauchamp. He never appeared to be overwhelmed by the loud buzz of conversation.

Mrs. Friday, too, seemed at ease, which Janice was so pleased to see.

"And how is Her Grace?" Mama asked in the first lull of conversation, which didn't occur until everyone had their cup of tea in hand.

Janice knew that Mama was extremely curious about what had happened to the dowager.

"Well, thank you," said Halsey, "as much can be expected for someone in her condition."

Everyone was too polite to ask him for more details.

Janice rushed in. "She's such a dear, and she's in a new bedchamber now—we moved her. I felt she was too cooped up—"

"By her own choice, of course," said Halsey. "Your daughter, Lady Brady, reminded Her Grace that there *is* a world beyond the confines of her room, for which I'm grateful."

Mama looked well pleased.

"A man doesn't always notice these things," Halsey went on. "I tend to hole up in my library, hunt, or hang about the stables when I'm out in the country. Speaking of which, I need to get you men out there to tour them."

"That's a fine idea," Daddy said with his usual affable charm, but behind it Janice could sense him taking the man's measure.

Sitting next to him, she could even *feel* the way Daddy was ready to protect her. It was his favorite thing, to look after his family, and he excelled at it.

"How's the estate faring?" the Duke of Beauchamp asked Halsey.

"Tolerably well," he said. "I'll be happy to show you around. We've made some improvements."

"Those are always good," Duncan said with a friendly smile. "We'll have to compare notes sometime."

"And backing up my father, I'm keen to see your stables," said Peter, who was horse mad, as all good Irishmen were.

Looking about the room, Janice was vaguely alarmed. Everyone seemed to *like* Halsey. Marcia and Cynthia were already beaming at him as if he were their new brother-in-law. Good God, everyone but Daddy was beaming, not just Janice's sisters.

Halsey took it in as if he expected it.

Which he did, of course.

Janice was so relieved that she'd already spoken to Daddy, or she'd have felt very alone. It was going to be extremely difficult to disappoint this entire room of people.

"You wrote to us of your grandmother's orchids," Mama said to Halsey. "Do we have time to see them today?"

"Mama's been talking of nothing else," said Marcia, "and I confess, I'd love to see them, too."

"Peter and I can stay behind," said Robert, "to tour the stables. Would you mind, Mama?"

"Not a bit," she said. "In fact, let's break up—the women shall see the orchids, and the men may go see the duke's horses."

Halsey agreed that this was an excellent plan, although Beauchamp overrode it and said he'd prefer to stay behind and visit with the dowager. Another cacophony resounded as everyone spoke at once.

"We'll find a moment to talk," Janice overheard Halsey tell Daddy.

"Of course," Daddy replied.

Janice sighed, dreading the eventual conflict. She hoped Halsey would bow out gracefully, but she doubted it. He'd promised a good fight, but if he was clever he'd see that Daddy was no man to roll over and give up if he had something at stake.

Which he did—Janice's happiness, as he'd reassured her.

She would trust in his skills as patriarch of the family.

Meanwhile, she had to think about when to tell Mama and her sisters. She dreaded the carriage ride to the stove house and the inevitable questions about her whirlwind courtship with the duke.

Chapter Thirty-two

Janice needn't have worried about the ride to the stove house. Cynthia told her all about her latest shopping activities in London, and then Marcia outlined all the details about the upcoming Christmas pageant at Oak Hall, which they began preparing for months in advance. Mama even had a story to share about one of the servants, who had married a servant from a neighboring house.

It was all very breezy and comforting.

When the carriage passed the Oriental gazebo and Cynthia rhapsodized over it, it was Janice's first uncomfortable moment. The memories she associated with that gazebo weren't at all fond ones.

But she maintained a cheerful expression anyway, especially when they arrived at the dower house and were greeted warmly by the house staff. After Mama graciously declined tea on all their behalfs, they strolled down the stone path—now clear of all traces of snow—to the stove house, where the elderly gardener welcomed the ladies with his usual good cheer.

The introductions were made, and he rubbed his hands together in obvious delight. "You've caught me at a good moment," he told them. "I'm potting quite a beauty."

"Show us," said Mama.

"An orchid man always likes an enthusiastic visitor," he told her.

"No one is more keen to admire and learn about orchids than my mother," Janice told him.

Marcia and Cynthia followed behind and looked about the stove house in wonder.

"Isn't it amazing?" she asked them.

"Yes," they both said together.

All of them listened in rapt attention while the gardener told them how difficult it had been to grow the variety of orchid he was working with in that pot. "Let me show you what it looked like a month ago."

"How will you?" Mama asked him.

"I illustrate them." He walked to his shelf and took down a book. It was the same one he'd shown Janice.

"He does beautiful drawings," Janice explained.

They crowded round to see the sketches. Mama was especially taken with one variety that he no longer had in the stove house.

"It died," he said. "Sometimes you do everything you can, but we're not in their native habitats, so often, they don't thrive. It makes the ones that survive all the more precious."

"Yes," said Mama.

"I do have some other pictures of that variety," he said. "And I know exactly what notebook it's in."

They waited patiently while he brought back another. When he flipped through the pages and they oohed and aahed over his pictures, Janice couldn't help noticing that it was an accounting book. The pages on the right had numbers on them. He wrote only on the pages on the left.

"Why do you have this accounting book?" she asked him.

"I scrounge about for paper." He chuckled. "My

mother taught me never to waste a thing. Whenever His Grace's secretary finishes with one, he copies it over into a fancier book for the duke's review and gives the old books to me. Occasionally, I'll buy a new one, but most of these are used."

Janice's heart thudded hard against her rib cage. "Does—does anyone else give you half-used notebooks?"

"Hm-m-m . . . not really. Although the dowager did once, and the vicar at Bramblewood had a brand-new one he gave me out of the kindness of his heart. On the dowager's behalf, I'd given him an orchid for the church and a picture of one for his mother."

"How kind of you," said Mama. "The duke is fortunate to have you in his employ."

"I'm going to sketch a special orchid for you," he told her shyly.

Mama had won over another man without even trying. She always did.

But Janice couldn't care at the moment. No, her heart was pounding so fast, her hand trembled when she laid it on the gardener's forearm. "Did you burn the notebook the dowager gave you?"

"Of course not," he said proudly. "I never do." He looked at Mama again as if she understood him best. "And Her Grace came in here raving like the Queen, the poor old thing, demanding it go straight into the bowels of the oven. I waited until she left and popped it on the shelf with the others."

Marcia and Cynthia exchanged shocked glances.

"Find it, please, sir." Janice knew she sounded shrill. "I need that notebook!"

"All right," the gardener said slowly. "I'll get it right now."

Janice let out a little sob.

"What is it?" Mama took her arm and squeezed it. "You're scaring me."

"Yes," Marcia said, her eyes registering alarm. "Janice, you're white as a ghost."

"And you're on the verge of tears." Cynthia was always one to point out the obvious.

"Can I get you some water?" asked Mama.

"No, thank you." Janice inhaled a breath. "I'll explain in a moment. First—"

The gardener was already upon them with a pale blue notebook. "Here it is, my lady."

"Thank you," Janice whispered, and took it with trembling hands. "It never occurred to me to ask you if you had it—the dowager said it had been destroyed, and she was so convincing, I never dreamed you wouldn't have followed through."

"The Good Lord likes us to use things up, don't He? So I wasn't disobeying, exactly." The gardener scratched his head. "All right, I was, but don't go telling the dowager." He chuckled. "Her Majesty might chop off my head."

Her sisters looked to Janice to explain, but she'd no time. She'd do so later. As she flipped through the notebook, her fingers shook more and more. A woman's scrawl filled every page of the first half. The second contained sketches of orchids. "I need a moment, please, everyone. And then I promise to explain oh, so much. I know you're worried, but please bear with me."

"Take what time you need," Mama said.

Quietly her family moved away with the gardener.

Passages in the notebook leapt out at Janice as she progressed, forming a basic story.

It was shocking. Terrible. And the courage of Emily March so moving that Janice found herself crying.

But the most shocking part of all?

Learning that Luke—her Luke—was the rightful Duke of Halsey. Now not only were her fingers trembling; she began to shake all over.

"Mama!" was all she said before they were upon her. A black curtain fell before her eyes, and she fainted.

When she awoke, Cynthia held her in her arms.

"I caught you," her little sister said with a sparkle in her eye. "You fell onto Mama's shoulder and then sort of went backward and I was there."

Janice felt awful, but she had to smile. "Good for you. Thank you, dear."

Marcia was already at Janice's side with a cup of water from the gardener's own pitcher. Janice took a sip and felt instantly better.

Mama took her hand. "Darling, what happened? What's inside that notebook that's upset you so?"

"Oh, no." Janice's eyes flew wide open, and she sat up. "Where is it? I need to hold it all the way back to Halsey House."

"I've got it." Marcia reassured her with a smile. "And I'll hold it for you. I promise."

"Good." Janice exhaled a shaky breath. "You won't believe how important it is. I'll explain in the carriage."

Of all the ridiculous moments of his life, this one had to be the most extreme, thought Luke.

Grayson—damn his filthy soul—demanded that Luke be the groom to accompany the men on their perusal of the estate on horseback.

"You'll come with us," Grayson ordered that morning.

Luke should have quit right then and there. His cousin was taking a great deal of spiteful glee in exposing Luke to the pain of losing the woman he wanted. Now the farce at the gazebo made so much more sense—Grayson had found out the evening previous about Luke and Janice.

Nothing was keeping Luke here anymore. The notebook was destroyed. His only hope now was to go to every church in each corner of the kingdom and look at their registries to see if his parents' marriage had been documented. He'd already searched all the parishes within a three hours' ride of Halsey House, but there were hundreds more to check.

It would take him at least a year, probably more.

And meanwhile, Sister Brigid and her orphanage would have to keep Grayson at bay as best they could. Luke hoped that his cousin's fervor to find his uncle's missing child would wane as the mantle of duke weighed heavier upon his shoulders—if it ever did.

In a man with integrity, it would.

Luke ignored the inner voice that reminded him that if he was ever able to prove his own ducal rights he'd take the money and run, leaving all ducal responsibilities behind in the hands of solicitors, accountants, and managers.

But that's different, he thought. *I'm not able to do the job.*

He had no real education. He had no experience in the glittering world in which a duke moved. Indeed, it would be laughable—a true farce—to expect him to take the reins of power.

Anyone in his path should go running and screaming away if he was ever deluded enough to believe he could honestly be the next Duke of Halsey with any measure of success.

"Groom!" Grayson called now.

They were approaching one of the estate farms.

Luke wished he could feel a burning hatred of the man, but all that was in him was disgust and annoyance. Grayson was like a sticky piece of tar stuck to one's shoe.

"Yes, Your Grace?" he answered politely enough.

"Lead the way over this ditch," Grayson said. "It's spongy from all the snow."

The implication was that Grayson didn't want to face any unexpected holes in the ground. His prize horses were too valuable to lose one to a broken leg. Luke did as he was asked, carefully walking his horse across the sunken area—the ground was firmer than he expected—and everyone followed behind.

He'd come on this little expedition for one reason only: He wanted to get to know the men in Janice's family a little better before he left her for good. He couldn't do so with a clear conscience if she was returning to the protection of selfish bastards or absent-minded fools.

He was almost sure they must be all right before he'd even met them, because Janice obviously loved them a great deal. And he was nearly certain they were satisfactory replacements for his protection upon first observing them in the stable block.

But a little extra reassurance wouldn't hurt. And what he'd found was that he outright liked them: the marquess; his son-in-law, Lord Chadwick; and the marquess's two sons Lord Peter and Lord Robert.

Luke grew more convinced, as the ride progressed, that Janice would be—if not happy without him—at least well taken care of. He could trust these men to cajole her into rejoining their world and making a good life for herself among her own kind, supported by the bosom of her family.

While Luke remained in the saddle, the others alighted from the horses and met a tenant farmer in his field to discuss some improvements he was making. Lord Chadwick—the one his brothers-in-law called Duncan, seemed particularly interested in the conversation. Indeed, he and the farmer got so deep into it, the others wandered off. Lord Peter and Lord Robert went back to their horses to admire them. And Lord Brady and Grayson stood off to the side, talking. But it was actually Grayson doing all the talking. Lord Brady appeared to be listening intently.

Lord Brady's wary stance set off alarms in Luke's head. They were discussing Janice. He was sure of it. At this very moment, Grayson was making an offer for Janice and Lord Brady was being a cautious father, as he should be.

Luke felt almost dizzy and clung to the pommel of his saddle. Slowly, carefully, he exhaled a shaky breath. *Don't get soft,* the old mantra came back to him for the millionth time. *Get ahold of yourself.*

But it wasn't working. His heart slammed against his ribs. Sweat clung to the shirt inside his coat, which felt heavy and too hot.

Lord Robert approached, almost shyly. "Some of the fellows in the stables told us you were a prize knuckle boxer. Is that so?"

Luke nodded. "It is."

His visitor asked him another question, but Luke was distracted. He couldn't stop looking at Grayson and the respectful way Lord Brady was nodding in response to his words.

No!, everything in Luke shouted. *No!*

"What was that you said?" he asked Lord Robert.

The young man chuckled. "I asked your name."

Finally, Luke looked down to him, into those light-hearted eyes. He saw a boy who was almost a man, Lord Robert hadn't quite grown into his skin—the same way Aaron hadn't.

But Luke was nearly thirty.

By now, he should have become a man.

But he wasn't. Not yet.

He'd thought he was, yes. For many years now, he'd been the tough boxer, the soldier in the trenches, and the man in the stables his workmates called upon to lift the heaviest equipment.

But he wasn't fully a man.

He hadn't claimed his name. He'd only learned it a short while ago from Sister Brigid, and he thought he hadn't needed it. He was a wanderer, after all. But he'd not only been drifting through the world—he'd been running away from standing up for who he was and what he believed. He'd given himself no real power beyond his fists.

They'd only served to protect him from his own self-doubt.

Doubt that he could truly help the nuns in the way they needed help—from a person of authority willing to speak up on their behalf, not a midnight visitor who left them money on their doorstep on the same day each year and then fled until the following year.

Doubt that he could be of any help to Aaron, a boy only looking for some decent guidance and some hope.

And doubt that Luke could win the love of a good woman. He had never even considered it—

Not until Janice came along.

The enormity of this revelation—that he was frightened, that he believed himself unworthy of *happiness*—

was tempered by the knowledge that she'd told him just that in the cellar.

She'd pitied him. She'd seen straight through to his heart and recognized who he really was—a man on the run from life.

And she'd loved him all the same.

"Are you all right?" Lord Robert squinted up at him.

"I'm fine." He slid off his horse. "And my name's Luke."

Really, Lucius Seymour Peter George Hildebrand. Not that Lord Robert needed to know such a long name—yet.

Luke began to walk toward Lord Brady and Grayson.

Lord Robert trotted after him. "Would you mind giving me a boxing lesson? When we get back to the stables?"

"I'll be glad to," Luke allowed him to catch up, and they walked side by side. "Only if you remember this—most boxing matches aren't about fighting at all. They're about defending your body and your pride. But if you don't have anything to be proud about—nothing deep inside you that you're willing to fight for—what's the point in defending yourself? You might as well let them break your nose."

He'd be sure to tell Aaron that—and, while he was at it, give the boy a hug. A real one. And he'd tell Aaron that he wanted him to consider Luke his father—or older brother. Whatever he preferred. For now, Luke slapped Lord Robert on his side with the back of his hand. Boys liked that kind of rough treatment, too.

The young man grabbed at his waist too late and laughed. "You have a point there."

"I bloody well do," said Luke.

Now Lord Brady was talking. Grayson's brow

furrowed, and he began to speak again. Lord Brady
crossed his arms and nodded gravely.

"Wait," said Lord Robert. "I don't think we should
join them. They're probably discussing Janice."

"Yes, you wait here," Luke said.

Lord Robert stopped. "But Luke!" he called. "I really don't think—"

Luke ignored the boy's protest and continued on.

Grayson called out to him, "Don't interrupt us,
groom. Get back to the horses!"

Lord Brady watched Luke with interest.

Luke didn't break his stride. "I'm not going anywhere until I talk to the marquess."

"How dare you?" Grayson put his hands on his hips.
His expression was aggressive, to say the least. "Get the
hell away from here before I fire you, you bastard."

"I quit anyway." Luke came up to the two of them
and stood his ground as only a practiced boxer could.
He put every ounce of intimidation he could into his
own stance.

Lord Brady's face took on a new, hard-edged qual-
ity. Gone was the affable gentleman entirely. "I don'
know what's happening here—"

"I can tell you right now," Grayson said. "This man
seduced your daughter."

Before Luke knew it, Lord Brady had Luke's lapels
in his brawny fists. "What's His Grace talking about?"
He gave Luke a hard shake.

But before Luke could answer, Grayson said, "I offered for her anyway. In fact, thanks to me, the disgrace
will go untold. So I think you should reconsider, Brady
Your daughter may have said she didn't want me, bu
does she really know any better? She's in the throes o
calf love. She can't see straight—thanks to this scoundrel. I suspected she'd tell you to turn down my offer

t's why I brought him along today, so I could point him out to you."

From the look of him, Lord Brady was ready to throttle Luke to within an inch of his life. "Is any of his true? By God, if you've hurt her—"

Luke heard shouting behind him, the stomp of running feet. Within seconds, he felt the others at his back. He was in for a serious beating if things didn't go his way. Even he couldn't stave off five grown men and a boy.

Make that four men. Lord Chadwick quietly asked the farmer to depart. "Family matter," he said.

"Of course," answered the farmer.

Luke waited a few seconds for the man to go, then said, "I ask that you hear me out, Lord Brady."

The older man's eyes smoldered with banked fury. "That's not a good sign. No, indeed, it's not." His Irish brogue was stronger than it had been earlier at the stable block.

"Listen to him, Father," Peter said. "Every man deserves a chance to defend himself."

Lord Brady still held to Luke's jacket. "But you don't know the crime he's accused of," he chastised his son. "I'm ready to rip him from limb to limb."

"I can guess," Peter said coolly. "Even so, you know t's only fair to give him a chance to speak."

Lord Brady pushed Luke away. "All right, then." He waved a belligerent hand at Luke. "Commence explaining." He looked at Robert. "Get out of here, scamp."

"But Father, I'm nearly a man," Robert protested. "Let me stay."

"Yes, let him," said Lord Chadwick. "He needs to learn what it means to be a proper man."

"Do I have no authority here?" Lord Brady shouted. "Do my own sons challenge me?" He glared round the collection of males behind Luke. He could only imagine the extent of their dismay—the marquess was fierce when he was angry, like an Irish chieftain chastising his wayward foot soldiers.

"I'll go then, Father," said Robert, sounding disappointed. "But I like Luke. I don't believe he's done anything wrong."

Luke was touched by the young man's faith in him. He didn't deserve it, however. He'd done his share of wrong, and he was willing to own up to it.

"Aw, stay," Lord Brady said to his youngest with a scowl.

"Thank you, Father." Lord Robert's voice cracked. "But if you all think to gang up on Luke, it's only fair he have a man on his side. That would be I."

"And I'm lucky for your support, Lord Robert," said Luke without looking back at him.

Grayson eyed Luke with a sneer. "Go ahead and make excuses, you lout, but they won't work. Lady Janice herself tacitly admitted to what I just told Lord Brady."

Luke folded his arms and gazed steadily at the marquess. "I'm here to say I'm guilty of loving your daughter, my lord, and I want her to be my wife. I'm asking you for her hand in marriage right now. She loves me. And I love her. I'll fight until I win her. And for the rest of our lives together, I'll fight to make her the happiest woman on earth."

There.

He was standing in the truth. *His* truth. And it felt like nothing he'd ever done before.

Lord Brady's face registered shock, but he managed to get it under control almost immediately. He exhaled a deep breath and skewered Luke with an ominous look. "Will my daughter back up your claim?"

"Yes," he said. "She will."

"Then I'll withhold judgment until I speak to her," the marquess said.

"Wait, Brady." Grayson's scorn was palpable. "You're not actually considering his offer, are you?"

Lord Brady looked at the duke with a mildly annoyed expression. "I'm making no decisions about anything without hearing my daughter's say in the matter."

"He's a *groom*," Grayson said. "For God's sake, man, do you Irish have no pride?"

Lord Brady whipped around and grabbed Grayson's jacket. "Take it back," he said, "unless you want your face to look like one of those Irish potatoes you Sassenach love to partake of at all your meals."

"All right," Grayson said, clearly rattled. "I'm sorry."

Lord Brady shoved him hard—just as he'd done Luke—but Grayson couldn't hold his ground as well as Luke could. He stumbled and nearly fell. His cool aplomb was nowhere to be found.

It had been a long time coming. Only Luke wished he'd been in Lord Brady's place to deliver that ducal set-down.

"The ladies can't get back soon enough," Lord Brady muttered. "Let's go, boys."

He ignored Grayson.

Hell, Luke would, too. *Let him take care of his own horse.* It was a great feeling not to have to *Your Grace* the blackguard anymore.

Riding back, Luke let his horse gallop down the old farm road toward the stable block. Fighting out in the open was so much more fulfilling than making the occasional sneaky jab, he thought. It left him vulnerable to attack, yes, but *bring on your worst,* he thought—

He was ready.

Chapter Thirty-three

Janice knew her luck wouldn't hold out for long. The trip back to Halsey House in the carriage made up for the uneventful one they'd taken to see the orchids.

Mama was shaking her head. "Are you telling me you're in love with a groom?"

Janice nodded. "But he's really a duke. And I don't know if he knows it. Good God, I didn't know it until reading the notebook."

Marcia took her hand. "As outrageous as all this sounds, the sitting duke wouldn't be the first to hold a title he shouldn't be in possession of. I wonder what he knows about the whole business?"

"I wonder, too," Janice said. "Luke was very cagey about telling me anything about his search for the diary, other than the fact that his mother was likely mistreated and he wanted to find out more. But was he actually looking for it to prove his claim to the title?"

"You'll have to ask him," said Mama.

A dark shadow moved across Janice's heart. "I-I'm almost afraid to—because if he did know and he intentionally didn't tell me, then I can't trust him."

Marcia sighed. "Men often think that by shielding us from certain things they're protecting us. Don't be too hard on him if that's the case."

"Cynthia, put your hands over your ears," said Mama sternly.

Cynthia, eyes wide, did as she was told.

"Hum," Mama added.

Cynthia began to hum.

"You call him Luke," Mama said to Janice.

Janice blushed. "Yes."

"I presume that if you're in love with him and you call him Luke you two have had opportunity to spend private time together."

Janice was hesitant to nod, but Marcia squeezed her hand. "Yes, Mama," Janice said, "we have, but you don't have to worry."

Cynthia cast a sideways glance at her mother. She was still humming a nameless little tune that only added to Janice's agitation.

"Oh, take your hands off your ears." Mama pried up her youngest daughter's cupped palms. "You'll have to learn of these things soon enough."

Cynthia dropped her hands and grinned, apparently astonished at her good luck.

Mama looked round at the three of them. "As you well know, love is a necessary ingredient in a marriage, whatever the Polite World says to the contrary. And one of the best parts of loving your husband is what takes place between the two of you in the privacy of your bedchamber."

"And sometimes elsewhere," Marcia interjected lightly.

Cynthia's mouth stayed closed, but her eyes grew round as saucers.

Mama glared at Marcia. "This is not the time."

Marcia patted her mother's knee. "Mama, we mustn't make the girls too nervous. I know you don't mean to, but—"

"But what?"

"You sound a bit stuffy."

"Me?"

Marcia nodded. "Marriage can be quite amusing," she told her younger sisters. "Let's leave it at that."

Mama's pretty forehead puckered but quickly smoothed out. She couldn't stay angry for long when all three of her daughters were smiling at her. "My point is that if you love a man enough to want to be with him that way, I certainly hope you'll do every thing in your power to win him. Sometimes men can be a bit, shall we say, blind to the obvious."

Marcia nodded vigorously. "They're lovely just the way they are, but occasionally they need to be re minded of how lucky they are to have you in their lives."

"Yes," said Mama. "But it shouldn't have to happen often. He should be running after *you*—and not the other way around."

Janice's heart sank at that.

"Is he not running after you, Janice?" Cynthia's beautiful head tilted in curiosity.

Janice shook her head.

Mama and Marcia exchanged concerned glances.

"But it's because he's a groom," Janice explained. "A young lady of the ton can't marry a groom."

"You mean the way a marquess can't marry a seam stress?" Mama said coolly.

Cynthia gasped. "But Mama, *you* were a seamstress. And look at you!"

Mama patted her leg. "Yes, I know, dear. That's my point."

Everyone laughed.

"I'm sorry," Janice said to her mother. "I should have thought of you and Daddy."

"It's all right," Mama replied, "but if it's love—true love and not mere infatuation—then it's enough."

"I know about infatuation." Janice wasn't embarrassed to admit it. "I had that with Finn. He was handsome and witty, and he hung on my every word."

"Tell me about it," said Marcia, chuckling.

They exchanged a private smile.

"Just look at Daddy and me," Mama reminded them. "Whoever thought a lowly seamstress could rule his brawny Irish heart? And that I'd discover a marchioness in me just waiting to come out?"

All of them laughed so long that Marcia had to wipe her eyes with her handkerchief. "You did find her, Mama," she said. "Sometimes I forget that you weren't born and bred to your position."

"Neither were you." Mama smiled. "Neither as an earl's wife or as headmistress of a fine girls' school."

"But love changes everything," Cynthia piped up. "Pippa says it all the time. Her uncle Bertie told her so."

"Well, Uncle Bertie was right." Mama patted Cynthia's hand.

Janice sighed. "I wish Luke believed so, but he doesn't. I told him that he doesn't know any better. He's never been in a family. He's never seen that you can take an impossible situation and make it better. They were so busy at the orphanage, he never got much attention. And the nuns were always struggling. He saw nothing fixed. And then he ran away."

"That's a shame." Marcia sent her a solemn look. "Do you think he loves you?"

"I know he does." Janice gazed into her lap and thought about their time together in the cellar. "He admitted it, although he didn't mean to."

"He's afraid," Mama said.

Janice looked up at her. "That's what I told him."

The carriage rolled quietly on for a few minutes.

"What are we going to do when we get back?" asked Cynthia. "Janice, you can't marry the Duke of Halsey now. Oops, I mean the *pretender*."

Mama sighed. "Darling, we mustn't call him a pretender. He might know nothing of his family history. We need to give him the benefit of the doubt until all this is sorted out."

"All right." Cynthia leaned her head on her mother's shoulder. "I hope it's resolved soon. I want to celebrate *something*." She sat up. "Who ever thought you'd marry?" she asked Janice. "I was beginning to wonder. Your beaus dropped off last Season so precipitously, it was like you had the plague."

"Cynthia!" Marcia chided her.

Mama, too, glared at her.

"Sorry," Cynthia mumbled, two stains of red on her cheeks. "I didn't mean to sound rude. I only meant that it made no sense to me. Janice, you were as pretty and agreeable as ever."

"It's all right, little sister," Janice said. She could discuss that prickly issue with equanimity now. "I know my beaus disappeared. And one reason is because I was afraid to be myself. I was hiding and didn't want to make waves, to the point that I became invisible and . . . lost my own way. But no worries, I've found it again."

She'd never tell them the other reason—the malicious gossip about her sleeping with Finn. And now she wondered how much influence it had really had. Perhaps she'd seemed an easy target.

But from now on, she'd create her own impressions, and she'd start with singing. It was an important part of who she was, and she no longer wanted to ignore it.

Luke, too, was an important part of who she was.

If only he could see it, too.

"I can't wait to show him the diary," she told her mother and sisters. "I'd like to talk to him alone first, if you don't mind."

"Of course," said Mama. "We'll all exit the carriage as if we know nothing. This is a delicate matter, and I trust you, Janice, to handle it that way."

"Of course," she said. "By the way, Daddy already knows I don't want to accept Halsey's offer."

"He does?" Mama sat up straighter. "How did you manage that?"

"Before you even came into the house, I told him," Janice said.

"Before you knew Luke was a duke?" Cynthia asked.

"Of course," said Janice. "I don't care about that. If I did, I'd marry the current one."

Cynthia grinned. "That's right." She turned to Mama. "What will happen after Janice speaks to Luke?"

Mama looked round at them all. "We'll just have to believe what we believe—that love can work its magic, even if things get a bit messy."

"They're bound to," Marcia said with a shrug.

Janice looked out the window and saw the house looming. Her heart pounded as she thought of giving Luke the diary.

And then she thought of the dowager. What would she think of having a new grandson?

Surely she'd be pleased. And now Janice knew what the duchess had meant when she'd gotten confused about which young duke Janice was referring to. All along, somewhere in her memory, Her Grace had known she had a missing daughter-in-law and a missing grandchild.

In fact, she knew he'd been a boy.

Which made Janice wonder if the dowager had traced Luke as far as the orphanage and then lost the trail.

"Why are all the men out there standing in a half circle with their arms crossed?" Marcia craned her neck to see out the other window, where the stables were visible.

"Something's happening." Mama's voice was taut with concern.

"And that something looks like trouble," Cynthia whispered.

Chapter Thirty-four

"They're waiting for us," Janice said.

She was right. Halsey waved a hand. Instead of the carriage going straight to the front door of the house, it went to the stable block.

"It's a better place to fight," Cynthia said glibly. "Lots of open space. Near the house you have all those hard stone steps and those holly bushes. I'd hate to be thrown into one of those." She shuddered.

Everyone stared at her and said nothing.

She shrugged. "I'm only saying."

Janice hated to agree with her, but she was sure Cynthia was correct. Daddy must have had his talk with Halsey.

The carriage rolled to a rather abrupt halt. The driver, obviously, was excited by the scene awaiting them.

Janice peered up at the windows on the second floor of the stable block. Sure enough, there was Oscar's round face, Aaron's, and five other stablemen's, all watching from an open window—

And waiting.

Was anyone watching at the house? She imagined Isobel, Mrs. Friday, Mrs. Poole, and even the dowager and the Duke of Beauchamp might be. Heavens, probably everyone in the house was glued to a window.

"Here's the book." Marcia handed it to her and kissed

her cheek. "It doesn't look as though you'll get that private time to speak to him first. Good luck."

"Thanks." Janice said a quick prayer and got out first. But she waited until her mother and sisters were behind her.

She skimmed the faces in the semi-circle. Their gazes were grim and the mouths straight lines—save for Robert's. He couldn't help the glimmer of excitement in his eyes and a quirky little grin. He knew what was coming. Boys would be boys, so she couldn't fault him.

Janice swallowed the dry lump in her throat. What *was* coming?

A queasy stomach compelled her take a quick glance at Mama over her shoulder for comfort, and Mama smiled. *You can do it.*

But do what? Janice wasn't sure. She needed—

She needed Luke.

She swiveled her head back to meet his gaze and felt calmer. She'd been so nervous when she'd first descended from the carriage, she hadn't really looked specifically at *him*. But there he was—so distinguished with that slightly crooked line of his nose making his handsome face all the more endearing.

He was so manly.

And sweet.

He smiled at her, and immediately hot tears welled her vision.

She had hope.

Hope.

And this time he'd given it to her—not the other way around.

"You can be with other people, Luke Callahan," she said aloud to him. "And you're good for them. You're good for *me*."

Her words echoed off the stable block wall.

Halsey stepped forward and flung his gaze at Daddy. "What did I tell you? She's got stars in her eyes."

"That she does," said Daddy, his tone sober. But he didn't say more.

It seemed he was waiting, too.

Luke stepped forward. "I'll say it here before the world. I love you, Lady Janice Sherwood. And I'll fight for you with every last breath in my body."

He did? And he would?

Everything became a starry blur until she wiped her eyes. "But there are things we've yet to discuss. Things in this book." She held it up.

"Whatever it holds, it doesn't change anything," Luke said. "We belong together. And from now on, your story will be mine. And mine will be yours."

Their gazes locked, and she read in his a new boldness that had nothing to do with how well he could intimidate—which he could, of course. She knew that from her own first meeting with him. But where he used to push away, he now seemed open. His hands hung relaxed at his sides. His eyes, always so hooded with mystery, were clear and bright.

"The groom's desperate words mean nothing," said Halsey, richly dressed in fine riding tweeds. "I've already proved to you that I'll overlook your poor judgment. This is your last chance, Lady Janice: Will you say yes to the duke? The man who can give you everything you've ever wanted? Or shall you throw it all away"—he looked coolly down his nose at Luke—"on *him?*"

There was a long silence. Janice's heart was beating so hard, her knees almost gave out from under her. But she knew her answer very well.

"Janice?" Daddy called to her. "What say you?"

She straightened her shoulders, stood tall, and looked at her father. *"I say yes to the duke."*

There was another beat of silence before noise erupted from all corners. On the second floor of the stable block, words flew about the fight that was sure to ensue. The duke's hounds began to run circles around the crowd. Peter and Robert loudly exclaimed over Luke's tremendous boxing skills, which they lamented they'd now never have in the family. Duncan told them to shut up, repeatedly, and then he grabbed their arms and bent in to speak to them privately, after which they calmed down.

Halsey kicked a stone toward Luke and snickered. "Get lost, cretin. I should call you up before the magistrate for your willful disobedience. Go now, before I change my mind."

Luke ignored him. Janice could see Luke was puzzled by her declaration. But he wasn't terribly worried. At least not yet.

Daddy said nothing. But he scowled at everything he took in with that bright blue Irish gaze of his. He wasn't happy—he wasn't happy at all. And the world would know. Michael Sherwood, the Marquess of Brady, wasn't one to hide his strong feelings.

Janice's mother and sisters gathered around her.

Mama sighed. "You're torturing your father."

"I know," she said. "I couldn't resist. The Irish in him will love the irony when it's all over."

Marcia released a happy sigh. "Actually, I'm pleased Daddy's upset. This must mean he likes Luke. He always scowls like that when he's disappointed."

"I can't believe you chose Halsey," said Cynthia, and laid a hand on Janice's arm. "Please reconsider. Look how lonely Luke is. And he's so much more handsome than the duke. His Grace looks like he should be thrown into a mud puddle to loosen him up a bit."

"Be patient," Janice whispered, amused that her little sister didn't comprehend what she was up to. "You'll see."

She raised a hand in the air, and the noise died down. "I'd better explain further." She looked at Halsey. "I said yes to the *duke*. But I'm turning you down, Halsey. If I were you, I'd cling to your grandmother's affection. You're going to need it. You're going to need *her*."

"What the devil are you talking about?" Halsey's composure was cracking. Beads of sweat dampened that beautiful lock of hair over his eye.

"Yes," said Daddy. "What's this about, young lady?"

Duncan and her brothers also looked mystified.

Janice held the notebook aloft again. "Within these pages is an eyewitness tale of the origins of Luke Callahan, born to a mother and father separated by tragedy in a family with dark secrets. And that family is yours, Halsey."

"That's ridiculous," he said, but his face paled.

"There will be plenty of time to tell the entire story," Janice said calmly to the astonished males standing before her. Luke himself was riveted by her words. "But the duke I say yes to marrying is Mr. Callahan. He's Halsey's legitimate cousin—older by two years—and as such is the rightful Duke of Halsey."

Luke stared at the notebook and then at her, his dear face alternating between disbelief and hope.

"Is it so?" he asked her.

She nodded. "The church, the day, everything."

Halsey's expression was black. "You bastard," he said to Luke.

"Apparently not," Luke said. "I told you I'd protect this estate, and I am. I'm protecting it from *you* and your selfish aims. Your father knew I was out there somewhere and passed his worries on to you. Why else would the nuns at an orphanage two hours' ride away be subject to your threats?" He got up to Halsey's face and stuck a finger on his chest. "Stay away from St. Mungo's," he said in a murderous voice. "They're under my care now. It doesn't matter how many weeks, months, or years it will take to sort out this mess with the solicitors, but as of this moment, your harassment of them will cease."

"We'll back you up on that, Callahan," said Duncan. "Attempt to harm a hair on his head, Halsey, or cause the orphanage any more trouble and the Houses of Brady and Chadwick will seek you out and make you pay a severe price. That's a promise."

"Indeed, it is," said Daddy.

"And ours, too," said Peter, throwing his arm around Robert.

"I can speak for myself," Robert said.

"You're not allowed to promise to punish anyone, Lord Robert Sherwood!" called Mama. "You let the older men handle this!"

"Mama!" Robert's cheeks flamed. "All I was going to say is that we should stop calling him Halsey. That's *Luke* now."

He pointed at the groom who would be duke when everything was sorted out properly, which it would be, Janice knew.

"As he's to be Janice's husband, and my brother-in-law," Robert continued, "I'll be the best knuckle boxer at Cambridge when I go."

"That's years yet!" Cynthia called to him.

"Only three!" he protested. "Imagine how good I'll be by then."

Cynthia made an exasperated face, the kind only sisters can make at recalcitrant brothers.

Halsey scowled round at them all. "I won't let this happen, I'll have you know. I'll fight you every inch of the way." He pointed to Halsey House. "I'm going back there now, and *I will not be removed*. Is that clear?"

"Of course you'll stay." Luke's voice was quiet. "This is your home. We can't expect you to leave—and no one here wants that sort of estrangement. If *you* do, that's your choice. But you've got yourself a cousin. And soon, a new sister. Not to mention all of her family." He turned and gazed at everyone as if he couldn't believe his great good luck. "And I promise you that you're Halsey," he added, "until the world accepts our change in circumstance, and not before."

The duke who was not the duke glared at him. "I'd sooner walk the plank than admit our blood connection."

"Fine." Luke shrugged.

And everyone began to talk at once in the usual Brady way.

Janice had to chuckle. What Halsey said or did didn't matter anymore. It was going to be a rude awakening for him, and if he was clever he'd cling not only to his grandmother but also to the olive branch Luke had just offered him.

But he stormed off to the house, his coattails flapping behind him, his hounds nipping at his heels.

"I'm cold," said Marcia suddenly. "We're all cold. Let's follow Halsey inside and have tea. Perhaps we can convince him to join us. If the men desire something stronger, we've got Daddy's whiskey. Actually . . . all of us can have a dram. This has been quite a shock for everyone, has it not?" She spoke in her confident headmistress's voice that Janice knew she'd never be able to acquire, but she didn't care anymore.

She wasn't sure how she commanded attention, but she obviously had. A proposal from two dukes in less than three weeks! She was exhausted, quite frankly.

But the best part was that one of them she loved with all her heart.

Isobel was going to be over the moon with joy. So would the dowager, Janice hoped. And so would Mrs. Friday, her new friend.

Janice looked yearningly at Luke. Would he never come to her? She didn't want Mama and Marcia saying anything more about how a man should chase a woman.

He must have understood Janice's thoughts, because at that very moment he sent her a slow smile that made her warm all over, even the tip of her nose, which had been frozen till that point.

Come to me, her heart said. He'd done so in her dreams for years. And now . . .

Now she wanted it to happen here, in front of her family.

"As Lady Chadwick has said, this day is shocking," he reminded all the company. "I'm a duke." He glanced down at his dusty groom's jacket with wry amusement, but then his mood sobered. "It will take some very serious convincing of the legal system to claim my proper title, as you all know. And I'll need time to figure this new role out, too. But I intend to exceed everyone's expectations—especially my own—and there's only one way I can do so."

He caught Janice's eye, and her heart began to thump like mad and her breath came short as her one true love wended his way through various relatives to get to her.

At last, he was upon her. "I can only be duke if I can have you as my duchess," he said softly.

"I've already said yes to the duke," she said with a smile that trembled. "But I'm also saying yes to the groom, to the boxer, to the ex-soldier, and the rescuer of frightened dogs."

"Oh?" He grinned and captured her waist in his strong hands.

She looked up at the window where Aaron, happy and confident, waved down to her. "And yes to the man who'll teach our children that any strength worth having always begins in the heart."

"That's a lot to ask a brute like me," he said, "but I'm up to the challenge. Anything else?"

She eyed him speculatively. "How about yes to the man who'll learn to love a lonely old woman with a temper?"

"It will be an adventure. But how about this?" He leaned close to her ear. "You'll say yes to the man who comes knocking on your bedchamber door tonight, at two in the morning precisely."

He planted a lush kiss on her mouth, and her entire body suffused with delicious heat. "But Luke?"

"Yes?"

"Isobel will be asleep in the little closet of a room attached to my bedchamber."

"Oh."

"Plus, Mama and Daddy will be down the corridor."

"I see." He thought a moment. "How about yes to a quick elopement to Scotland then?"

"What a wonderful idea! But only if the whole family can come, don't you agree?"

"Of course."

She laughed aloud at the idea of all those carriages going to Gretna. And then she remembered. "Do you mind waiting for Gregory and Pippa? They're supposed to arrive in London from Paris any day now. I can't wait for you to meet Little Bertie. Oh—and there's Alice. In Ireland. If she has to miss the wedding, we need to sail to Ireland right afterward to see her, or she'll never forgive us."

He laughed. "I see that I'll have to say yes to the entire House of Brady."

"You understand me so well." She kissed him with such fervor she almost forgot—she reached into a coat pocket and pressed a key in his hand.

"What's this?"

"It goes to the new cellar lock," she whispered. "I pinched it from the pantry. I had to try seventeen different ones."

"Ah. Good work." Luke pulled her even closer and looked into her eyes with such tender passion, Janice was brought right back to their very first kiss. "Shall we steal away after tea?"

They both smiled. Then their mouths joined in an ardent celebration of the union they knew was to come. And so it was that Janice and Luke said yes—

To love.

Epilogue

"Read it to me again," the dowager said from her Bath chair. "It's like speaking to Emily March herself."

They were sitting in the dowager's bedchamber—she, Janice, and Luke—two days after Janice's family had arrived at Halsey House.

"Very well," said Janice. She opened the old notebook and cleared her throat:

"And so, Your Grace," she read, *"in addition to being your lady's maid, I am your darling Everett's widow, and I shall bear his child. We were going to tell you shortly, but he was waiting, you see, to find the right moment. You already had the shock of your dear husband's death to contend with. But if it's any consolation, if I bear a boy, he is the next Duke of Halsey."*

Me, Luke mouthed proudly to Janice, and pointed a thumb at his chest.

"Yes, you," said the dowager, her eyes lit with amusement.

Luke started, his cheeks red. It was obvious he didn't realize his grandmother was looking.

"And you're a scamp, just like your father," Her Grace added.

Janice stifled a laugh. And Luke, abashed as he was, grinned.

"Go on." The elderly lady waved a hand at Janice.

It was a gesture the Queen was quite fond of. But Her Majesty was nowhere in sight and hadn't been seen since Janice had first read the notebook aloud to the dowager, the same day she'd found it.

Janice sat up straight and continued: *"But I'm much too afraid of Russell to stay."*

When she looked up at the dowager, the old woman's eyes were crimped with pain. But there was also tremendous interest there. Somehow, reliving these events was good for Her Grace. This was the fourth time Janice had read her the notebook.

Luke put his hand on Janice's knee and squeezed.

"I saw him watch his brother drown when he knew how to swim to him to save him," she read. Her eyes stung every time. *"So you see how I'd rather my child grow up in obscurity than risk his life asserting his ducal rights. God bless you, Your Grace, and know that I wander the world with Everett's love in my heart and his blood in our child's veins. Your devoted servant and daughter, Emily March Hildebrand."*

"They were fishing," the dowager said. "The boat sprang a leak."

"Was that an accident?" Luke asked her softly.

"I don't know," said his grandmother. "We'll never know, I suppose."

"I'm going to hope it was," said Janice, "and I'm also going to hope that Russell was too paralyzed by shock to rescue his brother."

The dowager chuckled. "You're a good girl. But with the benefit of hindsight, even I, Russell's mother, believe it might have been planned. My younger son had been jealous a very long time, long before he became duke. After he assumed the title, he was cruel to me, cruel to Grayson, and he died a bitter man."

"That's so sad." Janice sighed and shared a poignant look with her future husband.

"Tell me again your part in all this," Her Grace asked Luke.

"Certainly." He settled deeper into the sofa. "Just two months ago, I was dropping off a pouch of coins at St. Mungo's. I do it every year on my birthday and at Christmas. Secretly."

Janice kissed his cheek.

Luke smiled, rather embarrassed again. "But Sister Brigid waited up late for me this time. She caught me in the act, and she told me the orphanage needed my help. It seemed that Grayson wouldn't leave the nuns alone. He'd been looking for Emily's offspring and was harassing them to reveal what they knew about me."

The dowager's brows lowered.

"So that dark night," Luke went on, "Sister Brigid told me the truth—that *I* am the Duke of Halsey. Not Grayson. Of course, I had no idea I was related to a peer at all. I was a boxer, a soldier—"

"And a groom," the dowager added, her eyes gleaming with pleasure. She clearly liked Luke's dramatic style.

Janice kissed his cheek again.

Luke winked at her, then went on: "Sister Brigid had promised Emily before she died never to reveal the truth to me of my origins. Emily was afraid it would put me in danger. But Sister told me she must. She said I was a man now and well able to take care of myself, as I clearly am. And St. Mungo's needed me to claim the title so that Grayson's harassment would cease."

Her Grace let out a frustrated sigh.

"Don't give up on Grayson yet," said Janice. "Surely he'll come round eventually."

"But it wasn't true that I wanted to stay up in that stifling bedchamber." The dowager pouted. "I can't believe he told you that."

Janice winced. "Well, you did say that, actually, Your Grace. You were so upset with me when I tried to take you out."

The dowager's eyes registered some confusion.

"It's all right, Granny," Luke said. "Part of you didn't want to face what had happened. And another part of you wanted to rejoin the world."

"And part of Grayson was looking out for you," said Janice. "And another part of him found it terribly convenient that he could tuck you away so that no one would bring up the awful events of the past."

"Go on," the dowager snapped at them both. Much like the Queen. But there were no sneezes. "Finish your story, Luke."

Apparently, she wasn't ready to analyze the situation or couldn't, which was fine. It was early days yet.

Luke nodded. "All right, Granny. So Sister Brigid had heard from Emily herself that Russell was responsible for Everett's death. But Sister knew nothing more than that—except for the very important fact that Russell would gladly kill me if he could find me. Somehow, he managed to trace me to the orphanage. But a kind nun put money in my pocket when I was eleven and told me to run. There was another orphanage in Bristol. But I never made it. I grew up on the streets, and after Russell died last year, Grayson started the search up again."

"Which takes us back to Sister Brigid," the dowager said.

"Right," answered Luke. "All that could possibly help me establish my claim was the missing diary. Emily had told Sister about it, but we didn't know if it still existed. But it did, obviously. Janice here found it."

"Good for you, Janice."

"Thank you, Your Grace." Janice put the notebook down, and Luke wrapped his hand around hers.

"Well." The dowager inhaled a deep breath. "That's a fine tale. And I'm glad it has a happy ending. Tomorrow we'll go over the part involving my stove house. I always knew that gardener was special."

"He is," said Janice.

Luke stood and pulled her up with him. "We're off now, Granny, for our daily walk."

Janice nodded. "But we'll come back later."

"Very good," said the duchess. "But before you go on this walk of yours . . ."

"Yes?" asked Luke.

"I have a favor to ask."

"Anything," said Janice.

"Is there anyone staying in the old wing?"

"No," said Luke.

"Oh, well, in the old wing, there's a fine bedchamber at the opposite end of my tiny one. I left a pair of spectacles there. Please look for them."

"But Your Grace, I've never seen you wear spectacles," Janice said.

Her Grace merely stared at her. Her silence spoke volumes.

Heat spread across Janice's face as she began to realize . . . there was no way the dowager was leading them to a trysting spot, was she? And then she realized the Queen would. Oh, yes, indeed, *she* would!

Luke cleared his throat. "Of course we'll look for them, Granny."

The dowager finally settled her gaze on him. "Very good. And if you don't find them, you'll have to look again tomorrow. I'm sure they're there."

Luke and Janice left the room feeling like two naughty

schoolchildren, and as they walked up the two flights of stairs and got closer to their destination their legs carried them faster and faster.

"There's something very strange about this," Janice said.

"I like her," Luke replied.

They both chuckled.

And when they got to that bedchamber, they actually looked for a pair of spectacles—

For about three seconds.

And then Luke shut the door, Janice flung herself in his arms, and they fell back onto the enormous poster bed, side by side, kissing all the while.

"This beats the cellar," Luke said against her mouth.

"But it had a charm of its own," replied Janice, running her hand down his shirtfront.

"Yes, and spiders, too." Luke sat her up and undid her laces.

"It did?"

"Only one," he said, "and I killed it. But I don't know about mice."

Janice shuddered, and she didn't know if it was from contemplating mice and spiders or from Luke's touch. His finger was running loopy circles around her nipple while he kissed the side of her neck.

She decided that it was Luke—and for the next three minutes they rolled and kissed and pulled and tugged until they were both naked and Luke was poised above her.

Already.

"This is awfully fast," he said, a bead of sweat on his temple. "We should stop now and start over. This time we'll take it much slower."

"No, let's not." Janice was a little short of breath. "That was yesterday. And the day before. Remember?"

He gazed down at her adoringly. "How could I forget?"

"My back remembers." She giggled.

"Mine, too," he said. "You demanded to be on top the second time."

"Well, a girl can take only so much cellar floor."

He laughed and brushed some hair off her cheek. "This is our first time in a real bed."

"I know." She felt shy of a sudden. "But I'm ready—if you meant that this signifies something more than a bed of hard-packed dirt would."

"I don't think it does at all." He kissed her softly. "But *you* mean more to me. Every time."

"As do you," she whispered. "Your grandmother told me love can't be measured. And she's right. I have no way to explain how loving you is bigger than anything I've ever done or been a part of."

He kissed her again. "Only this comes close for me," he said, and with a firm, loving kiss—one that claimed her as his own—he entered her.

"Mm-m-m." She wrapped her legs around him. "Me, too."

They clung and let their bodies speak what they couldn't say, riding to a sweet conclusion that was both wild and beautiful.

When it was over, Luke collapsed upon Janice's neck and she sighed with happiness.

Together they were love.